THE
PHOENIX KEEPER

THE
PHOENIX
KEEPER

S. A. MACLEAN

orbit

orbitbooks.net

Copyright © 2024 by Sarah MacLean
Excerpt from *Sorcery and Small Magics* copyright © 2024 by Maiga Doocy

Cover design by Rachael Lancaster / Orion Books
Cover illustration by Niall Grant
Map by Helen Cann
llustrations copyright © 2024 The Illustration of Niall Grant
Author photograph by Tiffany Doan

Orbit
Hachette Book Group
1290 Avenue of the Americas
New York, NY 10104
orbitbooks.net

First Edition: August 2024
Simultaneously published in Great Britain by Gollancz, an imprint of the Orion Publishing Group Ltd, a Hachette UK Company

Orbit is an imprint of Hachette Book Group.
The Orbit name and logo are registered trademarks of
Little, Brown Book Group Limited.

The publisher is not responsible for websites (or their content) that are not owned by the publisher.

The Hachette Speakers Bureau provides a wide range of authors for speaking events. To find out more, go to hachettespeakersbureau.com or email HachetteSpeakers@hbgusa.com.

Orbit books may be purchased in bulk for business, educational, or promotional use. For information, please contact your local bookseller or the Hachette Book Group Special Markets Department at special.markets@hbgusa.com.

Library of Congress Control Number: 2024933014

ISBNs: 9780316573092 (trade paperback), 9780316573108 (ebook)

Printed in the United States of America

CW

3 5 7 9 10 8 6 4 2

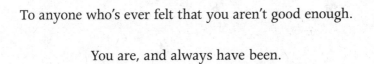

To anyone who's ever felt that you aren't good enough.

You are, and always have been.

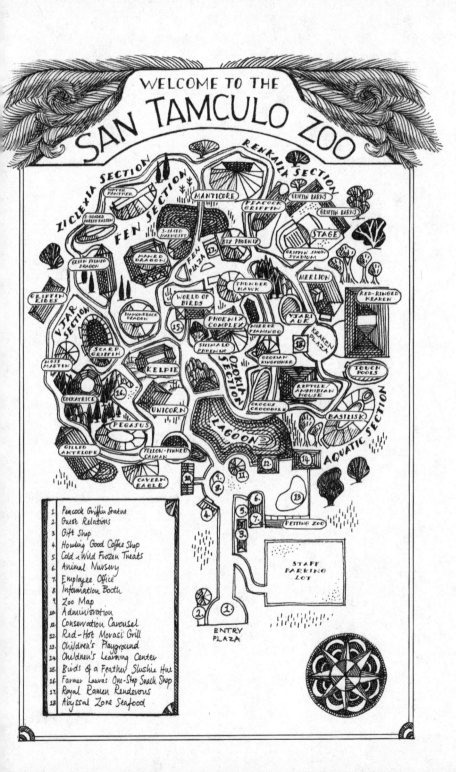

WELCOME TO THE
SAN TAMCULO ZOO

ZICLEXIA SECTION
RENKAIA SECTION
FEN SECTION
VJAR SECTION
OROKIA SECTION
AQUATIC SECTION

WATER PANTHER
2-HEADED FOREST FALCON
MANTICORE
PEACOCK GRIFFIN
GRIFFIN BARNS
GRIFFIN BARNS
3-FACED MEMOSIT
BIG PHOENIX
STAGE
MANED DRAGON
GRIFFIN SHOW STADIUM
GREEN FEATHERED DRAGON
FEN PLAZA 27.
THUNDER HAWK
MERLION
WORLD OF BIRDS
RED-RINGED KRAKEN
GRIFFIN RIDES
DIAMONDBACK DRAGON
PHOENIX COMPLEX
MIRROR FLAMINGO
VJARI AUK
15.
SHIMALO PHOENIX
KRAKEN PLAZA
18.
SCARP GRIFFIN
OZORIAN KINGFISHER
MOSS MARTEN
OROKIA SECTION
TOUCH POOLS
COCKATRICE
KELPIE
REPTILE/ AMPHIBIAN HOUSE
16.
UNICORN
CROCUS CROCODILE
BASILISK
GILLED ANTELOPE
PEGASUS
LAGOON
YELLOW-FINNED CAIMAN
12.
14.
CAVERN EAGLE
10.
1.
8.
11.
4.
13.
6.
5.
7.
PETTING ZOO
3.
STAFF PARKING LOT

1. Peacock Griffin Statue
2. Guest Relations
3. Gift Shop
4. Howling Good Coffee Shop
5. Cold & Wild Frozen Treats
6. Animal Nursery
7. Employee Office
8. Information Booth
9. Zoo Map
10. Administration
11. Conservation Carousel
12. Red-Hot Movasi Grill
13. Children's Playground
14. Children's Learning Center
15. Birds of a Feather Slushie Hut
16. Farmer Laura's One-Stop Snack Shop
17. Royal Ramen Rendezvous
18. Abyssal Zone Seafood

2.
1.
ENTRY PLAZA

PART ONE

Small tear under eye

wings are bright Red orange, yellow

The **SILIMALO PHOENIX**, once widespread throughout the rocky shrublands of the eastern Silimalo coast, was hunted near to extinction, their feathers illegally harvested for longevity remedies. Currently, the entire remaining population lives in captivity. Future reintroduction into the wild will depend on the success of our network of IMWS breeding facilities around the world.

Garumano et al. REVIEW OF BREEDING HABITS OF THE CRITICALLY ENDANGERED SILIMALO PHOENIX. Proceedings of the Magical Biology Society 148(3): 132–139

Chapter One

Aila Macbhairan's favorite time at the San Tamculo Zoo was early morning: cool, quiet, and—best of all—not a person in sight.

In the pre-dawn, an eggplant-purple sky hung over city streetlamps silhouetted with palm trees. Bird keepers worked the earliest shifts, their peckish charges awake at first light.

Aila swiped her ID card at the staff gate, then crossed the entrance plaza, hunched beneath a backpack of blue canvas and cartoon animal patches, work boots tapping terracotta bricks engraved with donor names. A bronze statue of the zoo's peacock griffin mascot stood sentinel in the fog, metal wings spread wide, back brushed gold from millions of visitors clambering up for a photo.

Already, the air warmed. Salt from the rocky coast of Movas mixed with asphalt, hay, and old popcorn, though not a kernel or crumpled cup strayed into sight. For a fleeting time before the gates opened, Aila enjoyed immaculate concrete paths, the main avenue of silent speakers and dark gift shops stuffed with everything from dragon plushies to candy cockatrice eggs, to those insufferable plastic toys that twirled with light-up phoenixes at the press of a button.

The shriek of an archibird sliced the quiet. Aila smiled, the zoo rousing to greet her.

Off the visitor path, hidden behind a screen of shrubbery, golden light spilled out a doorway. Inside, beige walls sported framed news articles and a bulletin board with flyers for the employee potluck, an advertisement for guitar lessons, a strongly worded note against storing unicorn deworming medicine in the human food fridge. Filing cabinets sprouted crowns of charging radios and protocol binders.

"Morning, Tom," Aila greeted.

From his corner desk, the middle-aged staff coordinator grunted in acknowledgement. He had brown and sun-weathered skin, a jaw patched with uneven stubble and a black uniform polo ironed to perfection. While he sipped his coffee and scrolled on his phone, Aila logged in at the computer, then clipped a radio to the belt of her cargo pants.

"Have a good day, Tom."

He grunted farewell.

Aila got along well with Tom.

Back into the budding dawn, a fog-muted sunrise filtered through leaves of eucalyptus and cypress. Aila's path cut through a food court and past the endangered species carousel, a menagerie of prancing pegasi and snarling dragons. During a school trip in third grade, four of Aila's classmates waged war over the coveted unicorn mount, ending in pulled hair and several detentions. She'd watched the skirmish from her lone perch on the carousel's thunderhawk, safe in a cocoon of resin wings and electric blue paint.

Beyond the entrance attractions, the walkway branched into narrower arteries. At Aila's passing, the yellow-finned caiman flicked open an eye, scales glittering with magnetized gold dust and tail dangling in his lounging pool. A pair of gilded swans honked a plea for handouts, trails of bioluminescence swirling the dark water in their wake. Ahead, a domed aviary rose from within the trees, panels of tempered glass ribbed with heat-resistant steel.

Aila's heart soared with it.

She'd collected her first poster from the San Tamculo Zoo at eight years old, a stylized print of the most stunning creature in the world: the critically endangered Silimalo phoenix, ruby wings spread in flight, tail swirling into flame. The prized possession held a place of honor on her bedroom wall throughout high school. It traveled with her in a packed sedan to Sagecrest College, the premier zoological school in Movas, motivation as she crammed her way to a degree in magical animal science. The edges crinkled yellow on her cubicle wall as she finished her apprenticeship at the Fablewings Rescue Center across town, as she poured her heart into the San Tamculo Zoo job application, then sobbed like a wrung sponge when the offer letter arrived.

Now, phoenix keeper Aila floated to work each day like a dream, eyes sparkling on the glass of *her* aviary.

Her jungle trees and concrete paths.

Her flock of birds chittering at the dawn.

Head held high, she mounted the slope to the World of Birds aviary and twisted a key into the outer lock, crossed the antechamber, then pressed the inner door to start another wonderful day of—

Her shoulder stalled against the push bar.

She planted her boots and shoved, but the door refused to open. From the other side of the steel mesh came a wry cackle. She looked up, glare settling on a stocky gray archibird—one of the more mischievous species under her care—peering down at her from behind a wide-leaved vine. He tilted his head, a crest of azure feathers raised to a rakish angle.

"Ha, ha," Aila said. "Very funny, Archie."

He replied with a puffed chest and a throaty sound like a deflating rubber chicken.

Aila shoved the door again, attempting to dislodge whatever twigs Archie must have jammed into the lock. Archibirds, native to the tropical islands of the Naelo Archipelago, had been hunted to near extinction in the wild. Some days, she understood why their beleaguered human neighbors did it. The feathered fiends obsessed over gathering shiny jewelry, light bulbs, bolts out of car hubcaps.

With gritted teeth, Aila strained against the push bar until her shoulder ached. No rattle of dislodging sticks answered her efforts. She gripped the metal mesh, craning to see the prankster's handiwork—then gaped at the glint of a metal rod jammed into the keyhole.

"Archie...you'd *better* not have torn apart your new enrichment item!"

She'd discovered the design for the swiveling mirror toy in a journal article, had labored over the construction in her free evenings for over a month. Fastening all the tiny pieces together with a soldering iron burned a couple of fingerprints off, but when she'd brought the toy in to work the day before, her reward had been Archie hopping and hooting like a mad bird.

Sneaky little con artist.

Above her, wings flapped. When Aila looked up, Archie froze on his perch, beady black eyes locked with hers. Another metal rod glinted in his beak.

The aviary had three entrances.

The moment Archie took flight, Aila set off at a sprint.

Her boots pounded concrete, frizzed auburn hair bouncing in her ponytail, backpack weighing her down like a turtle shell. The path around the aviaries curved past a slushie hut with a thatched roof and mannequin parrots, a garden of spiky cycad trees, several exhibits with animals locked in their overnight enclosures. Aila huffed up a flight of stairs and hit the aviary door at full force, fumbling for her key while the archibird landed against the inner screen.

"Don't you fucking dare, Archie!"

Two exhibits over, a three-faced marmoset mimicked back, *"Don't you fucking dare, Archie!"* followed by a whooping laugh.

Aila twisted the key in the lock. As she stumbled across the antechamber, Archie jammed the metal rod into the inner door, feet latched on to the mesh and body wrenching for torque. She hit the push bar and shoved as hard as her pale, skinny arms could muster.

It didn't budge. With each shove, the metal rod rattled in the lock.

Aila slumped against the door. Inside, Archie hopped along the ground, his triumphant cackles drawing a flutter of other birds peeking from the canopy: the translucent wings and purple feathers of the pixie wrens, the judging white eyes of the screaming mynas. The interior of the aviary was humid, hot, dense with wide-leaved cecropia trees and pod-bearing tamarinds to model a more tropical forest. As Aila pressed her cheek to the mesh of the door, the tang of moist soil and treated water thick in her nose, Archie poked through to nibble her fingers.

Nice going, Aila. How was she supposed to be a world-class zookeeper if she couldn't outsmart a single archibird? A single *door*?

"Aw, gee, Archie. You got me." Aila snapped her fingers in defeat. Could the archibird understand her? Logic said no, but considering what ratio of her conversations occurred with animals, she had to believe they got *something* out of it.

She backed away from the door. Archie watched with head tilted, a confused rise to his crest. Feigning indifference, Aila

7

slumped down the stairs and out of sight behind a screen of giant Renkailan reeds with feathery cream tips.

Stealth mode: activate.

As quietly as heavy work boots allowed, she snuck toward the third aviary door, shielding herself behind vegetation. She hopped through a garden of topiary pruned like flying birds. Flattened herself to a photo booth whose white LCD screen glowed eerily in the growing light.

The glass aviaries formed a central hub of the zoo, surrounded by sections themed after regions of the world. On this edge, the path cut through a forest of bamboo with stalks thicker than Aila's arm, native to Fen, their neighbor across the mountains to the north-east. Food shops were painted in a smooth gray with red trim, the plaza shaded by wooden pergolas dripping purple and white wisteria, feeding onto a low stone bridge across a pond. Not a bad place to relax, sans the screaming children who'd flood the grounds in a few hours.

She approached the main exhibit—a maned dragon in her own dome of ever-flowering cherry trees. Though the enclosure limited the dragon's ability to alter barometric pressure beyond the glass, a low fog clung to the ground, buckets of umbrellas on hand for any guests caught in an unexpected drizzle. In the plaza beside the exhibit, Aila ducked for cover within a giant replica dragon egg. The tourist trap consisted of jade resin, its hollow interior an invitation for tacky photos. Her nose wrinkled at the smell of shoes and stale waffle fries. Peering past scratched graffiti and the informational placard, she could just see her aviary door around a curve in the path.

In the canopy, Archie fluttered to a perch, bobbing his head as he searched for her, another metal rod in his beak. Waiting for a witness to his scheme? *Your love of theatrics will be your doom, my friend*. If Aila could get the door unlocked before he noticed her—

"Morning, Aila!" came a cheerful voice behind her.

Aila yelped and banged her head on the roof of the egg. Hand pressed to her far-too-easily-startled heart, she spun a glare on her betrayer. The woman stood tall in a black keeper's polo and work jeans, skin dark umber and hair gathered into a bun of slim braids beneath her cap, carrying a box of bird food pellets. Just Tanya. Aila slumped in relief. She'd have died from embarrassment if that gorgeous hunk of a dragon keeper found her skulking around his exhibits.

Or worse, that judgmental witch from the griffin show. Aila would never live it down.

"*Shh.*" She pressed a finger to her lips. "Not so loud!"

Tanya crouched beside Aila, balancing the box on her knees, ink-dark eyes scrunched to that patronizing angle reserved for misbehaving animals, obnoxious human visitors or, in this case, college roommates.

"What are we doing this morning, Ailes?" Tanya matched the conspiring tone.

"I need you to distract Archie."

"Archie?" Tanya lifted a penciled brow. "You letting that bird push you around again?"

"He dismantled the new toy I built him!"

"Mm-hm."

"Got the metal dowels loose somehow and jammed them into the doors! Do you know how long it took me to solder all those pieces?" Aila flexed her fingers, recalling the toil.

"You're talking about that contraption with all the shiny metal bits?" Tanya clicked her tongue. "Girlie, what did I tell you when you brought that thing in here?"

Aila frowned and studied the squishy ground, a mat of

recycled rubber dyed jade and gold to mimic maned dragon scales. A clever use of resources, though she could do without the smell of all the children who rolled around on—

"*Ailes.*"

"Right. Right! It was a bad idea. OK?" Aila slumped until her backpack hit the wall of the egg. "I just wanted to do something nice for him." As much as Archie could be a little shit, he was *her* little shit. Who could say "no" to that adorable, scheming face?

Tanya grinned, amusement dancing on high cheeks. She booped Aila's nose with a manicured blue nail. "Don't you worry, Ailes. You know I've got you."

She stood, her box of bird pellets rustling as she shuffled it back to a comfortable spot in her arms. As Tanya strutted down the path, she called out in a singsong voice, "Oh, what a lovely morning. And me, all alone with my big, exciting box of bird food! I hope there aren't any devious archibirds lurking up in the trees."

Aila grinned. She didn't have many human friends—too shy in grade school, too bookish in high school, too much of a barely contained ball of anxiety in college (and most days thereafter). How she'd lucked into a friend as stellar as Tanya was a cosmic wonder.

Peeking around the egg, Aila spotted a flutter of wings in the aviary. Archie took the bait, off to get a closer look at Tanya and her box.

Time to strike.

Aila sprinted for the door. As she ran, keys flashed in her hand, ready when she hit the lock. A jam. A click. Victory smelled like damp concrete and bird droppings as she lurched across the antechamber. Archie landed on the inner door in a panic of wings and croaks. Metal flashed in his beak. He gripped the mesh and angled the rod, thrusting down as Aila collided with the push bar.

She shoved. The door flew open, Archie squawking in retreat.

Momentum was a son of a bitch. Aila enjoyed her fleeting swell of triumph before losing her balance, flying forward into the aviary and toppling belly-first onto the pathway. Limbs sprawled, chin stinging from a scraped jaw, she accepted the embrace of cold concrete. Humid air stuck to her skin. Leaves rustled in the broad-leaved trees arcing toward the glass, in vines of pepper bushes and vanilla orchids encircling mossy path railings.

Aila grinned. She did it. She beat that conniving little—

A splat of bird poop hit her cheek. *Son of a bitch.*

She wiped the goop clean with a groan, careful not to smush any near her eyes or mouth, dripping a huge glop onto her work polo. Archie landed beside her and hopped a circle, chest wheezing, delighted with their game.

"You're lucky you're cute, Archie. Please tell me you realize that?"

Archie cocked his head, eyes beady. *Shoot.* Aila couldn't stay mad at that.

As the chaos subsided, the aviary fluttered to life. Purple pixie wrens hopped the branches, fluttering their dragonfly wings. A cinnamon bird peeked from behind a cecropia leaf, twirls of spiced bark accenting his tail. A pair of vanishing ducks waddled up from the pond, white tails shimmying in time with inquisitive quacks. From his neighboring aviary, the six-foot-tall Movasi thunderhawk landed on a perch, his crest sparking, beak clacking in annoyance at all the hubbub.

Despite her scrapes and the remnants of bird droppings clinging to her cheek, Aila laughed. She couldn't imagine herself anywhere else.

11

Archie squawked and flared his blue crest.

"Of course. I'll be right back with your breakfast. Don't break anything else? *Please*?" Aila hopped to her feet to start her morning routine—for real, this time.

After unblocking the doors and confiscating the pieces of Archie's toy (to his vocal displeasure), she finished her trek to the heart of the aviary complex. There stood another glass monolith, heat-tempered using powdered dragon scales, attached to a building of red stucco and gilded pillars. A pergola arched over the path, shaded with grape vines and olive trees. Above, a metallic art piece depicted a fiery bird in flight, flames flickering from gas valves in the tail.

The Silimalo phoenix.

Aila would never forget her first visit to the San Tamculo Zoo, eyes so wide on those vivid colors, those mesmerizing feathers. She forgot how much she hated school field trips. She forgot about holding back tears when none of her classmates wanted to sit with the nervous, quiet girl who kept to herself at lunch. Other visitors fawned over the gaudy tricks in the griffin show, the teeth of the diamondback dragon or jewel-headed carbuncles at the petting zoo, but what were all those theatrics compared to *this*? Something unique. Something vanishing. Hunted to extinction in the wild, Silimalo phoenixes lived on thanks to a coordinated breeding program across the world's zoos—from the pegasus-studded grasslands of Silimalo to the rocky plateaus of Movas, to the vast sand dunes of the Renkailan desert.

Of course, when Aila was younger, San Tamculo's phoenix breeding program was the best in Movas. A jewel of species conservation. These days...not so much.

The public façade of the exhibit sparkled—the well-trimmed grape vines, the wide observation window. But upon entering the back keeper complex, Aila was met with faded orange walls.

Metal counters were piled not with chirping fledglings, but boxes of food pellets that didn't fit in the main storage room. Cream linoleum, clean glass, but quiet. Too quiet. These facilities hadn't bred Silimalo phoenixes in over a decade. Since their last male passed away from old age, there'd been no compatible birds available to transfer within the conservation network, either from their Movasi sister zoos or farther abroad.

"Good morning, Rubra," Aila greeted, soft as a mother rousing her child from bed.

The female phoenix perched alone in a metal aviary, preening. She resembled a large red pheasant. Plumes of gilded crimson bobbed on her head as she ran an obsidian beak over her wing feathers, a sunrise gradient from red to tangerine to gold. Her tail was striped gold and ruby, nearly twice the length of her body, two straight central feathers and another pair curling on either side, the full lengths of them alight with perpetual flame.

The phoenix lifted her crest and gave a high-pitched chirp.

By all the skies and seas, Aila's heart cracked every time.

She slipped on a fireproof glove covering fingertips to shoulder. When the cage door opened, Rubra hopped onto her keeper's hand and fluffed her feathers in a puff of red down and a whiff of woodsmoke.

Careful to keep open flame away from her clothing (not always successful, as evidenced by a few old singes on her cargo pants), Aila walked Rubra to an observation window overlooking the public exhibit. While the phoenix preened on her glove, Aila pulled a laptop from her backpack, set it on the counter, and navigated to the bookmark she visited a dozen times a day. Maybe two dozen.

A video feed popped up on the screen: live footage from the second largest zoo in Movas, a few hours down the coast in

Jewelport. Center frame, a pair of Silimalo phoenixes roosted on a nest of charred branches.

"Look, Rubra," Aila whispered. "They should hatch any day now!" A shining achievement for any zoo. Watching the progress filled Aila with equal parts overwhelming joy and crushing envy, doubly so when Rubra pecked at the phoenixes on the computer screen.

"Don't worry, sweetheart." Aila stroked the bird's back, feathers warm as a hearth. "I'll find a partner for you one day. I promise."

On the wall above her desk hung a yellowed phoenix poster, the same one she'd carried with her since she was eight. Through college. Through apprenticing. Aila leaned against the counter, phoenix on her arm, scrolling through the video chat box to catch up on the latest highlights. Rubra watched with head cocked, a melancholy trill in her throat.

"I promise," Aila told her again.

Same as she did every day.

Chapter Two

Three hours remained until the front gates opened and flooded the Sam Tamculo Zoo with patrons. Aila had an army's worth of tasks to prepare her exhibits before then.

Her laptop stayed open to the Jewelport Zoo live cam, inspiration in the form of cute birds and childhood dreams. She set Rubra on a metal scale and checked her feather iridescence against a chart on the wall—crimson values only a nine out of ten today, but a papaya snack would boost those carotenoids. Some keepers found rote routines tedious, but Aila reveled in the satisfaction of filling numbers into a logbook. At a tap of her fingers, Rubra hopped back to her glove, rewarded with a juicy grape she crushed in her beak.

With check-in complete, Aila released Rubra to her public exhibit. The phoenix glided over a scrubby hillside and landed in an olive tree. The plants, like the bird, were native to Silimalo, the other side of the world from arid Movas, across the Middle Sea, on the western arm of the continent. These particular trees came from a Silimalo specialty nursery down the street.

Dawn light filtered through the glass dome, each panel outfitted with sensors and venting mechanisms to maintain the perfect temperature and humidity. State of the art. Yet no amount of fancy climate control technology guaranteed success at breeding captive Silimalo phoenixes. Somehow, the birds *knew* when they weren't in the right place.

The Silimalo National Zoo had the greatest success, their phoenixes content in a climate of mild winters and arid summers shared by few other regions. Movas was such a place: the same latitude, the same west-facing coast, the same scrubby biome. Another stretch of scrub in the southern hemisphere, on the west coast of Renkaila, participated in the breeding program, but hadn't produce a clutch. The two premier zoos in Movas— San Tamculo and Jewelport—were the only institutions to have successfully bred Silimalo phoenixes outside their native range.

Then, San Tamculo's birds passed away from old age—right as Aila was applying to college, mind you, causing a real jab of urgency for those personal statement essays. With so few phoenixes in the breeding program, Rubra barely got transferred, and the carousel of genetically optimized bird pairings limited the pool of male partners. A whole legacy, ended by administrative red tape.

Enter: phoenix keeper Aila. Here to kick butt, scrub aviaries, and revive the phoenix program from the ashes. If only she could get that second bird—three straight years of transfer requests, denied. Who'd take that gamble on an untested keeper and a defunct facility?

So Aila had to prove herself by doing a kick-ass job at everything else.

She cleaned Rubra's back aviary from floor to ceiling, collecting any molted feathers to dispose of according to International Magical Wildlife Service protocol (lest the plumes end up on the black market as longevity tea or chintzy cold remedies). Charred perches, Aila replaced with fresh olive foliage. Metal held up better against flame, but Rubra loved playing with leaves.

Though the Silimalo phoenix starred on her route, Aila oversaw several neighboring exhibits as well. Next stop, she returned to the World of Birds aviary, largest after the trio of dragon domes. With a high-pressure hose, she attacked the concrete paths and decorative rocks around the ponds, clearing every speck of bird poop that would be right back again tomorrow morning. Skies and seas forbid any visitors witness something so unsightly. On hands and knees, she raked leaves off the circulation outlet for the waterfall, emerging with mud beneath her nails and twigs clinging to her clothes. Clean zookeepers weren't doing their job right.

Food time. Aila dipped into a keeper kitchen and returned with arms laden. Into the pond went bowls of bird pellets and chopped fish for the vanishing ducks—native to wetlands of the tropical Pennja savannah, to the southeast—and, yes, Aila still jumped whenever they materialized beside her, thanks for asking. Fortunately, their teleportation was only good for causing heart attacks, not phasing through anything solid. They fluffed their white cheeks and cinnamon bellies, whistling in delight as they dug into breakfast.

Next, a hike up the hill, swatting aside leaves as worldly as the animal residents: giant gunnera from the Pennja sub-tropics, aromatic cinnamon from the Ziclexian rainforest. Aila set bowls of fruit and mealworms into strategic feeding stations viewable from the public walkways.

The next residents hailed from Renkaila, even farther south than Pennja, the lower tip of the continent. The purple pixie wrens, native to Renkaila's western shrublands, descended first, their gossamer wings fluttering like dragonflies. A sprinkle of magical dust from their feathers sent several pieces of fruit levitating, safe out of reach of other beaks.

Next, the pair of screaming mynas perused the offerings, large brown birds with eerie white eyes and yellow wattles.

In the thicker forests of Renkaila's east coast, superstition said the myna's human-like shrieks predicted death. Others claimed they mimicked the voices of deceased loved ones. For Aila, the birds were a nuisance, the source of too many calls to zoo security when patrons mistook them for people screaming bloody murder.

Once the rowdier crowd departed, a mouse griffin slunk out of the leaves. One of the aviary's most far-from-home residents, mouse griffins skulked the wide temperate forests of Ozokia, all the way on the southern continent. The palm-sized creature perched with rear mouse paws and front talons, wings of pastel blue and yellow, bird head marked by a comical white eyebrow. Aila offered a chunk of mango the size of her pinkie. *Can't let the extroverts get all the good stuff.* The mouse griffin squeaked, snatched the fruit, then fluttered off.

With paths cleaned, birds fed and waterfall switched on to a roar, the aviaries were ready for visitors. At least, Aila's exhibits were. Tanya handled the other half of the aviary complex, laying fish out for the Ozokian kingfishers and buckets of shrimp for the mirror flamingos.

Aila returned to the concrete path to find Archie perched on a railing, blue crest raised, cheeks puffed. Someone wasn't pleased about losing his latest toy.

Let him pout. Aila knew this game.

She pulled a shiny metal screw from her pocket, the last remnant of her doomed enrichment item. The threads were chunky, too thick to fit in any door mechanisms (she'd double- and triple-checked). Archie's feathers flattened, his neck raised in rapt attention.

"Are you going to behave now, Archie?"

The Archibird squawked and hopped from foot to foot.

"No stealing cell phones from visitors?"

A puffed crest, then another squawk.

"No pooping on them, either?"

This wheeze was less enthusiastic, but honestly, if Aila could vent her frustrations against the general public that easily, wouldn't she be tempted?

She offered the screw. Archie snatched it in his beak and flew off in a blur of gray, hooting in delight. As he dipped into the forest understory, Aila leaned over a mossy railing to view the clearing below. There, Archie landed upon his masterpiece, the instinctual calling of every archibird: a tower composed of every shiny object he'd collected.

The Naelo Archipelago lay along the equator, a collection of tropical islands arcing across the Middle Sea, starting off the coast of Silimalo and nearly spanning the distance to Movas. Archibirds originated in the islands' coastal mangroves. As cities grew, the birds found urban life remarkably to their liking, treasure troves of shiny objects to pilfer for their towers.

In the wild, archibirds attracted mates with the dazzling constructions (taller towers were, obviously, sexier). Thanks to the tranquil lifestyle of captivity, Archie had spent years raising his tower to over six feet tall. Some pieces were rewards for good behavior: brass buttons, metal sheets, assorted screws. The addition of jewelry, sunglasses, and cell phones produced no shortage of complaints from guests, but hey: they should have read the warning signs before entering the aviary.

Archie rolled the screw in his beak, coating it with spit—a physics-defying spit stronger than any human-crafted industrial adhesive. When he placed the metal piece on his tower, it stuck as if welded. Delighted, he perched atop his throne and hooted.

Aila smiled. If she could give him the cell phone of every visitor to the zoo, she would.

One hour left until opening. One exhibit left to prepare.

Though Archie was a scheming menace, his small bird body precluded him from posing any physical hazard.

The kelpie, on the other hand...

Beside the aviary domes, a pocket of dense fog clung to weeping fir trees, persisting even as the Movasi sun rose hot overhead. The air hung thick, stale, peat-scented like a pocket of real Vjari moor, transported from the sub-polar expanse of boreal forest that crowned the northern continent. She approached the exhibit from a side entrance hidden by bracken and sculpted rocks. Here was the only non-avian charge on her route, assigned partly due to proximity, partly because no one else in the zoo wanted it.

Aila preferred a carnivorous horse over other people most days.

She unclipped the radio from her belt. "Entering kelpie," she reported, standard protocol for any exhibit with a dangerous resident. In the coordinator's office, Tom would scribble down the time. If Aila didn't report back after a while, well... it would be too late, but at least they'd know where to find her body.

When Aila started this route three years ago, stepping into the kelpie exhibit left a skip in her heart. Now, it was just a matter of diligence—and *many* checks to the gate locks. The main metal gate lay submerged in water, a barrier between the pretty public exhibit where the kelpie spent her day, and the back enclosure where she slept at night. Modular exhibits let Aila work in one section without fear of fangs looming over her shoulder.

Mist eddied at her ankles as she entered the empty public exhibit, the kelpie still locked in her back holding. In a loop around the boggy habitat, Aila collected gnawed bones from yesterday's meal, scrubbed the bloody rocks clean, inspected the water level in the observation pool. Peat moss squelched beneath her boots, a smell of wet hair clogging her nose.

The fog? Natural. Zoo designers proposed a fog machine when the exhibit first came in, but as it turned out, the kelpie *affected* the air around her.

Satisfied with a clean exhibit, Aila exited, double-checked the door locks, then moved into the concrete hall of the back exhibit. The gate controls were down a flight of stairs, beside a tank of inky water separated by foot-thick observation glass.

The tank looked empty. When Aila approached, her reflection peered back at her, ghostly in the fluorescent backlighting. Then, the moor-black water rippled. Dark eyes replaced hers. Like wisps of algae, a figure materialized on the other side, snout long and eyes sunken, hooves pawing the water, mane and tail woven with kelp.

"Good morning, Maisie." Aila laid a hand against the glass.

The kelpie pulled back her mouth to reveal fangs, followed by a gentle press of her nose to the wall between them. More polite than some patrons. Part of that was thanks to the glass, a refracting structure that blocked the hypnotizing aura kelpies used to lure and drown their prey.

At the control panel, Aila held down a red button. Mechanisms grated. The water in the tank lurched as the gate slid open, granting access to the pond in the main exhibit. With the ease of a current, the kelpie kicked off, closer to liquid than solid as she swam through the gate and into the public observation tank. She had a long day ahead, producing mystical fog and startling children.

Aila pressed a second button to close the gate.

With all her animals released into their public exhibits, she shifted back to cleaning. Aila reveled in the rhythmic scrubbing of her broom, the frizz of fog in her hair, the stinging scent of disinfectant as she worked along the concrete slab beside the kelpie's back water tank. By the time the floor gleamed spotless, a new din had grown outside.

Opening time. From the exhibit came squeals of delight as the kelpie swam across the glass. Laughing families. Shouting parents. Louder by the minute.

Aila checked her watch and groaned.

If she could hide in her back exhibits all day, she'd do so. Unfortunately, she had "professional obligations" and a "responsibility to facilitate positive interactions with zoo patrons" and all those cheery lines that came up in the yearly HR training. With the enthusiasm of a horror movie zombie—the low-budget ones Tanya collected posters for, no less—she stalked upstairs to the kitchen. Half a goat carcass lay defrosted in the industrial sink. She'd pulled it out the day before, preparing for one of the zoo's most popular weekly spectacles.

Just get it over with, Aila. Then she could hide again. Like she always did.

Aila peered out from the keeper entrance, squinting like a bat. The gloomy Vjari moors were home to kelpies—and Aila's gossamer-skinned ancestors. Midday Movasi sun glared down harsh enough to sear a few new freckles across her cheeks, banishing the morning fog. At least, any natural fog. Mist still cloaked the kelpie exhibit, bog musk fighting an assault of buttered popcorn and fried food from the snack shack down the path. On the public walkway, patrons hiked past with sunhats and squeaking strollers, gathering in a horde beside the observation window of the main pool.

They clapped when Aila emerged on a platform above the exhibit, a dead goat splayed on a cart behind her, fake smile plastered to her face. She'd done this a hundred times. Her legs still wobbled like jelly.

"Ahem." Aila cleared her throat. Tapped the lapel microphone clipped to her polo. Zero words in, and her voice already shook. Why didn't speaking to crowds ever get easier?

"Hello. Yes. The...um...kelpie feeding will start momentarily."

The crowd buzzed with murmurs and crinkling lunch wrappers, whizzing toys from the gift shop and electric fans in neon colors. Within the exhibit, the pond rippled as if caressed by a breeze. *Focus on the animal*. Aila knew how to deal with animals.

A cable ran over the exhibit. After hooking the goat carcass, Aila heaved on a pulley, sending the bait over the water. Perplexed looks peppered the crowd. Expecting more pomp? Some sparklers or perilous music? Maisie had it covered. A snout emerged from the water, a flare of fog from black nostrils. The kelpie dipped below the water's surface.

The pond exploded in a thrash of hooves and algae-strewn mane. Fangs sank into the goat carcass. With a powerful twist, Maisie ripped her meal from its hook and dragged it into the pool. The crowd rioted, shouting and pointing and waving flashing cameras.

"No flash, please," Aila squeaked. No one seemed to hear her.

With slumped shoulders, she pulled out her phone and set a timer. Five minutes. She could survive *five minutes*. Forcing a smile, she exited the exhibit and waded into the crowd as Maisie ripped apart her meal behind the glass, playing with chunks of meat in the current. Oh, how Aila preferred the smells of bog and bone to popcorn and sunscreen.

"Hello!" At her microphoned voice, the shouting lulled. "I'm Aila, keeper for this exhibit. I've...uh...got a moment to answer some questions about the kelpie, if you'd like to—"

"What do you feed it?" A call from a woman in giant sunglasses, her blouse a blinding shade of tangerine.

Aila lifted an eyebrow, looking at the observation pool. "We feed her...meat? Kelpies are carnivorous. In the wild, they're known to eat—"

"Meat like what? Goats?"

"That is meat. Yes. Though stories from the Vjari moors say kelpies sometimes lure humans onto their backs, then drown them in the—"

"What about vegetables?" This time, a shout from a bouncing child, his hand buried in a bag of candied almonds. "My mom says I have to eat vegetables."

"That is...not meat," Aila answered.

"But where does it get its vitamins?" The child's scowling mother.

Deep breath. Deep fucking breath. "Kelpies acquire a balanced diet from the meat we feed them. Next question."

A hand shot up in the back. Aila pointed.

"What makes it magical?" asked a teenager, tone flat.

Better question. Aila straightened. "The International Magical Wildlife Service, IMWS, defines magical fauna as species with attributes and/or abilities beyond the explanation of current biology or physics—though scientific studies with IMWS-approved animal care protocols are constantly working to better understand these attributes and their ecological significance. Kelpies are classified with extrasensory abilities of hypnosis, as well as paradoxical water breathing and fog production."

"Why does the kelpie look sad?" accused a man with thinning hair.

Aila fought for a level tone. "Well, actually, she's a horse. Nowhere near the same facial muscles we associate with sadness in humans, nor should we be extrapolating human emotions or social constructs to animals, so it would be erroneous to compare..."

Blank stares looked back at her. Aila pressed her temple. She went to zoo college for her animals. Not this.

Her fake smile felt like spoiled sugar. "I can assure you, we take excellent care of all our animals here at the San Tamculo Zoo. Next question."

Five minutes took an eternity. Fortunately, Maisie and her severed goat head proved better entertainment than Aila's stumbling responses. When her timer rang, she excused herself, retreating toward her aviaries on swift strides.

"Exploratory design" was all the rage in zoos these days—Aila devoured every detail in journal articles and message threads on social media. Twisting walkways and screens of foliage gave patrons the allure of exploration, of discovering the zoo's animals in the fern-thick forests of Renkaila's eastern slope, the towering boreal forest of Vjar, the moss-wreathed marshes of Ozokia. Aila used the curving routes to skirt visitors, avoiding eye contact with anyone eager to snag a keeper with inane questions.

How was she supposed to revive a phoenix program when she couldn't *talk* to people?

Aila reached the back of the phoenix complex. A waft of dust and Silimalo olive leaves welcomed her, fragrant Movasi sage along the path. At the exhibit viewing window, a crowd gasped, probably watching Rubra fluff her feathers or hunt bugs amidst singed branches.

"Got a minute, Aila?"

She froze at the voice behind her, the door within reach. *So* close.

With slumped shoulders, Aila faced Roberto, one of the primate keepers in the Fenese section. He met her with a frown, work boot tapping concrete. Unhappy. Splendid.

"Sure," Aila said. "What's up?"

"I was hoping you could tell me why my three-faced marmosets have been shouting *'Don't you fucking dare, Archie'* at visitors all morning?"

Aila winced. *Rotten, three-faced snitches and their flawless mimicking abilities.* Reason number one hundred and fifty-two of why birds were better than monkeys. "Oh. That. Sorry, Roberto, I got a little carried away this morning, and Archie was being a real little shit. I made him this *amazing* toy, great enrichment piece, and I thought he'd love it, but instead..."

Roberto crossed his arms, boot still tapping.

Aila hung her head. "Sorry. Won't happen again."

"Thanks, Aila."

She slunk into her keeper sanctuary like an exposed worm, desperate to escape the judging eyes. The constant demands. *Smooth, Aila. Can't manage ten minutes out there.*

She retreated to the kitchen to chop several days' worth of fruits and vegetables, trying not to imagine the grapes as snarky patron heads smooshing beneath her knife. Not like she didn't *try* to do better with the public. When first hired, she'd been a disaster, clamming up under the simplest questions. Ask her to rant about natural history of phoenixes for an hour in her apartment? Easy. Get five words out in front of a crowd? Harder than diamondback dragon scales. For some people, the outgoing attitude came easy.

Not for Aila. Never for her. Animals had always been simpler.

She glanced at her laptop, set upon the metal counter, wreathed in a battlefield of kale stalks and mango. On the screen, the Jewelport phoenix pair preened on their nest. The chat box scrolled by, viewers all over the world debating when the eggs would hatch and proposing chick names. That, Aila could handle. Let the commenters keep their distance, and let *her* focus on more important work than stringing up goat piñatas.

After dicing a cornucopia of produce, she shifted to a pack of thawed fish in the sink.

What was she so worried about? She rocked her assigned duties, kept all her animals happy, volunteered most evenings researching the latest husbandry techniques and enrichment items. Last week, she froze fruit popsicles that had Rubra chirping in glee for *hours*. The week before, she'd hung peanut butter bait balls (with proper nutritional supplements) throughout the World of Birds aviary. Let someone else handle the public relations.

Aila scowled, picturing the epitome of excess: the zoo's wildly popular griffin show, luring patrons with dazzling lights and tacky music. As if a gaudy stage production would save any of these animals from extinction.

She scoured her diet list. Bird pellets next, measured into bowls for tomorrow's breakfast. Aila stalked into the main room, but someone had cleared the boxes off the counter. A snoop around the desks and back into the kitchen revealed the stash high atop a shelf. She pushed onto her tiptoes and reached, *reached*, spindly arms devolving to futile swipes.

A chuckle behind her. "What's wrong, Ailes? You're pouting as bad as Archie."

In the doorway, Tanya stood with arms crossed, mischievous eyes framed by aqua shadow that popped against her dark skin. Aila slumped against the counter.

"Did you put those boxes on the top shelf so I couldn't reach?" she accused.

"Me? Nah. Why would I ever?"

Tanya reached over Aila's head, nine inches of superior height letting her access the top shelf with ease. Box retrieved, Tanya flicked Aila's nose. Aila swatted back.

They settled into an easy routine, Tanya scrubbing dishes in the sink while Aila measured food pellets for both their routes. At least not every person in the world burnt her out. They'd found that rare familiarity in college, staying up late cramming notes on exhibit cleaning techniques and devouring boxes of chocolate bonbons.

"How's your morning been?" Tanya asked.

Aila chewed her lip, head buzzing with too many thoughts of phoenix cameras and jelly legs at her keeper talk. She shrugged and swallowed the stress. "You know. The usual. How about you?"

Tanya groaned. "Khonsu got himself into that little gap in the rocks again. Scared me half to death when I couldn't find him."

Aila nodded and dropped pellets into a dish. Tanya's main exhibit was the Bix phoenix, a long-legged cousin from river deltas of the massive Bix Desert in western Renkaila. Not as endangered as Silimalo phoenixes, but plenty rare, their silver plumes rumored to bring women good fortune in dating when worn on now-illegal hats.

"I'll have to seal the place up somehow." Tanya attacked a crusted bit of grape with a sponge. "Hard to get up in the back of the exhibit, though."

An obnoxious design flaw. The rocks of the water feature in the Bix phoenix exhibit *looked* gorgeous, but required a steep climb to access.

"No one's thinking these things when designing the place." Tanya clicked her tongue. "Some good chicken wire could do it. Or maybe a couple of plants, those ones with big frilly leaves. I'll have to ask groundskeeping if they've got spares."

"I can help," Aila offered. "Let me know when."

"You're too sweet, Ailes." Tanya nudged her shoulder. "Later this week? Project day?"

"Project day," Aila agreed.

Work to do and a friend to help—both welcome distractions from her own stress. With keen focus, Aila pulled off a grin, words bubbling with a socially adequate dose of enthusiasm.

Tanya still locked her down with a squint. The perceptive mink.

"Everything else OK, Ailes?"

On any normal day, the *thoomp* of the phoenix complex door would have flooded Aila with dread, rather than relief. Her salvation came as a squeak of boots on old linoleum tiles in the next room, the telltale creak of plastic animal carriers.

"Hello?" a man called out. "Any lovely phoenix keepers back there?"

Aila couldn't have asked a magic genie for a better Tanya distractor. Tanya abandoned her squint, beaming brighter than the fluorescent lights overhead.

Theodore appeared in the kitchen doorway, skin dark as walnut wood and stature equally trunk-like, thick-rimmed glasses perched above a lopsided smile, his orange T-shirt frayed at one hem—by teeth or claws, a toss-up. Big block letters read SAN TAMCULO HUMANE SOCIETY above a cartoon puppy snuggled against a carbuncle with giant fluffy ears and twin tails. The slogan: MUNDANE OR MAGICAL, ADOPT YOUR NEWEST FAMILY MEMBER TODAY!

In either hand, he balanced two large animal carriers. Zoo security was always finding pets abandoned in the parking lot, next to the entry turnstiles, even out by the dumpsters near the veterinary center. Poor things. The humane society came to pick them up. A call about a wayward palm dragon hiding under Tanya's car summoned Theodore to the zoo two years ago.

One hour-long conversation about animal ethics later, and Tanya laid her claim. Boy never stood a chance.

"Morning, Teddy Bear," Tanya greeted, dropping into a voice paradoxically softer and more devious than the cadence she used for any other human or animal. She pecked a kiss to his forehead—leant down to do so, Theodore standing several inches shorter than her.

"I go where duty calls," he said loftily. "Hey, Aila."

Aila froze in her attempt to slink out the door, pressed against the counter like a sneaking purserat, trying not to intrude on the happy couple who honestly flabbergasted any of her conceptions of romance, considering she'd never progressed past a second date. Theodore—entirely *too* similar to Tanya—was too kind to let her hide.

Teddy took good care of Tanya. That granted him a spot in Aila's rather selective book of *"people who are mostly pleasant to interact with."* Still, this was a burnt-out day.

"Hey, Teddy." She mustered another smile. Heroic. "What's in the crates?"

"Caller thought they might be phantom cats." He held up one carrier, revealing vivid yellow eyes against sable fur, almost too black to discern against the dark interior. He shrugged. "Turns out, just regular cats." At that, an indignant meow from the occupant.

"You need help carrying them to the van?" Tanya offered.

"I thought you kept me around for my muscles?" Theodore pouted, flexing an arm in demonstration—and visibly struggling with the weight of carrier and cat. As an equally noodle-armed individual, Aila commiserated (though even Teddy had an inch of height on her—unfair, both her tall parents passing on the lamest genetics).

He and Tanya laughed together, soft and easy as she took a carrier from him. She cooed to the entrance. The cat meowed back. Good. More likely to get adopted quickly.

On her way out, Tanya paused in the doorway, shooting Aila another squint. "You sure you're OK, Aila? Were you about to say something?"

"Why would you think that?"

"You've got your face all scrunched, like something's upset you."

Aila forcibly unscrunched her nose.

Panic, her closest friend (after Tanya, of course), pulled Aila's gaze down to the box of food pellets in her hands, the scratch of her nails against the cardboard, the dig of her boot against a pit in the linoleum floor. If she opened up, Tanya would listen. One of the few people who did.

But Aila didn't want to bother her. Not with the same worries day after day.

"Ricardo stopped by earlier," she said. "I guess I upset his marmosets."

Tanya rolled her eyes to the ceiling. "Don't let that sour blanket get you down. Those beasts will be chanting fouler things by closing time, all the school groups we've got scheduled today. You sure there's nothing else wrong?"

"Positive. You go on, I'll be done with food prep soon."

"Don't you dare touch those dishes. I'll be back to finish them." Tanya pushed out the door in a flash of sunshine, the murmurs of the zoo creeping into the phoenix complex as she called back. "If I see Ricardo, I'll flip him off for you!"

The door closed.

In the quiet, Aila's companions were the humming fridge, the clack of her knife as she scraped wayward bits of kale together on the steel counter. She shoved the morning's frustrations aside like discarded detritus, focused on finishing food prep, then washing a *couple* of dishes, just so Tanya wouldn't have as much work when she got back. Simple tasks helped soothe Aila's nerves. The prospect of helping Tanya with her exhibit later that week helped more.

But the phoenix cam on Aila's laptop never stayed out of her sight for long.

Chapter Three

Aila sprawled on a dirt incline, papyrus reeds crowding her vision and sticking up her nose, peering into a hole framed by sculpted rocks.

Beside her, the reeds shifted. A wild Tanya in the brush.

"There!" Tanya pointed, dark skin striped by reed shadows, morning light slanting through the glass aviary. "Got him. Back right corner."

Aila squinted into darkness, teasing out a patch of silver-blue feathers. For the past week, she and Tanya had worked to thwart the Bix phoenix from his favorite new hiding spot, employing every strategy from piling fish near the observation window to planting reeds in a screen along the waterfall slope. So far, the bird's determination outmatched them both.

Tanya pushed through the reeds now working against them, stiff fronds snaring her box braids and dust fading her black polo into brown. Despite plastering a cheek to the dirt, she couldn't reach the back of the hole. Aila snickered.

"Hey, let me try." She did a little wriggle. "Spindly arms, finally good for something."

Once Tanya backed off, Aila squeezed into the gap. Not a fan of enclosed spaces. She watched cave diving videos on the internet more out of morbid fascination than any desire to entomb herself. Fortunately, this was no cavern, just a gap in the rocks where dirt had eroded down the slope, perfectly Bix phoenix-sized.

Her fingers brushed feathers, followed by an angry croak. Bix phoenixes were ganglier than their Silimalo cousins, all heron-like legs and neck. Careful not to strain anything delicate, Aila hooked an arm around the bird's torso and heaved him out.

"There you go." Tanya knelt at her side, monitoring progress. "Turn him around a bit. Perfect. Now hold up right there."

Aila paused with the bird nearly out, scooching over so Tanya could grab the recoiling neck and spear-like beak. Khonsu didn't usually pose a threat, but under duress, she couldn't blame an animal for lashing out. Through his restrained beak, he let out an indignant croak.

"All right." Tanya shifted to a more stable stance. "One. Two. Three."

They pulled the bird out and released him to the air. His wings flashed lapis blue, bringing him down the slope to land on stilt legs, tail an angry fan of gray wisps.

At his irritation, all water in the exhibit rippled—a cascade down a rocky cataract, into a pool full of papyrus reeds and lotus flowers. The phoenix ruffled. Squawked. As he pranced into the water, the current rose at his command, washing over his feathers to clean the dust away.

A great trick to play on patron water bottles.

"You've got this whole lovely aviary, Khonsu!" Tanya arced an accusing arm over the sunny glass dome, the lush vegetation of a Renkailan river delta, the feeding tray brimming with fish. "Why you gotta keep shoving your ass in muddy holes?"

The phoenix squawked at her, then dipped into the pond for another wash.

With their mission accomplished, the keepers left the aviary.

Opening time had long passed, the public walkways swarming with patrons as the Movasi summer bloomed in full force. Khonsu's exhibit was modeled after the Bix Desert of Renkaila (largest in the world, with the interior desert of Movas a close second), but the zoo's wider Renkailan section followed the forested eastern coast, paths shaded (blissfully) by canopies of many-armed banyan trees. Tanya and Aila worked their way around the northern edge of the aviary hub.

One bend in the path transported them back to the northern hemisphere, the temperate forests of Fen, across the cloud-scraping mountains to the northeast. Movas itself was a habitat sandwich west to east: scrubby coast, then low mountains, then high desert, then *bigger* mountains, that second ridgeline defining borders with Fen and Pennja. Cypress and giant bamboo screened the paths. Three-faced marmosets hooted within their netted enclosure, flashes of gilded fur swinging through the branches. Human children hooted louder, careening through the lines of a food court and chasing feral (and thankfully, non-magical) pigeons around tables.

"We need to try something new." Tanya dodged a convoy of strollers without breaking stride. "Metal, maybe. Plants aren't permanent enough to block him out."

"Won't he just summon a current to break anything loose?"

Tanya groaned. Aila commiserated. Thwarting a stubborn animal was frustrating on the best of days, especially when that animal had magical control over water.

"He's just a bird, Tanya. With a brain the size of a walnut. I'm sure our combined human intelligence can outsmart him."

"Combined intelligence, hmm? We both know you're the brains of this partnership."

"Oh? And what does that make you?"

"The beauty, of course." Tanya batted lush lashes, folding

manicured nails primly beneath her chin. "Maybe if we get this volunteer program off the ground, we can get some fresh ideas in here, finally beat that bird at his game."

"You want to make your poor volunteers crawl around in the mud?"

"It's a learning opportunity. Builds character!"

Aila would admit, a great deal of her own character building had transpired while covered in mud, or hay dust, or whatever other substances one encountered in endangered species barns. The bulk of that, she hadn't experienced until college. Tanya's ambitious proposal (currently under consideration by the zoo director) was to form a volunteer keeper program, bringing young trainees to shadow real keepers and build the next generation of zoo superstars.

A very *Tanya* plan—generous, forward-thinking. Aila might well shrivel into hay dust herself if a stranger had to shadow her all day, but she supported her friend regardless.

Tanya carried the conversation, navigating the river of patrons while musing on volunteer prospects and how to combat the crafty phoenix. Aila nodded at the appropriate intervals. Most people thought her rude when she kept quiet, but sometimes, she just wanted to listen. Not have to be on all the time. Tanya understood how to give her space without leaving her behind.

"How's the Jewelport phoenix cam?" Tanya asked with practiced nonchalance.

Aila perked up. "Have you been watching?"

"Here and there." Tanya smirked, knowing the perils of phoenix-related questions.

"I haven't checked in yet this morning—*sooo* busy. But it's amazing, Tanya! The Jewlport Zoo has an incredible setup. All the nesting materials are imported from Silimalo. Real scrub olive! In addition to the trees from the Movasi nursery, of course. Their enclosure is all open-air. Natural climate. It keeps the feathers so healthy!"

"Mm-hm."

"The phoenixes laid their first egg four weeks ago." Aila tapped her fingers against the air. "Average incubation time of twenty-eight days. They could have chicks any day now!"

"Very exciting."

"A lot of people have been asking about the immolation, if the female is healthy enough. She'll have to burn to hatch the eggs, of course, and she'll reincarnate as a chick if everything goes right, but the keepers have valid concerns with her age. The process gets more uncertain the older the hen, but considering she's had a clutch before, she should have the experience required to . . . Sorry, I'm talking too much again, aren't I?"

Tanya laughed. "You, Ailes? Never. Skies and seas save us the day the breeding committee finds a mate for Rubra."

Aila might burst into flames herself if that happened.

"Maybe we will." Speaking the prospect aloud fluttered her chest. "With how successful the nest at Jewelport has been? IMWS is *bound* to ramp up other programs in Movas. Right?"

"That would be grand." Tanya sighed, wistful. "Now if only we could get excited Aila to show up in front of the general public, the rest of us would be doomed."

Aila stiffened. Dropped her eyes. "I've gotten better."

"Oh, girlie." Tanya squeezed her arm. "There's nothing wrong with being an introvert! You're not the best at the whole socializing thing. So what? I've never met another person who can recite two dozen feeding schedules down to the teaspoon."

"Sure," Aila muttered.

"Or someone who will drop her schedule in a heartbeat whenever I need an extra hand."

"Right, but—"

"It's just a shame, you know. So few people getting to see your passion."

Aila remained slumped. Funny, how often she'd been fed that exact line from her teachers. From her parents.

From the Fenese portion of the zoo, their path snaked into spruce trees, dense as the wide Vjari forest that spanned most of the northern hemisphere above Movas. Vanilla bark scented the air, paired with a tang of pine needles and misted concrete. Overhead, squeals of delight and terror joined feathered wing-beats. Griffin rides ranked among the zoo's flashier attractions, and though the saddled beasts were all domestic varieties bred for people and cargo transport. Their wild scarp griffin cousins could be viewed a couple exhibits over.

"What's wrong, Ailes?" Tanya asked. Too observant.

Aila clamped her mouth shut, studying the pattern of chewing gum and soda stains on the concrete.

"*Aila*. What have we talked about?"

Aila muttered under her breath.

"What was that?" Tanya pressed.

"*Bottling up your problems doesn't make them go away.*" Aila's therapist, annoyingly, said the same thing. "I'm trying, Tanya. Last time I gave a keeper talk, my legs nearly gave out on me. *Again*. What if I trip into the exhibit? That would be a show, Maisie eating me in front of everyone."

"She'd never."

"She's a carnivorous horse, Tanya."

"Carnivorous horses still know who feeds them."

Aila rolled her eyes. "I've *always* been like this. Why should I keep hoping something will change?"

"Don't give me that defeatist talk, Miss Ailes."

"It's true! In grade school, I spent more time talking with our class moss marten than I did with other human kids." The moss-crusted fur of the martens purified air, making them a staple of offices, reception lobbies, schools. Their wide black eyes made them good listeners.

Tanya shrugged. "You knew you liked animals. Is that a bad thing?"

"In high school," Aila went on, "while *normal* kids spent their lunches gossiping about crushes and movies? I sat alone in a corner. Reading zoo books."

"Must've been a sight."

"A boy tried to talk to me once. I stared at him so long without saying anything, he backed away and never spoke to me again."

Tanya stifled a laugh. "That's...Yeah...you've mentioned that one before."

The path sloped upward, lined by a railing of rough-hewn logs, info signs and building fronts decorated in bright geometric designs on dark backgrounds. In winter, the zoo dressed the Vjari section up with a snow machine, though nothing frozen lasted long in Movas.

"So maybe this is just me." Aila kicked a bit of gravel off the path. "Doomed to be antisocial. Forever."

Tanya clicked her tongue. "High school is no baseline to be judging the rest of your life. Took me most of high school just to realize I'm a woman."

Aila scrunched her nose. Point taken.

"And even college," Tanya continued. "We get shoved together as roommates, and how many days before you spoke to me? Three? Four?"

"*Five*," Aila muttered.

She'd applied for a single dorm room. Imagine her horror upon being assigned a double. As the only child of two working parents, she'd scarcely had to share a house, much less a room. Avoidance seemed the best strategy. If Aila burrowed deep enough beneath her phoenix-print comforter, maybe she could survive the year without interaction.

To her surprise, Tanya left her alone. And started decorating.

Onto their dorm wall went a dozen posters for the most obscure movies Aila had never heard of. *House of the Phantom Cat. A Cockatrice for Two. Krakenado.* What in all the skies and seas was a krakenado? Aila couldn't stop herself. She had to ask.

Tanya, the devious asp, had seized the opportunity, redirecting their conversation to what Aila thought about naturalistic exhibit design. Clearly a superior alternative to historic exhibits, any loss in patron visibility more than made up for in the well-being of the animals and—

Focus, Aila. You're doing it again.

"You've come a long way, Ailes," present Tanya said. "Change doesn't come easy. But you've got to keep testing that comfort zone. You'll grow with it. I promise."

"If I have to answer any more absurd questions from the general public, I'll combust."

"Oh? You're sure you can't make any exception?" Tanya's brow quirked up. "Not even for a smoking hot dragon keeper you've always got your eye on?"

"*What?*" Aila squeaked.

They'd reached the trio of dragon aviaries. The largest dome enclosed a Vjari cliffside, dark rocks coated in pine trees and purple lupine. The needles rustled with a scrape of claws as the diamondback dragon shifted behind the trees. By the observation window, a crowd packed tight, craning their necks to spot the elusive resident.

For once, Aila couldn't care less about the crowd.

At their center stood a keeper with the most swoon-worthy grin in the zoo. Tall with broad shoulders. Fair skin. Dark hair swept into a mesmerizing tousle, the lone curl against his temple enough to occupy Aila's thoughts for days.

"Welcome, everyone," Connor announced. "The afternoon keeper talk will begin soon."

Maybe Aila could stand listening to a keeper talk if she wasn't the one delivering it. Her somersaulting heart would give out on her if she risked anything closer.

"We should say hello," Tanya proposed.

"*Excuse me?*" Aila's heart ceased somersaulting and tried stopping instead. "No. Tanya. That's a terrible idea—"

Tanya grabbed Aila's arm and marched them toward the crowd.

Oh no.

Oh no no no no.

"*Tanya,*" Aila hissed. "I'm fine. Really. Let's go!"

"Nonsense!" Tanya sang. "One little distraction to clear your head. What's the harm?" She smiled, a glint of victory in her devious brown eyes. Not wanting to cause a scene, Aila slumped behind her like a boneless fish.

A quick listen. What could go wrong?

By the observation window, the crowd pushed into a ring around Connor. Children raced through the periphery, roaring as they flapped plush toys of diamondback dragons. Since adding the item to their inventory, the gift shops struggled to keep them in stock.

Whatever. Phoenixes were cooler.

"Good afternoon!" came Connor's voice over his lapel microphone. "If you're here for the keeper talk, please gather in front of me. If a few of the taller guests wouldn't mind making room in the front? There you go."

Aila and Tanya kept to the back of the crowd, where they could gawk at their leisure. Connor, the zoo's head dragon keeper, had joined the staff not long after Aila.

Horns and fangs. He was gorgeous.

That hair the color of ink. Eyes like aquamarine. Every keeper in the zoo wore the same black polo with a peacock griffin embroidered on the pocket, yet the way his fit that toned chest and broad shoulders...

"Mm-hmm," Tanya agreed. "That's one fine-looking boy."

Aila's nose scrunched so tight her cheeks hurt. "What about Teddy?"

"I said *one* fine boy, not *the* finest boy on the continent. You deserve something nice, too. Should go talk to him."

Aila would rather ask the fire-breathing dragon if she'd like a date.

She was awful at people watching. Tanya could look over a crowd and instantly spot the couples holding hands, the ones bickering over the zoo's map app. Yet even oblivious, hermit crab Aila noticed the bloom in Tanya's voice when she talked about Theodore. She noticed how he always looked at Tanya like a flame-wreathed queen (as he should).

And sure, Aila was lonely. And various levels of envious for her friend's much-deserved romance, especially when Aila's approach to dating better imitated a category five hurricane.

"Welcome to the San Tamculo Zoo!" Connor said with a dazzling grin. "How are you all doing this beautiful Movas morning?"

A round of cheers and overlapping answers sounded from the crowd. Somewhere, a child wailed. A mother shushed him.

"You're all here to appreciate this beauty behind me, the Vjari diamondback dragon." He gestured to the observation window. "Let's see if we can get her to say hello?"

How did he do it? He spoke without wobble, without hesitation. The crowd laughed, and he'd hardly made a joke. What Aila wouldn't give for an ounce of that confidence.

"Hello, Vera!" Connor held a theatrical hand to his ear, head tilted to the window. "We've got some visitors here who'd like to meet you."

He slipped a hand into his pocket, remotely triggering a bell within the exhibit. Pine needles rustled. Rocks scraped. The crowd gasped.

From behind the trees emerged a massive snout, black scales flecked with gold. Wide yellow eyes followed. After a scan of the crowd, the diamondback dragon slipped down from the cliffs in a serpentine motion, four clawed legs moving agile over the terrain, leathery wings folded at her back. She sprawled upon an outcrop of rock, displaying the yellow and red diamond pattern down her back.

In the crowd, phones shot up, pictures flashing.

"No flash, please!" Connor said. "For the comfort of our beautiful animals."

The flashes ceased. Fickle, all of them.

"Everyone, I'd like you to meet my friend Vera." Connor swept an arm to the exhibit. "Our female diamondback dragon. Unlike other dragon species, female diamondbacks are larger than the males. Our Vera is about thirty-five feet long, a whopping twelve tons."

The crowd bobbed their heads, transfixed. For once, Aila agreed. Watching Connor's infectious smile, the lilt in his voice when he talked about his dragons, her eyes glazed over with distracting thoughts.

"Diamondback dragons are native to the boreal forest of Vjar. Anyone here from Vjar?"

A few hands lifted.

"Welcome! We're glad to have you all the way down here in Movas. Of course, what we call cold down here has nothing on a Vjari winter. Dragon scales are resistant to both extreme cold and heat. Powdered dragon scales are the most widely used strengthening agent in modern construction." Connor tapped the glass behind him. "We use them in all our glass exhibits. Just make sure your powder comes from humane, naturally shed dragon scales!"

Skies and seas, accurate conservation facts, too? Aila could have swooned.

Connor clicked his remote. Within the exhibit, a trapdoor released a dead rabbit. Vera snapped up her treat in a single mouthful, followed by a contented growl.

"Now!" Connor clapped his hands. "I'd love to answer any questions about Vera."

A battalion of hands shot up. Connor pointed to a straw hat.

"Yeah, so, what do dragons eat?" the man asked.

What a dumb question. Who didn't know that dragons ate—

"What an excellent question!" Connor replied. "Dragons are carnivores. In the wild, they hunt primarily scarp griffins. Here at the San Tamculo Zoo, we feed Vera a balanced diet with several types of meat. Another question?"

He pointed to a young girl in the front row. She swayed back and forth at the attention, hands clutched behind her yellow sundress.

"I was . . . Well, I was just wondering . . . Well . . ." She spoke in a ramble, her attention flitting like an indecisive bird. Kids. The absolute worst at asking questions. During Aila's keeper sessions, she avoided them at all costs.

Connor leaned forward, eager.

"I was just wondering . . ." the girl continued. "How did Vera get here?"

"Another wonderful question! Unfortunately, if you look at Vera's right wing, you might notice something amiss."

As Connor pointed, the crowd craned their heads. The injury

wasn't hard to see: a swath of leathery webbing missing from the dragon's wing.

"When Vera was a hatchling, she was captured by poachers," Connor explained. "The International Magical Wildlife Service caught the culprits as they tried to smuggle her across the Vjari border, but by then, she'd suffered damage to her wing. Because she couldn't be released into the wild, she lives here as an ambassador for her species. Hopefully, your visit today will inspire you to support conservation of diamondback dragons in the wild!"

"Why's she on her own?" shouted someone else. "Isn't she lonely?"

"Ah, well, we used to have a male diamondback dragon. In fact, the pair was able to breed! However, females are only receptive to breeding once every several years, and outside of that, they're incredibly territorial. So our male diamondback moved on to another zoo. Vera is quite content with the single life. She gets all the rabbits to herself!"

Despite Connor's cheerful tone, Aila swore she heard a strain beneath the words. San Tamculo had, indeed, bred a clutch of diamondback dragons a year ago. Part of the reason why plushies were so popular in the gift shop—visitors flocked to see the hatchlings scampering over rocks and puffing smoke at pine needles. Even she had to admit, they'd been precious.

Then, when they were old enough, they'd been transported to a Vjari rehabilitation center for release into the wild. They never made it. In transit, the shipment was intercepted by poachers, the precious cargo no doubt sold off to black-market collectors—either as pets or in pieces. How Aila would have liked to throw those slimy excuses for humans into the dragon enclosure, see how much they liked it.

The next few questions took on a more lighthearted tone:

the heat resistance rating of dragon hide, how often she shed her scales, whether Connor had to brush her teeth with a giant toothbrush and if anyone had ever died trying to do so. As the crowd began to disperse, Aila fidgeted.

"Well, that was fun," she said. "We should get back to work, yeah?"

"What, you don't want to say hello?" Tanya teased.

"Why in the endless skies and seas would I want to do that?"

"Because every time that boy opens his mouth, you get this look in your eyes like you're thinking about—"

Aila tackled her. Tanya swatted back. After several seconds of wrestling like children, rather than professionals in their late twenties, Aila crossed her arms and pouted.

"You know I'm teasing." Tanya smirked. "Though I'd be so proud if you said hello."

The best friend guilt trip. What a low blow.

"*Just* hello," Aila conceded.

Tanya shooed her off like a fairy godmother. Or a wicked matchmaking witch. Aila marched toward the dragon exhibit with concrete steps.

There came the wobble. Aila focused on steady strides, but her brain struggled between proper posture and remembering how to breathe. By the observation window, Connor stood with eyes down, unfastening the microphone from his polo. Those eyes shone clear as a tropical—

"Hello!" Aila blurted out. She expected more words to follow. None did. Shoot.

Startled, Connor looked up. "Oh, hey. Something you need?"

"Me? Nah. I just..." Aila moved an arm to lean against something, discovered only smooth glass within reach, abandoned the motion and swung her hands at her sides. "Tanya and I were walking by. Listened to your talk. That's Tanya, by the way."

Aila pointed. Tanya waved back from across the plaza, brows perched high. Aila vowed to fill her socks with bird kibble later.

"Thanks," Connor said. "You're Aila, right? The phoenix keeper?"

He knew her name. *Don't panic don't panic don't panic.*

"Yeah, that's me?" Why did that come out as a question. Aila grinned. Too wide. "Amazing keeper talk. Wish I could give one like that."

Connor focused on his microphone. Oh no, was she being too weird? Too *boring*? Aila's heart tried to chisel its way out of her chest.

"I appreciate it," Connor said. "I should get going, though. Work to do."

"Of course. Yeah. Work."

"Take care, Aila."

"Same."

He left her with a half-smile. Aila returned to Tanya, cursing herself for going along with such a horrible idea. Why was she so vulnerable to peer pressure?

Tanya laid a hand on her shoulder. "We need a date night. Work on your small talk."

"Thanks, Tanya." As if that would do any good against this disaster.

They resumed their walk, Tanya with a thoughtful silence, Aila musing ways she could turn herself into a specter and never have to interact with another human. Her stomach squirmed as she looped over her chat with Connor, replaying every horrendous word. Coming up with the right thing to say was so much easier once she was alone, a moment to think. To breathe.

Hi, Connor! Wow, what an amazing keeper talk! You have a knack for this.

Thank you! Aila, was it?

That's me! Silly, how we hardly see each other. We joined the zoo around the same time.

You're so right, we did! Maybe we could keep up with each other a little better?

There's a great coffee place a couple of blocks over, down by the trolley station. My treat?

I'd love to.

Aila frowned. If she could manage half the competence in real life as she did in her imagination, she might stand a chance.

She and Tanya reached the phoenix complex, the cool interior a welcome reprieve from the hot morning—even if the air conditioner had started rattling more than it used to. And the door to the patio had jammed ajar. Functional, but nowhere near as updated as the facilities at the Jewelport Zoo. Some world-famous breeding center. A whole shipment of dragon hatchlings stolen, no male phoenix.

Aila pulled out her laptop to check the Jewelport nest cam, already planning how she could avoid people for the rest of the day. More cleaning to do. Food prep to finish. Easy.

Behind her, Tanya sighed. "You'll be fine, Ailes. You broke the ice today!"

"It felt like falling through ice, yeah."

"Don't pout like that." Tanya wrapped an arm around Aila's shoulder, hugging her close. "I just want to see you happy."

"I know. I appreciate the advice, but...maybe I'm not cut out for the dating life."

"Don't be ridiculous, Ailes. We'll sort this out."

"You've seen me flounder like a Vjari auk enough times, what makes you think...?"

Aila frowned at her laptop. The Jewelport live cam loaded as a black video screen, the chat in the sidebar frozen. She refreshed the page. Still the same.

"Weird," Aila said.

"Hmm?" Tanya squinted at the screen. "Camera's down? I'm sure they'll have it back up by lunchtime. All those fancy donors watching the cute phoenix nest on their breaks."

Maybe. Jewelport struggled through some technical difficulties when the camera first went up, but they'd had smooth sailing since their phoenix pair laid eggs, and why take the camera down without good reason? Unless...

"Tanya." Aila bounced. "What if the female immolated? The timing's right!"

"You think they'd close the camera for that?"

"Sure? Maybe they don't want the public freaking out, seeing her burst into flames? Necessary to hatch the eggs, of course, but you know how people can be. Or maybe they want to make sure all the chicks are healthy before going live again."

Aila whipped out her phone, struggling to type as her fingers jittered. It must be in the news. A clutch of phoenixes hatched in Movas! Jewelport PR would be daft if they didn't have this story ready to launch. She pulled up a search tab and typed *Jewelport phoenix nest*...

Jewelport phoenix nest raided, the autocomplete offered.

Aila stared at the screen.

She read it again, a pit in her stomach. A mistake. It had to be. She clicked the article. A choked gasp drew Tanya to her side.

"Ailes? What's wrong?"

No. No no no. This can't be right.

"Early this morning..." Aila's voice caught. She took a deep breath. "The South Coast Police Department responded to a tripped security alarm at the Jewelport Zoo. Upon arrival, responding officers found signs of forced entry through the west parking lot, as well as the building housing the zoo's breeding pair of critically endangered Silimalo phoenixes. Though the male bird was found unharmed, the female and her nest of five eggs are unaccounted for. The avian pair earned worldwide fame this summer as millions tuned in to watch..."

Aila's words trailed off. Her vision dimmed around the edges.

"Not a camera malfunction," she said, quivering. "Not immolation. They're..."

Tripped security. Forced entry.

She fell into a chair. Her legs never shook this bad except when she stood in front of a crowd, yet here she was, alone with Tanya in a derelict breeding building that suddenly felt much colder than usual. Her chest tightened. How was she supposed to breathe?

"Oh, Ailes..." Tanya pulled up a seat beside her.

"How could this happen?" Aila struggled with the words, struggled to make sense of them. "Someone took them. Someone *stole* the phoenixes?"

Saying it out loud made it real.

The phoenixes were *gone*.

Aila's world crumbled, taking her with it. Drawing her knees to her chest, she tightened into a trembling ball in her chair. Tears welled in her eyes. When she stared again at the black video feed, she wanted to scream, wanted to say anything.

Only a sob came out.

An entire nest of phoenixes. Gone.

Tanya wrapped an arm around her as she cried, nothing to say, a steady presence in a world falling to pieces.

Chapter Four

Aila drifted. Broken.

For the rest of the week, her phone stayed glued to her hand, doomscrolling through every article about the *Great Jewelport Phoenix Nabbing*, the *Chick Conservation Caper*, the *Firebird Tragedy*. Tacky titles, but Aila devoured every word, searching for meaning amid chaos. She found none. Article after article appeared with sensational headlines but scant details, the South Coast Police Department scrambling to catch up with perpetrators long gone.

One significant detail slipped out of the zoo's security footage, and it was the one that twisted Aila's heart the most: the female phoenix *had* immolated, had hatched her chicks in the way no artificial incubator could replicate. The thieves swooped in the same night.

"Ailes," Tanya chided. "How are more news articles going to help?"

She loomed over Aila like a concerned dragon mother—part sympathy, part "I will drag you up by the claws if it's for your own good." Above them, summer sunlight glared through the glass of a smaller aviary. Dust and sagebrush itched Aila's nose as she sat on the ground, back slumped against the gnarled trunk of a juniper tree, terrain typical of the rocky plateaus dotting the interior desert of Movas.

A six-foot-tall thunderhawk perched beside her, talons at eye level.

His plumage varied from stormy gray to electric blue, shifting with iridescence. Ozone drenched the air. Sparks danced within his crest, head cocked, aqua eyes looking down on Aila as if he might swallow her in a single gulp.

Looks could be deceiving. Cumulus wielded a hooked beak capable of slicing deer hide like cotton candy, could generate lethal electricity for subduing prey, but the aging bird's temper couldn't be gentler. At Tanya's prompting, he lifted one massive foot off the rock, placid as she gave the talons their monthly inspection (protected by rubber gloves on both hands, of course). Zoo safety protocol required a partner accompany her while doing so. Just in case.

"Clippers, please?" Tanya asked.

Aila hefted the shears out of their equipment box. While Tanya trimmed the thunderhawk's talons, Aila slouched and scrolled through her phone. Another news article popped up, bereft of new details. Only speculation about the phoenix poachers. *Who would do such a thing?* the useless final paragraph read.

Aila knew who was to blame. The same people who'd hunted Silimalo phoenixes to the brink of extinction, until the last wild birds had to be captured and brought to safety within the world's zoos. The same people who'd pushed prices on phoenix feathers higher and higher as the supply turned scarcer. A routine of phoenix feather supplements could extend a human life up to two decades, the effects more potent the younger the bird.

And most potent of all: a female who'd freshly immolated. Her fire hatched her eggs, and she emerged from the ashes as a chick herself. Male feathers weren't as valuable, or the thieves would have absconded with him as well. They still might have, if a Jewelport security guard hadn't noticed something amiss and come to investigate.

"Dremel?" Tanya held out a hand.

Aila plopped the battery-powered tool into her palm. Its drone filled the aviary as Tanya filed the thunderhawk's talons to an even point.

Poachers. Black marketeers. Selfish, greedy people.

No one would ever see those phoenixes again. They'd be smuggled out of Movas by now, distributed to wealthy buyers across both continents by the end of the month. That was, if the thieves didn't pluck their plumes on the spot and dump the leftovers in the San Tamculo Harbor. Live phoenixes weren't worth anything more than their feathers, and few facilities had the proper conditions to care for them long term.

"There's a good bird," Tanya cooed. "Almost finished." She popped open a tin of waxy balm and massaged it into dry patches on the thunderhawk's feet.

On her phone, Aila scrolled past another article, an interview with one of Jewelport's phoenix keepers. Those ones she couldn't bear to read. She clicked off the screen and rested her head against the juniper trunk.

Tanya stepped into her line of sight, hands on hips. "What's all this moping for, Ailes? You *love* visiting Cumulus."

"Cumulus is great." Aila pouted. "The rest of the world is terrible."

Beside her, the thunderhawk chirped. At least someone understood.

Tanya heaved a long sigh. "Let's clean up. Then lunch? Looks like you need it."

Aila did.

They left Cumulus a deer leg for his troubles, batted dust and sagebrush from their clothes, clicked their radios back on. Proximity to thunderhawk static made for ear-splitting interference (IMWS conducted annual surveys of wild thunderhawk nests, ensuring no conflicts with crucial radio towers, but cell reception in the Movasi interior was always hit or miss).

Few occasions made braving packed zoo food courts worthwhile, employee lunch discounts chief among them. Today's special: noodles at the Royal Ramen Rendezvous.

Aila and Tanya found a table shaded by a Fenese pergola, red beams dripping purple wisteria, overlooking a pond stocked with gilded swans and multicolored eel koi. Along the shore, patrons cranked vending machines to dispense food pellets. Feral pigeons prowled for stray mouthfuls.

Hunched over her food, Aila tried to tune out the din of vacationing families and boisterous tour groups. Noodles and savory pork should have been enough to hold her attention. Today, she idled her chopsticks through the mild broth. Spiteful genetics precluded her from enjoying anything spicier. Across the table, Tanya drenched her ramen in chili oil.

"What does this mean?" Aila's dreams of breeding phoenixes at San Tamculo seemed to plummet away, wrenched loose like a broken gate in the night. "For the Jewelport breeding program? For *our* breeding program?"

"I don't know, Aila." Tanya plucked a mushroom from her ramen. "We've just got to wait. See how things play out down there."

Aila didn't mesh well with waiting. Or patience. Or uncertainty in most capacities.

"We're already in a precarious position! San Tamculo's been out of the phoenix game for a whole decade. Everything in the public exhibit might be updated, but the breeding facilities are going to keep withering away if we don't *use* them."

Tanya's lips puckered. "Refrigerator in the kitchen *has* been making upsetting noises."

"It's more than the noisy refrigerator, Tanya."

"Smell, too. You think a purserat died back there or something? People say those things aren't magical, but how else do they manage to burrow into impossible places?"

"It's more than the *refrigerator*! The patio door that doesn't fit right. That crack in the linoleum that always catches our boots. I haven't seen our incubator boxes in over a year, and who remembers the last time we refreshed the fire-retardant interior paint?"

"Well..." Tanya stirred her noodles. "All that's obnoxious, sure. But we hardly use that building for more than the kitchen. And stashing our backpacks on the desks."

"That's my *point*, Tanya!" Aila gripped her chopsticks like a judge's gavel. "It's hard enough justifying a whole breeding building for one phoenix. It's hard enough rehashing the same stupid argument *every single year*."

Tanya's brow lifted. "Wait a minute. Are we...talking about Luciana?"

"*Of course we're talking about Luciana!*"

Aila's teeth clenched on the witch's name. Luciana, glittering star of their college class. Leader of the zoo's cash-cow griffin show. Employee of the month *eight times* in three years, and Aila had to suffer seeing that smug face on a plaque in the coordinator's office. Every time IMWS declined Aila's request for a second phoenix, she had to drag herself to the zoo director's office and argue against Luciana's *absurd* proposal to transfer Rubra to the griffin show.

Aila's tone took on a flippant impersonation, her hand batting imaginary hair cascading over her shoulder. "*What good is Rubra doing behind glass, Aila? Let her perform!*" Aila waggled her fingers in spite. "As if a phoenix is only valuable dressed up in ribbons and glitter."

"Aila—" Tanya tried to cut in.

"Luciana thinks she knows best about everything. Just because she has the perfect hair. And the perfect face. And the public speaking voice of an angel."

"Aila, this is a tangent."

"This is not a tangent!" Everything snowballed in Aila's brain. "We're barely holding on to one phoenix, one derelict building, Luciana breathing down our necks. What if Jewelport was the last straw for Movas? What if...?" Aila's voice caught. She turned small, hunching over the table. "What if I missed my chance? What if I'm not *good enough* to breed phoenixes? If Jewelport couldn't manage with their facilities and experience..."

Tanya reached for Aila's hand. The anchor didn't take the anxiety away, but it helped Aila catch her breath.

"You know that's nonsense," Tanya said. "This news hit you hard. You're allowed that, Ailes. But don't let some mishap all the way in Jewelport get you doubting yourself."

Aila's thoughts were angry wasps, but she didn't know how to wrangle them, didn't want to speak any more worries into existence for fear of them taking over her.

Tanya leaned in with a knowing look. "Finish your lunch, Aila. A tragedy, letting good noodles go to waste. Yeah?"

She clacked her chopsticks against Aila's, playful. The sounds of the plaza drifted back, shouting children and honking swans combating the noise in Aila's head. She mustered a smile.

"An unforgivable tragedy. I could never look you in the eyes again."

Aila dug into her soup, lukewarm now. She hoped Tanya was right.

With lunch devoured, they hiked back to the aviaries. The

path split near the kelpie exhibit, one side leading up to the phoenix complex, the other toward the zoo entrance. Tanya gripped Aila's shoulders and looked her hard in the eye, no room for escape.

"Now, Ailes. I *need* to pop over to the admin building and check on my proposal for the volunteer program."

Something tiny and tight squeezed in Aila's chest. "Yeah. I know."

"Which means I'm gonna need you to hold yourself together on your own for a bit. OK?"

No. It wasn't OK. Aila's world was shattering and she needed Tanya and—

"Sure. I can manage that."

Tanya squeezed her shoulder before parting ways. Alone, Aila hiked up the hill, beneath the metal phoenix sculpture and arbors shaded with grape vines, into the phoenix complex.

Her best therapy now would be losing herself in chores.

Hard to focus on that, even, when her boots chafed against yellowed linoleum, crackling where the adhesive had dried out. The public exhibit stayed immaculate for zoo visitors. But behind the scenes? She cataloged every patch of faded paint and countertop stain. Beside the observation window, two desks were crammed into a corner. Above Tanya's, the wall was decorated with cheesy movie posters, several new additions since their college dorm.

Above Aila's desk hung the phoenix poster she'd kept for twenty years. A distant dream.

She marched out the back door, onto a patio overlooking the phoenix exhibit. In the heyday of the breeding program, keepers would have sat out here for lunch, feeding hatchling phoenixes bundled in heated blankets. Now, all that remained was faded terracotta tile, a splintered picnic table, drifts of olive leaves clumped against the building's stucco. Aila carried out a bin of feeding bowls. The hose unraveled like a knotted snake (the on-call keeper who came in on Aila's days off always wound it up wrong, no matter *how many times* they'd argued). One by one, she sprayed down her dishes, then propped them against the railing to dry. Above her, a cloudless sky. Typical for Movas: scorching summers, not a drop of rain until winter.

The urge hit to pull her laptop out, that comforting routine of checking the Jewelport phoenix cam for updates. A comfort no longer.

This pang in her heart was unbearable, worse even than soggy socks from an errant hose maneuver. She wriggled damp toes and planned her afternoon. Finish meal prep. Fix that loose perch in Rubra's aviary. Then on to the closing routine, moving animals into their back exhibits, locking everything up for the night. Aila forced herself to keep moving, the sweet oblivion of manual labor promising to ease her nerves.

Before she could enact her plans, the radio at her belt clicked on.

A call came through loud and clear. Words to stiffen her in horror. The most harrowing summons imaginable, any plans for a mindless afternoon shattered like glass tossed to concrete.

"Griffin show, calling aviaries."

For a long moment, Aila stood still, as if lack of movement could shield her from the unpalatable words. The radio crackled, the message repeated with a hint of irritation.

"Griffin show, calling *aviaries*."

The words sent Aila rigid. She'd recognize that dulcet accent anywhere, the caramel tone with savage curls and painted nails lurking underneath.

Luciana.

The radio hung in Aila's hand, unanswered. Maybe she

wouldn't. Maybe she'd let Tanya deal with whatever that griffin show witch wanted.

Seconds dragged by. Why hadn't Tanya answered? Aila grimaced, realizing Tanya was in the admin building. If she'd turned down her radio to avoid interruption—

The radio clicked again. "I know you're there, dork. Answer me."

Aila puckered her lips. Well, she *definitely* wasn't answering now. She dredged her memory for zoo policy on radio communications, whether or not she could get written up for forgetting her radio in the other room and missing a call from another department.

Another click. "I can *see* you. Loser."

Aila jerked in alarm. She spun a circle on the patio, searching the trees between the aviary domes as if expecting to square off with a sniper barrel. Most of the view behind the phoenix complex was foliage, but sure enough, through a gap in the boughs she spotted a smudge of teak wood. The distant wall of the griffin show amphitheater curved through vegetation like a ship's hull parting waves.

Atop the stadium lookout stood a silhouette, black hair curling in the breeze like a movie villain, radio propped by her ear and fingers strumming the rail in impatience. Even at too far a distance to make out Luciana's face, Aila shrank beneath an imagined scowl.

She clutched her radio and put on her most condescending customer service voice.

Click. "Hello, this is aviaries. How may I help you today?"

A pause hung on the line like curdling cheese.

"Do you have any bird arthritis ointment?" Luciana radioed back. "The topical kind?"

"Doesn't griffin show have their own stock?"

"We're out. You're the only other bird-centered department."

"Just order some more."

"It's for Nimit."

Aila bit back her next complaint. Luciana's ageing peacock griffin, Nimit, hadn't been faring well. She could hate the woman's guts until her deathbed, but if an animal needed help...

"Sure," Aila conceded. "We've got extra. You can come pick it up."

"Bring it here."

Aila did a double take at her radio. "Why can't you come here?"

"Afternoon show's about to start. We've got to get ready. Bring the medicine before showtime. Thanks."

The radio clicked off. Luciana's silhouette disappeared from the amphitheater railing. Aila stared back, mouth agape.

That self-absorbed bitch.

As if Aila should expect anything else from the zoo's premier performer. The prodigy of the griffin show. *Why don't you two collaborate?* Aila's performance reviews always went. *The Silimalo phoenix would be an outstanding addition to the show!* Aila would sooner hurl herself into the cold Middle Sea than throw her lot in with that shallow excuse for a department. The mission of the San Tamculo Zoo was to save endangered wildlife, not pimp them out for tourists.

Only the thought of a poor, ailing peacock griffin spurred Aila to clip her radio to her belt and duck inside the keeper building. Armed with angry mutters, she dug into the cabinet of medical supplies in the kitchen. She and Tanya used their stock so rarely, she had no trouble finding an unopened box of the bird-friendly arthritis ointment. Unexpired, even.

Now, to deliver it to Luciana on a gilded platter. *Won't she love that?*

Aila slunk out of the keeper building, head bowed beneath an onslaught of patron voices and scorching sun. She'd put on no sunscreen since morning. If she kept getting dragged outside, her pale skin would fry.

She'd blame Luciana for that, too.

Sure, go ahead and assume no one else in the zoo is busy. Just because Aila's schedule wasn't crammed with three public shows a day didn't make her routine less hectic. Or less important. She got plenty of visitors to her exhibits. Not the same crowds that packed the griffin show amphitheater, but there was something to be said for quality education over cheap thrills—

A shriek sounded from the World of Birds aviary.

Aila jerked to a halt. The screaming mynas should be dozing in the afternoon, roosting high in the cecropia leaves, biding their time to screech at visitors at closing time. Then came another call, a frantic hooting.

Archie.

Aila stuffed the tube of ointment into her pocket and diverted to the aviary.

The antechamber doors squealed as she pushed her way inside (mental note to grease that later). A wall of humidity hit her, sweltering despite fans blowing in the ceiling, air dense with wet leaves and decomposing soil. The railed pathway wound through forest foliage, slanting past the pond and alongside the waterfall.

Ahead, a crowd gathered. Never a good sign. There'd been a weird trend in teenage visitors recently, some fad of taking videos with the screaming mynas to post on Griffingram (their calls were perfect mimics of human shrieks, but the exact voice sounded different to every listener, even in recordings). Aila pushed her way through the onlookers, no apologies for jabbed elbows or crushed toes. When she reached the front, her mouth fell open.

"Hurry up! Get a good photo!"

On the path stood two college-aged men in board shorts and flip flops, hair gelled to douchey coifs. One held up his phone, giggling as he lined up a photo. The other man had corralled a periwinkle prairie goose.

The pair of purple geese were one of the odder aviary residents, not native to any near-tropical forest, but rather the flat tundra of Niplik that made up a large swath of the south continent. In other exhibits, the meek-mannered geese tended to get picked on. So they enjoyed a balmy vacation in World of Birds. Oil on their feathers produced a lavender scent, well known for its aura of drowsiness. A couple of birthdays ago, Aila's parents—always worried she was working too hard—gifted her a pillow stuffed with periwinkle prairie goose down (sustainably harvested, of course). She'd never slept so well.

No tranquil aroma filled the aviary now. The goose honked in terror as the patron scooped it up and held it to his chest, wings pinned, fighting webbed feet and thrashing neck as he leaned into a pose for the photographer. For three full seconds, Aila froze, too affronted to process the atrocity. Then, she transformed into a raging mother manticore.

"Turn this way!" the photographer said. "I can't see your face."

"I'm trying! This stupid thing—won't—hold still."

"What in all the skies and seas are you doing?" Aila shouted.

Their attention snapped to her, annoyed.

"Hey," the photographer complained. "What are you shouting for?"

"Put that goose down!"

The patron did so—though Aila didn't flatter herself into thinking she'd persuaded him. Holding the goose too close, he breathed deep of the lavender feathers. His eyes drooped. More than aromatherapy, the sleep-inducing aura was a predator deterrent, wild geese nesting in dense colonies that scientists could only study while using specialized breathing equipment.

The goose wriggled out of his weakened grasp, whopping a wing into his face. He yelped, blinking back to wakefulness.

"Dumb bird! What was that for?"

He moved to kick the goose. Aila snatched his arm, letting the goose escape with startled honks.

"*What are you doing?*" the patron demanded.

"Touching zoo animals is expressly prohibited!"

"Says who?"

Aila released him, too smoldering to stand still. She pointed at her uniform polo. Next, a placard beside the path with DO NOT TOUCH OR FEED THE ANIMALS in bold red letters. The man rolled his eyes. His photographer friend giggled.

At least, until the second goose arrived. With its harassers distracted, it waddled up to nip the man's ankle.

"*Horns and fangs!*" He jumped. The phone lurched from his hand and shattered against the path, shiny innards spilled across concrete.

Serves him right.

"Dumb bird *bit* me!" He knelt to salvage the pieces. "The zoo better pay for repairs!"

"Are you out of your mind?" Aila said. "Get out of here before I call security!"

"This is destruction of personal property!"

His next mistake was looking away from the phone. A split-second opening.

Archie swooped from the canopy like a gray spirit of vengeance. Silent. Focused. Before the man had time to react, Archie snatched a piece of shiny phone case and flew off, hooting like a Movasi outlaw with a posse on his heels.

"My phone!" the man shouted.

Aila had felt more sympathy for aviary slugs. "Oh, I'm sorry. Maybe you'll remember this the next time you think of harassing innocent birds?"

"Innocent? One bit me, and another stole my phone!"

By now, the other goose napper had recovered. He scowled down at Aila, entitlement drenching his face like sweat. "What's your name?"

Aila's mouth clamped shut.

"Forget it," he said. "You're in charge of the aviary? We'll be sure to tell HR all about how you assaulted us and refused to help with stolen property."

The pair skulked off, snickering as if they'd won.

Aila wrapped her arms over her chest, fighting the slimy feeling left on her skin. Fine. Let them tell on her. She'd been written up plenty of times. She'd get a reprimand, maybe a mandatory workshop on proper patron relations. *No one* hurt her animals.

As the onlookers thinned, Aila ducked under the railing and off the path. She waded through the damp foliage, careful not to slip on slick rocks around the pond. When she reached the shore, she found her two periwinkle prairie geese hunkered beneath a bush.

"Oh, babies," Aila cooed. "It's OK. They're gone."

The geese shrank away from her, shaking in fear.

"Sweet birds." Aila's voice came soft. "It's OK. Just me."

Aila trembled like her geese. Careless people were the reason these animals were here. The diamondback dragon and her lame wing, injured by poachers. Rubra alone in her aviary. Vanishing ducks harvested for weight-loss oil. Thunderhawks killed for threatening livestock. Archibirds and screaming mynas trapped as pests. Periwinkle prairie geese weren't the most endangered species in the zoo, but even they'd been overhunted before captive breeders developed more sustainable ways to harvest the therapeutic feathers.

The zoo, of all places, should be safe. *Her* aviary should be safe.

Not as safe as she'd thought. The theft at Jewelport proved that.

Aila moved slowly, extending a hand to appear unthreatening. At the stroke of one finger against soft purple feathers, the goose relaxed. Lavender laced the air, accompanied by a drowsy aura that tugged Aila's eyelids, but she was careful not to press the oil glands directly.

Kneeling beneath the leaves, legs folded in damp dirt, she sat with her geese for as long as it took to stop them trembling.

Chapter Five

Did Aila regret kicking those two assholes out of the aviary after harassing her geese?

Never.

Did the detour delay her in reaching the griffin show with the requested ointment?

Sure as rancid dragon spit.

Aila hurried away from the World of Birds aviary, hoping she wasn't too late. That hope shattered at the blare of an intercom.

"Good afternoon, ladies and gentlemen!" came the recorded message. "Please find your seats. The world-famous San Tamculo Zoo griffin show is about to begin!"

The paths of the Renkailan section wound beneath massive banyans and lemon-scented curry trees, bordered in fences of red teak latticework. One could get lost in the maze of leaves and concrete, if not for one central marker: the griffin show amphitheater rising like a vine-coated ruin, height rivaling the tallest trees, pale wood spires carved with thousands of miniature creatures and flowers.

Any illusion of antiquity was shattered beneath electric lights along the eaves, the hidden speakers blaring drums and flute music. As the notes soared, a gasp went up from the crowd inside. A flock of mirror flamingos looped overhead, flicking in and out of sight, sun reflecting off silver feathers like shards of polished glass. The squawk of a flightless Vjari auk echoed within the amphitheater. Up next, the dueling trills of a two-headed forest falcon.

Then, the most astonished gasps yet.

A Movas thunderhawk landed atop the highest minaret— Stratus, one of the griffin show's stars, a couple of decades younger than Tanya's aging charge at the aviaries. Lightning webbed the bird's feathers, building to a blinding bolt that pierced the sky and cracked with ozone. Energy surged through a lightning rod, flaring every light in the amphitheater blue.

Aila hissed a curse. The griffin show had begun.

She avoided the main amphitheater entrance, mortified at the thought of appearing in full view of the patron-packed seats. Instead, she circled around to an employee side entrance.

Just pop in. Drop off the ointment. Then leave.

Behind the scenes, the griffin show moved like well-oiled chaos. Aila slunk like a thief into the staging area, the click of the door lost within a swarm of bodies and feathers. She dodged sideways as the massive thunderhawk swooped past her from side stage, landing on a wheeled perch. He snapped up a mouse tossed by a keeper, then thunderhawk and handler disappeared toward the back aviaries. A dozen more birds and other creatures lined the room on perches or in boxes, waiting for their cue. Through another hall, Aila spotted a pair of keepers seated at a dizzying array of switches and screens, headphones over their ears, controlling the lights and music on stage. Busy with their tasks, no one paid Aila any heed.

Except for one person. *Of fucking course.*

At the center of the storm stood the human version of a lightning rod, a woman of tight curves and perfect stature. Perfect Movasi brown skin. Perfect jade nails. Perfect black curls falling glossy past her shoulders. Dark eyes and heavy lashes surveyed the milieu around her with the intensity of a basilisk.

Luciana scowled at Aila, a delicate twist to her coral lips.

"*Before* the show, I said." She brushed her hair back with a hand flip, then clipped a microphone to the collar of her polo.

"Yeah," Aila said. "I caught that. But I do sort of have other things to take care of, so—"

"Wait here. Try not to get in the way."

"But—"

Luciana strode past, through a gap in the wall and onto the stage.

"Welcome, everyone, to the San Tamculo Zoo!" Her voice soared over the speakers, clear and confident. "I'm Luciana, your host for our incredible, our awe-inspiring, our one-of-a-kind griffin show!"

The crowd applauded.

Aila contemplated throwing the arthritis ointment onto a counter, then leaving. Better for her ego, but she couldn't stop her thoughts devolving into worst-case scenarios of the precious medicine getting lost in the chaos. Of a poor, sick peacock griffin, in pain because of her. *Stupid conscience*. She scowled and backed herself into a corner to wait. Around her, keepers swarmed like a hive of beryl bees. The show was a choreographed dance, timed to the second.

Impressive. Still tacky.

"Let's start things off with a pop!" Luciana announced. Aila pictured the honeyed smile. "Give a warm welcome to our troupe of vanishing ducks, the Transparent Quackers!"

Backstage, a keeper slid open a large carrier. Four vanishing ducks waddled out, disappearing through a duck-sized tunnel in the floor. The crowd cheered as the actors appeared on stage, followed by delighted gasps as the ducks disappeared and reappeared along platforms of an obstacle course. Aila had seen them practicing on the lawn some mornings.

Whatever. Her vanishing ducks were just as cool without the cheap stunts.

A Vjari auk waddled onto stage next—dense birds in body and disposition, clubbed near to extinction thanks to poor survival instincts and tasty breast meat that never rotted. A cockatrice followed in a case of one-way glass, a fluffed chicken body with bat wings and lizard tail, turning objects to stone with a glare. The gift shop sold the trinkets as souvenirs.

"Could you step aside, please?" whispered a keeper backstage.

Aila did so, clearing a path for a green-plumed dragon. The dog-sized creature scampered after its keeper on wide-padded gecko feet, wingless, blunt snout packed with tiny teeth. Iridescent green feathers coated its body, accented by a red and yellow neck ruff. At a sign from its keeper, the dragon darted onstage in a blur of color. The crowd cheered louder.

Then, a rumble outside. Aila knew that heavy wingbeat anywhere, that call dipping low before soaring into ear-splitting decibels.

"And now," Luciana announced. "The star of our show. The mascot of the San Tamculo Zoo. Our peacock griffin!"

This one didn't fit backstage. A thunder of wings sounded outside, shaking the walls as the griffin took off. Ashamed by her curiosity, Aila edged toward the gap looking onto the stage. There stood Luciana, hands raised to the sky, green and pink spotlights dancing over her glossy hair. A wave of gasps from the crowd tracked the griffin as it circled the amphitheater, landing center stage in a hurricane of color.

The peacock griffin reared on paws of golden fur, sleek as a leopard. In the spotlight, his cobalt head feathers sparkled like sapphires, dark eyes framed by snowy white brows and cheek patches, crowned by a cluster of stiff bristles with pom-pom tufts. His wings spread with warm rufous tips, and at Luciana's command, his tail fanned with even greater resplendence, an explosion of iridescent green with blue and gold eyelets.

It was a stunning creature—the jewel of the Renkailan savannah, icon of long-gone dynasties, feathers hoarded by celebrity dressmakers now that IMWS regulated the supply. Enraptured, Aila inched closer, trying to get a better look at the gorgeous beast.

That was her mistake.

Beyond Luciana, beyond the stage, a dozen tiers of seating wrapped the amphitheater, filled to near capacity with *people*. Eyes. No way could they see Aila within the shadows of backstage, yet her knees wobbled. Her throat tightened. Hard to swallow, hard to breathe.

In an instant, she was back in college. Back on the faux stage in their animal outreach course, a Ziclexian sunburst hummingbird perched upon her hand, her classmates staring and snickering as her tongue refused to work. Words vanished. Her fingers shook. Her heart pounded so fast, she worried she'd faint in front of everyone.

"Isn't he splendid?" Luciana announced in the present. "All the way from the Renkailan plains. Let's get a closer look at those feathers, shall we?"

She pointed to a platform across the lawn from the stage, closer to the audience. The griffin cocked his head and paced a confused circle around her.

Luciana didn't miss a beat. "Uh-oh, looks like someone has a little stage fright! I think he could use some encouragement, don't you?"

The crowd chuckled. Luciana tossed a dead mouse to the

platform, reminding the griffin of his cue. He jumped forward, wings and tail spread to the cheering audience.

How did Luciana do it? Stay so calm? So confident?

Aila's stomach rioted, unable to watch any more. She hurried away from the lights and the crowd, pushing out the door into the side yard where she could gulp salty Movas air until her head stopped spinning. A pair of griffin show keepers waited nearby, eyeing her with concern. Self-conscious, she stared at the packed dirt beneath her boots. Ridiculous. She was *ridiculous*.

She'd always been ridiculous. Barely a functional human being.

Her parents had worried about her since... probably third grade? Whenever it was they'd realized she wasn't growing out of her "shyness phase" (still a solid decade before she'd gotten an anxiety diagnosis, thank you health care system). Skies and seas, she loved them both to death. But even little Aila knew she was letting them down, noting their frowns when they asked about her friends at school (or lack thereof). The concerned glances when she sat in a corner for family gatherings, more comfortable reading a book than talking to people.

Her parents had always smiled, though, when she brought home good report cards to hang on the fridge. They'd beamed when she started talking about phoenixes, clueless about zoology, but willing to buy her every book she asked for. They'd cried and hugged her when she got her college acceptance.

Aila couldn't tame her nerves around people. But grades? Books? Applications? Those were things she could control.

Work had always been something she could control.

If only her heart rate was so easy to master. Aila leaned against the griffin show wall and focused on slow, deep breaths. That was supposed to help, her therapist kept telling her. Pressing her hand against the wall was supposed to help, feeling the smooth teak wood against her skin. The grounding didn't calm her heart completely, but it helped her think a little clearer.

Heavy wings beat the air. Applause trailed the peacock griffin as he soared out of the amphitheater, circling the crowd one final time. Performance complete, he banked around the building, landing in the side yard with a spray of gravel. His keepers met him with kind words and a dead rabbit (excellent pest control, so much that Renkailan farmers often built nesting platforms to encourage griffins roosting near their fields). He trilled and snapped up the prize, prancing in delight.

Energetic. Young. This must be Ranbir, the least experienced of the show's peacock griffins. That explained the faux pas on stage. Why fill a prime-time slot with a trainee rather than their star, Nimit?

The aging griffin must be faring worse than usual.

Music swelled in the amphitheater. Luciana's honeyed voice announced the end of the show, followed by an invitation to hand donations to an adorable mouse griffin who'd stuff bills into a box while patrons posed for photos. Aila hunkered down in the side yard, content to never have to face another human again.

Luciana offered no such peace. She strode out the side door with the self-importance of a queen, surveying her colleagues as they led the peacock griffin away. Then, she appraised the cowering phoenix keeper. Sculpted brows knit in disapproval. Aila plucked her own eyebrows in an attempt to look present-able, but she could never achieve such laser perfection. Even Luciana's sigh came out elegant.

"Horns and fangs," the witch said. "After all this time? I thought you'd have some handle on that stage fright. You weren't even *out there*."

Aila wrinkled her nose. Easy for *her* to say. In college, Aila had to suffer every one of Luciana's flawless presentations, the delight of her instructors. Why couldn't Aila be like that?

She didn't need to be. Luciana could keep her applause, so long as Aila had her phoenix.

"You want this, or not?" Aila brandished the tube of arthritis ointment. Luciana waved a hand, beckoning her across the yard, and *of course* Aila followed without protest. Not like she had a spine, or anything.

The barns behind the amphitheater matched the Renkailan architecture—teak latticework, red paint trimmed with gilded flowers. Carved griffins reared on the doors. Luciana slid the wood panel open and stepped inside, the room dim and dusty with hay.

Nimit, the zoo's oldest peacock griffin, lay in a corner, feathered tail curled around him in a swirl of green. Though he didn't stand for his visitors, his cheeks fluffed as he trilled a greeting. Aila grinned. *What a cutie.*

Beside her, nails clacked. Luciana gathered the cascading curls she'd worn for the show and tied them into a more zoo-appropriate ponytail. The glossy tips teased her shoulders. Skies and seas, why couldn't Aila's hair act that luxurious? She self-consciously stroked her frizzy auburn locks, the errant gray hairs she scowled at in the mirror. Way too young for gray hairs.

Luciana held out a hand. Feeling petty, Aila tossed the ointment, which Luciana caught without fumble. Obnoxiously toned, those arms, the perfect balance of muscle and soft lines (same as Tanya, and *many* zookeepers who didn't have noodle arm genetics). She knelt at Nimit's side and offered a hand for him to sniff. Must be a crazy day, the queen deigning to get her khakis covered in hay dust.

Stop it, Aila. You're not here for her.

"How's Nimit doing?" Why did she bother asking? Why not

hightail it out of here while the basilisk wasn't looking? *Stupid, mushy heart.*

Luciana massaged arthritis cream into Nimit's front talons. Her reply came quick. Clipped. "He's doing as well as any thirty-year-old griffin can be."

Which was to say, not well. Even late twenties would be considered a long, happy life for a peacock griffin. Luciana must take good care of him.

Stop it. Don't give her that.

Nimit bore the treatment with head lowered and posture tense. When Luciana touched his back leg, he hissed and sidled away, lax wing feathers brushing hay off the floor like the world's fanciest broom. Though docile around humans, any creature this large required caution. Luciana eased off, speaking in calm tones, but he refused to let her reach for him again.

Just leave just leave just leave.

Aila stepped closer.

"What are you doing?" Luciana demanded.

"Calm your candy-coated ti—" Aila stopped herself, cheeks molten.

Luciana's glare, equally so.

"*What* were you about to say?"

"Nothing! Just let me..."

Aila hid her embarrassment by focusing on the griffin. After sniffing her hand, Nimit let her scratch beneath his chin. She moved lower, into the soft blue underfeathers of his neck. His posture relaxed. He stretched his neck to give her better access, a contented trill in his throat.

Luciana's mouth fell open. "How do you know his favorite spot?"

"I've seen you petting him, when you don't think anyone's

watching." Aila dropped to a murmur. "And when you're not worried about chipping a nail."

Luciana scoffed, a flick of black curls in her ponytail. "There's nothing *wrong* with taking care of my nails. Or do you have a phobia against proper hygiene, too?"

"Will you just put the ointment on?"

Luciana's sneer was calculated, careful not to leave too many wrinkles on that star-studded face. She returned to work. With the griffin distracted by neck scratches, he allowed her to massage his hind legs. She shifted, leaning past Aila to reach the final limb.

What was that smell? Not the dust of hay or griffin feathers, but something . . . sweet. Strawberry? Pear? Mango? A whiff of tropical shampoo, mixed with the warmer smell of—

STOP IT. Why are you smelling her?

"Well! If that's all." Aila retreated toward the door. "I'll be going now. Birds to take care of, you know."

Luciana wiped the remnants of arthritis cream from her fingers. "Thanks. If you ever want to work on that stage fright, let me know. You do work at a *public-serving* institution."

Aila huffed. Not everyone was made for the spotlight (as if Luciana would share it). "I'll stick with my phoenix, thanks."

"Sure." Luciana's voice dropped. "Until Rubra ends up where she belongs."

Aila's hand froze on the barn door. *Don't do it. Not worth it.*

"Are you still on about that?" She reeled on Luciana. Not to the dramatic effect she'd hoped for. The witch rolled her eyes.

"That Silimalo phoenix would go to much better use as part of the griffin show."

"So she can do what? Jump through hoops for your audience like a trained carbuncle? No way does she deserve such a demeaning—"

Luciana pushed Aila outside, so as not to disturb the senile griffin. In contrast to the manicured façade she put on for the public, her sneer could make a dragon flinch.

"Get over yourself," Luciana said. "Rubra is *wasted* on exhibit, sitting around doing nothing all day. You don't even have the excuse of the breeding program anymore. But put her in the show? She'd be a star overnight."

"Rubra's not *wasted* on exhibit. The whole point of the zoo is to gain appreciation for endangered animals, not to see them paraded around doing cheap tricks."

"People come to the zoo for spectacle, Aila." Luciana's whisper turned venomous. "You know as well as I do, the griffin show brings in more conservation donations than any exhibit."

Aila stiffened at the verbal slap. Her exhibits pulled in respectable revenue at their donation boxes, even more from virtual supporters excited to "adopt" an endangered phoenix or a flesh-eating kelpie. Nothing came close to the money brought in by the griffin show.

Luciana leaned in, looming over Aila with several inches of superior height (seriously, though, why was *every* human in this zoo taller than her?), taunting with her tropical shampoo. "You think Rubra's better off locked up like a museum specimen? People care about what they can connect with. We're here to leave impressions. And patrons seeing a live Silimalo phoenix flying over their heads? That's an impression no one will forget."

"Rubra deserves better than that." Aila's hands curled into weak fists. "After what happened in Jewelport? She's more important to the breeding program than ever!"

"Last I checked, you need *two* phoenixes for a breeding program."

"So we wait for IMWS to transfer another bird to San

Tamculo!" One step closer to the dream Aila had clutched since childhood.

"Stop living in your dream world. Why would IMWS transfer birds to a breeding program that hasn't run in a decade? If anything, they'll move Rubra to Jewelport."

If Luciana's last accusation was a slap, this one pummeled Aila in the gut. Bad enough, she had to worry about losing Rubra to the griffin show. But to see her phoenix stolen away to another zoo? The prospect was too incomprehensible to have crossed her mind.

They wouldn't. They *couldn't*.

"I will *never* let that happen," Aila said through clenched teeth.

Luciana looked down on her through smoky eyes, a delicate scoff flaring her nose. Always right. Always in control.

"It isn't your choice, Aila."

She left without further argument, the last word hers, Aila's stomach pitted as deep as an ocean trench.

Chapter Six

Aila prepared herself for war. Her weapons: a scrub brush and a bucket of animal-safe cleaning solution.

Within the World of Birds aviary, Archie's contraband tower had dulled beneath mud and forest algae. Not to mention the coat of bird droppings. This oddity of archibird engineering was a photo magnet on Aila's route, which meant she had to scrub the conglomerate surface of bolts and buttons and stolen cell phones once a month to keep it shining. Today, she imagined Luciana's smug face on every tarnished surface as she attacked with her bristles.

"What if that witch is right?" Aila asked, teeth gritted, stance wide as she tackled a stubborn crust of chewing gum.

Archie listened from atop his tower, blue crest raised, a diva artist ensuring the janitor didn't harm his masterpiece.

"She's usually right." Aila hated to admit it. "About dumb PR things, at least."

Archie squawked, pecking Aila's finger when she tugged a bit of metal wire. She let it be. Not like she could remove anything if she wanted to. Engineers had been trying to replicate archibird spit for decades, producing a bevy of industrial and household metal adhesives, but never as strong as the real thing.

"She *can't* be right."

Aila closed her eyes and rested her head against the tower. She wasn't a perfect zoo employee (farther from it in some aspects than others), but she gave her heart to her animals. If IMWS transferred Rubra to Jewelport like Luciana suggested... Aila didn't know what she'd do. The prospect rattled in her chest like an unbalanced washing machine, tumbling over and over and—

A *clink* sounded from Aila's belt.

She opened her eyes to see Archie staring up at her. Frozen.

He'd pulled her keyring halfway off the belt clip.

Before she could react, the archibird yanked a key and smacked it against his tower. He flew off, cackling, leaving Aila to heave and twist, but the saliva-slathered metal was welded in place. With a groan of defeat, she fumbled waterlogged fingers on the keyring, twisting off the lost key and stashing the remaining ones safe in her pocket. Just a kitchen key. She'd have to visit maintenance to request a replacement. Or two.

Aila finished cleaning and stalked out of the aviary, thoughts buzzing. IMWS *could* take Rubra away. What could she do to stop them?

She couldn't even keep a key away from an archibird.

It must have been one of those days the animals all conspired against their keepers. Not far along the path, Aila found Tanya. Scowling. A shovel in one hand. Covered in mud.

"How's Khonsu?" Aila asked.

Tanya threw up her hands, narrowly missing Aila with the shovel. "All that work we did yesterday to fill that hole in the Bix phoenix exhibit! All that hauling dirt across the zoo and up that hill. Do you know what he did?"

Aila appraised her friend's muddy uniform. "Did he dig it—"

"*He dug it out, Aila!* Less than twenty-four hours!"

The keepers made a gloomy pair walking past patrons in

summer hats and sunglasses, heads buried in maps, a mother shouting at her son not to toss kettle corn into the stone fox exhibit. Aila kept her eyes on the concrete, trying to narrow the world to something manageable. Beside her, Tanya muttered about phoenix deterrent strategies.

"Metal next time. That's all we've got left to try."

"Sure," Aila said, unconvinced. "But we're dealing with an animal who can command water. Won't he just erode away whatever we—*Oh, hello! Good afternoon!*"

Aila froze mid-stride, voice shooting to a squeak. *Fuck. Again?*

The dragon keeper, Connor, paused in the path, that adorable curl caressing his temple, brow furrowed in either alarm or confusion. Tanya shot a side-eye, one even Aila could interpret. *The fuck are you doing, Ailes?* rang in her head as clear as if Tanya had spoken aloud.

Aila begged herself to relax. To smile. *Not that wide. Griffin shit.*

"Hello," Connor said. What a gorgeous grin, flashing teeth like pearls. Never mind him looking at Aila and her nervous bouncing as if she were a wild animal.

A wild animal would flirt better.

"Good to...uh...see you again," Aila said. Why were words so *hard*?

"Small zoo, sometimes," Connor returned.

"Sure is."

"Did you need something, Aila?"

"Need something? No, no, I just..." Aila cringed at Connor's bafflement, at the mental screams from Tanya's direction. "I just wanted to say hello. See what you're up to."

"I'm pretty behind on morning rounds, actually."

Connor shifted a bucket in his hands, the handle creaking with the weight. A pungent smell wrinkled Aila's nose. It was all she had to work with. She scrambled for a joke, something to salvage this train wreck.

"Is that fish I smell?" Aila chuckled, nervous. "Or just you?"

Horns and fucking fangs, that wasn't supposed to come out like that.

Beside her, Tanya's stenciled eyebrows threatened to jump off her face. Maybe Aila could crawl into Khonsu's hole with him.

"Um..." Connor drew out the sound, frowning at his bucket. "It's fish. For Daiyu."

He nodded down the path beyond Aila, past a bamboo plaza and replica dragon egg. The maned dragon paced the glass of her aviary, serpentine body coated in jade scales, antlers sprouting from a mane of onyx and gold. She ignored the patrons fawning for photos, hungry eyes focused on her keeper.

The patrons yelped and ducked for cover as a mini rainstorm brewed beside the exhibit. Dragon-sewn storms were the backbone of the Fenese agricultural industry, a hurdle when designing zoo enclosures.

"Right. Of course!" Aila could have slapped herself.

"Sorry," Connor said. "But I should get going."

"Sure thing. We'll let you get to that. She looks hungry."

"Thanks. Good to see you, Aila. Tanya."

Looking more perplexed than when the conversation started, Connor hurried toward the dragon exhibit. Aila thanked the endless skies and seas for the escape.

Tanya swatted her arm. Fair.

"What was *that*?" Tanya demanded.

Aila slumped. "Better or worse than last time?"

"*Is that fish I smell?*"

Worse than last time. Without question. Forget a muddy hole, Aila would be better off fleeing to the remote tundra of the Niplik south pole. Or maybe to the other side of the world in Ziclexia, the largest rainforest of either continent, hidden away where she'd never have to attempt small talk again. She bore Tanya's chastisement in silence as they left Connor behind, winding up the path to the Silimalo phoenix complex.

When phoenixes courted, the male and female performed an elaborate dance: the male hanging from a tree branch, exchanging gifts of leaves in their beaks, bobbing heads and stoking fire from their tails. If the moves came out right, the pair bonded. Simple. Straightforward. Researchers had documented every step in the performance.

Why couldn't human romance be like that? Aila might stand a chance.

"...and we'll get you some practice talking to a poster or something," Tanya said, wrapping up the lecture Aila had zoned out for most of. "Wasting opportunities with cute boys like that. Tragic."

"Yeah. Tragic's what I am."

When they reached the breeding complex, the zoo commissary had dropped off tomorrow's food order on their doorstep. Tanya set her shovel aside, then grabbed a box of kale and grapes from the pile, shuttling it to their rattling refrigerator in the kitchen. Aila hefted her cleaning tools onto the counter. Beyond the observation window, Rubra perched in her exhibit, a queen of fire within her tidy little world. Still alone. One thing they had in common.

"I know people are nerve-racking, Ailes." Tanya said from the kitchen doorway.

Aila huffed. "Understatement."

She pulled out her phone to find a blinking email notification. The last thing she needed. Aila contemplated ignoring it until she built back more mental bandwidth, but better take a look, in case it was important. After swiping a few mud flecks off the screen, she opened the message.

"And I'm not trying to convince you otherwise," Tanya said. "But if you want to get better at something, the only way to go about it is to practice...Ailes? What's wrong?"

Aila had stopped breathing. Her fingers trembled. Suddenly, a lost key seemed a stupid thing to mope over. Her conversation with Connor, she could have repeated a dozen times.

This was a nightmare.

"*Aila*," Tanya pressed when no reply came.

"It's an email from IMWS. They're requesting immediate status reports on all Silimalo phoenixes in the conservation network..." She skimmed the words, moving too fast to make sense of them. She tried again. "'An internal review...seeking the best possible distribution of birds to ensure the longevity of the species...Movasi program status to be evaluated...'"

The email's language was curated to the letter, bureaucratic, masking any broader purpose. Aila read between the lines. IMWS was performing an emergency program evaluation. They'd move phoenixes wherever the birds would do the most good.

"Tanya?" Her voice squeaked. "What does this mean for us? For Rubra?"

"You know exactly what it means," came a velvet reply.

That taunt. That *intruder*. Aila spun around too fast, betraying a blur of tears in her eyes as she faced the doorway. Luciana stood on the threshold, flawless posture and flawless hair draping her shoulders, an insult of perfection as Aila shriveled like a punctured water balloon.

Tanya donned a dragon-mom scowl. "What do you want, Luc?"

Luciana flinched at the college nickname. A brief slip. The

queen had her public façade back up in a heartbeat. She held up a new box of arthritis ointment, cobalt nails clacking against the cardboard.

"Replacing your medicine. Wouldn't want you to think we're freeloaders at the griffin show." She hesitated, her expression unraveling to the verge of soft. That must be a mask, too. "Best of luck with the review. Director Hawthorn mentioned it when we chatted this morning."

"Appreciated," Tanya said. "But if you don't mind, we could use a moment to—"

"What have you heard?" Aila smeared tears and snot across the back of her hand in one ill-advised swipe. "Any other statements from IMWS? News from the director?"

"Calm down," Luciana said. "I don't know any more than you do. My guess for what happens next?" She shrugged. "Extrapolation."

Aila's heart clawed into her throat. "What do you mean?"

"Like I told you the other day." Luciana's gaze slid to the observation window. Out in the exhibit, Rubra preened in a charred olive tree, fluffed and content, no idea how her world had gone up in flames this week. "Jewelport has a working breeding program, and you don't. Now, they're short one female phoenix."

"They can't take Rubra." Aila would say it over and over in the hope it might be true. "San Tamculo is her home. She *belongs* here."

"Are you saying that because you want what's best for her? What's best for conserving the species?" Luciana hardened. "Or because *you* don't want to let her go?"

The accusation silenced Aila. Another verbal backhand, delivered with sucrose insincerity. She might have stood there for eternity, a statue to abandoned dreams, ensnared in Luciana's thorned glare until one of them dared to blink.

Tanya interceded before the barbs could tangle any tighter.

"Thanks for the ointment, Luc. I think you ought to be on your way." Tanya nodded to the boxes of produce piled on their doorstep. "We're busy here."

"Of course." Luciana's tone lightened to customer-service sweet. "Glad I could pop by. Always happy to help our sister department."

She left. But the damage was done. Luciana's words dug into Aila like manicured nails, threatening to strangle her.

For the rest of the day, Aila moved like a phantom. Tanya offered to take over her keeper talks, leaving Aila to drift in bleach-scented back hallways, slump over fluorescent-lit cutting boards, waver at the railing of the patio as if the salty breeze might carry her away like a discarded meal wrapper.

Inside the phoenix complex, the old linoleum had never looked so jaundiced. The dust amassing in every corner made her want to choke.

"Nothing's decided yet!" Tanya assured her. "Rubra's been at San Tamculo all her life. Female phoenixes are way more territorial than males. You're the one who told me that, Ailes! IMWS would be crazy to transfer her."

Though Aila craved reassurance, hope seemed dangerous. Though she fought against Luciana's words, they cut like fangs masked in coral lipstick. That witch had always been better at politics, at the infuriating dance of PR. If she thought Rubra would be better off elsewhere . . .

No. Aila refused.

But what could she do about it? Not like the world cared for what was fair. Nothing more than the broken heart of a reclusive keeper with more HR write-ups than accolades, pitted against the future of an entire species. Luciana was wrong about one thing, though. If IMWS did decide Rubra would serve better at another zoo? Aila would let her go. She'd shatter in the process, but she wouldn't be selfish, would never stand in the way of saving the birds she loved.

All Aila wanted was a chance to prove herself. She couldn't inspire crowds or flirt with cute dragon keepers, but let her show how well she could take care of phoenixes. Let her prove she could be worth something.

As the zoo closed for the night, Aila locked her animals in their back enclosures—the kelpie swirling in her water tank, Archie and his neighbors dozing in their aviary. When she put Rubra away, she checked the locks on the aviary five times, made sure the closed-circuit TV monitors were running, swiped her ID card at the door and heaved on the handle to make sure it wouldn't budge. Derelict building or not, the security measures for the Silimalo phoenix exhibit outclassed any others at San Tamculo. Jewelport must have had something similar?

Aila stalked out of the zoo, across the street to the crosstown train.

The city of San Tamculo wrapped a crescent around the bay, lights blurry through the fogged train window. The coast was hot and dry, but sheltered from the harsher interior desert by a low mountain range. The first inhabitants sent ships out into the Middle Sea to hunt red-ringed krakens, though today the harbor was all restaurants and tourist shops. Walnuts and citrus trees once coated the valley floor, now replaced by sprawling suburbia. Aila leaned her head against the glass, a screech of rails rattling beneath her, watching the world speed past.

She'd worked all her life to get here.

From the train station, Aila kept her head down and followed the sidewalk, boxed in on one side by electric cars humming down the pavement, on the other by LED signs and smells of frying oil. Restaurant patios glowed beneath string lights floating with pixie wren dust. Lines trailed out of bars. All around, people laughing and talking as they swirled past her like sea foam.

A few blocks over, the world quieted. Streetlamps stood over yards of sage and sun-baked gravel, stucco houses in tan and terracotta. Aila nodded to a passer-by walking a levitating poodle, another with a non-levitating schnauzer (not everyone had the stamina for magical pets). She keyed herself into the lobby of her apartment building and climbed the stairs to her hole on the third floor. When she flipped on the light, her care-taker routine began all over again.

"Hey, everyone. How was your day?"

From amid the jungle of plants and thrift shop furniture, the patchwork quilt on the sofa, stacks of animal care books teetering on every surface, a bolt of silver appeared. Aila's pet carbuncle, Tourmaline, greeted her with fox teeth bared into a smile, two gray tails wagging. A gem on his forehead changed color with emotion, an overjoyed pink and gold whenever she returned home—brighter, when she scratched his fluffy ears.

"Sorry for another late evening, sweetie. Summer's so busy. And today, there was..."

The thought of lost phoenixes carved out her heart, left prickles in her eyes. If she cried any more, she'd have a migraine tomor-row. Aila's to-do list was too long for migraines.

"Today was hard." She forced a grin. "But we're still on for the dog park this weekend. Maybe I can convince Auntie Tanya to come?"

Tourmaline yipped and spun a circle, dull claws padding carpet.

He trailed her around the apartment as she tended her other roommates. Crickets and a spray of water went into the fern lizard terrarium, his scales shifting to mimic leaves. Edible rock pellets for the volcanic salamanders. Check the temperature in the hot spring axolotl pool to make sure it was boiling. Mango for the mouse griffin in her aviary, and a handful of shredded paper for the purserat to add to her nest.

The carbuncle was the only one Aila had adopted herself, a wide-eyed pup with bad mange from the San Tamculo Humane Society. The purserat, Tanya caught in their work kitchen and insisted Aila dispose of. The rest came to her. Get into an animal husbandry career, and one became the go-to for any friends or distant acquaintances looking to get an unwanted pet off their hands. Aila couldn't turn any of them away.

Once her animals were cared for, she microwaved a bowl of condensed soup, curled up on the couch, and stared through what was visible of the window through the screen of plant fronds. Tourmaline lay in her lap, a bundle of warmth and musty fur.

Aila wasn't much for curios. Her apartment decoration scheme consisted of plants, books, and assorted animal care products. She wasn't much for photos, either. Most of her life, she hadn't had friends to take photos with, few exotic excursions to document.

With one notable exception.

On the wall above her desk, propped on a shelf between five potted plants, sat a framed photo of Aila and her parents on vacation in Silimalo. Her mom had bushier, redder hair than Aila did. Her dad was a tree of a man with a kind smile. They'd never traveled much when she was a kid. Could never afford it. But when she got her college acceptance, they'd surprised her with a trip for her high school graduation. She'd sobbed. It hadn't been pretty.

One week had been life-changing. They'd snorkeled coral reefs off the rocky coast, spotted pegasi on the grassy plains, toured the dormant volcano. And, of course, the highlight of the trip: a visit to the Silimalo National Zoo, Aila running around the paths like a little kid while her parents tried to keep up. The photo showed the three of them in front of the Silimalo phoenix exhibit, smiling and showing off their matching phoenix T-shirts.

Now, as Aila studied the photo in the dark of her apartment, the memory felt bittersweet. No matter how much her parents had worried about their quiet daughter, no matter how much her obsession with phoenixes perplexed them, they'd supported her every step of the way. She was the first in her family to attend college. This meant, of course, that both her parents were super duper proud.

But that also meant she had to figure out a lot on her own. Studying for placement exams. Finding internships. Learning how the fuck a college application worked. Nothing ever came easy. Aila had to work and scrape at every step.

So what should she do now? Wait and see what happened in Jewelport—if they'd come for her phoenix to replace the one they'd lost? She'd go mad twiddling her thumbs.

And nothing ever came out of doing nothing.

Careful not to disturb the snoozing carbuncle, Aila opened her laptop and browsed for updates. The Movas National News posted an article that afternoon, a statement from IMWS extending sympathy to the Jewelport Zoo and assuring the public that the Silimalo phoenix breeding program would continue after thorough evaluation.

With the article was a photo of a middle-aged woman speaking at a podium, black hair bound into a starched bun, brown Movasi skin contrasting lilac-rimmed spectacles and a matching business suit. Maria Rivera, director of the IMWS Movas Division, coordinator of the regional phoenix breeding program. A year ago, Aila spent a solid hour working up the courage to say hello to the esteemed conservationist at a zoo gala. The woman was as intimidating as a lion-headed manticore, but passionate for her work. She'd even encouraged Aila to keep applying for phoenix transfer, had shared her email in case Aila ever needed . . .

Aila froze on the webpage. Thinking. Scheming.

As the idea came together, her heart pounded in her ears. She could mope on her couch all night, waiting to see what happened in Jewelport and whether they'd steal Rubra away.

Or she could fucking *do* something.

With jittery fingers, Aila pulled up Director Rivera's email, then stared at the blank message box until her eyes ached. As the scramble of words came together in her head, she started writing.

Dear Ms. Rivera.

Too formal? Not formal enough? Horns and fangs, Aila hadn't had to write such an important letter since college applications.

As the head Silimalo phoenix keeper at the San Tamculo Zoo, please accept condolences on behalf of myself and my colleagues. We were all devastated to hear the news from Jewelport earlier this week.

Aila hated small talk. That had to be enough of a lean-in. She took a deep breath.

I understand you face many tough decisions over the coming weeks, and we're all working together for the good of our phoenixes. To that end . . .

Aila laid it all bare: Rubra's lifetime of acclimation to the San Tamculo Zoo, the territoriality of female phoenixes, a somewhat embellished account of the breeding center and its security systems. Her heart poured into the words, raw and aching with each syllable.

Then she made her request. Rubra shouldn't be transferred to Jewelport. Their male phoenix should be brought to San Tamculo.

Beyond Aila's window, the city stilled. Slumbered. Her carbuncle snored at her side, the rest of her animals quiet in cages and terrariums. Aila sat awake for too long, reading and rereading the email a hundred times, making sure it had everything she could put into it. Her life's dream distilled into a few paragraphs of black and white pixels.

She hit *send*—and her future flew out of her hands.

PART TWO

Did you know?

Male ARCHIBIRDS attract mates by building elaborate towers of metal objects. Though different birds have individual preferences for items, all archibirds are attracted to metal, and can discern true metal from similar materials.

The saliva of ARCHIBIRDS is a magically soldering adhesive. When a metal object is coated in archibird saliva, it can be instantaneously welded to any other piece of metal, regardless of the type of metal of either object.

Bright Blue Hair

Tiny yellow feet

....

Naelo Archipelago Department of Fish and Wildlife.
WHAT HAPPENED TO MY HUBCAP? FREQUENTLY ASKED QUESTIONS ABOUT ARCHIBIRDS IN URBAN AREAS.

....

Chapter Seven

The next morning, Aila sprang from her bed like an uncaged water panther, clawed her phone off the bedside table, and pulled up her email to check for...

Nothing important. She scowled at the new messages in her inbox as if each one had done her personal insult: a monthly internet bill (drab, unnecessary, who didn't use automatic payments nowadays?), a notice from the San Tamculo Humane Society about an open house to raise awareness for illegal carbuncle pup mills (Teddy would probably drag her and Tanya to that), a newsletter about rescued Vjari auks in knitted sweaters that Aila didn't remember signing up for (but they were very cute sweaters).

No reply from Director Rivera or IMWS about the phoenix transfer.

It had, she supposed, been less than eight hours since she sent her request. And most of those hours had been during the middle of the night. She could be patient.

Surely, Aila thought, there'd be an update by lunchtime.

But there wasn't. She dragged the app screen to refresh a dozen times, ignoring Tanya's judgmental squint from her desk.

Surely, Aila hoped, there'd be an update by the end of the day.

But there wasn't. She scowled at her phone for the entire train ride home, checking inbox, then spam folder, then trash, then archives, then inbox again.

Surely, Aila begged, there'd be an update by the end of the week.

But there wasn't. Each time a new email notification appeared, her heart skipped. Each time it turned out to be nothing, she felt like crawling into Khonsu's muddy hole to hide with him. The tiny message icon haunted her dreams.

She could only wait as one week slipped into two. As midsummer came and went.

Summer hit hard in Movas. Along the arid western coast, there'd be no drop of rain for months. Heat and sweltering sun turned spring blooms into dry scrub upon the hills, sent the people of San Tamculo flocking onto sandy beaches—and into the shaded gardens of the zoo.

Aila added an extra ten minutes to her morning routine, time to slather every exposed inch of pale, freckled skin with sunscreen. Damn Vjari genes. Just because her distant ancestors were lucky to see sun once a month in their foggy, sub-polar moorlands didn't mean she deserved to suffer for all eternity.

She arrived at work just after dawn. Already, the sky tinged yellow, the air sweltering, only the balm of the ocean to provide meager relief. The crowds would be packed today, draining the zoo of slushies and novelty unicorn-head ice cream pops like an invading army. Aila needed to check the misters at the phoenix observation deck. Skies and seas forbid one of them went out, or her exhibit comment box would be inundated with complaints.

She nearly slammed into another keeper at the staff office.

Aila snapped out of mindless-walk-and-think-mode in time to shrink out of the way. Past averted eyes and a murmur of "excuse me," she registered the face of one of the griffin show keepers. Aila averted her eyes *harder*.

Mercifully, her colleague shuffled past without attempting conversation. Most people around here knew to leave her alone like a liquefying starfish—prone to transform into jelly and hide in the nearest crevice when startled (a neat trick at the zoo's touch tanks, though).

At least it hadn't been Luciana. Aila had steered clear of the Renkailan section in its entirety, still haunted by the witch's words about Rubra being transferred.

She pulled out her phone for a glance at her email notifications. Still nothing.

Her morning routine passed without incident. Aila—working at heightened speed thanks to stress—was ahead on her weekly tasks. Time to tackle one of her monthly chores. She dragged a rake and waste bin into the World of Birds aviary to deep clean the waterfall outlet.

"You know. This would go a lot faster if you could help, Archie."

The archibird perched on a molded waterfall rock, crest half-raised as he inspected her tools. He replied with a low wheeze.

"You, too." Aila faced the vanishing ducks bobbing in the pool. "Don't think I don't know that half these leaves got dragged in here because of you."

The pair quacked, then vanished. They reappeared near the waste bin, white tails wiggling, inspecting the gray plastic with inquisitive bill nibbles.

Aila heaved the valve to shut off the waterfall. As the rumble of water subsided, the glass-domed aviary settled to an odd quiet. Dew pattered on the wide forest leaves. The pair of screaming mynas rustled branches as they hopped through the canopy, observing Aila while muttering muffled shrieks that sounded uncannily like her late aunt.

Raking leaves off the waterfall outlet grate was the easy part. Aila's longer task was power-hosing the pool, then climbing into the rocks to remove more stubborn clumps of detritus and vegetation.

"Miss?" A group of patrons stood on the observation deck. "Why's the waterfall off?"

Aila gritted her teeth and heaved at a tree branch wedged between rocks. "Maintenance."

"Can you turn it back on? We want a photo."

"No." She planted a boot, seeking better leverage.

"But—"

A myna screeched from the canopy, the cadence a perfect imitation of a small child. The patrons huffed and continued down the boardwalk. If only Aila could scare people off that easy.

The branch came loose with a wet *slurch*, sending her staggering backward and nearly onto her ass. She added the refuse to her pile and trudged onward.

Sweat beaded her brow in the humid aviary air, more suffocating than the dry heat outside. Mud and pond grime splotched Aila's arms. She felt at least one cool slick on her cheek. Her efforts yielded a growing pile of tree limbs, leaves in various states of decomposition, novelty soda cups, and a lost hat that Archie deposited as a show of helping. She didn't ask where he'd gotten it.

Her phone buzzed in her pocket. Aila swore and fished it out with her driest fingers.

A fleeting hope surfaced. Maybe IMWS wouldn't send a reply as a lowly email. Maybe they'd call Aila to tell her about their ground breaking decision to transfer five new phoenixes to the San Tamculo Zoo. She fumbled to unlock the screen and—

Shit. It was just Andrea. Aila's therapist.

Shit. Was their next telephone appointment *today*?

When Aila was a kid, all her problems came back to being too quiet. *She's excelling in every subject!* her report cards read. *But she doesn't participate well in group activities.*

Her reading level is above average!

But her math instructor has complained about her reading books during class.

She has a bright future ahead!

But we have concerns that she'd rather sit in the classroom during lunch than socialize with her peers.

Aila's parents were never neglectful. They just didn't know what to do, other than smile and reassure her she'd grow out of it. They sent her on playdates in elementary school (literally torture). Signed her up for sports in high school (who thought it was a good idea to let Aila anywhere near a tennis racket?).

When Aila went off to college, she became aware of this weird concept called "therapy," and how sometimes people went to therapy when they had trouble talking to people and stayed up at night planning out worst-case scenarios for every event in their lives. She'd tried out a counselor at the campus clinic.

The room had been dimly lit. It smelled of calming cinnamon bird incense. The feathers magically absorbed and enhanced any scent they came in contact with—cinnamon in their native Ziclexian rainforest, but captive populations could be trained with other scents. Aila had asked the therapist if the incense used humanely molted feathers from a sustainable population. The woman had smiled blankly and said she'd have to look into it.

She'd told Aila that worrying was a natural part of the human condition. Had recommended swinging in a hammock as a form of reconnecting with the serene headspace of a child rocking in the womb.

So, yeah, Aila didn't go back for another session.

She suffered in silence through the rest of school, spent her time bottling everything up and berating herself for not just acting like a normal person for once. This, to her equal perplexity and annoyance, didn't work, either.

It was Tanya who'd finally sat Aila down. They'd combed through a list of local therapists together, even created a color-coded ranking system that made the process feel less impossible. Aila had to try a few more out before she found Andrea, someone who actually listened and offered more tangible strategies than positive thinking.

Aila adored her. And telephone appointments were great for a busy schedule.

Just maybe not right now, while she was covered in waterfall sludge.

She swiped the screen to accept the call. "Hi, Andrea."

"Hello, Aila," came a bright, soothing voice. "So good to hear from you. How's your week going?"

Aila considered the mud in her hair. The email notification icon haunting her like a vengeful phantom cat. She sighed and sat on a rock, beyond view of the public deck.

"Oh. You know. The usual."

"Why don't you tell me what you've been up to?" Andrea said, undaunted.

"I went to a staff meeting last week."

"How was that?"

Aila had spent a full day before the meeting working up the courage to wave at Connor if he looked at her. He'd never looked at her.

Luciana *had* looked at her, dark eyes and black eyeliner honed like daggers. Aila spent the rest of the meeting staring at the carpet beneath her chair, privately rolling her eyes as the zoo director regaled the meeting with the latest attendance records the griffin show had broken.

"Nothing important," Aila mumbled. She propped her phone between chin and shoulder, leaving her hands free to pick mud from her nails.

"Did you try talking to your coworkers, like we discussed?"

"Umm..." Aila scavenged her memory. "Someone asked 'Is this seat taken?' and I said no, so they took the chair and carried it to sit somewhere else. Does that count?"

A pause. Aila imagined her scribbling notes. "How did that make you feel?"

"Minor panic."

"Why do you think that is?" Andrea pressed, that soft but firm tone zookeepers used to talk to animals. "What sort of situation were you envisioning during the conversation?"

"Well, I don't really *envision*, I just sort of—"

A man's shriek cut through the aviary. Then, a wheeze. In the canopy, a screaming myna carried the hat it had stolen from Aila's pile. Archie followed, breast puffed and crest raised in indignant anger.

On the phone, a longer silence passed.

"Aila. Are you at work?"

"Well... yeah. It's the middle of the day, Andrea."

"We've talked about scheduling sessions during work. It's important to set time aside for your mental health. To approach our meetings without distraction." Andrea never used the disappointed tone Aila was used to hearing from other people, but this was still firm.

"I'm really busy." Aila knew that wasn't a good excuse.

"Yes, you work very hard. But it's important to maintain a healthy work-life balance. What self-care have you done for yourself this past week?"

"I..."

On the phone, Andrea was silent. Waiting. Curse this woman and her professionalism.

"Well...I...um..." Aila ran down her list of scrubbing food dishes, ordering produce, staying after hours to finish their monthly equipment inventory, then getting home so late she barely had the energy to..."I watched a new documentary about Silimalo plains pegasi."

"That's good, Aila! How did that make you feel?"

"Kind of a waste of time, honestly. I knew most of the info already."

"Why do you feel like that's wasting time?"

"Because I could have been doing something else," Aila said. "Something more productive. Like catching up on phoenix papers. Or researching a better nesting box for the pixie wrens, so they don't accidentally levitate up to the ceiling again." Once she started, the words cascaded out, as if she'd opened the valve to the waterfall. "And I still haven't gotten a reply to my email about the phoenixes, and I still feel panicky whenever I see a notification, and I don't know what I should do, whether I should leave it alone or follow up or *what*."

Aila winded herself. Tension wound into her shoulders, her jaw, making her want to scream like one of her mynas. Why. *Why* was this always so *hard*?

"Would you like to try a mindfulness exercise?" Andrea said, calm as ever.

No. "Sure," Aila said, gloomy.

"What topic would you like to focus on?"

"The phoenix email."

"All right. So when you think about the phoenix email, what comes to mind?"

Aila hunched over her knees and let the string of consciousness flood out. No filter. "Waiting. Too long. Failure. I'm a failure. I'm not good enough. What if I could have worded the email better? What if they never reply? What if I lose Rubra?"

The list went on, each item worse than the last, until Aila fought a prickle in her eyes.

Andrea didn't speak until she'd finished. "Do you notice any tension in your body?"

Literally. Everywhere. Aila was nothing but nerves, mud, and sunscreen.

"Now let's do some grounding," Andrea said.

Aila sprawled upon the rock, staring up at canopy leaves and the glass of the aviary.

"I invite you to close your eyes, if you're comfortable," Andrea instructed.

Aila did so.

"Start with one deep breath in. Then out. Another breath in. Then out. Focus on the feeling of each inhale and exhale."

Aila breathed in, then out, lungs filling with warm air and the scent of damp loam. And waterfall muck. And a bit of bird poop.

"Next, focus on your body, the places you're holding tension, how your weight feels in the position you're sitting . . ."

Aila took another slow, deep breath. Following Andrea's guidance, she focused on relaxing her shoulders, then the feeling of her back against the stone, then the rough texture beneath her fingernails, then the drip of dew in the canopy. As she filled her thoughts with physical sensations, her worries receded—temporarily, at least.

"OK," Andrea said. "When you're ready, you can open your eyes. Then describe your topic again."

Aila blinked her eyes open, squinting at bright light through the glass. She reached again for the thought of her email to Director Rivera.

"Waiting," she said. "Impatient. Uncertain..."

The descriptions came smoother this time, still anxious, but not in that debilitating way that brought her to the brink of tears before. Aila was always a *little* annoyed when the process worked so well. Like some weird mental magic trick.

"That sounds difficult," Andrea said. "Why do you think this email is so frustrating?"

"Because I can't do anything. I have to sit here and wait."

"And why is that a negative mindset?"

Aila heaved the world's biggest, most resigned sigh. Then, she repeated, "It's unhealthy to base my self-worth on goals outside my control. Centering myself in the current moment will help avoid triggering my brain's fight-or-flight response."

"And what's one thing you appreciate in your current moment?" Andrea asked.

A flutter of wings crossed the canopy. Archie swooped down to land beside Aila, his stolen hat reclaimed. With a triumphant honk, he dropped his prize on the rock and dug his stubby black beak into the fabric, trying to detach the shiny metal fastener in the back.

Aila grinned. "Archie's pretty cute. In the current moment."

She wrapped up their call and scheduled her next appointment—not during work hours, at Andrea's stubborn insistence. After another tranquil minute of breathing in her aviary, Aila pushed herself to her feet. She turned the waterfall valve back on and cleaned up her tools with a lighter chest than before. Amazing, how much better she felt after talking things out.

"Hello? Do you work here?"

Aila froze on the boardwalk, arms laden with rake and waste bin, stomach sinking like a stone. Amazing, yes, how much better she felt after taking a moment to breathe. And equally amazing how swiftly the real world came crashing back.

She plastered on a smile and turned. A middle-aged woman stood behind her, dressed in enough bright purple to put the pixie wrens to shame, sun visor tight on her forehead.

"I do work here." Aila's words came out malevolently chipper. "How may I help you?"

"Do you know much about birds?"

Aila winced. "Yep. I sure do." She only had every single magical ornithology textbook published within the last twenty years, plus several editions of each major field guide, plus—

"Can you identify a bird for me?" The woman approached, cell phone in hand.

Aila went clammy in horror. Oh no. It couldn't be. Not here. Not the eternal curse of every bird enthusiast in the world, the shackle clasped to their wrists the moment they dared pick up an avian field guide. Aila tried to back away, but the woman already had her photo gallery open. She came closer, fingers swiping through images as she muttered to herself.

"No...not that one...not that one...I could have sworn I had it right...here!"

She beamed and held up her phone.

Aila squinted at the image of smudged trees, a pixelated brown blob in the center. Her fear, realized. By the endless skies and seas, blurry bird photos were the *worst*.

"It was far away," the woman explained.

"I can see that." Aila squinted harder, trying to make sense of the stretched proportions, the wide tail...

"It was very big," the woman said proudly. "I think it was some kind of hawk."

"It's a squirrel."

"Excuse me? No, it was definitely a bird."

"Definitely a squirrel." It usually was. Aila picked up her waste bin and resumed walking. "Enjoy your time at the zoo, miss."

"But . . ."

"Next griffin show is at two p.m.," Aila called back, not pausing. "Consider making the most of your visit today by applying your entrance fee toward a zoo membership. See the front kiosk for more information. Thank you."

Aila was gone before anyone else could stop her, back into the safety of her keeper quarters. Talking with Andrea always helped—she just wished the effects lasted longer.

She checked her phone one more time. Still no email about her phoenixes.

Chapter Eight

It was a productive summer, if nothing else—though Aila was pretty damn focused on the *nothing else* that continued to haunt her inbox.

The cinnamon birds in the aviary had their yearly chicks, little puffs of brown feathers now fledged and fluttering around the forest vines. In fall, they were set to transfer to a zoo in Pennja with a new aviary exhibit (and sure, IMWS processed *that* paperwork just fine).

Aila and Tanya rated all the zoo's seasonal novelty ice cream pops. The strawberry-mango Silimalo phoenix pops were, obviously, the best. Blackberry diamondback dragon pops were tarter than Aila expected. The blueberry limeade peacock griffin pops were, to her annoyance, the perfect blend of sweet and sour. She ranked them lowest, out of principle.

Tanya won second prize at the staff salsa contest and only stewed about it for a week. The first-place winner—Ricardo from the primate department—was declared a nemesis.

Now, late summer scorched through Movas, turning the hills beyond the city from green to scrubby brown. On its heels came fire season. Vjar and Niplik had winter blizzards. Eastern Renkaila had monsoons. Tornadoes swept the Ozokian plains. Movas spent two months a year burning.

The familiar smell of woodsmoke puckered Aila's nose. The San Tamculo Fire Department started a small blaze in the south hills overnight. The controlled burn would sizzle through the shrublands and clear the heat-desiccated brush, seeding the soil for healthy regrowth. Unlikely that the fire would threaten the city proper, but the bulletin board in the staff office posted a note reminding keepers to review their evacuation protocols.

Aila and Tanya sprawled their binders over a metal lunch table. The zoo's main food court was modeled after a Movasi villa, paved in cream tile, colorful flags strung overhead and planters brimming with red carnations. The buildings were white stucco and clay shingles, light colors to diffuse the heat, accented in bright yellow doorways and a larger-than-life thunderhawk mural by a local painter. A pack of children climbed a three-tiered fountain, ignoring the shouts of parents sprawled in the shade beneath electric fans.

A louder din came from the petting zoo across the plaza, foolish families letting their children play with jewel-headed carbuncles, a trilling moss marten, a calm old domestic griffin who loved belly scratches, dooming themselves to endless pet requests on the drive home (Aila's parents had to endure the onslaught for years).

An even *louder* din came from the conservation carousel, melding laughter and upbeat carnival music as passengers twirled on resin replicas of a serpentine maned dragon, a prancing plains pegasus, even a manticore with snarling lion head and barbed tail.

Aila tuned out the ruckus, focused on one of the greatest culinary creations of mankind: fries piled high with grilled meat, melted cheese, and the mildest red sauce she could get her hands on. She dug a fork into the mound of food while flipping through her binder.

"OK," Aila said around a mouthful. "Order of priority for evacuation, page three."

"Mm-hm." Tanya munched a fish taco piled with cream sauce and cabbage. She opened the same page in her binder.

"Silimalo phoenix and Bix phoenix are highest conservation priority, first in the carriers."

"We've only got five carriers in the back room, since griffin show borrowed a few."

Aila rolled her eyes. Not freeloaders, her ass. "Thunderhawk has to go on the zoo truck. Archibird next on carrier priority. Then periwinkle prairie geese. Could jam the mynas and a pixie wren in one carrier."

Tanya arched a brow. "And the rest? We leaving those behind?"

"Tanya, how dare you say such a thing? You know full well if we ever have to evacuate, I'm cramming every animal possible into my backpack."

She chuckled. "I don't think that's acceptable zoo policy, Ailes."

"Try to stop me." She skewered a fry in a meager attempt at intimidation, polo muddied from the aviary pond she'd cleaned that morning, pale arms spotted with sunscreen to avoid frying like a lobster. *Some sight.*

"I tell you what." Tanya flipped her binder closed. "We better not ever have to evacuate. I'm not looking forward to helping you dredge that kelpie into a trailer."

Tanya brandished a pair of churros to finish their meal, cinnamon-sugar sifting off the paper wrappers. Another of Aila's favorites—the perfect crunch on the outside, soft on the inside. She eyed the pastry with a frown.

"It does seem ridiculous, all this planning for fire safety. This close to the coast, fire would have to tear through most of the city to get to us."

"Mm-hm," Tanya agreed. "Gotta be prepared for anything, though."

"What we *should* be doing is evaluating our security."

Tanya paused, churro halfway into her mouth. "Ailes..."

"I finished updating all the CCTV monitors. Most are working fine, but a couple still get blips in the feed. Then there's the issue of night security. Can you believe, still one guard for the whole zoo? How's he supposed to cover everything? And don't get me started on those old bolts on the aviary."

Tanya listened in silence, humoring the rant. For two months since the break-in at Jewelport, Aila had been more jitters than person, burning her anxiety by deep-cleaning exhibits and combing through their security systems. What if someone tried to break into San Tamculo?

Since the catastrophe, two IMWS Phoenix Program newsletters had rolled through Aila's email. Still no formal announcement on the future of the Jewelport Zoo breeding program. No email replies. Aila could have kicked herself, thinking that pipe dream could amount to anything.

With lunch devoured, she and Tanya returned to their aviaries. Patrons packed the paths with sunhats and soda bottles, scents of sunscreen and sweat swimming on the fire-laced air. This time of year, the kelpie's foggy exhibit skyrocketed in popularity. Visitors flocked to the maned dragon aviary to delight in localized drizzles, or crowded around the marine touch pools to poke at liquefying starfish and ruby axolotls (gentle zookeepers harvested any precious gems that grew on their gill frills before putting them on exhibit). Other patrons piled beneath misters at the Silimalo phoenix exhibit, children miming themselves bursting into flames in the heat. Rubra's popularity had grown tenfold since the tragedy at Jewelport.

Tanya had war to wage with her Bix phoenix, her latest attempt of blocking his hole with chicken wire collapsed beneath a flood. Aila planned a challenging afternoon as well: snagging the vanishing ducks for their yearly checkup. The pair were hide-and-seek champions, but she had some enticing fish-and-berry treat balls to tip the scales in her favor.

"Sure you don't want to join me this weekend?" Tanya asked. "Air-conditioned mall. Get smoothies, browse that retro DVD store." Her words quickened in excitement. "Word on the forums is, they got a new shipment from the old rental place that closed downtown."

"Sorry, Tanya, I..." Aila grasped for a socially acceptable excuse, only to remember this was Tanya. She didn't have to fake. "I'm sticking to the sofa this weekend. Could use some recharge time."

Tanya gave a knowing smirk. "New textbook?"

"On phoenix habitat studies, yeah. Looks *really* interesting." Aila hadn't been able to resist a peek or two, but she looked forward to reading in earnest.

"Next time, then." Tanya bumped her shoulder.

When they rounded the path to the phoenix complex, Aila and Tanya slowed in unison, surprised by a visitor waiting at their door. The staff coordinator, Tom, greeted them with his usual grunt, jaw grizzled and polo immaculate. Spotting him outside his office was like a rare animal sighting, even odder without a cup of coffee in hand.

"Hey, Tom," Tanya returned. "Something we can help you with?"

"Director wants to see you."

Aila puzzled at that. Tanya must have another meeting for her volunteer keeper program, but why hadn't she mentioned any updates? She must have things under control. Of course. She was Tanya, the unflusterable sea eel. Aila flopped like a fish out of water.

"Go ahead," Aila said. "I'll start on the protocol updates."

"No, Director wants to see *you*." Tom nodded to Aila.

She puzzled *harder* at that. A slow blink of shock followed. Aila had been called to the administration building any number of times over HR complaints or mandatory training, but lofty meetings with the zoo director meant...

Her phoenix.

Aila gulped a surge of panic. "Sure? When?"

"Now, I suppose." Tom grunted and set off down the path.

"*Now?* What for? Hold on, give me a second to..." Aila flashed wide eyes at Tanya, who returned a shrug. With Tom disappearing around the corner, Aila hurried after him.

She assumed something horrible awaited her. That was how these things went.

Her thoughts scrambled as they walked, Tom weaving through patrons with the ease of an merlion in a current, Aila crashing into elbows like a manticore in a porcelain shop. What had she done recently? Nothing *too* disruptive. There was that pair of douchebag college boys a couple of months ago who'd promised to report her over Archie breaking their phone. A mother she'd gotten snippy with at a keeper talk last week, wrung out at having to explain why the kelpie would not, in fact, be healthier on a vegan diet.

Dread coiled in her stomach as they entered the sliding glass doors of the administration building. Crisp linoleum squeaked beneath her boots, one wall decorated in a panel of mounted succulents spelling out *San Tamculo Zoo*. The other wall displayed framed photos of the zoo's charitable conservation work throughout the world. An image from a Renkailan tea farm showed workers building peacock griffin nesting platforms for pest control. Another photo showed a patch of replanted Zi-clexian rainforest, a team of researchers working with the local community to learn sustainable methods of harvesting orchid viper venom to amplify plant fertilizer. An older, more faded portrait captured a pair of biologists on a scrubby Silimalo cliff-side, affixing a wing ID tag to a phoenix, one of the last in the wild.

A receptionist in a frizzy updo and peacock-feather blouse sat behind a desk, all smiles for Tom. All glares for Aila. Last time Aila got called here for a patron complaint, she may have had...well...some might call it a "spirited argument" with said patron in the middle of the lobby.

"Welcome back, Tom." The receptionist greeted him like sugar. "And Miss Macbhairan," she added like a cracked jaw-breaker. "Director Hawthorn is waiting for you."

Tom grunted. Aila scuttled after him like a cockroach fleeing a boot.

The director's office sat at the back of the building, a corner of windows overlooking the yellow-finned caiman lagoon. Fit-ting—haggling with one's boss while toothed reptiles swam outside. The room smelled of wood polish and office carpet. A stone carving of a peacock griffin perched on the desk. A wall of bookshelves housed more curios: a framed diploma from Sagecrest College, photos of keepers and their animals, a merlion sculpted of driftwood, a phoenix feather in a glass case. Spider plants dangled tendrils down the wall, a familiar sight.

OK. OK. Not bad so far.

"Miss Macbhairan? Good to see you."

The zoo director, Clement Hawthorn, greeted her from behind his desk. He was a stout man in a button-down shirt and jeans, cool black skin wrinkled from years of sun. During his time as a keeper, he'd run San Tamculo's aquatic section. Though his pioneering of the world's first red-ringed kraken exhibit had been his claim to fame, everyone at the zoo knew the crocus crocodiles were his personal favorites. The giant lilac lizards grew flowers along their scaled backs, capable of photosynthesis to supplement their fish diets. A replica crocus flower carved of purple stone sat on his desk, some kind of paperweight.

"Thank you for coming on such short notice," he said. "Please take a seat."

He gestured to a pair of armchairs across his desk, upholstered in shiny green leather. One of them was empty. In the other sat—

Aila's heart shriveled.

Looking up at her was Maria Rivera, director of the IMWS Movas Division, head keeper of the San Tamculo Zoo phoenix program during its peak over a decade ago. She perched hawklike on the edge of her chair, her black business jacket paired with a skirt that fell in fiery waves to her calves, warm tones against brown skin. Even more intimidating in person than in photos. She sat tall, hands folded in her lap, black hair gelled into a bun.

Aila turned to Tom for support, but got only a nod as he shut the door. She squeaked like a trapped purserat.

Director Hawthorn drew a pointed look between her and the empty chair. With nowhere to flee, Aila sat. The deep cushions tried to swallow her. A preferable demise. She hazarded a nervous smile toward Rivera, met with piercing eyes behind lilac spectacles, appraising Aila like an animal in a behavioral study.

Director Hawthorn's tight grin was little better. Aila was not the *best* employee. A hard worker, but more of a wave churner than HR would like. She bounced in her seat, heart fluttering like pixie wren wings.

Rivera leaned toward her with a smile. "Good to see you again, Miss Macbhairan. I believe the last time was the Plumed Gala last year?"

Aila blinked, part of her surprised the IMWS Director would remember their brief conversation, the other part panicking as a grand total of zero words offered themselves in reply. She nodded, a toy unhinged at the neck.

"I was surprised to receive your email," Rivera said. "Apologies for the delay. I contacted Director Hawthorn as soon as we were ready to discuss next steps."

Next steps?

Horns and fangs, this really was about Aila's phoenix.

"And I was *equally* surprised to hear about this request," the director added.

Aila cleared her throat. "Um...surprised, Director?"

"A petition to IMWS for a phoenix transfer should have gone through official channels."

Oh boy. Aila hadn't thought about that.

"I'm so sorry! I didn't think...I mean, I didn't *mean*..." She clasped her trembling hands. *Not like this.* She couldn't lose Rubra without trying to fight it. "I think our breeding program should be given a chance. We've been on the transfer list for years. And Rubra is happy here! Healthy appetite. Feathers always in the upper range of the iridescence scale."

Oh, stop it, you idiot! How is random trivia going to help?

Aila had to stop anyway, a prick of tears threatening her eyes. Crying in front of her boss, not high on the to-do list. She shifted a pleading look to Rivera.

The woman listened with a polite smile. Once Aila fell silent, the IMWS director reached into her briefcase and pulled out a tablet and pen.

"I'm sure you understand," Rivera said. "IMWS has been working hard to decide how to move forward with the Movasi breeding program. In light of the security breach at the Jewelport Zoo, we're evaluating alternative facilities, at least until we can pinpoint what went wrong." She tapped her tablet screen, a flash of white light as a notepad popped up. "Remind me, please. When was the last successful phoenix breeding year here at San Tamculo?"

Aila's brain stalled so hard, she thought she smelled smoke drifting out her ears.

"Um...It was...ten years ago. Almost eleven." Rivera, of all people, would know that. "Four clutches after the last nest you oversaw, Ms. Rivera."

Rivera's brow lifted. "You know your zoo history. And the breeding facility is still functioning?"

"Sure? It's a little dusty, but..."

Great sales pitch, Aila. Wouldn't qualify for advertisement accolades anytime soon.

"Director Hawthorn and I have been discussing the zoo's security measures." Rivera looked up, snaring Aila in oil-slick eyes. "Those were updated recently. Five years ago, yes?"

"Yeah." The fuck was happening? Aila didn't dare believe it.

"How do *you* feel about the current security measures?" Rivera asked.

Skies and seas, at least Aila had rehearsed that one with Tanya about twenty times. "Our CCTV monitors are all functioning, but I'd like to see them updated with a remote access system, preferably incorporating motion detection in key areas of the aviary. You know, like those cameras people use to watch their pets at home."

Could have left out that last part. Somehow, Rivera still smiled. She scribbled on her tablet, screen angled so Aila couldn't snoop.

"How long have you worked at San Tamculo, Aila?"

"Three years."

"Your education?"

"Sagecrest."

"Good school. How about your familiarity with the current breeding practices?"

"Our building is compliant with the replicate climate model, within one degree of temperature variance per year, which is well within the Silimalo phoenix breeding tolerance based on the latest research from Garumano and Kuprik. We import our olive trees from the Crescent Bay Nursery, just like Jewelport. And we have automated double glass in the viewing exhibit to offer privacy from patrons."

The words gushed out like the aviary waterfall, leaving Aila scant space to breathe. This couldn't be happening. It was all a cruel trick, a distraction to take her phoenix away.

Rivera's brows lifted at the details. "It sounds like you've done quite a bit of reading, Miss Macbhairan. Always good to see that in a young keeper. I'll need to schedule an inspector to tour the facility. Can we decide on a date about two months from now?"

"*Excuse me?*"

Aila's outburst earned her a chiding look from Director Hawthorn.

"An inspector," Rivera said. "To evaluate whether this facility would be a suitable transfer candidate for the male phoenix. Given the territoriality of female phoenixes, we typically prioritize male transfers, and your proximity to the Jewelport Zoo makes you an attractive contender. Less disruptive for the bird. But we need to ensure you're up to the task."

Aila opened her mouth, dismayed when only a squeak came out.

"We're humbled by the opportunity," the director replied for her, mustering the warm tone he put on for galas and well-dressed donors. "The San Tamculo Zoo is proud of our successful partnerships with IMWS breeding programs for several threatened and endangered species. We'll be excited to demonstrate that our Silimalo phoenix facilities are suitable as a transfer candidate."

"I look forward to it." Rivera turned to Aila. "Thank you for your help, Aila, and for your time today. Director Hawthorn and I can iron out the details. I look forward to reviewing the inspector's report."

Aila nodded. She rose from her chair. Walked out of the office with some passing semblance of knowing how human legs were supposed to work. When the door closed behind her, she stood in the hallway. Linoleum squeaked under her boots. An unobtrusive jingle drifted from a speaker in the ceiling, static thoughts buzzing in her head.

Holy. Shit.

Aila left the lobby in a power walk. She shifted into a jog past the gilded swan lagoon. She came into the aviary hub at full sprint, exploding through the door of the phoenix complex.

"Tanya! Tanya! *Tanya!*"

Tanya stumbled out of the kitchen. "Aila? What's wrong? Don't tell me someone got bit again?"

Aila slammed into her at full force, throwing them both off balance. Tanya's superior poise kept them standing. She gawked as Aila dissolved into tears in her arms, some heinous sound between laughing and sobbing.

"Tanya! They're considering a phoenix transfer."

"OK. Right. We knew that, though?"

"They're considering transferring a bird *here*!"

"Oh, Ailes, that's great news! I'm gonna need you to breathe, though. There we go."

Tanya backed her toward a chair. Aila plopped onto the cushion, too bouncy to sit still.

"Maria Rivera came herself! She read my email, Tanya. Said

San Tamculo is an *attractive contender*. They're sending an inspector to look at our facility in two months!"

Tanya blanched. "They're sending an inspector in *how long*?"

"She said in . . ."

Aila's thoughts caught up to her in a landslide.

She followed Tanya's horrified gaze over the derelict breeding facility. Beneath their boots, the linoleum cracked and faded. On the walls, the flame-retardant paint was expired by at least a year. Dust blanketed shelves and counters, clumping atop cracked protocol binders, storage boxes, rags.

Not just cosmetic fixes, either. Crates of bird food pellets sat atop the counter where the egg incubators should have been. The refrigerator rattled in the kitchen. A questionable smell drifted from behind the cupboards when the weather turned damp.

At its construction, the breeding center had been state of the art. Though Rubra's public exhibit remained pristine, the remaining facilities hadn't bred a phoenix in over a decade. Now, Aila had to whip the place back into shape . . .

"In two months," she said, sobering.

Oh no.

Chapter Nine

"All right, here's the plan of attack!"

Aila stood before her whiteboard like a military commander, brandishing an olive branch at a list of to-do items.

"The IMWS inspector comes in two months. If we want to look like a world-class facility ready to receive a critically endangered Silimalo phoenix, we've got a shit-ton of work to accomplish in a ridiculously short amount of time."

"Yes, ma'am!" Tanya quipped from her chair, muddy boots propped on the counter. If this was a real army, she'd have been written up for insubordination. Aila let it slide.

"Our plan of attack." Aila whipped the branch against the top item on the list. "Order new olive trees from the Crescent Bay Nursery to replace those two charred ones in the exhibit. Set up a new order for fresh boughs delivered every week."

"Roger that," Tanya said.

"Next, deep clean interior. Replace cracked flooring and countertops."

"Don't forget fancying up the patio. Need a ritzy place for the donors to sit and eat their tea sandwiches."

An unsavory prospect, but Aila would bear it, if she got another phoenix out of the deal. "We also need to replace the refrigerator in the kitchen, the one with the dead purserat stuck underneath."

Tanya rolled her eyes. "Thank the skies and seas."

"And repair the crack in the observation window glass where that kid played 'hide the rock' a few months ago."

"The audacity of the youth these days." Tanya shook her head.

Now, on to the hard ones. "The dragon facility has our egg incubators from when they were hatching diamondbacks. We'll need to move those back here, figure out what repairs need to be made. We also need to increase our talon-mite dusting schedule, which means borrowing the sprayer from griffin show." She'd rather swim the kraken-infested Middle Sea than tackle that one. "We should focus on the incubators first."

"Skies and seas, what a cruel fate!" Tanya threw up her hands. "You'll have to talk to that hot dragon boy again? Think you can say something without sticking a foot in your mouth?"

Harsh. But fair.

Aila eyed the extensive list with beetles buzzing in her stomach. Building renovations weren't her only hurdle. Already, she'd assembled an extensive reading list of every book and scientific paper on phoenix breeding she could get her hands on.

Breeding.

And social introduction.

And pair bonding.

And male feather health.

Aila might be doomed.

The door clicked open. Aila stiffened by her whiteboard. Tanya tipped her boots off the table and jumped to her feet as Director Hawthorn stepped inside.

"Good morning, keepers," he greeted. "I'm not interrupting, am I?"

Aila's nose scrunched. "Well, actually, we were just about to—"

"Of course not!" Tanya piped back.

Aila locked eyes with her. *Not* avoiding human contact, today? *Shoot*. Missed the coordination on that one. "We were reviewing our itinerary, Director Hawthorn."

He stepped up to peruse the whiteboard, a hum in his throat, a bend in his knees from too many years scrubbing aquarium tanks. Aila twiddled her olive branch as he read, uncomfortable in the silence, staring at the wall, the floor. She nudged a crack with her boot, producing a louder squeak than intended. Panicked, she held still.

Behind the director, Tanya glared at Aila and shook her head like a scolding mother.

"An ambitious project," the director said at last. He ran wrinkled knuckles through what remained of his hair, thinner at the top than the sides. "It's in the zoo's best interest to support you. Getting the breeding program running again will be fantastic for our conservation portfolio. I just wish you'd run this by me sooner. We could have had more time to work with."

Aila had spent so many years begging for a male phoenix, she hadn't expected any more support this time around.

"I spoke with the donors yesterday," he continued. "They're...supportive. But it's a bit of a gamble for their liking. What if we sink a chunk of funds into the restoration, but IMWS decides to go with another facility? I can move some money around for essential equipment repair and installation, but most of the elbow grease, we'll have to keep in house."

Aila's nose wrinkled. Donors. Budgets. Not her cup of tea. She'd get done what she had to, on her own if needed.

"Have you reached out to griffin show yet?" the director asked.

Aila looked at him like a two-headed falcon. "Why would I do that?"

"They're your sister department. I'm sure they'll be eager to help."

Over Aila's dead body would she go crawling to Luciana's pedicured feet. *I don't see why you're bothering,* she'd say in that honeyed voice. *Rubra would be better off dressed in a tutu and doing fire flips for a crowd.*

"We'll get on it, Director," Tanya interjected. "Appreciate you stopping by. We should get working, though. Got to check the phoenix drinking spigot, been fritzing again."

The Silimalo phoenix did not, in fact, require a water spigot. Phoenixes required less hydration than most animals (a tendency for internal combustion made them bloat with steam if they drank too much). They acquired most moisture from their food. As part of standard zoo compliance, a water spigot had been installed in the phoenix exhibit regardless. The pipes ruptured any time Rubra neared them. Aila and Tanya gave up on that repair years ago.

The excuse remained a useful code phrase to escape unwanted conversations. Easier to flee human interaction under the guise of official business.

"Of course," Director Hawthorn said. "I'll let you get to that."

Tanya, you sublime, magnanimous sunfish.

They escaped into the fall heat. The morning smelled of sage and wet concrete beneath the misters, voices growing as the first patrons trickled into the zoo. Hidden around the corner of the building, Aila slumped against sun-warmed stucco. All she wanted was to rescue an entire species from extinction. Why did that involve so many *logistics*?

"That's just out of one fire, Ailes," Tanya chided.

Aila moaned. "I don't have to get the incubators *now*. Not like they're going to sprout legs and wander off."

"The quicker we get them, quicker we know what we need to repair."

"I don't even know where Connor is right—"

Their radios crackled in unison. "Entering plumed dragon," Connor announced, as he did every morning while cycling through the dragon exhibits.

Griffin shit.

"Fine!" Aila threw up her hands. "I'll go *talk* to him." She chewed the words like gristle.

Maybe one of his dragons would eat her instead.

Aila left the safety of her phoenix complex with a trudge to her step.

Skirting strollers and absent-minded patrons, she passed the diamondback dragon aviary, climbed the pine-shaded hill of the Vjari section, until stiff conifers gave way to broader-leafed tropical palms and rubber trees. An aviary lay ahead, smallest of the three dragon enclosures.

The glass dome of the green-plumed dragon exhibit was fogged with humidity, its interior obscured by Ziclexian nut trees and thick-trunked kapoks. A public pathway tunneled through the center of the dome, an arch of glass overhead, snaking through a rainforest understory of cacao trees, orchids, and tufted pink chenille, all webbed in vines and knots of surface roots.

Aila stepped into the tunnel, embarking on an expedition to the other side of the world. Sunlight dimmed beneath the canopy, air thick with a smell of moist soil. An information placard along the walkway gave background on the Ziclexian cloud forest, its high montane jungle wreathed in fog and dripping moss, remote from most human settlements. Aila would love to visit one day, the vast rainforest one of the few places in the world with magical beasts likely still undiscovered (that, and the deep ocean, but fuck the ocean, it always creeped Aila out).

Another placard showed a diagram of green-plumed dragon feet, the toes splayed with climbing claws and wide, gecko-like pads that let them scramble over massive jungle leaves. A resin foot model beside the glass was perfect for visitors to take photos against their own hands.

Then came a placard about green-plumed dragon feathers. The red, green, and yellow quills of the neck ruff contained some magical pigment that enticed the viewer—both other dragons *and* humans. There'd been some fiasco in the art world not long ago, a few prominent painters discovered to have slipped pow-dered dragon feathers into their paints. This sparked a debate on whether the paintings were *truly* masterworks, or just enchant-ing people to think they were. Aila had never really understood art.

No patrons shared the tunnel, yet. Alone, she enjoyed the quiet, the giant trunks that made her feel as small and wide-eyed as when she'd visited as a kid. That was the fun of it: creeping along, searching for iridescent green plumes amid the foliage. She peered through the glass, scanning for movement.

In her pocket, her phone buzzed.

Aila sighed. So much for her jungle escape. If this was Tanya texting her advice on how to talk to boys, Aila would . . . prob-ably take it. She needed all the help she could get.

It wasn't Tanya. Aila swiped open her phone to find a mes-sage from her mother, an image of a wooden counter messy with chopped green peppers and fresh herbs.

Dad is trying a new recipe! Will update you on results.

Aila smiled. A single picture, and she was back in that kit-chen, smelling the sage bushes outside the open window and the pomegranate dish soap her mom always used, listening to her dad talk as he chopped at the counter. It was a warm feeling, one of the few places that had always been safe.

At the same time, guilt twisted Aila's stomach. Though her parents lived right here in San Tamculo, she hadn't visited in too long. Always busy, and with this new renovation project...

She texted back.

Looks great! I'll call this weekend so we can catch up?

Before the reply came, something rustled inside the dragon exhibit. Aila looked up.

Connor stared back at her from the other side of the glass.

Aila shrieked in surprise, the sound echoing down the tunnel. She clutched her heart as Connor's brow lifted.

"Connor! Hello! I...Wow, didn't see you there!" Off to a superb start.

"Morning, Aila." Humidity dotted Connor's cheeks. It glistened like stardrops on the lock of dark hair curled against his brow. "Sorry, didn't mean to startle you."

"Startled?" she returned. "Me? Never. No idea what you're talking about."

"Oh. Is there something you need, then?"

"Yes!" The reply flew from her lips with no semblance of punctuation. "The incubators I mean the egg incubators the ones you borrowed from the phoenix building I was wondering if we could maybe get those back." She gulped a breath. "You know. If you have a free moment."

She forced a smile, legs wobbling.

Connor smiled back. Her legs turned to jelly.

"It's true, then?" he said. "What everyone's saying? You're going to restart the phoenix breeding program?"

"People are *saying* that?" Ludicrous. Aila hadn't thought... Skies and seas, she needed to pay closer attention to zoo gossip. A swell of pride kept her from collapsing. "Yeah. We are."

Aila, restarting the breeding program. Her eight-year-old self squealed inside.

Her eight-year-old self wouldn't understand the other reason she wanted to squeal. From across the glass, Connor's smile didn't fade. His blue eyes fixed on her through a brush of thick lashes. No drifting focus. No uncomfortable side-eye. In that moment, Aila realized he'd never *looked* at her before. His attention knotted a string around her heart, a kite thrown to the wind.

"I'd love to help," he said. "But first, I've got to get the plumed dragons out on exhibit. Give me a hand?"

Aila jerked a nod.

By the time she walked around to the aviary's keeper entrance, her legs had resumed functioning. Her thoughts teetered like tops. *Animals. Focus on the animals.*

This back enclosure was taller than any of Aila's, the concrete floor new and smooth. On one side of the room gleamed a stainless steel fridge and counters. On the other, a flock of five green-plumed dragons trilled behind the bars of their aviary, yellow eyes following Aila like a shiny new toy. Most dragons were territorial, but these were an unusually social species, happiest in groups. Also, flightless. Their aviary stretched floor to ceiling, a resin tree trunk twisting through the center like a climbing gym, wreathed in chew toys tied on metal cords. The dragons scrambled over the boughs on wide footpads and strong claws, down to the closed door to their public exhibit, eager to be let out.

Connor lifted a rope from the counter and slung it over his shoulder. Five chicken carcasses were strung along the length like party decorations.

He grinned. "Not squeamish, I hope?"

Around people? Sure. Dead animals? Never.

Aila followed Connor into the exhibit, soil soft beneath her boots, humidity frizzing her hair. She smoothed vagrant tendrils behind her ears. What she wouldn't give for Luciana's sleek curls. And no, she'd *never* admit that out loud.

Once they were in sight of the viewing tunnel, Connor looped one end of his rope around a tree. Aila clambered up another mossy trunk to do the same with her end. Jungle chickens on a string. Talk about a neat party game (for a dragon).

Once Aila and Connor returned to the keeper room, he locked the exhibit door and slid open the gate keeping the dragons inside. They darted out in bolts of green and red feathers. Aila pressed herself to the aviary bars, wriggling to get the best view out the gate as the dragons hollered in the trees, snapping at chickens like feathered piñatas.

"Look at that, they love it!" She smiled, a remedy to jittery nerves. "I bet Rubra would adore something like that. Maybe... apples instead of chickens?"

"I bet she would." Connor bumped her shoulder. "Hey, I think that's the first straight sentence I've gotten out of you."

Aila's cheeks blushed hot as phoenix feathers. "Oh, no! I mean, probably? Not the best people person. You know, animals are just..." Her voice dropped to a murmur. "Cooler."

Connor laughed. "I don't think that's an uncommon sentiment in this line of work."

"Shut up. I've heard your keeper talks. You're *great*."

"Loads of practice."

He winked. Aila gripped the bars to keep from disintegrating.

"Come on," Connor said. "Let's go look at those incubators."

Aila should have taken Tanya's advice and practiced talking to a poster.

If someone wrote an instructional guide to human flirting—a real one, not those fluffy romcoms on airport bookshelves—she'd read it cover to cover and still be oblivious. Aila had never pulled off a successful date. One time in college, she sat next to a cute boy in her zoonotic diseases lecture all semester, failing to find the courage to ask him out. He asked to borrow a pencil once. Most words they ever exchanged. Another time, attempting small talk with a barista, Aila spilled an entire toffee latte on the floor. Poor girl had to clean up the mess. Aila asked her out to a movie to make up for it, but when her "date" invited a gaggle of friends to the outing, Aila panicked and backed out last minute.

Then there were the dating apps. Aila abandoned that purgatory long ago. Did ninety percent of the world's hobbies consist of "going to the gym" or "long walks on the beach"? Neither of which she partook in, her daily exercise accounted for by hauling goat carcasses to kelpies, her gossamer skin as suited to beach weather as dry paper to open flame. On the flip side, she hadn't found a single match who understood the importance of naturalistic exhibit design and behavioral enrichment to the health of magical creatures.

All to say, Aila followed Connor's lead with a mix of dread and an airy feeling like floating. Maybe she'd be fine. And maybe she'd sprout wings and dragon scales.

Vanilla-scented conifers shaded their walk back to the Vjari section, a cool escape from fall heat. Cooler still in the keeper building behind the diamondback dragon aviary, a bunker of concrete from floor to ceiling, the air conditioning set low enough to prickle Aila's skin. In contrast, the back dragon enclosure was a garden. Stark walls were speckled with colorful lichen and delicate flowers. In the wild, diamondback dragons roosted in caves, their body heat enough to create near-tropical microclimates sheltered from the cold Vjari exterior. The flora and fauna living within dragon dens were completely unique.

Fluorescent lights shined on a well-swept floor, a desk with a granola bar and three bins with green-plumed dragon feathers, diamondback scales, and maned dragon hair. IMWS required all magical animal parts of black-market value to be collected, cataloged, and disposed of. An observation window looked out on the diamondback dragon exhibit, an alpine hillside sprinkled with...snow? White blanketed the rocky ground and mats of pine needles.

In Movas, snow never fell this low in elevation, confined to the mountains behind the city. Connor must have gotten the snow machine out, a treat for the dragon. Vera lay on her back in the deepest snowbank, wings spread, belly exposed like a sunbathing cat. What a sweetie. Aila would have been tempted to scratch her scales, if not for claws the size of her forearm.

"Here we are."

Connor pulled a tarp, uncovering a line of incubators on the counter. Each metal box stood half as tall as Aila, control panels dense with buttons and an LCD screen, windows capable of insulating molten lava. Phoenix eggs had to hatch from their mother's immolation, but once out of their shells, the chicks survived best via gradual temperature acclimation. Aila pressed her nose to the window like a child in a candy store, picturing baby phoenixes peeping inside.

"They still work?" Her words came out muffled against the glass.

"Worked for the diamondback eggs," Connor said. "Could use a checkup, make sure the heating coils still work. If you can find a cart to load them, I can help you move them up to the phoenix complex."

"That would be great!" Aila hopped in enthusiasm. Too much. She folded her hands and tried not to appear crazy.

But there came Connor's smile again. Aila had no defense for such things.

"No worries. Not like we're using these hunks of metal." His voice grew quiet. "Will be nice to see them working again."

Aila felt like an ass. The last chicks these incubators held were diamondback dragons, Connor's star species, a clutch of hatchlings who'd scampered around the exhibit for weeks. Connor had raised them, pampered them. When the time came to send the dragonlings off to the reintroduction center in Vjar, the entire zoo staff celebrated. Aila attended long enough to steal a piece of dragon-shaped cake with black frosting that stuck in her teeth.

Then the dragons were stolen in transit. Connor called in sick for a week afterward.

"I'm sorry," she said. "I hope I'm not bringing up bad memories. If that happened with one of my phoenixes, I'd . . ." Cry? Shrivel? Melt into a puddle?

Connor rested a hand atop an incubator. As his thumb brushed the metal, he looked over the dark panels and empty interior. Imagining the previous occupants, she guessed—fewer feathers than what she had planned, but equally precious.

"Thanks, Aila. That's kind of you to say." He looked up with a small grin. "About time someone put these to good use again. Can't wait to see them full of phoenixes."

Oh no. He was gorgeous, and smart, and funny, *and* he cared this much about his animals? *Keep it together, Aila.* This was the longest she'd ever lasted around Connor without face-planting onto concrete.

Connor's brow lifted. Too late, Aila realized she was staring. Frantic for any focal point other than dreamy blue eyes and that distracting curl on his temple, she scampered to the observation window, feigning interest in the dragon lounging on her snow pile.

Well, maybe not feigning. Who didn't like watching dragons?

"How's Vera?" Aila asked. "Since the hatchlings got sent off."

Connor joined her at the window. "Vera? She took it fine. Probably relieved to have some quiet. Not like she knows what happened to them."

Aila couldn't decide if that was less heartbreaking. She wondered sometimes if the animals *did* know, had some sense of their species dwindling, a few bad breeding seasons away from vanishing like a snuffed match. Or maybe that was a burden their keepers bore alone. Vera looked content, a rumble in her throat as she nestled deeper into snow.

Sunlight slanted through the exhibit glass, a ray into the keeper quarters. In the light, Connor's skin was crisp as Vjari snow, warmed by the softest blush.

"Why dragons?" Aila blurted out, thankful that those words emerged, rather than some harp on how handsome he was. "Are you from Vjar?"

"Me? No. My parents are. Got sick of the winters, moved down here. As for the dragons." He chuckled. "I...uh...applied to work with unicorns."

Aila's mouth fell open. "Get. Out. Of. Here. *Unicorns?*"

"What's wrong with unicorns?"

"I don't know, they're like, a kelpie but way less exciting."

His brow quirked. "Are you quantifying 'exciting' based on the criteria of eating flesh?"

"And making kick-ass fog all day! All unicorns do is stand around and look pretty." Her eyes narrowed. "Does that make Patricia, like, your mortal enemy or something?" Aila had never gotten along with the unicorn keeper. Too...peppy.

Connor laughed. "Patricia and I are fine. I took the next position that popped up. Dragons are pretty cool, too."

"Cooler than unicorns," Aila muttered.

"Hey, you know the business. Got to go where the opportunities are."

Aila made a whining sound. Connor leaned against the windowsill.

"No?" he taunted.

"No. Always phoenixes for me."

Not the most advisable career limitation, her college counselor had told her again and again. So what? Aila knew what she wanted, that she could put in the work to get here.

"Why phoenixes?" Connor asked. "You like the glamor?"

"What? No. Of course not. I mean...sure, they *are* one of the most critically endangered species on the planet. That's neat and all."

She stared out the glass, chewing her lip.

"People nearly drove Silimalo phoenixes extinct," she said. "*Our* greed. *Our* short-sightedness. All for a few feathers, we almost wiped out a species. But people *saved* the phoenixes, too. We captured the last wild birds and brought them into captivity. We started breeding them, trying to keep the species alive. For me, phoenixes are a reminder of how awful people can be... but also how much good we can do, when we put our minds to it."

One day, that kindness might pay off. Silimalo phoenixes in the wild once more, preening in olive trees along the rocky coast of their home country, a salt breeze ruffling their feathers and a fiery sunset in their eyes.

"Sounds like the new phoenix is heading for a good home," Connor said.

"We have to make it into a home, first." In under two months.

"Well." Connor nodded to the incubators. "If you need help getting those up and running, I handled the maintenance while the dragons were breeding. I'd be happy to help tune them up."

"Really? That would be amazing! I...Thank you, Connor."

Her heart fluttered. Her legs felt weaker than she'd like. But at some point, the words came easier. Talking to him was nice, not as terrifying as Aila thought it would be.

Tanya was going to be smug about this, wasn't she?

"I've stolen enough of your time," Aila said.

"Not at all. You're welcome to do so again."

Horns and fangs, Aila had to unmelt herself first. "I'll be back later with that cart!"

"I'll be here."

"Good. Great. Goodbye."

"See you later, Aila."

She waved in parting, backing toward the door like a wary animal. When she stepped outside, Aila restrained herself from skipping off into the sunset.

Incubators returning to phoenix complex: check.

Speaking to the hot guy for longer than thirty seconds: *check*.

Watch out, world. At this rate, nothing was keeping Aila from that phoenix.

Chapter Ten

The Phenomenal Phoenix Rejuvenation Plan (title pending, Aila really wanted that full alliteration) went like this.

Week one: Strategy.

Aila scrawled their to-do list across several dozen sticky notes and plastered them on the office wall. She inventoried every supply in the phoenix complex, down to the half-empty bags of food pellets in the back cupboard.

Week two: Acquisition.

Aila completed and filed the (frankly excessive) purchase order paperwork for a new refrigerator, new linoleum flooring, new fireproof paint, new olive trees for the exhibit, new towels and heaters and nest platform paneling and *anything* else the zoo would give her. Rubra deserved the best.

Week three: Deconstruction.

Ordering new flooring was exciting. Tearing up the old flooring required a whole week, several internet videos, a trip to the hardware store for tools, several more internet videos, all crammed in half-hour increments between Aila's normal routine. She dug out the charred olive trees in the exhibit, broke down the old nest platform.

Week four: Implementation.

The purchase orders started arriving, and the real work began.

Today, Aila's new olive trees were scheduled for delivery. She arrived at the zoo before the sun touched the palms, before Tom and his coffee settled into the corner of the staff office. The first fall rain had come in the night, distant lightning flashing in her apartment window. The morning came chill, the concrete damp as water dripped off the aviaries.

Aila flew through her morning routine of shuffling animals, feeding, cleaning, all in time to be at the zoo's cargo gate when the delivery truck arrived. Five young olive trees sat in the open cargo bed. Groundskeeping helped her move them to the exhibit on the back of a golf cart. A brief break for lunch—because Tanya *insisted*—then Aila spent the afternoon digging holes for the new plantings.

"Just a . . . little . . . straighter . . ."

Aila braced her shoulder against the gray trunk of a sapling, all her meager weight required to tilt the tree a couple of inches. Its roots strained in the soil, shifting until Aila was satisfied with the placement. Her opinion, of course, meant little.

"What do you think?" she asked.

Within the tangle of branches and silver leaves, a ruby head popped into sight. Rubra clucked, her highest form of endorsement. She toyed a leaf with her beak, the fiery plumes of her tail already scorching marks along the (thankfully) flame-resistant bark. Aila envisioned a pair of phoenixes frolicking through the boughs, exchanging leaves and trills for their courtship dance.

Or maybe that was the sleep deprivation. She'd cut her sleep schedule down, just a little bit, cramming a couple of extra hours each night to study phoenix papers. Nothing another afternoon coffee couldn't fix. She blinked until her vision focused back into a single bird.

"You like it, Rubra?"

The phoenix puffed her cheek feathers and chirped.

"Perfect. Let's hope the inspector likes it, too."

Aila assumed the human would be pickier, but Rubra's vote of confidence was a good start. The first month flew by with prep and paperwork. Only one month left to bring it all together. She surveyed her progress with a groggy grin.

In the exhibit, every olive tree had been pruned or replaced. The ground was raked, regraveled, planted with rock sunflowers that Rubra had played in for an entire afternoon, coating her plumage with yellow petals.

Most important of all, the nesting platform in the back corner had been rebuilt with cedar planks and a heated floor. Every year, instinct compelled Rubra to build a nest of woven olive branches, but she never laid any eggs.

Soon, that could change. If Aila kept her shit together for one more month.

She returned to the breeding complex covered in mud and smelling of olive. Not awful, on a scale of potential substances one could accrue at a zoo. Normally, Aila didn't mind smelling like kelpie bog or vanishing duck guano.

That opinion swiftly changed when she spotted Connor, waiting at the door with a swoon-worthy smile. She froze like a toad caught in a headlamp.

"Morning, Aila," he greeted.

Aila's brain went through a swift reset. Connor was here. At her exhibit. He'd just said hello to her. *Shit. Shit! Why are you gawking? Are you sure you don't smell like bog? Say hello! Say something nice!*

"Morning. Connor." Aila coughed. "It...uh...rained last night."

He eyed the damp concrete. "So it appears."

"Sure does."

Not the worst interaction she'd had with him. Sleep-deprived Aila would take it.

"I've got some spare time before closing," Connor said. "Want to test those incubators? I know you won't need them for a while, but nothing wrong with getting ahead of the game."

He smiled wider. Aila fought the instinct to hyperventilate.

The incubators weren't the only thing she wanted to take a closer look at.

Inside, the breeding complex smelled of bleach. Too much bleach. Needed to air out the bleach, or by all the skies and seas, Aila might pass out today. The linoleum had been ripped up, but not yet replaced. Her boots crackled on the grout-strewn floor as she pranced to the back counter, the stacks of bird pellet boxes replaced by incubators she and Connor had carted up from the dragon aviaries last week.

"Ta-da!" She waved her hand over the spotless glass, the gleaming buttons and knobs. They *looked* brand new. Whether they worked remained to be seen. Aila hadn't dared try them out without a mechanic on hand, lest one explode.

"Moment of truth?" Connor plugged in a machine and tapped the LCD screen. It blinked on with a white light followed by a flashing egg logo. Inside the box, a fan whirred. A bulb lit up, illuminating the inner chamber.

"Good sign." Aila touched the glass, a bloom of warmth against her finger.

"Do you know how to work them?"

"Well, I read through the manual about . . . five times. Could revisit the temperature calibration section. Don't quite have all the tables memorized yet, but handy to know how to . . ."

She paused at Connor's arched brow.

"Yeah," she concluded. "I know how to work them."

He chuckled. "Seems you're always on top of things."

"On top? I don't know, I've always considered myself more of a..."

Aila froze.

Connor's brows climbed higher. She didn't. She did not nearly say *that* right when he was starting to talk to her like a normal person.

"*Anyway.*" Aila cleared her throat. "Let's have a look at these incubators!"

She flicked the switch for the heater and tapped through the temperature settings, bumping the thermostat up to phoenix immolation heat—just a few degrees hotter than her cheeks currently, she guessed. The coils in the back glowed orange as the internal thermometer rose. While she worked, Connor plugged in the next incubator. The fan sputtered, a troubling wheeze compared to the first.

"Something loose." Connor popped open a side panel. "Should be an easy fix."

Aila sidled as close as she dared. "Would you...um... mind if I watched? To learn, of course. Don't want to have to call you up here every time something breaks. Not that I *mind* calling you up here. You're welcome any time. I just mean... You know."

"Of course." He grinned, flashing flawless teeth. "Happy to teach."

He didn't smell like mud. Or bog. Or duck guano. Pine drifted off him, a glob of sap clinging to his black polo. Beneath that, the warm dust of dragon feathers, a musk of aviary soil on his boots. Aila would take any one of them bottled like cologne, more pleasant than nose-puckering spice.

She leaned closer, impressed by his deft hands as he sorted incubator wiring. Entranced by the dark hair curled against his forehead, shifting into his eyes as he tilted for a better view of his work. He brushed the stray lock aside with the back of his hand.

His hair looked so soft. Perfect to run fingers through.

Aila's stomach swirled with butterflies. "You're pretty good at this."

"I had to learn on the fly with the dragon hatchlings. Necessity breeds innovation." He tugged a loose wire away from the fan. The whirring stopped. His grin widened. "There we go."

"Amazing." Dumb little things like that were never in the manuals. "Thanks, Connor. We're lucky to have your help."

"I'm sure you'll have the hang of it in no time. You're a quick learner, I can tell."

He looked at her. Aila could drown in the pools of his eyes. The soft curve of his lips turned the butterflies in her stomach to a swarm.

When had she ever been someone worth looking at?

"Still." Aila's throat was sandpaper. "Happy to have you."

"Happy to help. Us exhibit neighbors have got to look out for each other, right?"

Connor bumped his shoulder to hers. Aila couldn't breathe, her heart hammering into full-blown panic. He stood too close. Too stunning. Too long a pause as he stared at her. Why was he *still* staring at her?

This was the point it always went wrong.

What was she supposed to do? Lean closer? Run away? Tell him he was gorgeous and the mere thought of his smile made her legs give out? No, no, that was too forward. She needed to ease in slow, something more like—

The door across the room flew open.

"Fucking prissy bird and his fucking holes!"

Aila went rod-straight as Tanya stormed across the room,

raging like a drowned cat. And looking like one. Her clothes were drenched, boots squishing, squiggles of black hair plastered to her cheeks. The streaked mascara could have passed for low-budget monster makeup in one of the movie posters on the wall. All evidence pointed to her having plummeted into a pond.

Or having the pond dropped on her by a magical river bird.

"Smart-ass little feathered prick thinks he's being so clever." Tanya's muttering followed her into the bathroom. "See how he likes it when..."

The door slammed shut. Connor shot Aila a questioning look.

"She's fighting with her Bix phoenix," Aila explained. And losing, it looked like. "He likes to hide in holes."

"Holes?"

She nodded. "Any of your dragons like to hide in holes?"

"No. I can't say I've run into that one."

"Probably for the best." All the aviaries had a protective foundation of IMWS certified concrete underneath, but if a five-pound bird could prove so crafty, Aila shuddered to think what a determined dragon could accomplish.

The interruption fizzled any tension between them. Connor returned to work. Aila leaned against the counter a safe distance away, begging the heat in her cheeks to recede.

He was being friendly. A helpful colleague. Dangerous, to hope for anything more.

No matter how much Aila wanted something more.

When Tanya emerged a few minutes later, she'd refreshed her makeup and washed the mud from her braids. Her attire remained soggy, paired with a frown as she squinted between Aila and their visitor.

"Morning, Connor."

"Morning, Tanya. Sorry to hear about your bird troubles."

Her lips thinned. "He'll get what's coming to him. You helping with the incubators?"

"I was showing Aila how to do some repairs. She learns fast."

He flashed Aila a dazzling smile. Her heart twirled.

Tanya made a displeased hum. "Sure is kind of you. Mind if I steal Aila for a minute? Got to take a look at the water spigot outside, been acting up again."

Aila glared, a silent *what are you doing?* "Can't be that bad. I'm sure you can handle it."

"Please, don't let me keep you," Connor said. "I'm almost finished. I can take a look at the rest of the incubators, come get you if anything pops up?"

Aila gave him a tight smile. For Tanya, a scowl. "Right. Sure. Sounds perfect."

Fuming, she followed Tanya outside. They were friends. Best friends. How dare Tanya defy their most sacred of pacts, invoking their code phrase when *cute boys* were involved?

Out in the public viewing area, a group of teenagers gathered at the exhibit glass, snapping photos with their phones as Rubra rolled on the ground with an olive branch, setting each leaf alight like birthday candles. Tanya drew Aila past the crowd and into a secluded corner beneath the grape arbors, immune to Aila's glare, tapping an azure nail to her chin.

"Yes?" Aila demanded. "Can I help you?"

"Cute dragon boy's gotten awful friendly."

"Yeah. Of course he . . . Wasn't that the *goal*?"

Tanya made another long hum. "*Too* friendly."

Aila slumped against the stucco wall with a groan. "Tanya. Please. What do you want from me? Because we both know I'm not socially adept enough for whatever is happening in this conversation."

Tanya sighed. "I don't mean anything too serious by it, Ailes. Just you've got a lot to balance right now. Maybe trying to add romance on top is a little...precarious?"

Fair point, if not for one glaring oversight: Aila was *always* precarious. In all her meager relationship experience, there was never a right time, only panic and flailing and awkward monologues that should have stayed locked up in her head. Having someone reciprocate even a sliver of her affections was a rarity.

Didn't Aila deserve that? To not always have to stretch and scrape herself to fit the people around her?

"I just don't want him hurting your precious little heart." Tanya laid a hand on her shoulder. "Because if that happens, I'll have to feed him to the kelpie, and I chipped enough nails today already."

"No one needs to get fed to the kelpie, Tanya. And he's... It's no big deal. No hearts or anything. Just spending some time together."

"*Mm-hm.*" Tanya dragged the syllables out to an insulting length.

"OK, you got drenched by a bird this morning, so I don't want to hear it."

"Is that the game we're playing? How many hours of sleep did you get last night?"

"I'll have you know I got..." Aila paused. She tapped her fingers against the wall, counting. "Four. OK. But studies have shown that required sleep levels are variable across individuals."

Aila had managed tighter sleep schedules in college. And this was only temporary until the inspection.

It was fine. She was *fine.*

"All I'm saying is, you've been pushing yourself to the bone. Doing all this work on your own, and we've still got a plenty big list before that inspector comes."

"Yes. I'm aware. But—"

"Yet here you are dilly-dallying with cute dragon boy." Tanya crossed her arms. "Almost as if you're *avoiding* something in particular."

Skies and seas, sometimes Aila hated how well Tanya knew her.

"I will get that talon-mite duster from griffin show," Aila said. "In time for our scheduled application tomorrow. As promised."

"Oh?" Tanya dripped skepticism. "And how are you going to do that?"

"Relax, Tanya. I *totally* have a plan."

Aila's plan consisted of waiting until the zoo closed, then sneaking ninja-style into the griffin show complex while no one was around. Genius. She'd pat herself on the back later.

After hours, the amphitheater was less offensive. Quiet. Dark. A little spooky. Aila jumped when the first motion-sensing light snapped on behind the show building. Nothing to be concerned about. The performing creatures were locked away in barns and aviaries. All the keepers appeared to have headed home.

The only person Aila cared about avoiding was Luciana.

It was college all over again. Aila spent most of her freshman year skulking around the teaching exhibits and study halls, yearning for the abilities of a vanishing duck, heart skipping any time Luciana glinted past like a wayward star.

From the start, Aila had a hopeless crush on her. The flawless hair, that regal smirk, those eyes that disintegrated every flirting human who dared push into her orbit. But more than anything, the *confidence*. Luciana walked that campus like every blade of grass could sing for her, spoke without doubt that any person or beast would hang rapt to her words.

Aila had hoped they could be friends. Silly, naive Aila. She'd have a better chance coaxing a star to join her on the ground.

She'd aced all her college courses—except for *one*: Animal Outreach Practicum. An entire mandatory class dedicated to crafting educational presentations and *speaking* them in front of people. Aila hadn't known such agony since her parents signed her up for a theater summer camp in middle school as an attempt to help her make friends.

Except outreach class had been worse. Aila was supposed to be good at animals, at academics. She'd written her entire script about sunburst hummingbirds, spent weeks memorizing lines about the birds' native habitat in the Ziclexian rainforest, how they produced multicolored light to accent their plumage while singing, until she started reciting the speech in her sleep (much to Tanya's annoyance). The day of her practice presentation arrived. She'd stood in front of her entire class, demonstration bird perched on her hand.

She'd gotten one sentence out before the words froze in her throat.

Aila had stood in front of everyone as her legs began to shake. Speechless. Petrified. Helpless as the judging stares of her classmates bored into her, as her instructor frowned over their grading notecard. She'd looked like a fool. She'd looked like a pathetic little kid who'd never been able to do what came so easy for everyone else.

And what was the first sound to break that spell?

A laugh. A perfect, honeyed laugh.

Luciana. Flawless, confident Luciana, sat in the back of that class, laughing as Aila stood numb with stage fright. Years later, the wretched sound still rattled in her skull.

Then add the insult of the following day, when their group projects were assigned. Luciana and Aila, paired together. The witch hadn't waited thirty seconds before slinking to the instructor, whispering a request for reassignment. A shining comet, refusing to be tethered to a lump of coal.

Each memory churned hot in Aila's stomach as she crept through the griffin show barns. No people in sight, and she preferred it that way. Less chance for her to look like an idiot. Less chance to disappoint.

Yet when she spotted a barn door ajar, her path veered before she could stop herself.

Wasn't this where she'd visited Nimit, the aging peacock griffin? The other keepers ought to be long gone, and she'd hate to think someone left an enclosure open. Golden light spilled through the crack. Wary, she peeked inside.

Nimit lay curled in his stall, wrapped in a spray of blue and green tail feathers, breaths heavy as his head rested in the lap of a familiar figure.

Luciana. She sat with her back to the door, shoulders slumped and hair coated in hay dust, combing her fingers through Nimit's cobalt neck feathers.

Aila should have scurried off, grabbed the equipment she needed while Luciana was distracted. Confusion kept her rooted. She'd seen Luciana affectionate toward the griffin, yet assumed it an act, part of the stage persona. This was different. The silence of the barn tugged at Aila like claws, a gravity hanging between Luciana and her beast, pulling the proud woman's head down lower than it had ever hung. Lower than a star *should* hang.

Aila shouldn't be watching this.

Heart pounding, she backed away.

With new urgency, she dove into the storage barns behind the aviaries. A quick trip. That was all she'd meant this to be. No distractions, no run-ins with colleagues or their uncomfortable emotions. Without bothering to switch on the light, Aila scrambled into a shed and beelined for the talon-mite sprayer, nudging aside boxes of leather handling gloves and a couple of transport crates she could have sworn belonged to the phoenix exhibit. A battle for another day. She pulled the apparatus free, a long metal sprayer attached to a plastic backpack.

The light to the shed flicked on.

Aila gasped and clutched the sprayer to her chest like a busted jewel thief.

Her worst nightmare stood in the doorway: Luciana, with one manicured finger raised beside the light switch, coral lips pressed into a scowl, eyes like phoenix embers beneath veiled lashes. In the harsh light of the exposed bulb, Luciana's eyeshadow smudged into tired shadows. A blush of red puffed her nose.

Wait wait wait.

Had she . . . ?

Had she been crying?

"You could have asked," Luciana said.

Aila blinked, stumbling over Luciana's less than flawless appearance, her slumped shoulders in the barn.

"Hello?" Luciana snapped her fingers, breaking Aila's spell. "Were you going to let me know about taking our equipment, or abscond with it in the night like a skulking purserat?"

"I knew Nimit was getting old," Aila said, quiet. "I'm sorry, I . . . didn't realize he was that bad."

This was, it turned out, as far as possible from the correct thing to say. Luciana flinched, a flash of shock replaced by a dragon's snarl.

"You're sorry?" Luciana scoffed. "That's a first."

The words stung like a slap. This was what Aila got for trying to be *nice*? "Will you give it a break? You don't have to act all perfect and tough all the time."

Luciana laughed, humorless. "You're one to talk."

"What's that supposed to mean?"

"You know what I mean."

"No, please. I'd be honored for our star performer to *educate me*."

Luciana swept a hand over Aila's defensive stance, the sprayer clutched to her chest. "Everyone in the zoo knows about your renovation project. Yet have we heard a peep about it here at griffin show?"

Of course. Always about *her*. "I haven't had time to—"

"Of course you haven't. Instead, you think you can tackle this whole thing on your own. You come sneaking in here after hours when we'd have gladly handed that equipment over. Why is it always like this, Aila? Are you that embarrassed to ask us for help?"

"I just don't want to ask *you* for help!"

The words crackled between them.

Aila wanted to shrink away. Not the smartest tactic. Every survival guide said running from predators was the surest path to doom. Not to mention, Luciana blocked the door. Puffy-eyed or not, her glower weighed heavy enough to crack bones.

"If you need our help," Luciana said, too quiet, "we'd give it in a heartbeat. All you have to do is suck up your pride and *ask*."

The offer came out less like a kindness, more like a threat. It sank venomous into Aila's skin, prickling even after Luciana marched off into the night. Even after Aila was alone again, a trespasser caught in rumpled clothes and stark fluorescent light.

Fuck Luciana. Of course she could claim the high ground, the world revolving around her as usual. When she spoke, people listened. When she called, people answered. Aila had to claw her way here without all that. She'd keep clawing if she had to.

She fled in the opposite direction, sprayer in hand, determined to prove that witch wrong.

Chapter Eleven

Sleep, Aila decided, was overrated.

Tanya kept saying she *needed* sleep. But who could waste time on such frivolity when a deadline loomed? Aila organized every minute of her workday on her whiteboard in the phoenix complex, breaking out a new sixteen-pack of colored dry erase markers for the task. When she got back to her apartment each night, she used every waking hour to read.

First up was that instruction manual for the egg incubators. Aila read it front to back twice and skimmed it three more times for good measure, filling the pages with so many colored sticky notes the book no longer closed correctly.

Next, she reread every book she owned about Silimalo phoenix courtship, breeding, and chick rearing.

Next, a guide to Silimalo gardening, specifically the section on olive trees.

All it took was a little focus, a few extra cups of coffee. She could do this.

She'd prove to Tanya—to *Luciana*—that she could do this.

Normally, Aila loved working late. Tourmaline curled into a silver poof in her lap, her desk lamp the lone light in her apartment after all her animals went to sleep. There was a quiet serenity that only came at midnight and early morning, the whole world still and silent outside her window. No parents asking how school went. Not teachers telling her to put her book down and pay attention. No colleagues scheduling meetings or impromptu equipment drop-offs. A rare window of no expectations, where Aila could just...be.

Granted, her late-night sessions were made less serene by the never-ending stack of papers on her desk. Every manuscript on phoenixes published in the last ten years. IMWS reports. Care protocols by Giuseppe Garumano, director of the breeding program in Silimalo. A bevy of IMWS-approved studies on behavior, natural habitat, nest site selection.

Aila only had four weeks until the inspection. Then three. Then one.

The digital clock on her bookshelf read just past two when she laid her head down on the desk. Just for a moment. Just one more paper before bed.

Groggy, her eyes flicked over the mess of manuscripts. She'd emptied her coffee mug hours ago, a gift from Tanya bearing a cartoon phoenix and a "Fire me up!" speech bubble. Beside that was a blue-gray thunderhawk feather as long as her arm, molted by the first bird she'd worked with in college. Above, potted plants lined a shelf, perched alongside the framed photo of Aila and her parents on vacation in Silimalo—

Shit.

Aila dug beneath several papers until she unearthed her phone. A new message icon glowed on the screen. A text from her mom, unopened.

Hi honey, haven't heard from you in a while, hope everything is OK!

Aila had meant to reply earlier.

She'd just gotten a little...carried away with reading. Bleary-eyed, she stumbled her fingers across the keypad.

Sorry. Been super busy. Will call when I can.

She hit *send* just before her eyes drooped. Just before...

Aila jerked awake to a blaring sound.

What in all the skies and seas *was* that?

She floundered into a sitting position at...her desk? Hadn't even made it to bed. That would be murder on her back later, but first, she was more concerned with the loud beeping...

Alarm.

Aila's wake-up alarm was going off on her phone. She *never* slept late enough to need an alarm, her brain usually alert with a to-do list long before she had to rise.

It was dark outside her window as she scrambled to get dressed, scarfed a granola bar for breakfast, scratched Tourmaline behind the ears on her way out the door. She hit a cafe on her way to the train station, in and out the door just long enough to snag a coffee.

One more week until the inspection. She could do this.

She had to do this.

Aila readied a knife over the cutting board, a mango poised to meet its doom.

"Another one!" With that battle cry, she commenced chopping.

Tanya sat on the kitchen counter, shuffling through a stack of flashcards Aila had shoved into her hands that morning. "OK, let's see. Umm...incubation period of a Silimalo phoenix?"

"Twenty-eight days," Aila replied. "With a standard deviation of two days in the Silimalo population, three days in Movas."

Tanya flipped to the next card. "Key signs of imminent female immolation?"

"Increased shifting on nest." Aila slid her diced mango into a bowl, then started hacking a clump of kale. "Pecking at breast feathers. Begging for food from the male."

"Common ailments of phoenix hatchlings?"

"Flame foot. Ingrown feathers. Ash lung. Dammit!" Aila jerked to catch a bottle of bird antibiotics she'd nearly swatted off the counter in her haste. Archie always got a sinus infection when the weather turned cold. She measured a spoonful of medicine and mixed it with his favorite fruit and bird-pellet smoothie.

Tanya pulled the next card. "Diet of chicks?" She dropped the stack to her lap. "Ailes, we can print that out and put it on the fridge. You don't have to memorize—"

"One part cricket meal. Three parts softened phoenix pellets. One scoop Fiery Fantastic brand nutritional supplement."

"You should take a break, Aila."

"No. Another one."

"You need rest. Take a nap. I can finish the food prep."

"I need to be ready to impress the inspector."

"You can't impress anyone if you pass out!"

Aila slumped against the counter, fingers stained with fruit juice and nutritional slurry. One week until the inspector arrived, and she still had to paint the interior rooms with fire-resistant pigment. Organize a couple dozen protocol binders. Update the new software on the security cameras.

One week wasn't enough time.

"We've come so far." Aila straightened, a burst of adrenaline fighting fatigue. "Just one more week. We can do this. We can..."

She reached for the refrigerator handle but swiped air. *Oh. Right.* An empty space remained where the appliance had been hauled out the day before, purserat remains and all, several stains left behind on the floor.

Tanya handed Aila a bowl of vegetables they'd hauled up

from the lower aviary fridges, nails clacking against metal in what had to be the sassiest transference of cookware Aila had ever received outside of awkward family reunions.

"You know," Tanya said. "I hate to say it, Ailes. But if we need some extra hands..."

"No," Aila shot back. "I have standards, Tanya. I will not sully my honor by getting on my knees in front of that witch!"

Tanya bobbed her head at the choice of words.

Someone in the doorway cleared his throat.

Dragon spit.

Aila spun around to see a man in a delivery uniform, clipboard in hand, glancing between her and the upraised knife in her hand.

"Did you...? Uh...You the one who ordered the new industrial fridge?"

Aila set the knife down, giddy. Here was something going right, at least. She'd been on the phone for hours last week coordinating the delivery, but once the refrigerator came in, the kitchen renovations would be finished. All that left was... everything else.

The man led Aila and Tanya outside. At the junction of the public path and the keeper offshoot, a new refrigerator sat on the concrete: stainless steel wrapped in layers of protective plastic and Styrofoam. Aila's mouth fell open. She'd run all the measurements a dozen times, but the behemoth still impressed her. They could fit enough mangos for all of winter in this thing. And, best of all, no musty purserat smell.

"Your signature here." The man held his clipboard out as Aila scribbled her name. "Thank you, ma'am. Enjoy."

"Wait. Are you not...? How do we get it *inside*?"

"Paid for delivery, not installation. Have a nice day."

He lumbered off, leaving Aila's jaw hanging. Beside her, Tanya tapped the metal monstrosity with a frown.

"It's fine." Aila stepped a wide circle around the appliance, sizing it up. Several passing patrons paused to do the same. "There's two of us. We can totally move this inside."

"Aila."

"I know, I know, it will mostly be you. I can focus on logistics."

"*Aila.*"

"It's not my fault you have strong, gorgeous arms!"

Tanya grabbed Aila with one of those strong, gorgeous arms and yanked her into the keeper building.

"It isn't *just* a refrigerator, Aila."

Tanya pointed to the unpainted walls. The torn-up floors with rolls of new linoleum still in plastic. A desk full of empty binders and paperwork in various stages of sorting. New cork boards to be mounted. Boxes of donated towels and blankets to comb through.

"You can't do this in a week," Tanya said.

"But—"

"*We* can't do this in a week! Especially not while taking care of our animals."

Aila grasped for an argument. If she just finished her rounds a little faster today . . . or if she stayed an extra hour past closing . . . or cut another hour of sleep . . .

She groaned and sank to her knees, the floor crackling against her work pants.

"*Fuuuuuuuuck.*"

Tanya crouched beside her. "Ask Luciana for help. What's so bad about that?"

Aila glared.

"Remember in college," Tanya said, "when Luc and I got partnered for barn clean-up? She's not all bad, Ailes. Was always on time. Pulled her weight. Knew the animals as well as anyone there—dare I say it, as well as *someone else* I know. Yet somehow, the two of you got all tangled up in each other."

"Oh, yeah. *Somehow*, she acts like an entitled princess whenever she's not faking it for the public. Somehow, she has to be perfect at everything. Somehow, she tries to steal Rubra for the griffin show every single year."

Tanya gave a long-suffering sigh. "Sure. But she offered to help. And we *need* help. Get this over with, and we'll never speak of it again."

Aila's pride lumped in her throat. Tanya was right.

"Do you want me to come with you?" Tanya asked.

"No. No one needs to see this."

But of course, everyone in the zoo would hear about it.

Mid-morning sun trickled through the banyan trees of the Renkailan section. With the passing seasons, the light turned slanted, cool. Not unlike Aila's heart.

Do it for Rubra. She's all that matters.

When Aila arrived at the amphitheater, several hours remained until the next show. Two keepers stood on the lawn between the stage and the empty audience seating, leather gloves on their arms, training a cavern eagle to fly between them. One keeper snapped her fingers. The blind bird perked feathered ear tufts, swiveling to pinpoint the sound. With a beat of black and ruby wings, he leapt off his perch, flying straight to the keeper's glove and landing with a weight that made her sag. She dug a mouse from the satchel at her waist. The eagle snapped up his reward, followed by a happy chortle as the keeper scratched his neck feathers.

On the sidelines stood Luciana, hands folded, hair starched and woven into twin braids down her back. She nodded at the bird's progress.

Aila mustered her protest with scraping steps against the concrete, plodding over the damp lawn. Luciana never turned to face her, attention glued to her work. They stood side by side for what could have been the most uncomfortable minute of Aila's life, her boot tapping the grass, cavern eagle wings beating in time with her heart.

In the silence, Aila heard Luciana laughing at her in their college classroom, that honeyed sound like a knife through her heart.

"Good morning, Aila," Luciana said, brittle as ever.

"Luciana."

"Is the talon-mite sprayer working well for you?"

"As well as it always does."

"Glad to hear it. Something else I can help you with?"

Aila puffed a strand of auburn hair out of her face. "I think you know what you can help me with."

"Still, I'd prefer to hear you say it."

Wouldn't she, though. Wouldn't she love to lock that in her memory box along with every other time she'd humiliated Aila, a treasure to gloat over whenever she wished.

Do it for the phoenixes.

"I could use your help," Aila said. "Finishing the renovations. The inspector comes in a week. We're nearly there, but Tanya and I..." She took a steadying breath. "We can't pull it off on our own. An extra pair of hands would make a huge difference."

Luciana didn't look at her. Dark eyes slid across the lawn as the cavern eagle glided from keeper to keeper, a perfect performer thanks to those tidbits of meat dangled in front of him.

The longer Luciana remained silent, the more Aila's stomach twisted.

What if this had been a game all along?

What if Luciana wouldn't help? *Too busy training for the show. Why didn't you ask sooner?* She had every excuse, and even if she didn't lift a finger, she'd get to enjoy Aila's groveling as the cherry on top.

"Thank you for letting me know," Luciana said at last. "I'll see what we can work into our schedule."

Aila stormed off, unable to bear the smug twitch to Luciana's painted lips.

Chapter Twelve

"She's a cold, callous bitch!" Aila announced as she slammed a paint can upon the metal counter of the phoenix complex. "I'd rather face the spiked tail of a manticore than that feral woman!"

A venomous tail, no less. As venomous as Luciana.

A gloomy Tanya leaned against the counter beside her. She handed over a jar of powdered diamondback dragon scales. Next, a packet of *very* expensive, captive-molted Silimalo phoenix feather pigment. That one took a month of IMWS paperwork before approval, delivered in a suitcase by an armed guard. Aila dumped both contents into the orange paint and stirred. The resulting concoction would be fireproof to several hundred degrees, enough to protect against errant phoenix tails.

"First, she goes lecturing me, *all you have to do is suck up your pride and ask*." Aila waggled paint-speckled fingers in a pompous Luciana impression. "Then, when I do ask for help, she acts like she can't be bothered."

"Mm-hm," Tanya mused.

"Probably never wanted to help from the start."

"It does look that way."

"Putting on that stupid do-gooder act. How does everyone fall for it?"

"Careful with that paint, Ailes. It costs more than both our paychecks."

Aila paused, chest heaving, paint spatula brandished like a sword. Before she could waste any precious drops, she sighed and plunked it into the can.

"The paint should be mixed enough," she grumbled. "Let's give it a test."

Aila grabbed a square plank of wood from her desk and laid it on the counter atop some packing paper. Brush in hand, she dipped gingerly into the *very expensive* paint bucket. She'd only survived her elective art class in high school thanks to a very liberal interpretation of "abstract" design. That, and her instructor took pity when Aila broke down over her mixing colors turning brown for the twentieth time. She'd been trying to make green.

Fortunately, this was within her skill level. She painted the top side of the wood orange, dripping only a couple of spatters onto the surrounding paper.

Tanya drummed the counter with turquoise nails. "This just doesn't seem like Luc."

"What doesn't seem like her?" Aila said, dryly. "The part where she's a stuck-up witch? Or where she loves being the center of attention? Or where she gets off on making me grovel?"

Aila yanked on a pair of fireproof gloves, pulling them all the way up to each shoulder. Tanya grabbed the hand-held blowtorch from the counter and passed it over.

"The part where she refused to help," Tanya said. "Griffin show's our sister department. Luciana's never turned me down when I needed something. Not even that time you were out sick, and I needed extra hands to ground the Ozokian kingfisher while I treated him for electric mites. Luc was down here as soon as I called."

Aila scoffed and clicked the gas canister into the blowtorch.

"She's never turned *you* down, either," Tanya continued. "Rare as you ask for help."

Aila scoffed harder. "Unless you count her trying to drag Rubra into the griffin show for three straight years. Which I do, by the way."

She clicked off the blowtorch safety valve. Squared her feet. There was something therapeutic in pulling the trigger and letting a jet of fire loose, feeling the flare of heat upon her cheeks. Sure, mindfulness and breathing exercises were more "approved" methods of treating anxiety, but burning shit made for a strong runner-up.

Upon the metal counter, the packing paper combusted, shriveling into black cinders. The plank of wood charred on every edge. But the painted portion? Untouched. The top of the wood stayed pristine. Once all the inner walls got painted with this stuff, the phoenix complex would be fully up to date with IMWS code 40.04.b: Flame-Resistant Facility Requirements.

And the fresh orange would look pretty.

"When you talked to Luciana," Tanya said, "did you ask *nicely*?"

Aila's grip flinched on the blowtorch, nearly dropping it to the floor.

"What's that supposed to mean?" she demanded.

Tanya shrugged. "You've got a tendency to be...prickly around her."

"Because she's prickly to me!"

"That's what we call a vicious cycle, Aila."

Another scoff. Aila was on track to use up her quota today. "She started it."

"Ailes..."

"Well, she did!" Aila floundered a hand for emphasis. "She's the one who wouldn't give me the time of day in college. She's the one who laughed during my outreach presentation. She's the one who keeps asking Director Hawthorn to move Rubra to—"

"*Aila, you're on fire.*"

Aila paused. Blinked. She looked down and...sure enough, one of her gloves was on fire. She heaved the world's largest groan.

"Well. That's great. Now I need to order new fire-resistant gloves? On top of everything else?" Granted, each pair had a limited warranty, given the expected lifespan of the fireproof coating, but Aila could have sworn they were still within their operational period. She'd have to check her paperwork for—

"Aila," Tanya said, firm. "Inventories later."

"Right, right..."

It wasn't the first time one of them had caught on fire. Skies and seas knew it wouldn't be the last. That was what protocol was for.

Aila turned down the flame on the blowtorch and set it on the counter. The fingers of her burning glove started feeling toasty by the time she made it to the metal disposal canister in the corner. She peeled them off and dropped them into the empty bin. Tanya was ready with the fire extinguisher. One long spray of foam—infused with liquefying starfish gel, for extra density —and the flames went out with a hiss.

Aila scowled at the remains. "Damn gloves are always in low stock. I'll need to get that order in by the end of today to have any chance of shipping in time for—What's that sound?"

A crinkle. A pop. Aila turned.

Half her desk was on fire.

Now *that* was something new.

"*Fuck!*" she and Tanya said in unison.

They lurched into motion. On the counter, the blowtorch lay on its side. Aila must not have set it down properly. She hadn't turned the fire off all the way. She thought she had. She could have *sworn* she had, but all of it melded into a fog of fatigue and panic. The fallen torch had caught a binder on the edge of her desk. Fire crackled through paper and vinyl, spreading fast.

Tanya raised the fire extinguisher.

"Wait!" Aila pleaded.

Not just any papers. All the phoenix protocols. The work inventories. The logs of their building updates. Piles and piles on her desk, waiting to be sorted before the inspection. Now going up in flame. The fire extinguisher would soak the rest.

"We need to save it!" Aila shouted.

"We'll lose it anyway if we don't put this fire out!" Tanya clipped back.

Aila grabbed for whatever papers she could, anything the fire hadn't touched. Tanya worked at her side, snatching binders and pages out of the path of the flames. They salvaged as much as possible. Then Tanya hooked an arm around Aila's waist, dragging her away from the carnage as she swiped and pleaded. One more. Just one more page.

Tanya unleashed the fire extinguisher. Flames sputtered out beneath the foam. The remnants of Aila's paperwork turned to soggy ash.

In the aftermath, the room smelled of smoke, burnt paper, and the salt of liquefying starfish gel. Aila and Tanya sank to the floor, backs resting against the cabinets.

"All my paperwork..." Aila's hands shook. Maybe this was all a nightmare. Maybe she'd wake up any moment now, slouched over her desk at home, alarm blaring in her ear.

Upsettingly, she didn't.

"It's just paperwork," Tanya reassured her. "We can reprint the invoices, the protocols. Rewrite the building renovation logs."

"It took me over a week to get all that together."

"I know, Ailes."

"We don't have time." Aila's voice rose to a panicked squeak. "Tanya. What am I going to do? I don't have enough *time*."

Reprinting and filing the paperwork. Painting the walls. Putting the flooring in. Moving that behemoth new refrigerator inside. Updating the software on their security cameras. Aila didn't have enough time.

She'd never had enough time.

"Maybe this was a stupid idea from the start," Aila said.

Her shoulders caved. She pulled her knees to her chest and shriveled into a ball, tiny and useless. She wasn't supposed to shrivel. Aila was supposed to sit up straight, take a deep breath, not let the anxiety win. That was what everyone always told her.

How could she breathe, when nothing she did was ever good enough?

She'd been a fool, thinking she could pull off a stunt like this. A feat of desperation, mostly. Unable to bear the thought of Rubra being whisked away, it was enough to attempt something impossible. It didn't even matter that Luciana had turned her down. At this rate, Aila would need a small army of help to stand any chance of having this place presentable by the time the inspector arrived.

"We can still do it," Tanya said. "As best we can."

Tanya. That generous lunar moth. Aila groaned and clutched her knees tighter, fighting the itch of smoke in her nose and the sting of tears in her eyes.

"Hey," Tanya said, firmer. "Enough of that, Aila. Sit up."

Aila—against her will, spurred by Tanya forcibly unclenching her arms—sat up. She looked at her charred desk again. Groaned again.

Tanya wrapped an arm around her shoulder, strong and

grounding. Aila didn't understand how she kept her voice calm. She didn't understand how Tanya could look her in the eye without laughing, without pointing her finger and telling Aila her dream had always been impossible.

But Tanya had a way of making the impossible seem manageable. Whether it was salvaging Aila after her first energetic genetics exam in college, piling their dorm room with chocolate bonbons and potato chips until her anxiety boiled off. Or whisking Aila away after the cute boy from the library stood her up on a date, a cozy evening crashing on the couch with Tanya and Teddy to watch highlights of their cheesy movie collection. Or just a long talk into the night, Aila confessing how people terrified her, Tanya sharing the uncertainty of her transition, both seeking themselves and their place in the world.

"You can't quit now," Tanya said. "After torturing me for two months with your colored flashcards, ripping every wall and floor to pieces? We have to see it through."

Aila sniffed, fighting a wobble in her voice. "You still think we can do it?"

"Things may not come out perfect. But we'll give it our best try. You're used to tackling everything on your own, but you've got me to help at least. Hopefully, that's enough."

Despite the weight of existential agony crushing Aila like a toothpick, she nearly laughed at that. Enough? Tanya hoped she was *enough*?

Aila dove into a bear hug, sniveling like an idiot. Tanya's arms closed around her, cracking her ribs a little too tight.

"What kind of stupid question is that?" Aila wheezed into her shoulder. "Of course you're enough. You're *always* enough, Tanya. You majestic tropical orchid."

Tanya chuckled. Patted her back. "I don't think tropical orchids will be much help in moving that fridge inside. Might look nice on our desks, though. We should talk to utilities about getting you a new one, don't want any charred edges showing during the inspection. Now, are you done getting snot all over my polo? Are we getting back to work?"

One week. They still had one week.

Aila sat back. Forced a deep breath.

"Thanks, Tanya. I couldn't do this without you."

"Nah. You couldn't." Tanya patted her head like a small, anxious poodle. "We'll get it done."

"Even without that witch?"

"You've got to stop calling her that during work hours."

Then, from across the room, "Do you...uh...need some help?"

Aila jerked straight. Connor stood in the doorway, dark hair curled against his temple, sunlight pooling behind him like a gift from the sky. She wiped a hasty hand over her cheeks, under her nose, coming away with too much snot.

"Connor! Hello! What brings you here?"

His attention lingered not on Aila, the wreck of a person, but instead on the wreck of a room surrounding them—the counters in disarray, a fire extinguisher in the middle of the floor, charred paperwork covering her desk. "Haven't heard any updates for a couple of weeks. I'll be honest, I was expecting a little more progress. Is that...? Was something on fire in here?"

"Just a little bit," Aila said, meek. Tanya jabbed an elbow into her ribs. "*Ow!* But yes, now that you mention it, we are indeed accepting offers of help. If you would be so inclined."

Connor surveyed the damage, settling on the roll of linoleum flooring. He nudged a boot against the plastic wrapping. "I've helped my dad lay some of this before. Could give it a try?"

Aila could have flown. Could have burst into flames. Could have pranced across the kelpie pond like a wisp of fog.

"Maybe he isn't so bad after all," Tanya muttered.

Of course he wasn't. He was wonderful. Gorgeous. Kind.

"You're a lifesaver!" Aila said. "I mean it. We'll pay you back in whatever food you want. Even a couple of extra hands, and we might be able to finish—"

Aila froze as the door creaked open one more time.

Yes, stand perfectly still. That's what panicked animals did when they spotted a predator, wasn't it?

Luciana entered with slow strides, hands folded behind her back, eyebrows threatening to leap off her face as she inspected the battleground. Aila blinked, yet the apparition remained. A knot tightened in her chest. Luciana was cold, but would she come here just to gloat?

Another griffin show keeper stepped through the door. Then another. And another. By the time a small army of five had amassed behind Luciana, Aila convinced herself she must have tripped and hit her head. A hallucination. Any moment now, she'd wake up, Tanya leant over her with that *I told you so* expression.

"Oh, hey, Luc," Connor greeted. "What brings you all the way up—"

"*Don't call me that.*" Luciana's words sliced like talons. Not a hallucination, then. She sniffed the air like a hunting basilisk. "Was something on fire in here?"

"Just a little bit." Tanya hooked the fire extinguisher with her foot, nudging it underneath the counter.

Luciana's brow quirked. She faced Aila. "Well?"

"What are you doing here?" Aila blurted.

"You asked for help. Here we are. What do you need?"

Aila scrunched her nose. This could be a trick. A cruel game. "We've got new security software for the cameras. Needs to be installed."

Luciana pointed to two keepers: a brown-skinned Renkailan woman with a slim build and a pale young man with slumped shoulders. "Nadia. Jericho. On it."

Aila recognized them from the griffin show's technical booth. They moved to the computer monitors at Tanya's desk and set to work without a word, barely glancing at the charred carnage of the desk beside them. It was a phoenix complex, after all.

"What else?" Luciana demanded.

"Well, uh..." Aila flinched as Tanya poked her with a paint-brush handle. "New coat of flame-resistant paint?"

Luciana snapped, and two more volunteers came forward, one snagging the paintbrush, another inspecting the can on the counter.

The last bent over the mess of binders and paperwork they'd salvaged, stacked haphazardly on the counter. "Standard IMWS organization?"

Tanya hurried over. "Yeah. We had a little setback, need to reprint some records, let me just..."

The room buzzed with voices. With work. Aila watched with wide eyes, processing the change—the flicker of hope in her chest. Five minutes ago, this had all seemed impossible. Sudden-ly, they might stand a chance, all thanks to...

Luciana's ice queen glare provided a reality check.

"Why are you doing this?" Aila hissed, low enough for only her to hear.

"Regardless of what you think of me, I keep my word."

Aila fought an eye roll. Of course, Luciana was always so *generous*.

"And besides..." Luciana flicked dark eyes to the observation window. Beyond the glass, Rubra swung from an olive branch, snapping at leaves. "Would be nice to see that bird put to good use for once. We'll get this place in shape. For the phoenixes."

The final words came out hard as concrete. Pointed like fangs.

A truce, then. A phantom laugh echoed behind Luciana's offer, a reminder not to trust too easily. Aila only had to bear it for a week.

"For the phoenixes," she agreed, eyes locked with Luciana's, refusing to flinch.

Chapter Thirteen

On the morning of the inspection, dawn drowned beneath a blanket of fog.

Aila—or rather, the bundle of raw nerves formerly known as Aila, now masquerading as a human in work boots and an animal-patch backpack—arrived at a dark zoo. The mist frizzed her hair into a rat nest bun. The peacock griffin statue in the entry plaza swam through the sea of gray, condensation clinging to bronze wing tips.

Aila flipped on the light in the coordinator's office. She started Tom's coffee, signed in at the computer, clipped a radio to her belt, then leaned over the desk with a deep, hitching breath. She'd tried burning calming cinnamon bird incense the night before. Tried doing her mindfulness exercises. Tried burying her face in her periwinkle prairie goose pillow until lavender drowsiness took over.

Her morning chores offered little sanctuary. She sprayed down the World of Birds aviary. Set out food she'd chopped the day before. Sat Archie down for a firm talking-to about being on his best damn behavior because mom couldn't handle any distractions today.

She moved the kelpie onto exhibit.

How did time slip by so fast?

Aila slept little the night before. Why bother with an alarm? She'd set her phone to wake her, yet still she'd woken up an hour before the chime to stare at her ceiling and catalog everything that could go wrong. What if she missed something on the IMWS checklist? Froze up during the inspector's questions? What if a meteor crashed out of the sky, releasing the animals and turning the zoo into a frenzy?

She flipped on the lights in the phoenix center. Despite her nerves, Aila had to admit one thing.

The place was beautiful.

New linoleum squeaked beneath her boots, an easy-to-clean surface patterned after Silimalo tile. Orange paint brightened the walls. Multicolored protocol binders lined the shelves. The incubators sparkled on the counter, all polished and functioning. A week of back-breaking work, but they'd pulled it off.

Aila dropped her backpack at her desk and stepped up to the aviary. Rubra roosted on a perch wrapped in fresh sisal, her abode decorated in fans of olive leaves like some ancient queen of the Silimalo coast, a heater casting her puffed feathers in a rosy glow. She greeted Aila with a half-open eye and a muffled chirp.

"Today's the day, Rubra. The inspector will love you, of course. I'll do my best to follow your lead."

Tanya finished her rounds a half-hour later. They sat in their clean new chairs at the clean new desks they'd bartered from facilities, staring at a clean new clock on the wall. The hands were little phoenix feathers. When Tanya brought it in as a surprise, Aila squealed with delight. Now, her stomach felt sick.

"You'll do your best, Ailes," Tanya said. "Whatever happens today, we'll be fine."

Aila nodded, half-hearted. An old poster hung above her desk, an abstract phoenix with a tail of fire, the paper yellowed and crinkling at the edges. WORLD FAMOUS SAN TAMCULO ZOO, the script read, HELP SAVE THE SILIMALO PHOENIX. This wasn't just an inspection. This was Aila's lifelong dream. If she earned bad marks with the inspector today, she risked more than losing Rubra. She could set the San Tamculo Zoo back on the transfer list for years.

She didn't expect any other visitors that morning. When Connor poked his head through the door, a smile broke through Aila's nerves. Wider, when he held up a brown paper bag, grease stains an obvious show of quality. And the *smell*.

Aila might have forgotten to eat that morning. *Oops.*

"Morning, ladies. Time for breakfast?"

Two months ago, Connor and Aila hardly spoke. Over the past week, he'd become a fixture at the phoenix center, donating his precious time to help them roll out flooring and shove a behemoth refrigerator into place. How did this happen? Sleep-deprived Aila hadn't dissected that mystery. Non-sleep-deprived Aila would have managed little better.

He dropped the bag on the counter and pulled out three breakfast burritos.

"What's the occasion?" Aila asked. A dumb joke. She knew the occasion. It was a heart-throttling, terrifying occasion.

"Celebration, of course." Connor dropped into a chair. "For how much you're going to amaze the inspector today."

Aila crinkled open her wrapper and poked at the eggs and cheese. "Well, I don't know about that."

"Are you kidding? This place looks fantastic!"

"Couldn't have done it without your help."

Or Luciana's help, but Aila would sooner bury herself in bird droppings than say that out loud. Everyone had worked their asses off this week. And for what? To help *her*?

No, that didn't make any sense. To help the phoenixes.

Yet when Aila dared look up from her food, Connor's eyes had her pinned. Skies and seas, her stomach couldn't afford any more somersaults.

Sure, he'd started visiting more. Sure, Aila no longer went full puddle mode the instant she had to share a room with him. That didn't mean they'd *talked* much. Where could she have found the time? Their interactions were confined to awkward elbow bumps while laying down the linoleum, Aila's nervous laugh when Connor made a joke about her hair matching Rubra's feathers (which was, consequently, one of the most flattering things she'd ever been told).

Friendly? Sure. Romantic? Aila hadn't a clue. More and more, she commiserated with the zoo's Vjari auks, bumbling around on stubby legs and useless flippers, big dumb eyes unable to tell a rock from a human hunter.

"Aila," he said. "You've memorized those protocol binders front to back. You're *brilliant*. That phoenix is as good as yours."

No, no, no, not romantic at all. It couldn't be.

Aila buried her face in her burrito and pretended it was the hot sauce turning her cheeks red. Beside her, Tanya conceded a nod. Dragon boy had a steep climb to earn best friend approval, but compliments and food offerings were strong marks in his favor.

As they ate, the clock kept ticking.

Then it was time.

"Get these wrappers out of sight," Aila said. "Everything has to be perfect."

"Aye aye, ma'am," Tanya replied.

Connor saw her off with a grin. *Remember how to breathe, Aila.* And for the love of the endless skies and seas, stop shaking. She stepped out into fog.

The paths were empty. Quiet. Normally, her favorite time at

the zoo, that blissful calm before the gates opened. Aila wound through mock jungles and replica lagoons, off to face her own beast.

Ahead of her, a figure emerged from the gloom.

A drift of mango teased Aila's nose.

Luciana halted in the path, condensation kissing her hair like strings of diamonds, dark lashes drawn into a squint. Aila stared her down, the world silent around them.

"Now or never," Luciana said, then kept walking.

"Now or never," Aila whispered once she'd gone. She headed for the zoo gates.

"I always love this time of year," Director Hawthorn said, and for the life of her, Aila couldn't fathom how he sounded so calm. Maybe it was an old person thing.

They stood in the fog-soaked entry plaza, drum music playing from speakers above the turnstiles. The first patrons trickled in, noses buried in crinkled maps or phone apps, parents shouting at children not to run for the peacock griffin statue, a din of haggling over stroller rentals and memberships at the guest relations counter. The director split his time between greeting guests and attempting small talk with Aila as she stared at the bricks beneath her boots, trying not to hurl her breakfast burrito.

"The change of the seasons," he said. "Invigorating."

"Sure is."

"Not as stark here in Movas as some other parts of the world, such mild winters, but you come to appreciate the subtlety."

"Right. Subtlety."

"Crocus crocodiles love the fog. Floating in their ponds without a care in the world."

"Sounds wonderful." Maybe Aila would make a better crocodile than a human. Of course they could keep calm, no inspectors to impress.

"Ah! Here's Director Garumano now!"

Aila's head snapped up so fast, she felt a couple of vertebrae crack.

For two months, she'd snooped and begged, trying to discover who the inspector would be so she could add their information to her flash cards. Upon being told for the dozenth time that such information was "a surprise" or something equally atrocious, Aila gave up and researched all of them, every inspector and coordinator in the IMWS phoenix program. But Garumano? *The* Giuseppe Garumano, director of the core breeding program in Silimalo? Co-author on every significant study of phoenix habitat in the past decade?

A distressed squeak escaped Aila's throat.

The stocky man maneuvering himself through the entry gate wore a snug navy suit, a clipboard clutched to his chest to protect it from the mist. He was around the director's age, wrinkles creasing bronzed skin, bald, with a bushy gray mustache curled on the sides. On his lapel, a phoenix pin glinted in red and gold.

"Welcome back to the San Tamculo Zoo, Director Garumano." Hawthorn met him with a firm handshake, the kind Aila's dad was always harping on her to practice. "We're delighted to have you. I hope your flight went smoothly?"

"My pleasure as always, Clement." Garumano's mustache wriggled like a furry animal as he spoke. Aila couldn't look away. "Always a *long* flight to your side of the world." He chuckled. "I am eager to stretch my legs."

Hawthorn chuckled back. "I'm sure we can help with that. This is our head phoenix keeper, Aila Macbhairan."

Garumano extended his hand. Aila snapped her eyes off the

whiskery beast on his face long enough to return the gesture. Her shake felt like a clammy fish.

"Good to meet you, Aila," he said in a thick Silimalo accent. "Whenever you are ready, we may begin."

Aila shot a panicked look to Director Hawthorn. So soon? Surely, they could waste more time with pleasantries? Breakfast? A comprehensive zoo tour?

"I'm sure Aila is eager to show you the results of her hard work," Hawthorn said with a magnanimous smile. "Once your inspection is complete, please find me in my office. I have lunch blocked off before our meeting with Director Rivera."

He headed for the administration building, leaving Aila and Garumano alone. Another distressed sound fluttered in her throat, higher pitched than before.

Beside her, the inspector clicked his pen and scribbled a note.

When they reached the phoenix complex, Tanya and Connor had made themselves scarce. Any evidence of their morning stress meal had vanished. Tanya even stowed Aila's patch-plastered backpack out of sight. Bless her.

Aila stood near her desk, trying to remember how to hold her arms at her sides, silent to the point of physical pain. Director Garumano stood in the center of the room. Not a word. Not a sound except the *scratch scratch scratch click* of his pen scribbling notes on his clipboard. He flipped to the next page. Continued scribbling.

The fuck was he writing? He'd hardly looked up from his notes since arriving.

Aila scanned the room, searching for what could have inspired the essay. A rogue woodroach beneath the cabinets? Impossible.

They'd sprayed a dozen times. Incorrect ratio of flame retardant in the paint? How would he even notice such a thing? She eyed the clock, watching the seconds tick by.

"These incubators. Model 5s?"

Aila jumped at the break in the silence. The inspector didn't appear to notice, too busy studying the incubators.

"Um...Yes. Model 5s...er...Inspector...Sir."

He scribbled approximately fifty new words on his clipboard. Aila craned her neck to see, but his handwriting was dragon scratch.

"Very well, then." Garumano flipped to a new sheet of paper. "Let's have a look at your bird."

Aila had kept Rubra off exhibit that morning. She slipped shaking fingers into her flame-resistant glove (rush ordered to arrive just in time). With every move, the pen continued to scribble. Garumano trailed her to the aviary, where Rubra eyed him with cocked head and flattened feathers. Aila typed a code into the lock to open the gate. More scribbling.

"Morning, Rubra." Aila whistled. Rubra hopped onto her glove. What a good bird. A beautiful, sweet bird.

That scribbling pen was going to be in Aila's nightmares.

She held Rubra on her fist as Garumano eyed the bird from every angle, compared a color scale against her neck feathers, pulled a tape measure from his pocket to hold against her flaming tail. Aila was back in presentation class all over again. Her legs wobbled.

"What is her typical diet?" Garumano asked.

"Um..." Aila cleared her throat. The inspector lifted a wispy eyebrow. Rubra cocked her head. Not her, too. "One cup of phoenix nutritional pellets per day. Supplemented with fresh vegetables and fruits."

"Such as?"

"Kale. Seasonal squash. Grapes. Mango."

"Mango?"

"I . . . Yes?"

"Not native to the Silimalo region."

"Well, no." Mangos came from . . . Renkaila? Aila wasn't an expert on produce origins. "But she likes the taste. And they're high in carotenoids, which is good for feather health, so . . ."

More scribbling. Aila could have screamed, if her legs didn't give out first. What was she doing? Two months preparing, and she hadn't envisioned anything like this. On her glove, Rubra trilled in concern.

Aila took a deep breath. She focused on the scratch of the glove fabric against her arm, the warmth off Rubra's tail. *Do it for her. Do it for her. Do it for—*

"Standard daily schedule?" Garumano asked.

"Minimum eight hours outdoor aviary time."

"Natural climate, or artificial?"

"Both."

He paused, waiting.

"Natural climate summer through fall. Supplemental heaters in winter and spring to account for slightly cooler coastal temperatures than Silimalo, with regular venting of the aviary panels through the mechanical system."

He nodded. Scribbled. A good thing, or bad? The man's face was *granite*.

"You may return the bird."

Thank the endless skies and seas. Rubra weighed under five pounds, yet Aila's arm felt ready to collapse beneath the strain. She returned Rubra to the aviary. Slipped off the glove. Underneath, her palm was slick with sweat.

Garumano flipped to a new page. "Assuming you were approved for transfer of the male phoenix, please walk me through your introduction protocol."

Aila closed her eyes. Visualized her flashcards.

"Miss Macbhairan?" he pressed.

"We'd begin with scent introduction, the protocol developed by the Silimalo National Zoo. We've outfitted the back aviaries to allow vision exclusion. The birds can be placed side by side to get used to one another's presence without physical contact, in case of territoriality."

Garumano scribbled as fast as she spoke. Aila hoped she got the details right. *He'd* written the research paper, after all.

"From there," she continued, fighting the tightness in her throat, "we introduce the male in a carrier within the exhibit. Once the female appears receptive, we can allow short periods of monitored interaction."

"And how will you address any territoriality by the female?"

"Rubra has an excellent temperament. I'm sure we won't—"

"Female phoenixes are far more territorial than males," Garumano chided. "And yours has had a territory to herself all her life. How will you intervene if she fails to accept introduction of the male?"

Aila's tongue froze. She hadn't thought of that. How had she not thought of that?

"W-well," she stuttered. "In that case. I suppose we'd have to—"

The radio at her belt crackled. From the speaker, a honeyed voice struck her heart like an arrow.

"Griffin show, calling aviaries."

Aila stared at the radio in disbelief. In horror. That heartless, undermining witch.

"As I was saying," Aila pressed on, "we'd have to separate the male and female and start the reintroduction process over again—"

"Aila," Luciana called over the radio. "Pick up."

She and Garumano stared at the radio, his look confused, hers akin to a plucked phoenix being throttled by a narcissistic woman who didn't understand the importance of personal boundaries.

"If you'll excuse me for just a moment," Aila said in her sweetest, quivering voice. She unclipped her radio and replied in terse words. "*Luciana.* I'm a little busy right now."

"I'm aware," Luciana returned. "You need to come to the World of Birds aviary. Now."

"She most certainly does not!" Connor clicked in from his radio.

Aila's mouth opened. Closed. At the sight of Garumano's twitchy mustache, she gave a nervous chuckle and held up a finger.

"Connor," she said into the radio. "What's wrong?"

"Nothing. Focus on your inspection. Tanya has things under control."

"I most certainly do not!" came Tanya's muffled reply. In the background, other voices were shouting, followed by a whooping bird call.

Aila's heart fell clear out of her chest. Archie.

It took her all of three seconds to weigh the inspector's annoyed expression against the panic in Tanya's voice, the agitated note in Archie's call. Before her eyes, she watched two months of work crumbling to pieces. Rubra being whisked away.

But something was wrong with one of her birds.

"I'm so sorry," she said. "I am *so* sorry. I'll be right back."

Aila was out the door before he could argue.

Chapter Fourteen

Aila wished she could claim a coherent strategy for her retreat, rather than the mental scream drowning every thought as she sprinted away from the phoenix complex, leaving Director Garumano behind, with brow furrowed and mustache twitching.

A quick absence. Make sure Archie was fine. Then she'd be back.

No harm done.

Please, let there be no harm done.

Patrons shot startled looks as Aila wove between them, dodging strollers and wobbly toddlers like road mines, trying not to add child assault to her list of indiscretions for the day. Though the sun had risen, the fog remained thick, a gray cast upon aviaries speckled in condensation, cold morning air prickling Aila's bare arms.

When she burst into the World of Birds aviary, the humidity of a tropical forest bowled her over, air thick in her lungs, the smell of pungent soil clogging her nose. As she huffed up the path, the periwinkle prairie geese honked in alarm, wafting lavender in their wake as they retreated for the safety of their pool. The screaming mynas shrieked murder in the canopy.

The shouting patrons weren't any better.

Aila found a group clogging the path. Connor hung to one

side, frowning as Luciana addressed the rioters, her honeyed voice paired with calming hand gestures.

"Now, now," she cooed, as if to a raging griffin. "We appreciate your patience. Please, wait here while we take care of—"

"What's wrong?" Aila elbowed her way through the onlookers.

The people, she couldn't care less for. Her scrunched nose and glare were for Luciana. That woman knew how important today was, *knew* the consequences of calling Aila away from the inspector. Yet Aila saw no animal in peril. No dismembered patron crying in a pool of their own blood (though that would be a paramedic issue, not an Aila issue). What kind of emergency could have summoned her?

"Your bird stole my engagement ring!" a beleaguered patron shouted, tears smudging her mascara, pointing to the canopy where...

Archie hopped from branch to branch, a low hoot in his throat, a diamond ring clutched in his bill.

That conniving little thief. Aila's shoulders slumped, her sigh the long and pained sound of a disappointed mother whose child was caught gluing candy to a classmate's hair. Horns and fangs, Archie, they'd talked about this *earlier that morning*.

Luciana folded her hands together, using her metered public voice that masked all but the most subtle edge of annoyance. "It would seem one of our valued zoo guests decided to propose. Your archibird stole their ring."

Aila gawked first at the tear-strewn woman, then at a scowling young man beside her, then at the gray-socked aviary that smelled of bird droppings.

"You proposed *here*, of all places?"

Something Aila would do, but a normal person?

"Aila," Luciana said, a click on her tongue like she was training an animal. "Perhaps we ought to focus on *alleviating* the situation." Her word hardened, a chunk of crystalized sugar to crack the teeth. "And get this lovely couple's ring back."

Fat chance of that. They were lucky Archie hadn't already glued the metal to his tower. In fact, that was downright miraculous. Aila pushed her way to the railing, leaning over for a view of the clearing below.

Tanya stood in front of Archie's trinket tower, using her body to shield the bird from his goal. He hopped through the canopy in annoyance, honking at her every few steps.

"Aila!" Tanya shouted. "Do something about your bird!"

Do something? *Now*? On today of all days? Aila's grip tightened on the railing, damp wood beneath trembling fingers. She hadn't stopped shaking all morning. The inspector's scratching pen, the crackle of the radio, had all carved shivers beneath her skin.

But now, the arguing patrons dimmed to a murmur. Luciana's fake smile fell out of sight. Even the screaming mynas in the canopy receded to background noise as Aila forced herself to pause and *breathe*. She drew strength from the loamy smell of her aviary, dug her fingers into the railing until cool moss covered every nail.

Birds, Aila could deal with.

And this one wasn't getting any treats for a week after pulling this stunt.

Aila stepped away from the railing. "Archie!" she called up in her sweetest voice, followed by a whistle and a hand to perch on. "Archie, come down here and let me see what you've found. It looks delightful."

Archie considered her for a moment before resuming his hopping with a grunt, the archibird equivalent of a middle finger. Right. Aila hadn't expected it would be that easy. She leaned back over the rail.

"Have you tried trading something with him?" she called down to Tanya.

"What do you think I've got that's shinier than a *diamond*?" Tanya snapped.

Not a small diamond, either. Aila could make out the hunk of a rock from down here, facets glittering in the diffused light, clasped in a ring of gold. Archie wasn't giving up a treasure like that without excellent incentive.

"Do you have anything else shiny you could give him?" Aila asked the woman with ruined mascara. "Something less important?"

The woman buried her face in her hands and resumed crying, prompting her fiancé to scowl at Aila. Hey, at least she was trying.

Connor slipped out of the crowd. "Aila. What about the inspection?"

"I'll get back to it as soon as this is settled," she hissed back.

"Let Tanya handle things here."

"But Archie is my bird."

"So what? The inspection is more important!"

Luciana stormed between them. "For the love of endless skies and seas, enough of this." She unclipped a pair of silver loops from her ears and shoved them into Aila's hand.

Aila stared at the offering. "What's this?"

"Give it to your bird."

"But why would you—?"

"Do it!"

Luciana wanted this annoyance over with. That was the only sensible explanation. Never mind the question of what she was doing in the aviary to begin with. Or how she'd noticed Archie's preference for silver in his tower of trinkets. Aila had no time to dissect such things, nor to dwell on the warmth of the earrings in her palm. The hint of fruity perfume.

Aila held the treasure aloft. "Archie! Look at this!"

He hopped down to a lower branch, azure crest raised in curiosity. With a dramatic head tilt, he examined Aila's offering, then clacked his beak, adjusting his hold on the diamond ring.

Archie hooted and fluttered back to the canopy, unswayed, searching for a path to his tower. Tanya mirrored his movements.

"Need something better than that, Ailes!"

Aila frowned at the earrings. Shiny, high-quality (as if she'd expect anything less from Luciana). Unfortunately, looks wouldn't cut it. Archie had found a treasure valuable not only in appearance, but also prestige. Who could put a price on something forbidden? Something he wasn't supposed to have?

The idea came to Aila like a jolt from thunderhawk feathers.

"I'll be right back!" She returned the earrings to Luciana, then ran for the aviary door. "Keep him busy!"

"What do you think I'm doing?" Tanya hollered. Aila would owe her a smoothie when this was over.

She hoped her prize was where she thought it was.

Aila bolted into the aviary kitchen and flipped on the lights. The space was smaller than their facilities at the phoenix complex, a staging area to store prepared food and medications for nearby exhibits. Now and then, Tanya made a show of clearing out the miscellaneous "trash" that accumulated along the shelves. A travesty. Aila should be entitled to keep her junk.

Especially at a time like this. She gasped in delight upon unearthing a box she'd shoved underneath the sink. The jumble of metal jingled as she pulled it out. A month of work to assemble Archie's enrichment toy, and he'd torn it apart overnight. After Aila confiscated all the pieces from the aviary floor and keyholes, she'd kept the parts on the off chance she could devise a more clever, archibird-proof construction.

She grabbed the shiniest metal rod from the bunch and ran back to the aviary.

"Archie! Look what I've got!"

Aila ran through the crowd with the metal rod held high like a baton in a championship footrace. Patrons watched the spectacle with confusion. The ring-thefted couple scowled their deepest yet. Luciana pressed jade nails to her temple and shook her head.

In the canopy, Archie went stone-still. Aila held her breath as his beady black eyes widened. His head tilted in one direction. Then the other.

He dropped from the trees like a lead weight, lighting on the rail beside the path. He squawked once, loud enough to silence even the screaming mynas. As Aila stepped toward him, he watched the metal rod in her hand, eyes gleaming on the forbidden treasure.

"That's a good bird," Aila cooed. "What do you need a dumb ring for?"

She held out the rod. Archie hopped toward her and, ring still in his bill, grabbed the rod with one foot. He tried to abscond with both prizes. All Aila had to do was hold on, his bird weight inadequate to free the rod. Archie fluttered and honked in indignation.

"Stop being greedy, Archie!"

He paused with chest puffed, crest flattened.

"You want the shiny metal rod?" She held out her hand. "Ring. Now."

Aila had never met an animal who could pout like an archibird. Thank the skies and seas he wasn't great at mimicking, or he'd spend all day cussing patrons out of his aviary.

Head bowed, chest emitting a disgruntled wheeze, Archie

dropped the diamond ring in her hand. She closed her fingers on it first. Released the rod second. Archie flew off with his prize and a triumphant hoot.

"Tanya!" Aila called over the railing. "Let him have it." Last thing she wanted was to find another rod jammed into a door lock.

The moment Tanya retreated from the tower, Archie fluttered down and spit-glued his new piece to a place of honor on the pinnacle. Safe and sound. Aila breathed out enough relieved air to fill a cart of animal-shaped zoo balloons.

When she returned the wedding ring, the young couple stormed off with half-hearted promises not to report her to HR. *You're welcome*, Aila mouthed to their backs. A few onlookers clapped at the resolution, but once the drama passed, they dispersed, revealing a lone figure standing at the rear of the crowd.

Garumano scowled at his clipboard, mouth hidden beneath his curled mustache, scribbling notes with the most gusto yet.

Aila couldn't shake the pit in her stomach. With a tight smile, she offered to take him back to the phoenix complex to resume their inspection.

What was the point?

The damage had already been done.

Several hours and several million questions later, Director Garumano scribbled his final notes. How he'd avoided cramping his hand off, Aila had no idea.

"Thank you for your time, Aila. You'll hear back from us soon regarding a decision."

Once he left, Aila collapsed on a chair and groaned loud enough to shake the observation window.

He'd asked everything on her flashcards and then some. And *then* some. Scenarios for bird introduction. Layout of the nesting platform. Feeding schedules at each stage of female incubation. Immolation protocol. Evacuation plans for fire and earthquakes and tsunamis and tornados. Movas didn't even *get* tornados.

Aila tried her best. She couldn't shake the dread in her stomach, the certainty that even her best hadn't been good enough. So many questions. So many scribbled notes and twitching mustache hairs, never so much as a nod of affirmation. If her oral exams in college had been half as brutal, she'd have flunked out from nerves alone.

The door clicked open. Aila didn't move from her puddle state as Tanya collected her belongings in preparation to head home. Not even when a firm hand landed on her shoulder.

"Come on, Ailes," Tanya said.

"No." Aila swatted her.

"It's time to go."

"Leave me. Let my bones become one with the concrete."

"No one's bones are becoming one with anything in here. We just put new floors in."

Aila groaned and turned herself to a rag doll as Tanya attempted to drag her out of the chair, but superior strength won out. Tanya slipped Aila's backpack over her shoulders like a scowling schoolchild. Led her, moping, out of the building. Once they'd exited the zoo gate, Aila tried to scurry toward the train station. Tanya snagged her arm.

"Nah-uh. Where are you going?"

"Home. A blanket cocoon large enough to swallow me and never—"

"You're coming with me, Miss Mopey Pants."

An attempt to lift Aila's spirits, no doubt. She wanted no part in it. "Really, Tanya. I need some sleep."

"You know I'd accept that decision and the sanctity of your personal space on ninety-nine percent of occasions. Not tonight."

Aila wrinkled her nose as she was shoved into the passenger seat of Tanya's car.

"This is kidnapping," Aila complained.

Tanya clicked her seatbelt, then pressed the ignition button for the electric engine. "I don't see you calling no police."

"A violation of our friendship."

"Ailes, this is the *epitome* of our friendship, and you'll thank me later."

"What about Tourmaline?" Aila clicked her seatbelt extra loud in protest. "He has a standardized feeding schedule, and if I'm not home in time, you know he'll start gnawing on my sofa and spread the stuffing all over—"

"We will make a *brief stop* to get your damn carbuncle!"

Aila said no more, letting her pout speak for itself as the city lights blurred past the car windows. When they reached her apartment, she considered making a break for it, running inside then locking the door. Tanya might break it down. Plus, the mere suggestion of a trip sent Tourmaline into a twirl of pattering paws and dual tails.

They returned to Tanya's car, Aila grim, Tourmaline panting on her lap. His forehead jewel glowed orange in excitement as he braced his paws on the door, watching every passing car and streetlight. Aila stroked his soft gray coat and rested her forehead against the window.

"What if I let you all down?" she whispered. "All that work for nothing."

"You've never let me down," Tanya said without missing a beat.

"What about that time I lost both our lab reports and we had to redo the entire assignment?"

Tanya clicked her tongue. "You bought me a brownie to make up for it. We're cool."

"Or the time I ruined your favorite dress by spilling shrimp meal all over it?"

"Now why do you have to go bringing something like that up again?"

"Or the time I accidentally hit you in the head with a shovel while we were cleaning out the aviary pond?"

"All right, that's enough. Here I am trying to help, and all you've got is memories of vandalized property and attempted murder."

The smallest grin cracked through Aila's gloom. Wider, once she realized where Tanya was taking her.

They pulled into a parking lot a couple of blocks from the San Tamculo Harbor. The street was packed with striped restaurant awnings and bright shop windows. A bookstore had a display of star-shaped lights floating with pixie wren dust, a propped up *Guide to Movasi National Parks* with a stylized thunderhawk on the cover, another stack of fantasy novels where a woman embraced a weirdly handsome man with antlers. A flower shop showcased unnaturally stunning blooms in ceramic pots, a sign boasting ALL PLANTS AUGMENTED WITH ORCHID VIPER VENOM FOR ENHANCED GROWTH AND LONGEVITY!

From the harbor, a cold salt breeze carried aromas of waffle cones and fried potatoes. Strongest of all, though: lard. Corn meal tortillas. Boiled beef. Above the sidewalk, a sign shone in fluorescent green and red outline, a central strand of black neon looping into letters: MACBHAIRAN PUB AND TEQUILERIA.

Most people in San Tamculo had no idea what Vjari-Movasi fusion food entailed. To be fair, most patrons left without the clearest idea, either. Aila's parents claimed heritage from the fog-soaked moorlands of western Vjar, and blending their bland national dishes with the spice of Movasi cuisine came off as a family joke at first.

Twenty years later, the restaurant served as a marvel as much as an institution.

Tanya heaved open the wooden door, handle a knot of woven iron twisting into the head and tail of a diamondback dragon. Inside, they were struck by an onslaught of guitar music. Voices echoed off wooden beams and concrete walls with murals of Vjari sheep in festive sombreros. String lights dangled over tables and the scalloped tiers of a fountain, creating the illusion of an outdoor patio beneath twinkling stars. Clunky beer mugs and slim-necked margarita glasses peppered the tables.

From out of nowhere, a woman appeared to sweep Aila into a bear hug.

"There's my lass! Tanya said you were on your way."

Aila's mother had even paler skin, more time spent inside tending tables than out in the sun. Her frizzy auburn hair made for a chaotic bob, the same hazel eyes with a few more laugh lines crinkling the edges. Tourmaline danced at their feet, unsure what everyone was excited about, but excited nonetheless. Aila tried not to let her smile crack into tears.

Her parents had never been animal people. They'd never quite understood what drove their daughter to pursue a career of meager salary and daily exposure to mud and bird droppings.

That never stopped them from being Aila's biggest fans. On every trip to the bookstore, they escorted their daughter out with a tower of discount animal encyclopedias and field guides. They suffered a menagerie of pets, from purserats to snapping shrimp, to a vocal emerald cockatoo whose shrieks launched a war with the Homeowners' Association.

Aila had been so busy with the renovations, she'd hardly

talked to her parents in weeks. Their warm smiles welcomed her all the same.

"It's good to see you, Mom," Aila mumbled, cheeks too squished by the hug to enunciate properly.

"Well, have at it, then!" Her mother released her, punctuating her words with energetic hands. "How was the inspection? Just grand, I'm sure. With Rubra involved? Who couldn't love that sweet pea of a bird?"

"Oh, you know," Aila said. "The inspection was...long."

"Which is why we're here." Tanya swung an arm around Aila's shoulders. "To relax. And celebrate."

"Celebrate?" Aila's nose scrunched. "But we don't even know what the inspector decided. What if I didn't—"

"You did your best, Ailes. And now, you deserve a break."

"I'll let your pa know you're here," her mother said before Aila could protest. "He'll be whippin' up your favorite. Potato nachos, extra bacon n' cheese." She winked and ushered them to a table of thick wood, heavy lacquer. "And how *is* your lovely Rubra? Pretty as ever? I saw her in the news, you know! Just the loveliest photo, all puffed up and grand."

Aila settled at the table, making a show of perusing the laminated menu she had memorized front to back. After two months of non-stop work and anxiety, her fingers jittered. She shouldn't be sitting here. She should be doing something.

Then the first plate of food arrived: fried potatoes in three types of melted cheese, chopped bacon, sliced jalapeños and a glob of sour cream. One of Aila's comfort foods since she was a kid, followed by a spread of corned beef and fish tacos in creamy sauces and crunchy chopped cabbage. Last, a chocolate chili torte, rich Ziclexian cacao spiced with hot Movasi peppers, enough to leave a fire on Aila's tongue.

As she stuffed her face, her mother asked endless questions

about her, about Rubra and all her other animals. Tanya went on and on about how tidy the phoenix complex looked, how well Aila had handled Archie during their disaster earlier that day.

They had done a lot of work, hadn't they? Now, to wait for the verdict.

At least Aila had Tanya to lean on. And another giant hug from her mom as they left.

Though the prospect of failure loomed, a full stomach and an evening of smiling faces soothed Aila's nerves enough to collapse into bed the moment she returned to her apartment and finished tending her animals. She curled up with Tourmaline and slept like she hadn't in two months, dreaming of phoenixes.

Chapter Fifteen

One week. Two weeks. Three weeks.

After the inspection, Aila kept herself busy with every menial task on her backlog, plus several new ones daydreamed while folding towels on the patio. She had a shiny new phoenix complex. Why not clean everything else in her exhibits?

A power wash of the kelpie pool left Maisie swimming somersaults, seaweed-strewn mane and tail billowing around her like a stormy ocean. From the commissary, Aila bartered an entire crate of watermelons. Archie nearly fell off his perch when she dragged the feast into the World of Birds aviary, and patrons spammed Griffingram for days with photos of periwinkle prairie geese munching melon flesh, the screaming mynas shouting over scraps, the pixie wrens levitating leftovers with their magical feather dust.

Luciana stayed at the griffin show where she belonged. Everything back to normal.

Also back to normal (unfortunately): Aila's agony, waiting for a call or message with the inspection results.

"Do you think they lost my email?" Aila worried aloud as she and Tanya donned their rubber wading boots. "Or maybe they sent the results to the wrong email address? Macbhairan is a hard name to spell. People are always forgetting the *a*. Or putting the *h* in the wrong spot."

Tanya cut her a long-suffering look. "You think IMWS forgot where the zoo is, too?"

Aila mumbled something about her making a good point, then finished with her boots.

The morning was chill, overcast. Tanya and Aila were due for their monthly scrubbing of the mirror flamingo pond.

Tanya's exhibits made up the east side of the zoo's aviary hub. At the edge of the Ozokian section, surrounded by marshy walkways and high-kneed cypress trees dripping in gray moss, was the Ozokian kingfisher, smallest of the aviary domes. The exhibit contained a pool where the kingfisher could hunt for tiny fish, stunning them with his electrical pulses.

Next door was the larger mirror flamingo aviary. The interior mimicked their native Pennja savannah, south-east across the mountains from Movas, a subtropical savannah of low scrub and spiky acacia trees. The central pool made up most of the exhibit, shallow and warm and mildly salted, for optimal flamingo foot health. The edges were caked with smelly shrimp residue and smellier flamingo shit.

Tanya opened the valve to drain the pool, then they set to work cleaning.

As Aila crouched, scrubbing rocks along the pond periphery, the disgruntled occupants strutted past on spindly legs, silver feathers clinking like shards of glass. Her reflection stared back in the polished plumes, complete with frazzled hair and mud splotching her cheeks. Occasionally, a squabble between two birds made them flash out of sight, feathers angled to refract the surrounding light (but leaving the unfeathered beak and legs still comically visible). They reappeared, squawking and pecking at one another.

"We need to trim those palms earlier in the season." Tanya dredged an armful of soaked fronds out of the pond drain. "Keep blocking up the circulation."

Aila sat back on her heels. "I'm *not* climbing up there again. You know how I feel about heights." She shuddered at the thought of the ground any farther than a foot or two below her.

Tanya tossed a frond at her, splattering Aila with more mud. "You're making me do all the hard work?"

Aila grabbed a hose and held it up, threatening. "Don't make me do it, Tanya. I'd hate to see our friendship end like this."

Tanya brandished her own hose. "You always knew it would come to this, Ailes."

The flock of mirror flamingos honked in annoyance as the two keepers squared off, hands ready to draw on their respective hose nozzles, their dueling ring an empty pond slicked with algae and uneaten shrimp meal.

Before shots could fire, Aila's phone rang.

"Fuck!" She dug into her pocket, cringing at muddy fingers, then sprayed her arms clean and wiped a hand on the driest patch of shirt she could find. "What are you laughing at?"

Across the pond, Tanya clutched her stomach, shaking with giggles. Aila pulled out her phone and scowled at the unfamiliar number. Who would call her at work? Did she forget another therapy appointment? No, she'd just spoken to Andrea last week.

"Hello?"

Beside her, a mirror flamingo honked in response. She shooed it away.

"Hello, Aila Macbhairan?" came a crisp, professional voice. "This is Maria Rivera, at IMWS. Do you have a moment?"

Aila's world came to a standstill. Tanya sobered at the sight. Even the mirror flamingos fell quiet, their heads snapping from side to side.

She'd had weeks to prepare for this. Weeks to analyze every moment of the inspection and write mental essays of how she could have done better. Spoken more clearly. Held herself with greater confidence. She wasn't ready for another failure.

"Yes." Aila's throat constricted. "Of course, Ms. Rivera. How are you?"

"Excellent, thank you! I apologize for the impromptu call, but we've finished reviewing Director Garumano's report. He was impressed by the status of your facility, as well as your familiarity with the Silimalo phoenix breeding system. I'm excited to let you know, we'd like to move forward with San Tamculo as our leading recommendation for the phoenix transfer."

Aila's mind went blank.

Words? What were those?

Functioning legs? Barely.

This couldn't be real. Aila would write it off as a dream, if not for the pinch of an ornery flamingo at her arm. She flinched, biting back a curse before it spewed into the phone.

Tanya leaned toward her. *Aila?* she mouthed.

"Miss Macbhairan?" came a concerned voice in her ear.

"I...Yes...*Yes!*" Aila's voice shook. "I'm still here. Sorry. Are you...*sure?*"

Rivera chuckled. "Of course I'm sure. Why else would I call?"

"Sure, sure, dumb question." Aila winced at her informality. "I'm so sorry, Ms. Rivera, it's just...This is *wonderful* news!"

Unfathomable news. Aila spun it every way, looking for the caveat. The disaster.

"I thought you'd be eager to hear it. I've just spoken with Director Hawthorn about starting the process. We'll need to schedule a few more visits over the coming months, opportunities to update some protocols and prepare for..."

The logistics hummed through Aila's brain, stowed away for later, not yet sinking in. Rivera finished with hearty congratulations. A promise to talk again soon. Aila thanked her with a numb tongue, then ended the call.

Tanya had snuck close enough to press her ear to the phone beside Aila's. They shared wide eyes.

"Aila," Tanya said, hushed.

"Tanya," Aila returned.

"*Aila!*"

"*Tanya!*"

Aila squealed and leapt into Tanya's arms, who lifted her off the ground and spun them in a laughing, mud-drenched circle. The mirror flamingos resumed their disgruntled chorus. Aila didn't care. She couldn't stop smiling. Even when Tanya released her, she bounced in her muddy work boots.

This was real.

It was *happening*. A second phoenix.

Aila squealed again, just for good measure.

Chapter Sixteen

Once the excitement of the call faded, Aila's bureaucratic nightmare began.

She sat through hour-long lunches with Director Hawthorn, reviewing protocol binders Aila could already recite verbatim. Conference calls with IMWS facilitators, walk-throughs for the San Tamculo Police Department, an assigned watchlist of Silimalo phoenix documentaries that were outdated by fifteen years and *why* had no one made a new Silimalo phoenix documentary in *fifteen years*? Aila added that to her list of offenses she'd have to right one day.

And paperwork. Skies and seas, the *paperwork*. Aila's eyes turned fuzzy the moment she looked at a protocol confirmation, breeding registry, endangered wildlife transportation passport. Any break from the drudgery should have come as a joy.

Except when that "break" finally came, it required social interaction. Once the phoenix transfer passed the final stages of IMWS approval, Director Hawthorn insisted on hosting a private celebration at the zoo.

"It will be fun!" he'd said.

"A welcome reward for all your hard work!" he'd said.

Aila would rather celebrate with a pint of ice cream and a carbuncle curled in her lap at home, yet Tanya's batting eyelashes conned her into agreeing to host the shindig at the renovated phoenix complex.

"A little higher!" Tanya ordered.

Aila groaned from atop her ladder, eyeing the tiles too far below her before risking another step up. She tossed the last string of decorative lights atop the wooden pagoda on their patio. Without waiting for Tanya's approval, she hurried back down to solid ground, then huffed a warm breath into her hands.

The dead of winter had arrived. At least, as wintery as San Tamculo got. Movas had an arid coast, a desert interior, but the low mountains in between were dusted with snow, crowns of white overlooking the city. This month's zoo celebration was a manzanita festival, the red-barked shrubs some of the first to bloom in the surrounding hillsides and the zoo's manicured plant beds. The string lights on the patio mimicked the bell-shaped flowers in white and pink.

Tanya plugged in the last string, a dainty glow as the sun sank behind trees.

"What did I tell you?" Tanya beamed. "Fancy patio for fancy folks."

Aila couldn't argue with that. Beyond the lights, they'd dressed the patio with tables draped in crimson cloth, catered by the zoo's best kitchen. Cubed cheeses. Sliced meats. Crackers shaped like phoenix feathers, coated with cayenne sesame seeds. Fancier hors d'oeuvres included dragon-shaped puff pastries coiled around a hoard of Vjari mushroom stuffing, fruit arranged like peacock griffin feathers, a coffee-flavored Silimalo layer cake, cookies shaped like flowers and coated in rich Ziclexian chocolate. More than once, Tanya smacked Aila's hand to keep her from raiding the food before their guests arrived.

"Just one?" Aila complained. "I'll rearrange them so no one notices!"

"Ailes." Tanya straightened a vase of fragrant sage and white lilac flowers. "Why have you got to act like a gremlin at your own party?"

"It is not *my* party!"

Tanya's brow lifted.

OK, maybe it was a little bit Aila's party. That made things worse. She'd have to stay and talk to people instead of piling a plate full of food, then absconding to a corner. The strategy had helped her survive every party she'd ever attended. Dread for social interaction rattled in her head, squeaking like rusty wheels on a—

Oh, wait. No. That was just Teddy pushing along a metal trolley cart.

He eased the old contraption over the doorjamb and onto the patio, double tiers piled not with the usual bowls of food pellets and chopped vegetables, but bottled water and soda cans dropped off by the caterers. Tanya had invited her beau to enjoy the fancy food, a thank you for his patience through several dozen hours of overtime and at least one interrupted date night, when Aila had called Tanya in a panic about ordering the proper thread count of dish towels.

In light of the classy decorations, he'd swapped faded work jeans for less faded formal jeans, had thrown his Humane Society T-shirt beneath Tanya's desk in favor of a plum button-down that pudged a little at his rounded middle.

"Hey, Tani," he said over the creaking trolley, "where do you want these?

"On that end of the table. Thanks so much." Tanya pecked a kiss down to his cheek, then zipped inside like a jeweled hummingbird, arms piled with trash wrappers to throw away.

Always so easy, the two of them.

Teddy wheeled the trolley beside the banquet table and

started setting the soda cans out in neat little lines. "You know, when you two invited me," he said, light with amusement, "I was told it would be a fun night, not that I'd be conscripted into— *Aila, no.*"

Aila froze like a racoon caught with its paw in a trashcan, her moderately less grimy hand reaching for a feather-shaped cake pop—one behind the others, less likely for Tanya to miss.

"But she's not looking," Aila hissed at Theodore.

"*I'm* looking," he returned.

"You'd betray our friendship so easily?"

"Aila. What's clause one of the BFF–Boyfriend Contract?"

He spoke like the thing was a physical object.

Because it was, of course. Aila had demanded he sign it before granting her blessing to the relationship. Tanya, the coy pigeon, refused to sign as their witness—in part because she said it was ridiculous, but also she was laughing too hard. Didn't matter. Aila got a notary in town to take care of it.

Clause one was simple. "Tanya comes first," Aila grumbled. She scrunched her nose, thwarted by her own paperwork.

Teddy nudged her, armed with a conspiring grin. Clause three: no holding grudges.

"Thanks for letting me steal Tanya so much," she said, soft and earnest.

"Clause two," he answered smugly.

Clause two: *Tanya makes her own decisions. We the undersigned agree to work in coordination to support those decisions.*

"Tanya never would have let you do this alone." Theodore donned a surprisingly sage air for someone squinting over thick-rimmed glasses, laying out soda cans. "Will be nice to see her with some more free time, though. Needs to work on her own program."

Aila blinked. "Her own program?"

"Sure. The volunteer keeper program? She's been working on it most nights, trying to get ready for that big grant deadline. You know."

Aila nodded like she did know. Like her heart wasn't climbing to an unhealthy *pit-pat*.

She combed her thought archives, sifting for any sticky notes of Tanya comments she'd let fall under the cabinets. They'd been so busy getting the phoenix building ready. Sorting the paperwork. Prepping for this celebration.

There'd been no talk of volunteer programs or grant applications.

Tanya had everything under control. She'd snag whatever grant she applied for, would get this program running and have bright-eyed volunteers swarming the zoo in no time. Aila had no doubt of that—though a little twist went through her chest, thinking Tanya hadn't shared these latest developments with her. Had Aila been too busy? Too sleep deprived?

Then she heard footsteps, and all her side worries scattered like tadpoles spooked by a predatory bird.

The first guests stepped onto the patio: a flock of griffin show keepers in their black zoo polos. Normally, Aila gave the crew as wide a berth as she did their wicked queen, but with how much sweat and elbow grease they'd volunteered to get the building ready for inspection, she conceded a smile and a wave as they beelined for the banquet tables. Tanya, the excellent host, ran them through the culinary offerings. With the festivities underway, Aila eyed the spread with renewed hope.

Before she could strike, a sparkling smile snagged her from the doorway.

Connor waved. Directly at her.

Aila waved back, eyes wide. Without the excuse of the renovations, he hadn't been around the phoenix complex as often.

Obviously. That made sense. Connor had his own exhibits to tend to. Why should she expect him to waste time over here? Sure, he'd congratulated her when news of the phoenix transfer came through. Standard workplace behavior.

Connor's brow tilted.

"Aila," Teddy whispered, urgent. "Put your hand down."

Shit. Aila was still waving. Why was she still waving? She lowered her hand, then became utterly flustered as to what to do with it.

"Oh no. Not this again." Tanya cozied up to Teddy's side, voice a conspiring hush, keen eyes darting between Connor and Aila as a little pastry dragon perched in her aquamarine nails.

"Should we do something?" Theodore said.

"You've got to let those poor, blind-eyed kittens stumble their way to independence at some point," Tanya said.

"You aren't *helping*," Aila said.

Tanya pressed a firm hand to her back. "You can do this, Ailes."

"I absolutely cannot. What in all the skies and seas makes you think—"

Then Tanya gave her a firm push toward the banquet table, her and Teddy hanging back like smug goose parents watching their chick stumble into oncoming traffic.

Aila kept her eyes down. *Food. Focus on the food.* Intent on stuffing her face with everything in sight, she'd piled her plate several inches high when Connor appeared beside her. He wore his zoo uniform, polo crisp black against his pale skin, the tousled curl of his hair as delicious as anything on the banquet table.

"Connor! Hello!"

Across the table, a couple of griffin show keepers snickered. They could choke on their puff pastry.

"Long time no see, Aila!" Connor nudged her arm. "Thanks for the invite. And congratulations again on the phoenix transfer! Always seems to be exciting news coming from you these days."

"Oh. Well." Aila blushed and shoved a pastry into her mouth, continuing before she'd swallowed. "Thank you. We've been pretty busy."

"I bet. A new Silimalo phoenix, right here in our zoo? That's *huge* news." His eyes lit up as he reached across the table. "No way, are these those spicy phoenix crackers? Catering usually only whips these out for donor dinners."

"You've been to the donor dinners?" Aila had received an invite once or twice, but a crowd that fancy scared her more than the kelpie.

"Of course," Connor said. "Good food. Classy company."

Aila chuckled. "Oh yeah. Not exactly the lifestyle of a zoo-keeper salary."

"Sure." Connor gave a theatrical eye roll. "But we all knew that signing up, right?"

OK. This was OK. Aila had made it how many words without messing things up? One...five...ten...twenty...

That didn't matter.

This was her chance, free of deadlines and obligations for manual labor. Tonight, she could talk to Connor, and not as her usual bumbling self who'd once asked a girl out for candlesticks instead of coffee. She'd be clever. Charming. Watch out, world, Aila had a phoenix coming her way, and she might as well be a new woman.

"Hey," Connor said. "Is that Director Rivera?"

"*What?*" Aila coughed up a flake of puff pastry. Off to an excellent start.

Maria Rivera stepped onto the patio with a clack of heels,

dressed in a black blazer and a pencil skirt printed with crimson phoenix feathers, black bun glinting in the string lights as she tilted her head to admire the decorations. At her side, Giuseppe Garumano sported what could have been the same navy suit he'd worn for the inspection, his mustache gelled into swirls.

"We can catch up later," Connor said with a wink. "Don't want to keep you from your important guests."

"Oh, no, not at all, I'm sure they're fine on their own."

The plea fell on empty ears. As Connor left her to talk to the other keepers, Rivera strode toward Aila with a smile. Compared to all the keepers in their work uniforms, the IMWS director's poise made Aila feel like a child masquerading at the adult table. She clutched her plate, seeking an anchor.

"Aila! So good to see you!"

Rivera shook her hand. Garumano followed. Aila tried to come off as less of a dead fish than last time, though at least she could blame clammy hands on the season.

"Thank you so much for coming, Ms. Rivera. Mr. Garumano. We're so honored to have been selected for the transfer. It..." Aila chuckled, half nerves, half genuine. "Still feels like a dream."

Felt like a dream, because it *was* a dream. How could so much have changed since Aila was a (less?) awkward new keeper meeting Rivera at a zoo gala? Since she'd sent that email on a whim? Since being dragged to the zoo director's office, certain she'd face her doom?

Rivera's smile verged on proud. In a weird way, it reminded Aila of her mother.

"A dream?" Rivera chuckled. "I'm glad to hear it. Though don't discount your hard work, Miss Macbhairan. Giuseppe had the most glowing things to say after his inspection."

Aila shouldn't have gawked. "Glowing? *Really?*"

Garumano nodded, his expression swathed in mustache. "Intimate knowledge of the species. Detailed contingency plans. The building is old, but brought well up to code."

Could have mentioned that during the inspection and not given Aila a heart attack. Still, was that a swell of pride in her chest? Maybe just heartburn. She downed another pastry.

"We're delighted the phoenix will find a good home here," Rivera said. "And of course, please consider this just the beginning of our relationship. Everyone in the breeding network will be eager to help you succeed."

Aila shrank at the prospect but managed a nod. Just the entire future of a species resting on her shoulders. No big deal.

"We can only hope," Garumano added, grim. "After what happened at Jewelport, we could use some good news."

Aila fought a pull of morbid curiosity. Despite following the news with a fine-toothed comb, few details ever came out of the investigation into the stolen Jewelport phoenixes.

"Does IMWS know what happened?" She realized her inappropriate enthusiasm and reined it back. "I mean, from a learning standpoint. To avoid repeating the same mistakes. Not that I'm saying anyone in Jewelport made a mistake, I'm sure they all did their best."

Rivera's smile tightened. "Let's not talk about such grim things. Tonight is supposed to be about the future."

"And why not, Maria?" Garumano said. "We need to prepare her, in case it happens again!"

Aila's stomach sank. As awful as the events at the Jewelport Zoo had been, she hadn't thought . . .

It could happen again. The male phoenix was coming to her. She'd be responsible for both of them. The poachers wouldn't risk nabbing another clutch of chicks, would they?

"That's why security was so important to the inspection,"

Rivera said. "And why we updated our protocols across the board."

"Jewelport thought they were prepared," Garumano argued. "Yet the thieves found every blind spot in the security cameras. Phone jammers to keep the police from being called."

Director Rivera touched Aila's arm. "We don't mean to worry you, Aila. For now, all you need to focus on is the birds. We're sure you'll do us all proud, and IMWS is here to support you every step of the way."

Aila's stomach had turned to a swarm of orchid vipers. She wasn't good at hiding her unease, judging by Rivera's worried look.

"I'm sure a lot of information is still confidential," Aila said. "But did you ever find the phoenixes?"

Rivera and Garumano shared a long look before shaking their heads. Aila's stomach tied a fresh knot, imagining the poachers making off with the feathers, no need for the beautiful birds they'd been plucked from.

"What about who did it?" Aila asked, harder.

"The thieves, no." Rivera lowered her voice. "Though the Jewelport police brought one of the zoo's food workers in for questioning. He confessed to providing advice on how to enter the zoo unnoticed, in return for a handsome monetary reward."

Garumano's brow furrowed. "That blasted live camera let the thieves know exactly when to strike, after the female immolated. But to think one of our own opened the door? Unacceptable. And probably not an isolated incident."

Aila swallowed hard, a bit of pastry stuck in her throat. "What do you mean?"

She knew the answer the moment she asked. The San Tamculo Zoo had endured its own theft, not as sensational in the news as a phoenix nabbing, but the disappearance of those diamondback dragon hatchlings was a sore wound. The shipment should have been discreet, the dates kept quiet. Yet even oblivious Aila had caught the rumors around the zoo. How easy would it have been to slip a tracker in the box when no one was looking, then grab the dragons once they were in transit?

Someone in the zoo. *This* zoo, maybe. Who could be so heartless they would—

Her thoughts crumbled, scattered like dust to the Movasi desert.

Luciana stepped onto the patio.

Despite Aila's esteemed company, her mouth hinged open to an unflattering angle. She often attached facetious mental descriptors to the witch—strutting, preening, glowing. Mostly to make herself feel better.

Tonight, Luciana strutted onto the patio in heels she must have changed into after work. She preened in a maroon dress with frilled hem, tasteful enough for a professional function, accentuating every curve and the warm brown of her skin. She glowed in golden eyeshadow and black curls, catching every sparkle of the string lights.

Aila no longer felt the cold of the season. For some reason, she found herself quite warm.

Along with Luciana came Director Hawthorn, both laughing as they entered. Aila had no sooner donned her suspicious squint than the director headed their way.

"Maria!" He greeted her with a kiss to each cheek. "Giuseppe." A firm handshake. "We're delighted to have you visiting tonight. Have you had a chance to enjoy the zoo this afternoon? Perhaps I could show you our new pair of orchid vipers in the reptile house? Gorgeous specimens."

While the visiting dignitaries exchanged pleasantries, Aila

squinted her displeasure at Luciana. The witch's elegant lashes narrowed in return.

"But first, where are my manners?" Director Hawthorn said. "This is Luciana Reyes, head of our griffin show. And recently nominated for a Public Outreach Award by the Movas Society for Science Education. For the second year in a row!"

Aila held back an eye roll.

Luciana put on a dazzling smile. "My pleasure."

They shook hands. Luciana's grasp looked obnoxiously firm.

"Miss Reyes and I have been discussing the Silimalo phoenix transfer," Hawthorn continued. "She's agreed to join the project as a public relations coordinator."

What was that ringing sound in Aila's ears?

The reactions in the circle could have been night and day. Rivera smiled in delight. Garumano nodded. Aila puckered as if she'd downed a bag of extra sour lemon candies.

"What a wonderful idea!" Rivera said. "After all this terrible news from the Jewelport Zoo, we could use some good press with the transfer."

"Luciana will see to that," Hawthorn said. "Since she took over the griffin show, attendance is up sevenfold. We've had to look into expanded seating in the amphitheater."

Garumano's brows shot up. "Is that so? Most impressive."

Luciana gave an airy laugh. "Oh, you're all too kind. I'm delighted to be part of such a momentous occasion for the zoo."

"But I see you've yet to try our fine catering!" Hawthorn ushered them to the banquet tables. "Please, we can chat more with proper accompaniments."

The three important people shuffled off, gathering plates as Director Hawthorn boasted over every ingredient (all sourced from local San Tamculo farms). Aila was rooted in place, glaring up at her maroon-clad nemesis with the ferocity of a water panther (unfortunately, none of the chameleon-like fur to match). Luciana's smile dropped.

"The fuck was that about?" Aila hissed.

"Right. Well." Luciana inspected her ruby nails. "It seems we'll be working together a while longer. Believe me, I'm not thrilled about it, either. But I suppose there ought to be *someone* around here who can spin more than two sentences together in front of the press."

Aila scoffed. "I could memorize two sentences. No problem."

Luciana lifted an elegant brow.

"*And*," Aila continued, "I don't need you hanging around here after you tried to sabotage my inspection."

"Sabotage? What in all the skies and seas are you talking about?"

"You called me away in the middle of Garumano's visit!"

"Oh." Luciana waved a hand. "You mean that part where I dragged you out of what I can only imagine was an awkward conversation so you could demonstrate your animal handling abilities and crisis management in a real-life scenario?"

Aila blinked, speechless. That couldn't be right. Luciana just happened to be in the World of Birds aviary, even though that wasn't her department. She'd just happened to be the one to radio for help when Archie stole the ring. She'd just happened to defuse the situation until Aila arrived.

Every second she remained silent was another victory for Luciana.

"You did what?" *Smooth, Aila.*

"Don't worry. I'll stay out of your way." Luciana clicked her tongue, then her heels, as she joined the dignitaries at the banquet table, stepping into their midst with a smile.

How did she always make it look so effortless?

Suddenly, the patio felt too crowded. Too hostile. Aila

retreated, a wave of stress reverting her to typical party gremlin behavior. No one seemed to notice as she slipped away. No one ever did.

Inside, the empty phoenix complex met her with blissful quiet. No judging eyes. Rubra perched in her aviary, dozing with beak tucked under her wing. Just in case anyone wandered in to appreciate the magnificent bird, Aila cloistered herself in the kitchen, safe within four walls and stark overhead lights.

She leaned against the counter and breathed.

Horns and fangs, how had she gotten this far as such a mess of a person?

Luciana saved her ass with the building renovations. That should have been the end of it, one last chink in Aila's pride, then on their separate ways again. Now, Aila had to deal with her as PR director? The decision made sense. Aila knew her birds, enough to impress Director Garumano. Closet her in a back room, and she'd flourish like a mushroom in a tray of dirt.

Luciana was a sunflower, beautiful and confident. Brilliant with the public. The phoenix program needed someone like her. It *deserved* someone like her, someone to smile and spin engaging tales of phoenix conservation as cameras snapped. Aila didn't need to feel intimidated. They each had their own strengths, and there was nothing wrong with hers.

Except sometimes, Aila wished she could be better at talking to people. Even a little bit. Maybe then, Tanya wouldn't have to babysit her at important parties. Aila could *tell* people why Rubra was so amazing.

"Hey, Aila?"

She startled at the voice from the door. Usually, Tanya was the first to notice her scamper off at social functions, the one to slip her sweets from the banquet table while Aila built her energy back up.

This time, Connor leaned through the doorway. Aila's heart flipped.

"Hi, Connor." She tried to muster enthusiasm. After so much draining interaction that night, a small hello was like squeezing a dead battery.

"Are you all right?" Connor asked. "I noticed you'd disappeared."

"I'm fine. I'll be right back out." A smile, half-formed.

Connor's came out so much better. Softer. "You aren't great with people, are you?"

"I mean... That's not..." Even lying was too much effort. She sighed. "No. Not really."

He joined her in the kitchen, a casual lean against the counter beside her. "You're fine. Last I checked, Director Hawthorn was still talking about the menu. You know how passionate he gets."

"They are very nice snacks."

"Only the best locally sourced ingredients."

They shared a laugh. Aila sat a little easier. Maybe tonight wasn't so bad.

"So..." Connor said. "I overheard Luciana..."

Yep. There it was, all that tension back again. "Can we not talk about it?"

"You two have some sort of history?"

That sounded an awful lot like talking about it. "Gee. What gave you that idea?"

"Whenever the two of you are in sight of each other, you both glare as hard as a pair of mating diamondback dragons."

Not hard enough.

"Well, you know." Aila sheltered behind crossed arms. "It's just that she's better than me at everything and always has been. That's all."

"That's not true."

Aila made a long, unflattering sound, blowing air over her lips. He didn't have to say dumb, nice things like that. Not as if they were...

Standing in a room together.

Alone.

So very close. An inch of lean to the side, and Aila's arm would brush his.

She cleared her throat. "Why would you say that?"

Connor grinned. If not for the counter, jelly legs Aila would have been on the floor.

"Come on, Aila. You're smart. Determined. You passed that inspection with flying colors, from what I heard."

Every introverted muscle in Aila's body screamed at her to look away, to play with her fingers or wiggle her toes. She couldn't. Not with Connor staring at her like that.

"You helped," she whispered. Instant regret. Whispering sounded far too... *intimate.*

"A lot of us *helped*," Connor said. "But you're the one who convinced IMWS the phoenix will be safe here. Also, Tanya showed me your flashcards. That stack was scary thick."

Aila couldn't hold out any longer. Her eyes dropped to the linoleum floor, seeking refuge, a blush burning her cheeks.

She flinched when cool fingers cupped her chin, tilting her face up.

"Why do you always do that?" Connor said, soft.

Aila might have stopped breathing. Her heart might have disintegrated in her chest. All her panicked thoughts could register was the touch of Connor's fingers. The smell of pine, a sweet vanilla spice. His eyes, clear and blue and inches from hers.

Skies and seas, his *face* inches from hers.

"Do what?" Aila squeaked.

"Look away, like you have something to hide from. You

should be proud of what you've accomplished." That grin sliced her heart clean open. "I know I am."

His gaze drifted, down to her mouth.

"*Would you like to go out for dinner some time?*" Aila blurted, much too loud for two people sitting alone, inches apart. "I mean..." Her blush deepened, threatening to melt her cheeks. "If you're into that kind of thing."

Connor's grin widened. "Yeah. I'm into that kind of thing."

And then he kissed her.

Fortunately for Aila's exploding heart, it was a short kiss. A light press of lips as his hand cupped her cheek, scarcely enough to savor the moment, ending with that beautiful ache for more. She sighed low and wistful, something hot in her belly, hand bracing the counter to keep from swooning onto the floor.

Aila hadn't had many kisses in her life. This...wasn't a bad one.

Connor pulled back, his fingers slipping off her chin with one parting, shiver-worthy brush. "Dinner, then? Tomorrow at seven?"

Oof. Late dinner. Usually, Aila would be home in pajamas by seven. She could make an exception. "Sure. Sounds like a—"

Her throat closed up. Connor's brow tilted.

"A *date?*" he finished.

"Yes. That."

"I'll see you then."

With a parting grin, Connor disappeared through the door, back to the party.

Aila melted onto the floor, managing to catch her back against the cabinets. Her heart had to be beating a thousand times a minute. Her lips tingled where Connor had kissed her, warmth creeping through her like a spring thaw.

"Skies and seas," she breathed to herself.

A date with a handsome boy. A new phoenix on the way. Alone in a dim but renovated kitchen, Aila smiled. Luciana could have her precious PR.

For this moment, Aila's life was perfect.

Chapter Seventeen

Aila sat on a rock ledge, legs dangling, fingers fidgeting with the radio on her belt.

"What if this is a fluke?" she worried.

"How could this be a fluke, Aila?" Tanya shot her a dry look from downslope, brandishing an electric drill, shoulder jammed against a metal screen as she attempted to bolt it to the rock.

Khonsu, the Bix phoenix, perched above her, staring down his long heron bill with an annoyed puff of white cheek feathers, nibbling at the entrance to his favorite hiding hole.

"I don't know," Aila said. "Maybe Connor didn't mean to ask me out. It could have been an accident."

"Did he kiss you on accident, too?"

"Stranger things have happened."

Tanya rolled her eyes and shoved the screen in place. Her drill let out an ear-splitting whine as she tried to force a screw into stone. The only hardware they'd dug up at the zoo's equipment barn was meant for wood.

"What do you think, Khonsu?" Aila asked, turning to the more receptive bird. "Maybe we should reschedule. Cancel, even."

The phoenix croaked. Tanya let out a groan that could have been for Aila or the rock.

"You can't cancel on that poor boy, Ailes. You're worrying too much."

Aila was, indeed, worrying. Who could say it was too much, given her disastrous dating history?

"What if we have nothing to talk about?" Aila worried as Tanya gave up on the metal screen with a cry of defeat.

"What if he thinks I'm boring? Or weird?" Aila worried as they returned the equipment.

"What if I clam up over dinner?" Aila worried as they stood in line for lunch, Tanya's eyes rolled to the ceiling.

"What if I choke while we're eating?" Aila worried around a mouthful of cheese fries. "Or what if I trip, accidentally punch a waiter in the face, get us thrown out of the—"

"*Aila!*" Tanya pointed her fork like a weapon.

"OK, maybe that's a little extreme." Aila slumped and poked her food. "But not by much, Tanya. This is *me* we're talking about."

Tanya sighed and finished her lunch.

As they walked back to the phoenix complex, a griffin show keeper passed them on the path. Nadia, the technology goddess who'd updated the phoenix security cameras in a single afternoon. She glanced up from her phone, followed by a wave that had gotten much friendlier since their collaboration.

"Oh hey, Tanya, Aila—"

Aila shoved Tanya into a brisker walk. "So good to see you, Nadia! Please excuse us, we have a leaking faucet in the phoenix exhibit we need to fix. Have a nice day."

Tanya sighed the loudest yet but went along with it.

When they reached the phoenix complex, Aila dropped into her desk chair. Flailed her arms. Groaned. How was she supposed to get any work done when she had a *date* with a *boy* later *tonight*?

"Aila," Tanya said. "I love you. But I'm going to need you to take a deep breath and stop being weird."

"But I'm so bad at this," Aila whined.

"Everyone's bad at dating. All those hormones and awkward nerves."

"I'm *only* awkward nerves. Always."

"Which is why you've got to practice." Tanya softened. "Dates are scary. But also *fun*. Make sure you have some fun tonight, Ailes."

Aila wasn't sure. Being swallowed by a crater and consumed beneath the bowels of the dirt sounded a lot easier. "I thought you weren't crazy about Connor?"

Tanya shrugged. "It's a high bar to be worthy of my best girl. Only way to find out is if you talk to him. I expect a full play-by-play afterward. Obviously."

"Obviously," Aila grumbled. "I'll recount every excruciating detail of me blundering a cup off the table, spilling scalding coffee all over him, having to call an ambulance for—"

She squeaked like an over-inflated mouse when Connor poked his head in the door.

"Afternoon, ladies! Just wanted to . . . Oh geez, Aila, sorry, I didn't mean to startle you?"

Aila clamped a hand white-knuckled to her desk, the other to her sternum, zero words running through her brain beyond a high-pitched buzzing sound. At her outburst, Tanya nearly fell out of her chair. She swiveled, searching for the escaped zoo animal or freak tsunami that must have prompted such hysteria, settling instead on the puzzled hunk of a zookeeper standing on their linoleum threshold. She snapped a stern look onto Aila, a silent *say something*.

"Good afternoon to you, Connor!" Aila said. Several decibels too loud.

Tanya abandoned subtlety, pressing a hand to her temple. Stop worrying. All Aila had to do was *stop worrying* for ten seconds. Maybe twenty. Sixty would be exceedingly generous.

"Hope I'm not interrupting." Connor smiled at Aila, those flushed cheeks digging a slight dimple, that lock of dark hair deliciously wayward across his forehead. Every rational thought turned to porridge. "Could I snag a minute with "

"Mm-hm." Tanya headed out the door to give them privacy, a smirk on her lips. Traitor.

Aila loved her to death.

Then they were alone. Butterflies tried to erupt from Aila's belly, stirred by the memory of lips pressed to hers. Cool fingers brushing her chin. She straightened in her chair. Maybe he'd come to back out. Maybe he'd realized his mistake.

Connor smiled again. Her bones nearly disintegrated.

"Still on for tonight?" he asked.

"Definitely," she squeaked. "Seven o'clock."

"Enough time for you to change?"

Aila's nose scrunched. "Change?"

"Well, yeah." Connor chuckled. "You weren't planning to wear your zoo uniform to dinner?"

No, Aila would never do something like that.

Never.

She forced a laugh.

"I was thinking the Merlion Bistro," Connor said. "You know the place?"

Aila startled. "The Merlion Bistro? Of course I know it. But that's, like..." She grimaced. "A fancy place."

"Well, yeah, that's kind of the point?"

Aila had envisioned something lower profile for a first date. A cozy coffee shop. Maybe a diner. Somewhere easy to hide, easy to escape if things went bad.

"That's very thoughtful," she said, "but we don't have to..."

"Please, Aila." He grinned, a lopsided trump card. "I insist. You'll have a great time."

When Connor left, Aila spun in her chair until dizzy, even more jittery than before.

Aila discovered, to her horror, she owned only two dresses.

Expecting anything more had been, perhaps, optimistic, but Aila wore nice clothes so rarely, she dove into her closet after work hoping she might be surprised by the contents. No such luck. She pulled out a simple blue dress with a crumple of fabric flowers at the waist, a relic she'd worn to a cousin's wedding. The second was a floor-length black thing Tanya bought for her after Aila lost a bet, then laughed her ass off through an entire night of opera as Aila moped in her slinky skirts.

Simple blue it was.

Aila owned a single hairbrush. A couple of phoenix barrettes and a curling iron she had no idea how to use. Best not to tempt fate tonight. She smoothed her auburn frizz as much as it would tolerate, pinning back unruly bangs.

Skies and seas, who even invented high heels? Aila ignored the single pair in her closet and threw on some flats.

She tapped them against the train floor for the entire ride to the harbor.

When Aila emerged from the stairwell of the downtown station, cold air blustered the sidewalk, making her shiver. Should have brought a jacket. Her collection of fashion accessories was too slim. She clutched her arms and waddled down the street like a Vjari auk, desperate for every heater she passed on restaurant patios. Her parents' pub was a couple of blocks over.

Two blocks made a world of difference. Aila's zone of comfort had fluorescent store fronts and frying oil. Here instead were smoky interiors. Trees dressed up in string lights and painted sidewalk planters. Wheels of griffin-pulled carriages clacked cobblestone, transporting tourists in sparkling evening attire that made Aila's rumpled dress look like a thrift store reject.

The Merlion Bistro held the place of honor at the end of the pier, name lit up in swooping script almost too elegant to read, harbor waves lapping the pilings. At the door, an attendant in a three-piece suit waited by a podium, too busy flipping through a reservations book to note Aila's approach. All the better.

No sign of Connor yet. Nerves compelled Aila to arrive several minutes early. She could head inside the ritzy place on her own...

A bark from the waterfront snagged her attention.

She scuttled away from the lights and mood music, salt breeze tangling her hair as she leaned over the railing. San Tamculo started as a fishing harbor, hauling krakens from the depths of the Middle Sea. Most boats nowadays served tourists. The coasts here had no coral reefs as grand as the Naelo Archipelago, but the Movasi kelp forest was stunning for its own sake, home to such charming creatures as... A smile lit Aila's cheeks when she spotted a pod of merlions lounging on the rocks below the pier. Golden fur coated lion snouts and paws, tapering into a hind flipper. She propped her head in her hands and watched.

Awkward creatures. Like her. They sprawled their blubbery bodies without a care for fancy dresses or fancy restaurants, their world as simple as wriggling to a comfortable spot and barking at any neighbors who approached too close. What a life. The ability to breathe air and water interchangeably wasn't bad, either. What Aila wouldn't give for the option to hide beneath the depths of the ocean now and then.

"Well, look at that. Don't you clean up nice?"

Aila spun, an unintentional twirl of her dress.

She almost didn't recognize Connor in an unstained button-down. Tailored slacks. His dark hair was slicked sideways with gel, accentuating that distracting curl against his temple. *All of him* was distracting. Her cheeks burned beneath his unfair onslaught of formal attire and work-toned physique.

And then there was her.

Self-conscious, Aila smoothed the wrinkled fabric flower at her waist. When that proved fruitless, she pointed to the harbor. "Have you seen the merlions?"

Connor's head tilted. "The merlions?"

"Yeah. Down by the water. I think they're the south coast subspecies, based on the coat color, but it's kind of hard to tell in the dark—"

When Connor took her hand, Aila's world narrowed to the bloom of heat in her palm. The brush of fingers rough with work calluses. He leaned in so close, she thought she might freeze in place, chiseled to the pier for the gulls to perch upon for all eternity.

"Come on," he said, low, breath tickling her ear. "You must be freezing. Let's get you inside." He pulled her away from the merlions, head shaking in bemusement.

Aila pouted but went along with him.

As fancy as the Merlion Bistro looked from the outside, the inside was worse. White tablecloths coated every surface, decked with glittering silverware and tea candles in frosted glass cups. The burgundy carpet had no stains. Violins played from the speakers. A wall of windows overlooked the harbor, bordered in dim lights and portraits of boats.

This was the type of place Aila and Tanya might visit once in a blue moon, just for the ridiculous factor. A night masquerading as fancy people eating fancy food, but with the comfort of a friend to laugh with. Connor, she didn't know as well. As the host led them to a table, she focused on not tripping and smacking someone's champagne to the floor.

The menu was thick—cardstock pages in plastic sleeves and a cover of shiny leather, no discoloration from old salsa spills. Connor ordered a glass of white wine. Aila didn't often drink wine, but she imagined a place like this wouldn't be big on fruity umbrella drinks. Wine it was.

Her nose wrinkled at a strong, spiced smell. Connor was wearing cologne. He never wore cologne at the zoo, though no surprise, given how sensitive dragons were to scent. Aila preferred him smelling of aviary musk—then chastised the thought away. She was supposed to act like a *normal* person tonight.

"Cheers." Connor lifted his glass. "To your new phoenix."

Aila returned the toast, then sipped her wine. Oaky. Dry. She stopped herself from smacking her lips.

"Have you had dinner here before?" Connor asked.

"No. Not that I have anything against it. I mean..." She set her glass on the tablecloth and toyed a finger around the edge. "I don't eat out all that much. Too tired after work."

"Sure, we can all commiserate on that." His smile flashed, bright in the dim dining room. "Got to let loose sometimes, though? You work hard all day, ought to enjoy your time off."

"It's not so bad. Picking up after birds, at least. The kelpie gets muckier, but it could be worse. I assume dragons are more of a handful."

Connor shrugged.

"Not that dragons aren't incredible," Aila continued, more comfortable as she fell into her safe topics. "But phoenixes have always had my heart. Rubra, obviously. I could spend hours watching her play in her olive trees. Some of the posts I've seen pop up on Griffingram are to die for. Can you believe someone got a photo of her catching leaves in her beak?"

"Mm-hm."

"And the Bix phoenix is amazing, too. Still giving Tanya a load of trouble, but honestly? I'm impressed at how crafty he's been. Tanya and I have both put our heads together on this one, and we haven't figured out how to plug that hole. Tanya thinks that if we try blocking the entrance with metal sheeting—"

Connor sipped his wine with a muffled sound, something between a scoff and a laugh.

"Oh." Aila turned quiet. Meek. "Sorry. Was I talking too much? I get like that when..." She studied her glass. "When I'm excited."

"No, no, it's just..." He chuckled. "You want to talk about *work*? When we've been there all day?"

Of course she did. Aila could talk about her animals all night and still be eager to see them again in the morning, bright and early before the sun rose. She dropped her hands beneath the table and fidgeted with her dress, nerves returning in full force as she thought back to every time she'd single-handedly turned a date to disaster by talking too much or too little.

People always said to be yourself. But Aila's self was awkward, obnoxious. If she could figure out what Connor wanted her to be instead, maybe she stood a chance.

"What do you do outside of work?" she asked.

Skies and seas, Connor looked gorgeous when he smiled, when he stilled, even when he turned a bashful gaze to the wine swirling in his glass. Why couldn't Aila pull off cute awkward? All she ever managed was *awkward* awkward.

"You'll probably think it's silly," Connor said. "Past couple of years, I've been poking into stock trading."

Aila fought her brain's immediate attempt to tune out. Like

a slap on the hand. *Bad, Aila. Pay attention.* "That sounds... cool?"

"A grind is what it is." Another laugh, this one strained. "My dad used to be into it. Wasn't any good, mind you, but the hobby bled over. Most of the safe trades are in tech these days, microchip companies and those new tidal energy generators."

"Mm-hm." Now came Aila's turn to frown.

"The real fun is picking out riskier stocks. Magical creature goods go up and down like crazy, with seasonal supply and shifting regulations. Restaurant industry's great as well."

Aila floundered for the lifeline. "Oh! Restaurants? My family owns a place nearby, the Macbhairan Pub and Tequileria. Have you heard of it?"

"That little hole in the wall? Yeah, I think I've walked past."

Connor's laugh hit the wrong pitch—a little too far from jest, too close to mockery.

Aila tried to laugh with him, but the sound came out hollow. Her parents put their lives into that restaurant. They worked as hard as she did, slaving over grills and tables rather than concrete exhibits, all their savings gone toward putting her through college. The pub wasn't fancy, but it was home. People loved it.

She ought to be able to laugh at a harmless joke.

That, or find the spine to tell Connor he'd misspoken, give him the chance to explain he hadn't meant any offense.

She couldn't. Aila didn't know the right answer, feared one wrong word would careen this date onto even rockier territory. She bit her tongue until it ached. Her fingers clamped into her scratchy dress beneath the table.

Their food arrived to save her. Aila dug into a plate of lemony shrimp and pasta, thankful for the distraction, berating herself for overreacting. Connor talked as they ate. Investments he was excited for. Other fancy restaurants he'd tried. A couple of nonfiction books she'd never heard of. Aila tried to stay attentive, tried to nod and express interest at the appropriate times.

"Is everything all right?" Connor asked.

"Of course." Aila stirred her pasta. "Fine. Go on."

"You're super quiet."

"Yeah. I am sometimes."

Connor deflated, studying her with probing eyes—like a keeper studied a troublesome animal. They all did it. Easy to recognize.

"I'm sorry, Aila. I must have said something wrong. First date nerves and all that."

He spoke so soft, so genuine, that handsome brow shriveled into concern.

All because of her.

Aila's nerves flared to full-blown panic. *She* was the one who talked too much about work. *She* shut down when he shared his interests. Now, she'd made Connor feel guilty, which made her feel guilty, which made the whole room spin a little and . . . Why was this place so stuffy? They could afford fancy menus but not airflow?

"Are you excited for the phoenix transfer?" Connor asked. "Have they scheduled a date?"

Aila forced down the too-large forkful of pasta she'd stuffed into her mouth. "Yeah. Well, nothing definite yet. Spring most likely."

"What else do you need to get ready?"

"Oh, you know. Just a couple things. No big deal."

Aila was a lost cause. A dead battery. A popped balloon, all her air gone, no clue how to get it back as she slumped deeper into her padded chair.

Connor's words tipped even softer. "You're still worrying about work?"

That was an easier topic than all the noise in Aila's head.

"I guess," she peeped. "I know I should be happy about the phoenix transfer. And I am. So incredibly happy, and fortunate. It's just..."

She hadn't said the next part to anyone. Hints to Tanya, of course, but nothing so blunt, so vulnerable. Everyone kept telling her not to worry, but Aila *was* worried.

"It's a huge responsibility," she blurted. "I'm nervous. And scared for how the introduction will go. I've been working toward this all my life, and I know I'll put my all into it. I just hope that will be enough. That *I'll* be enough. You know?"

Connor reached across the table and laid his hand on hers. It was warm, a slow brush of his thumb urging calm as she tensed like a spooked mouse.

Then came that grin. That easy head shake. "You'll be *fine*, Aila. You worry too much."

Of course she did. She always did. Aila nodded and dropped her eyes to her food, stomach tied in too many knots for an appetite, thankful when Connor picked up the conversation on his own again.

She soldiered through dessert: a cake drowning in caramel and a puff of whipped cream, normally one of her favorites, now cloying on her tongue. Connor kept talking—another cup of coffee, another dive into some obscure tech start-up she'd never heard of.

Aila nodded along. She tried to keep her eyes from drooping, tried to excuse herself three times before she finally got the words out. Connor protested, proposing a walk on the pier, but she was full. Tired. A long day of work ahead of her.

Aila had every excuse ready to go.

Outside, Connor bid her goodnight with another kiss, longer than the first. She pressed into it, waiting for that tingle of excitement. The fireworks that never came.

Aila took the train home.

She climbed the stairs to her apartment on leaden feet, shoes pinching her toes.

Tourmaline greeted her at the door. The carbuncle spun circles around her legs, smelling every city aroma she'd brought home. Aila scratched his ears. Slipped off her flats. Sprawled on her bed and stared at the ceiling, dissecting the latticework shadows of spider plant tendrils cast from the window. Even in the quiet, the dark, her stomach wouldn't stop churning.

Tonight was supposed to be perfect.

It wasn't.

PART THREE

Compared to scarp griffins, PEACOCK GRIFFINS are smaller, lighter, and not as well suited to human riders. For these reasons, they were never fully domesticated, and most are wary of people.

Once acclimated, however, PEACOCK GRIFFINS have surprisingly docile temperaments.

"Once you earn their trust, they're some of the most loyal and inquisitive creatures in the world," says Pavina Kressali, a researcher at the University of Southern Renkaila.

Blue pom-pom crest

Long eyelet feathers

....

Renkailan
Geographic Magazine.
THESE FEATHERS ARE MORE THAN EYE CANDY.
HOW PEACOCK GRIFFINS ARE CHANGING OUR
UNDERSTANDING OF ANIMAL INTELLIGENCE.

....

Chapter Eighteen

Aila had never spent so much time cleaning the back of the kelpie exhibit.

Squelch went the mop into the bucket. *Swish* across the concrete floor, gathering chunks of wet horsehair and algae and jawbones from yesterday's meal. Her cleaning solution smelled of pine, acrid to the nose and a little too familiar.

A date with a cute boy. A phoenix on the way. What more could she ask for?

When Aila's phone alarm went off, she groaned. Time for her keeper talk.

With the enthusiasm of a slug, she dragged the goat carcass to the platform above the kelpie's public exhibit. Onlookers awed and clapped as she lashed the meal to the hook.

"Behold"—Aila spoke in a monotone and swept a hand through the air—"the incredible, carnivorous water horse."

She had nothing more to say. Fortunately, Maisie took over the show. The kelpie emerged from her pool like a hurricane, dragging the goat into the water amid a storm of fog and kelp fronds. The crowd cheered and snapped their photos as Aila slunk away, unnoticed. Thank the skies and seas for that.

Morning chores complete, she returned to the phoenix complex, thankful to retreat into the safety of—

"*Where have you been?*"

Tanya exploded as Aila entered, a tiger waiting to pounce, leaving her desk chair swiveling behind her. Aila froze like a startled deer.

"I was...doing my morning rounds?"

"Moping through morning rounds, more like it. You're half an hour late getting back!"

"You *time* me?"

"When you've got a date to tell me about?" Tanya crossed her arms.

Aila dreaded the debrief. She'd texted bare details the night before, but a deeper delve seemed better in person. Aila plopped into her own desk chair, grimacing as she felt a clump of wet algae stuck to her pants.

"Sorry, Tanya. Feeling burnt out this morning."

"No apologies." Tanya's tone turned annoyed. "You aren't the only one late."

Aila noticed the open door to the patio. An unfamiliar woman sat at the table, brown skin with cream blouse and black slacks, a recorder and notepad in front of her. Upon catching Aila's eye, she waved. Aila froze like a startled animal once again.

"Good morning!" the reporter called. "Isabella Lopez, San Tamculo Valley News. I have an appointment to speak with Ms. Luciana Reyes, but would you happen to be Aila? The phoenix keeper? If you have a moment, I'd love to ask you a few questions."

The recorder in her hand might as well have been a noose. Aila hopped from her chair, fleeing her eyesight.

"I'm so sorry. We're busy at the moment. I'm sure Luciana will be here soon!" With a brittle smile, Aila ducked behind the cover of the wall, pulling Tanya with her as she dropped to a hush. "Luciana will be here soon. *Right?*"

Tanya clicked her tongue. "I don't have a GPS tracker on that woman."

"You're right." Aila squinted, calculating. "That would make things much easier."

Tanya swatted her. "We aren't putting a tracker on a fellow zoo employee."

Before Aila could argue the merits of the plan, Luciana burst into the room.

Or was it some strange doppelgänger? Aila's alarm flashed to confusion as she took in bits of hay dust marring the Queen of Perfection's polo. Hurried strides sent her curls askew. Luciana smoothed the frizz with a hasty hand swipe, then beelined toward the patio, shooting Aila and Tanya a sharp look before snapping on a smile.

"Isabella! So good to see you. Apologies, I hope I didn't make you wait long."

As the women chatted outside, Aila and Tanya snuck back to their desks, a discreet vantage point to the patio. Luciana settled into a seat with ease, legs crossed at the knee. The reporter clicked on her recorder.

"Why's she got to use our patio?" Aila complained.

"Looks more official?" Tanya shrugged. "She *is* our phoenix PR lady now."

Aila groaned at that. At her shitty outing the night before. At everything. The only rescue from her reverie was a zipper whirring, a crinkle of plastic as Tanya retrieved something from her bag. Tanya scooched her chair close and set a container on Aila's desk, revealing a massive custard tart on golden pastry, crowned with glazed berries.

"I love you," Aila moaned.

"I know." Tanya offered her a fork. "Now, tell me. *Everything.*"

Aila stuffed her face with tart. In between bites, she ran

Tanya through her date in excruciating detail, not omitting a single word or facial expression. By the end, her stomach had returned to knots.

"So, there you go." Aila poked the remnants of tart crust. "Another horrible date to add to the list. Someone ought to give me a punch card or something."

Tanya sat beside her, tart forgotten, face puckered. "Hmph."

"I guess I do talk about work too much."

"Of course you talk about work," Tanya said. "That's your passion."

"It's boring."

"Only boring to a person who can't appreciate it. Can't appreciate *you*." Tanya tsked. "That boy ought to know better. Knew something was off with him."

Aila blinked at her. "Tanya. *What* are you talking about? I'm the one who can't hold a normal conversation for more than thirty seconds!"

"You manage that with me. All the time. Ought to be able to manage with a boy taking you on a date, if he had half a mind to listen."

Tanya was kind. Too kind.

"He took me to a ridiculously fancy restaurant. Looked so worried when things started going to shit." Aila dropped to a mutter. "Even texted this morning to say he had a nice time."

That part in particular blew her thoughts to smithereens. No one had ever done something like that for her. No one cared enough.

"Did you text him back?" Tanya asked.

"Well, yeah, I didn't want to be rude! I told him I had a good time, too."

And not a word more than that. Aila wasn't sure if she could survive another date. At the very least, she'd need a few days to bank up courage.

Tanya looked ready to strangle her. Or maybe, to strangle someone else. Even with the renovations out of the way, Aila couldn't afford to lose her partner to manslaughter charges. They had a phoenix to prepare for.

"It's fine," Aila insisted. "Maybe I'll do better next time. I'll try not to—"

Clacking heels cut the conversation short. On the patio, Luciana shook the reporter's hand, then led her back through the main room.

"A pleasure meeting you, Aila," Isabella said, slowing as she passed. "I'm sure you're very busy preparing for your new phoenix, but when you get a chance, I'd love to pick that brain of yours! Maybe once the new bird arrives?"

Aila smiled too wide, painfully aware of Luciana glaring behind the reporter's back.

"Thanks," Aila said. "I'll keep that in mind. Once the bird arrives."

She'd hoped Luciana would depart with their visitor. No such luck. As soon as the reporter left, Luciana slumped—actually *slumped*, something Aila had assumed that haughty posture incapable of. Luciana ran a hand through her curls, still sprinkled with hay dust.

"You missed a spot," Aila said.

Luciana's painted lips curled into a snarl, nails transformed to tangerine claws as she raked the tangles from her hair. "Have you got nothing better to do than sit here and judge while other people publicize *your* program?"

Aila's nose wrinkled. "Have you got nothing better to do than show up late and glare at people?"

Tanya jabbed her arm. Her tone for the witch was softer. "Everything OK, Luc? You seem . . . distracted."

Luciana's fingers slipped through her hair once more,

smoothing already flawless curls. "I've just been..." Her gaze flicked to Aila. Hardened. "Busy. I've got to get to a show."

She was out the door again on hurried strides, curls bouncing back to chaos. Stretched too thin, hopping between reporters and griffin shows? Shame. Not like this was Aila's idea.

Tanya swatted her again.

"Ow! What's that for?"

"You could be nicer, Ailes. We're supposed to be working together."

Sure, and Aila's volcanic salamander would freeze up at home. Luciana's honey-barbed words were still rattling in her head when her phone screen lit up on the desk, the flash of a message from Connor. Aila whimpered. People were just *too much* sometimes.

"I'll take you up on those 'how to speak to cute boys without looking like an ass' lessons you offered," Aila told Tanya. "After work? Get some junk food, make a night of it?"

Tanya's brows dug together. "I wish I could, Ailes. Another time. I've got a meeting with Director Hawthorn this week to discuss the volunteer program, still need to polish my proposal."

Aila's mouth made a little crinkle shape. That couldn't be right. Tanya was *always* there when Aila needed her.

"But you already had a meeting," Aila said, confused.

"I have another one. Pitching a new program takes a lot of meetings, Ailes."

"Sure. I know that. It's just, you haven't mentioned anything."

"Because we've been so busy with the phoenixes."

The fleck of annoyance in Tanya's tone silenced Aila like a slap. Panic crept up her throat, a chokehold that wouldn't let go. It was one thing to fumble her date with Connor. Missing the mark with Tanya was another disaster entirely.

"But what about the phoenix transfer?" Aila said.

At the sight of a startled Aila, Tanya softened, a low but stern voice that sounded uncannily like what she used on her Bix phoenix—as if talking to a silly little animal who didn't know any better. "We've got the building up to code. You have Luciana to do the talking. You've got this, Ailes. I just need a *little* time to work on my own project."

Tanya collected the empty tart tin for the trash, their forks for the sink, gone into the kitchen while Aila curled up in her chair. She listened to the hum of the sink and stared at her hands. Stared at the stack of protocol binders on her desk.

Stared at the flashing notification on her phone. Aila groaned and opened the message from Connor.

Glad you had a good time! You free again next week?

She weighed the blank reply box, fingers hovering over the keys. Aila typed out a polite refusal. Deleted it. Typed a longer paragraph about how their first date felt off. Deleted *that*. Connor was so nice. So handsome. *She* was the weird one, too frazzle-brained from everything else to enjoy their dinner.

I'll get back to you. Have to check my schedule. So busy!

She hit *Send*. An ellipsis popped up on Connor's end, the reply immediate.

Let me know :)

Aila dropped her phone to the desk, and her head with it. She was just nervous about screwing up with Connor. Riled up by Luciana. Worried she'd upset Tanya. Her thoughts would be clearer once the phoenix arrived.

At least she had that to look forward to.

The time came at the start of spring.

Another careful calculation (i.e. more paperwork) by IMWS.

Phoenixes bred during the heat of summer, timing their chick hatching to the warmest months. A spring introduction would land close to the start of breeding season, maximizing Rubra's receptiveness to a new aviary mate while allowing time for the pair to bond.

Connor asked Aila on another couple of dates. She declined and deflected, the phoenix preparations a convenient excuse, indecision hanging over her like a guillotine.

But on that morning, nothing in the world could bring her spirits down.

A clear sky blanketed the aviaries, sun turning the glass to crystal. No visitors yet. Just Archie's whooping calls within his forest, fast and deep like Aila's anxious heartbeat as she waited at the loading dock of the phoenix complex. A truck backed to their doorstep. The couriers donned heat-resistant gloves and carried a large metal box inside.

"Right in here!"

Aila's fingers shook as she punched in the code to the back aviary. They'd added a screened partition down the center, separating the quarters in two while the phoenixes acclimated to one another. Aila bounced on her feet as the couriers set the box on the floor.

Her heart shouldn't beat this fast. She made herself pause, breathe. Hard to do, past the smile splitting her cheeks.

Heels clacked the linoleum as Maria Rivera inspected the endeavor. Once the couriers left, she gave Aila a smile and a squeeze on the shoulder before opening the lock on the box, sliding away a metal transport plate to reveal a mesh door.

"Would you like to do the honors?" the director asked.

Happily. And with too many jitters.

Aila opened the door to the crate, a brush of warm air hitting her hand, a scuffle of feet on the padded interior. Not wanting to startle their new resident, Aila backed out of the aviary, then joined Rivera peering through the bars.

A ruby head poked out. Tentative steps drummed the concrete, head cocking in every direction to inspect the new room.

Carmesi, the male phoenix, was a gorgeous bird. Smaller than Rubra (as male phoenixes tended to be), and in contrast to her solid crimson neck and breast feathers, his were scalloped in metallic gold. As he emerged from his carrier, his long tail lifted off the ground, red and gold plumes coated in flame.

Rubra was going to love him.

Though the screen prevented the phoenixes from seeing each other, Rubra perched in her half of the aviary with head tilted, aware of something amiss. She clucked, sharp and inquisitive.

Carmesi pecked his box. A docile temperament, even more than Rubra. Aila met him once during a tour of the Jewelport Zoo a month ago, a whirlwind of protocol demonstrations and interviews with the keepers that left her head spinning. Carmesi had been the highlight of the trip, perched on a keeper's glove without a care in the world, cheeks puffed and eyes dozed as everyone lauded what a pleasant phoenix he was to work with.

Now, he was here. Aila beamed at her old poster on the wall, the curling yellow paper and faded ink of the phoenix print. Eight-year-old Aila would be squealing with delight. Adult Aila was barely more professional.

"You can remove the visual screen while keeping them separated?" Rivera asked.

Aila nodded. The design had been crucial to their inspection.

"Let's give it a try," the director said. "To gauge their receptiveness."

Still in a dream, Aila slid out a panel of the screen, leaving a metal mesh the phoenixes could see through. Rubra hopped to the closest perch, peering into the other aviary. At the sound, Carmesi lifted his crest feathers. Aila returned to a bounce, eager to see how they'd react.

Rubra puffed her breast and let out the most heinous sound Aila had ever heard.

The angry cackle reverberated throughout the aviary, throughout the building. To accompany her vocal onslaught, Rubra raised every single feather, a monstrosity of crimson and flame, looking as large and intimidating as possible as she bobbed on her perch. Carmesi flattened his feathers and skittered back into his crate.

Rivera frowned. Aila showed her shock more openly, mouth agape, hands clutched.

"Oh no," she whispered.

Chapter Nineteen

This was a disaster. An unqualified tragedy. Proof that romance was an overblown sham.

Oh, and also Aila's phoenixes were fighting.

She dropped her phone to the counter, ignoring Connor's latest text message. Like a coward, she'd spent another two weeks avoiding him. At least she had an excuse. For two weeks, every minute of free time had gone toward convincing Rubra to tolerate Carmesi's presence.

Not going well.

Aila slumped with her head in her hands and elbows propped on the counter, staring out the observation window into the phoenix exhibit. She'd tried letting them acclimate in the side-by-side aviaries, but Rubra cackled like a mad bird whenever she could see the intruder. Next, Aila tried setting Carmesi outside in his carrier while Rubra was on exhibit, but Rubra dropped olive branches onto the box until it was hidden from sight. For her last, most aggressive attempt, Aila released both birds out on exhibit at once, monitored to make sure they didn't attack each other.

Rubra perched in one corner of the aviary, feathers puffed. Carmesi crouched on the opposite side, trying to hide in a corner. Whenever he dared move, Rubra chirped in agitation.

"Rubraaaa," Aila moaned, channeling the heartbreak of a parent whose child refused to play well with others. In this case, the fate of a species depended on that stubborn child. She dropped her head to the cold metal countertop, listening to the rhythmic *crunch* and *tap* of Tanya chopping food in the kitchen.

Luciana was late. Again.

As if angst over Connor and uncooperative phoenixes weren't already turning Aila's hair grayer in the bathroom mirror each morning, that griffin show witch insisted on breathing down her neck. *We have another request for an interview, Aila. You need to get these phoenixes comfortable with each other, Aila.* Like the solution was as simple as flailing her arms over a candlelit ritual circle.

Aila had a couple of scented candles at home, birthday gifts from her mother. Cranberry spice. Vanilla latte. Not exactly cult materials.

For the third time that week, Luciana had demanded Aila meet her at the phoenix complex. For the third time that week, she didn't have the decency to show up on time. Some PR specialist. When the door finally opened, Aila swiveled in her chair with a weaponized scowl, prepared to give Luciana a piece of her mind.

Connor stood in the doorway. Aila deflated like a popped balloon.

"Oh. Hello," she squeaked, not unlike their early meetings.

Skies and seas, he was as handsome as ever, especially with that concerned furrow to his brow. The languid curl of hair against his temple. *Focus, Aila. Be strong.*

"Morning, Aila. Do you have a minute?"

In the kitchen, Tanya's chopping came to an abrupt halt. She appeared in the doorway with eyes narrowed and knife brandished. Connor reacted with fitting alarm.

"What do you want, Connor?" Tanya demanded. "We're busy over here."

"Yeah, Aila's told me, very busy with the introduction." He moved to the observation window. "How are the phoenixes?"

The trepidation in his voice snared Aila all over again. Even by her socially diminished standards, she'd been awful to him since their date. And she'd always had a weakness for poor animals with pleading eyes.

"It's all right, Tanya," Aila said. "I've got a minute. At least until Luciana shows up."

Tanya gave her a sympathetic look. Raised her knife. Aila wasn't sure she wanted to know what that meant, but she appreciated the support. She returned to a slump on the counter.

"The phoenixes are awful."

With Tanya back in the kitchen, Connor pulled up a chair. "Still fighting?"

Aila nodded.

"I'm sorry, Aila. I'm sure you're doing everything you can."

"And then some! IMWS, the Jewelport keepers, even Garumano called to give me advice. None of it works." She extended pleading hands to her bickering birds on the other side of the glass. "Rubra's having none of it. And Carmesi is fucking terrified of her."

Connor laughed. "If I was courting someone with a fire tail, I'd be pretty intimidated."

Despite two very shitty weeks, Aila chuckled. What was she doing? She was supposed to be aloof, distant. He wasn't supposed to make her laugh so easy.

"Even worse," she said, "Luciana's insisting I get a new live camera set up." She waggled her hands, imitating Luciana's haughty tone. "*Stop being a stick in the mud, Aila. The live camera is crucial to our publicity. What's the point of having phoenixes if you won't show them off?*"

That was the kinder version of the tirade Aila had to stomach no less than ten times in the past two weeks.

"So what's the problem?" Connor asked. "A live camera sounds like a great idea."

Not him, too. "What are the viewers going to watch, Connor?" She gestured to Rubra puffed on her perch, Carmesi cowering beneath a branch.

"Any phoenix camera is bound to be popular." He smiled, slow and encouraging and far too dangerous for Aila's heart. "And once the pair come around to each other? All the better."

As if Aila hadn't heard that line from Luciana already. That was only half the issue.

"And what about protecting the phoenixes from poachers? IMWS thinks the poachers at Jewelport must have watched the live camera to keep tabs on the birds, waited until the female immolated so they could grab the chicks."

Connor looked away from her, out the window, a scrunch to his mouth. "Maybe. But, Aila, you don't think anyone would try that again? Those thieves probably counted themselves lucky to get away so clean the first time."

Aila wished she could believe that. She wished her recurring nightmare hadn't become waking up to a news broadcast, Rubra missing and her exhibit trashed. No one seemed to agree with her. Luciana wanted the spotlight a camera would bring to the zoo. IMWS supported the idea, hoping to smooth over the bad publicity of the phoenix nabbing.

Now, Connor.

Hard to push back against him. The way he smiled. The way his brow furrowed as Aila shared her concerns. Why hadn't their date gone this smoothly? Maybe that night was a fluke, a misunderstanding. She ought to give him another chance.

"So, Aila," he said. "I know you've been busy, and I don't

want to get in the way. But maybe we could grab lunch some-time? Right here at the zoo, nothing fancy. Just something to give you a moment to breathe?"

Aila's thoughts scrambled for excuses, but none came out. A quiet lunch sounded...nice. Talking to him again sounded nice. Memories of that frustrating evening faded under scrutiny, too hard to remember while he was smiling at her now.

Despite Aila's avoidance, Connor had kept after her for weeks. That ought to count for something? No one had ever pursued Aila before. No one had ever made her feel wanted.

Before she could open her mouth, the door burst open.

Luciana entered with brisk strides, commanding the room in an instant. Eyes like smoky quartz darted over the observation window, the chopping from the kitchen, the counter where Aila and Connor sat too close to one another.

"Oh, hey, Luc," Connor greeted, and skies and seas forbid if the tension in his voice didn't make Aila adore him more. "How are you—"

"Out," Luciana ordered. "We've got important business to discuss."

So important, she'd arrived twenty minutes late. Aila resisted an eye roll.

Connor didn't. He leaned closer to Aila. A brush of his thumb against her hand sent her heart spinning. "Let me know about lunch?"

He left. The glare he shared with Luciana was like two moun-tain ranges colliding, ridges steep as the north Movas Plateau. Aila couldn't decide whether to be intimidated or enamored.

Luciana pulled out her phone, gilded nails clacking the screen. She'd always been the kind of person whose hair stayed curled even during the frizziest rainstorms. Who'd remove her gaudy hoop earrings while drawing blood tests from scarp griffins in their training clinic, then pop the jewelry back in for a stroll to the coffee shop, flanked by her adoring fans.

Aila savored some small victory seeing Luciana's hair pulled into a tight tail, curls limp, oily at the roots. Her gold-dusted eyeshadow was only stunning, not flawless. Her black polo was peppered with barn straw. Dark circles framed her eyes.

Still trying to do too much, running a griffin show and a phoenix PR campaign? Oh, how even the mighty fell. Except this fall could take Aila with her.

"I've gotten two more interview requests," Luciana said, staring at her phone. "The *Chaparral Bulletin*, local. And a bigger request from the Movasi National News."

Aila groaned. She'd taken three years to deliver a keeper talk in front of a crowd without fainting. What did these reporters expect out of her in front of a camera?

"Sounds great. I'm sure you'll do fine on your own."

Luciana looked up, armed with a menacing eyebrow. The woman glared like a cockatrice, like she could turn the world to stone. Maybe that was what Aila needed—to become a statue for the next century, free of interview requests and dating angst. A hundred years from now, when someone invented an antidote to cockatrice glares, she could snap back into existence with no one left to disappoint.

"You want me to handle *all* these interviews?" Luciana said.

"That's what you were hired for, wasn't it?" Miss Fancy Pants PR Director ought to be loving all the attention. She always had.

"I'm here to help," Luciana said. "Not to be the sole face of *your* program."

"*My* program would be better off without me freezing up on camera. Or is that what you're hoping to see?"

In the pit of her mind, Aila heard that honeyed laugh, saw Luciana seated in the back of their outreach classroom while

Aila trembled on the stage. Her hands clenched as the older, angrier version of Luciana glared her down.

"You're the head keeper for this exhibit, you dork. I can only field so many requests on your behalf. The reporters want to hear from *you*. Their audiences want to hear from *you*. At least once." Her nails glistened, an accusing point to the window. "Or did you think you'd get a phoenix transferred here and never have to show it off?"

"In case you hadn't noticed"—Aila waved a less elegant noodle arm toward the exhibit—"there's nothing to show off. Not while our phoenix pair refuse to come within twenty feet of each other. So how about I focus on doing my job and getting these birds acclimated, before the whole program goes up in flames?"

Aila's dreams with it. Her career.

Luciana should have snapped back like an orchid viper, a gorgeous creature armed with fangs and venom. Instead, her fingers went to her temple. She breathed out. For a second, Aila thought she heard that breath hitch. What in the widest skies and seas was this act?

"I'll take care of the interviews." Luciana's words came quick. Crisp. She stuffed her phone back into a pocket. "How about the live camera? Have you made a decision?"

Aila turned to a puddle in her chair. If one more person nagged her about this camera, she'd scream.

"I already told you. We don't need one."

"Don't need one? Or you don't *want* one?"

"How is that any different?"

Luciana's hands clenched and unclenched, claws at her sides. Somehow, that made her less scary. Angry animals, Aila could deal with.

"The zoo wants that camera, Aila." Her voice rose. "IMWS wants that camera. The visitors want that camera."

"I care about the birds. Not them."

"Then get your head out of your ass and stop pretending these are separate issues!"

In the kitchen, the chopping stopped. Tanya spied around the doorframe, shooting mental knives at Luciana's back. A silent look to Aila. For once, Aila didn't take the way out. Her chair spun as she stood.

"The phoenixes are supposed to be our focus. Not some pimped-up production for news cameras and live chats."

Luciana scoffed. "Do you have any idea how much zoo visitation has increased since that male phoenix got transferred? Of course not. You haven't been to a staff meeting in months, holed up here like a cavern eagle."

"What do I care about zoo visitation?" More crowds. More litter. More people tapping on Rubra's glass and flashing photos when she needed to focus on romance. "I care about the phoenixes!"

"It's the same thing, Aila! All the money for your renovations." Luciana swept an arm over the pretty linoleum, the orange walls. "All from zoo admission fees. Those visitors are funding your phoenixes."

Aila balked, eyes on the ground. "Sure. Some of it. Even without that, IMWS would have given us a grant to—"

"Where does IMWS get its funds? Ten percent zoo revenue from the partnership program. Another *seventy* percent donations. And who's donating, Aila? The people who visit a zoo and get inspired by seeing a Silimalo phoenix in person. The people all over the world watching a live camera of a bird sitting on a nest. The Jewelport live cam had the highest revenue generation of any IMWS publicity project in the past five years."

Aila's mouth clamped shut. Of course zoo visitation funded their conservation programs. Maybe she hadn't known the *exact* numbers. Horns and fangs, was it that much?

Not the point. All this fanfare, all this pomp and showboating. Aila couldn't stand it. She couldn't stand that they *needed* it, that she was expected to wave her phoenixes around like theater props to convince people they deserved to keep existing.

"Look," Luciana said, as condescending as if she were addressing a child. "I know you're shit at this, OK? But if you care about those birds, at some point you need to suck up your own pride and start reaching out to people."

Oh, no.

Oh, she did not just say that.

On a less grumpy day? Aila might have cowered. Retreated. Fallen mute into the corner where Luciana always pushed her. Today, she was mad at her phoenixes. Anxious over Connor. Now here came Luciana, the most convenient punching bag.

"Oh," Aila snapped, "and you would know *all about* sucking up your pride and reaching out to people?"

Luciana's pretty nose wrinkled. "What do you mean?"

"Look at me, I'm Miss Perfect Luciana." Aila waggled her unpainted nails, batted imaginary earrings. "Tyrant of the griffin show. Best phoenix publicist in the world even though I've only been at it a few weeks. Doesn't matter, because I'll do everything myself, even if that means I can't be on time for an appointment to save my life!"

Luciana's lips curled into a snarl. "That's not the point. You'll only get better at talking to people if you practice."

Just practice.

Just try harder.

Just be a different person.

As if Aila hadn't heard all that a thousand times. As if she hadn't tried a thousand times to be *normal*. Her heart raced at the mere thought of an audience filled with judging faces. Of words stalling, scratchy, in her throat.

"You think I haven't tried!" Something sharp pricked her eyes, but Aila refused to cry in front of *her*. "I've spent my whole life trying! But not all of us can talk to people like it's nothing. Not all of us are born perfect and successful like you."

Luciana reeled. "I never said I was *perfect*."

"No? You just act like it! Prancing around here as if everything is easy." Aila smacked a hand to her chest. "It isn't easy for me, Luciana. So let me do what I'm good at and focus on the phoenixes."

"You can do both! Just one interview. That's all."

"Why? So you can laugh at me again when I mess up?"

The room went fuzzy—too much blood to Aila's head, too many memories clawing at her stomach. That stage in their outreach classroom. Her legs shaking, words refusing to form. An arc of chairs in front of her, the instructor with a quizzical look behind her clipboard, the other students watching with mortified fascination, not a single one willing to help.

And Luciana. The class star, Luciana, sitting in the back row. How had Aila ever looked up to this woman? Idolized her. How had she thought they might be...?

Aila could have shouted at her. Could have burst into tears.

Except now, standing in the phoenix complex, Luciana's eyes went wide. She paled as if she'd seen a phantom.

"You...remember that?" she whispered.

Aila warred against her tears. One slipped out anyway. She swiped it with the back of a hand.

"Of course I remember! I was terrified, embarrassed, and what did you do? You laughed at me. Was I that funny to you? That pitiful? Have I always been?"

Luciana shook her head. "That's not—"

"And then you had the nerve to come around the next day and abandon me for our group project?"

That snapped some fire back into the witch. "Why would you say that?"

"What? You remember how much fun it was to laugh at my expense, but ditching me as dead weight is bland enough to slip your memory? We were supposed to work together. I was looking forward to it!" Despite everything, that was the truth. How pitiful. "Everyone's favorite, Luciana. Then you ran to the professor to get reassigned. Am I that insufferable to you? Is that what you think of me?"

It shouldn't have mattered. Aila survived college. She landed her dream job. What did it matter, having the approval of someone like Luciana?

"What I think of you?" Luciana snapped. "How about what *you* think of *me*? Since the moment we started working together, you've treated me like some conceited, self-absorbed bitch. Is that all I am to you?"

"You could have given me a chance, rather than abandoning me!"

"I didn't abandon anybody!"

Luciana had tears in her eyes.

Aila did a double take. Those flawless lashes. Those warm brown cheeks. They weren't made for crying. Too haughty, too proud. The tears glinted like a rim of crystal, a sparkle against black eyeliner and golden shadow, a perfect accent, yet perfectly out of place.

"You think I backed out on you?" Even wounded, even trembling, Luciana's voice boomed. "My best friend had just lost her dad. I spent a month with her sobbing her eyes out on my shoulder, watching her hardly eat. I asked to get reassigned to her group so I could look after her. Make sure she finished the assignment so she wouldn't have to drop out. The first in her family to get into college." Luciana sniffed, wiping her eyes with

253

the spite of a woman waging war. "What would her dad have thought if I let her quit when she was so close?"

Aila's words stalled on her tongue.

Her own tears dried, her surprise too numbing. In an instant, a decade of angst-hewn mental pathways bucked their borders, straining beneath this new information.

She'd never thought...

She'd never heard...

"Luciana. I—"

"It's not always about *you*, Aila. Other people have problems, too."

Luciana wiped her eyes one last time. Her breath came deep, the shake gone by the exhale. She didn't look at Aila again. Her boots thudded the linoleum as she swung open the door, a sliver of midday sun swallowing her silhouette as she disappeared outside.

Aila stood rooted. Mouth gaping. Brain processing.

"Well... shit," Tanya offered from the kitchen.

Aila swayed until her desk chair caught her. The slow spin matched the tumbling in her head. Luciana. Proud, perfect Luciana. "Did she just... *cry* in front of us?"

"Sure did," Tanya said.

Tears Aila had seen before, at the griffin barn. Inconceivable. Too human.

"And she said... all that about her friend. I never knew." How could Aila not have known? Luciana's life was always on stage, poised and successful. On the surface. Distracted by her own inadequacies, Aila never bothered wondering what else might lurk underneath.

Should she have?

"Ailes." Tanya clicked her tongue. "Are you still on about that group project years ago? Sometimes, you've got to let little things go. Bad for your blood pressure."

"Did *you* know? When you two were on barn duty together?"

Tanya's eyes dropped to the floor. "No. Luc, she...doesn't talk about herself much, you know? I never pried."

Aila dug hands into her hair. What did it matter? Luciana had laughed at her. Stuck her nose up at her. Treated her like a bug in her path at every opportunity. What difference did it make if the witch had a secret heart buried beneath the make-up and hair gloss?

Except this time, Aila was the one who'd made assumptions, said nasty things. She'd treated Luciana like a plague, fueled by an anger she'd bottled up for years. Part of it, unfounded. Aila had never imagined Luciana might have another reason for abandoning her. Too easy to assume it was Aila's fault. To take things personally.

She couldn't leave things this way.

Aila groaned. "Shit. I have to go apologize, don't I?"

"You're going to do *what*?" Tanya's brow shot up.

Aila stood. "Can you keep an eye on the phoenixes?"

"Well, sure."

"Super. I'll be right back." Assuming she didn't keel over from embarrassment in the process.

Aila plunged out the door, into the glaring sunlight, off to apologize to her mortal enemy. Worst decision she'd ever made? Possibly.

After several weeks of bad decisions, she hoped the only way left to go was up.

Chapter Twenty

For how popular the griffin show ranked among patrons, Aila marveled at how she seemed to visit the amphitheater exclusively under duress.

Even with several hours until the next show, the Renkailan section bustled with visitors. Aila kept to the edge of the paths, giant banyan trees and red teak railings boxing in either side, a flood of sneakers and stroller wheels churning alongside her. Early summer often saw packed crowds, but spring should have been a lull, people occupied with work and school. Instead, group after group crowded past, families and unburdened adults in equal numbers.

Aila had never seen so much phoenix merchandise.

The twirling light-up toys had always been popular in the gift shop, perhaps a ruby fan or two in the hot months. Now, patrons munched phoenix feather cake pops, the fancy cayenne-chocolate kind the zoo usually only busted out for holidays. Children pranced in feathered face paint. T-shirts showcased phoenix prints with stylized feathers, others of cute cartoon versions with sparkling eyes. One toddler stumbled past with a feathered headband, giggling as he pulled a phoenix kite behind him.

All of it rang a bell. Spreadsheets and order forms Luciana had shoved in front of Aila over the past several weeks, a publicity campaign launched in tandem with the phoenix transfer. Aila listened with half an ear. Bickering birds had consumed her attention.

All this excitement for a phoenix? *Her* phoenix? Maybe Luciana did have one teeny, tiny, valid point about Aila keeping her head in the sand.

This apology was going to sting.

The vine-swathed walls of the amphitheater made Aila feel tiny, insignificant, a carbuncle with tails between its legs, come to apologize to a woman she'd sparred with for years. The faster she got this over with, the faster she could go back to watching her two phoenixes want nothing to do with each other.

Behind the amphitheater, a thunderhawk called from the aviaries, the sound leaving static on the air. Aila rounded the empty stage and ducked into the prep area. A lone blue light glowed from a computer screen in the tech room, accompanied by the clatter of keys. Nadia sat at the sound control panel, headphones clamped over her ears.

"Hey, Nadia?" Aila called in.

The woman kept typing, her head bobbing in rhythm to some unheard music.

"*Nadia.*"

She startled. Slipped off her headphones. "Oh, hey, Aila. What's up?"

"I was just...um..." Aila dug the toe of her boot into the floor. "Wondering if Luciana passed through here?"

Nadia frowned. "Haven't seen her since she headed your way. But if she's back..." Her voice dropped, fingers fidgeting on her headphones. "She's been spending a lot of time in the griffin barns. You know."

That explained the hay clinging to Luciana's shirt. Aila thanked Nadia, then skittered back outside. Should have guessed

Luciana would be in the same spot as Aila's last two visits, tending her ailing peacock griffin. Having poor, sweet Nimit to fawn over was bound to lower Aila's guard. She steeled herself as best she could.

She arrived at the griffin barn to find the door cracked open. Aila paused on the threshold and imagined herself tall, fierce, a majestic dragon in meek human clothing. One simple apology for a simple misunderstanding. She could manage that much, even if it seemed a little dumb. After Luciana had laughed at her. After years of snide remarks and condescending scowls. Why did Aila have to be the better person?

Focus. One simple apology. Then she could leave. Maybe a show of civility would bring the ice witch down a peg.

She gritted her teeth and slid open the door. Sunlight slanted through the windows, catching every mote of dust and hay that swirled at Aila's entry. Luciana sat against the wall, legs sprawled over swept concrete, arms clutched across her chest.

The stall was empty.

This had always been Nimit's barn. Aila frowned at the clean floor, no bed of hay piled in the center. No bowl of lettuce or griffin protein cakes. A smell of feathers lingered on the air, fading beneath something clean. Sterile.

From the corner, Luciana sniffed.

"What the fuck do you want now?" she demanded.

"Luciana . . . where's Nimit?"

Aila thought she'd seen the woman angry before, but *now*. Luciana snarled with perfect painted lips, her eyes slitted and raw and rimmed with smeared mascara. "Are you fucking serious? You're so caught up with your special little phoenixes, you can't bother to give a shit about the rest of the zoo?"

"What happened?"

"What do you mean, *what happened*? He was the oldest

peacock griffin the zoo's ever had." Luciana's breath shook, head cradled in her hands. "We lose them all, eventually."

Aila stared at the empty room, a pit sinking deeper in her stomach than she knew there was space to drop. Nimit had been old. Ailing for so long. She'd missed the last staff meeting (or several), but she should have heard . . .

"Luciana," Aila whispered. "Skies and seas, I . . . I'm so sorry."

Luciana laughed, cold and humorless. "Are you? Well, doesn't that make me feel all warm and fuzzy."

"When?" Aila stared at the room, trying to force the empty space to make sense.

"Two weeks ago."

"*Two weeks?* But you've been handling interviews for us. Setting up our whole PR program. Why didn't you say anything?"

Luciana wiped a hand over her tear-glistened cheek, too calm. "Sometimes, staying distracted is a good thing."

Aila imagined how it would feel. Just the thought of losing Rubra, or Archie, or any of the animals who'd become the foundation of her life. Her heart twisted in a nest of barbed wire, tight in her chest, hard to breathe. She'd be a wreck. A sobbing mess on the floor.

Luciana hadn't betrayed any of that. A few late appointments. Some tired circles under her eyes. Though she didn't always show it, she had to have cared deeply about Nimit, yet her mask remained immaculate. All glamor. All confidence.

Just like their group project, Luciana faking a smile while aiding an ailing friend no one knew about. Always bottled up. Always close to the chest. Impossible, sometimes, to know what other people were going through.

"If that's all," Luciana said, flat, "I'd appreciate some time alone."

No sobs. No hiccups. Tears trickled silent down her cheeks, eyes distant, a tired sorrow.

"No. That's not all." Aila sank to her knees, the floor too cold and clean. "Look, Luciana, I...came to say sorry. I shouldn't have said those mean things about you. And I shouldn't have assumed your intentions with that group project. I..." She picked at her nails. "I guess I was just being insecure."

Luciana didn't look at her. "It's fine. That was a long time ago. What does it matter?"

"It does matter. At least to me." Aila rocked on her heels, uncomfortable with the silence. She shifted to stand up. "So. Yeah. There's that. I'll leave you alone to—"

"I'm sorry, too."

The words came meek, Luciana's fingers pressed to her temple. Aila sat back down, wary. "Sorry about what?"

"I remember laughing at you in class."

Oh. Aila clenched her hands. How had a simple apology spiraled out of control?

"I shouldn't have laughed," Luciana continued. "It just came out, before I thought better of it. When I was learning how to fight my nerves in front of a crowd, my teacher told me to laugh. Something quick to break the tension, to make everything feel a little less scary. I had no idea how bad your stage fright was, that I'd make things worse. I'm sorry. I guess I do come off as a bitch a lot of times."

Aila went ramrod-straight as she listened to the most earnest thing Luciana had ever told her. With too many revelations to process all at once, one above all leapt out at her.

"*You* used to be afraid of talking in front of people?"

Luciana scoffed. "Of course. Everyone's afraid at first."

Aila's eyebrows tried to touch the ceiling.

"Don't be ridiculous," Luciana said. "Some people handle social situations better than others, but standing on a stage is scary. What—you think I just popped into the world ready to give presentations?"

Of course not.

Maybe.

Aila didn't know. Seeing Luciana on the griffin show stage, tall and proud and exuding confidence, the idea of her with wobbling legs seemed impossible. Aila swayed until her back hit the wall, an anchor as she attempted to process this new, raw Luciana sitting beside her.

"You should still do the interviews," Aila said. "If you're up to it. You're so much better with people."

"You could be, too."

Aila puffed disgruntled air.

"I'm serious, you loser," Luciana said. "It won't be easy to step outside your comfort zone. Maybe it never will be. You could still learn the basics."

Aila slumped against the barn wall. She'd tried to learn. Maybe she could learn.

"I'm just..." She chewed her lip. "I'm afraid. OK?"

"Afraid of what?"

"Afraid of failing!" Aila threw up her hands. "Failing the zoo. Failing the phoenixes. Failing Tanya, and Connor, and all the people who helped from the griffin show, and..." She swallowed her pride. Today was weird enough already. "And failing *you*. Everyone who's put their time and effort into this."

"And afraid of failing yourself?"

"What?" Aila scrunched her nose. "Well...sure...I guess that, too."

Luciana stared her down.

261

"You know, it's just my childhood dream," Aila said. "The goal I've worked toward my entire professional life. And if I fail, I might never get to try again."

That last part, Aila hadn't confessed to anyone other than Tourmaline. As excellent a listener as the carbuncle was, speaking her darkest fear to another human left her jittery. And the first time came out for Luciana, of all people? Was Aila trying to get laughed at again?

She had no idea how to handle quiet Luciana, pensive Luciana, who for all the world appeared to *listen* to every word. What a weird feeling, being listened to. Aila's words fizzled like bubbles, stable so long as she kept them bottled safe inside her, an explosive mess when they escaped. Most people let the ephemeral thoughts vanish like the timid girl who spoke them, that reclusive creature more eager to slink into a corner than to press a point. Easier, in a way. Fewer judging eyes and ears.

When Aila finished, Luciana tilted her head back. A gorgeous beast, even with tear-streaked mascara.

"Of course you're afraid," Luciana said. "You'd be insane otherwise, all that responsibility. But that doesn't matter now."

Aila clutched her knees to her chest, trying to become small. To vanish and never show this vulnerability again. "Why?"

"Because the phoenix is here, Aila. He's yours. No matter how afraid you are, no matter how many things go wrong, you have to act to make this work. And you will. You'll mess up a few times along the way. But you'll push through it because you have to, because those phoenixes need you. And you'll have people there to help you every step of the way."

Aila unshriveled. A timid caterpillar emerging from its cocoon, not sure how much of it was butterfly, how much remained useless insect goo. In a single afternoon, Luciana had said more nice things to her than in the seven years they'd known each other.

More nice things than most other people had said to Aila.

Shit. That meant Aila was supposed to say something nice back. She waded through her knee-jerk insults, her witch commentary, desperately searching for something more...

"Your friend," Aila said. "Is she OK now?"

Luciana knit her slim, unfairly perfect brows in confusion.

"From college," Aila stammered. "That group project in outreach class. You said you wanted to work with your friend. You said she was having a hard time. Is she OK now?"

"Oh." Luciana spoke soft as phoenix dander. "Yeah. She made it, graduated and all that. Kristina Laro. If you remember."

Aila did. Kristina. They'd never talked, really. Aila hadn't talked to much of anyone, other than Tanya. But they'd had barn cleaning duty together once. Kristina had hardly said a word. Aila blamed her usual social awkwardness, had never thought Kristina might be...

"She's at a zoo in Ziclexia now," Luciana went on. "Which is *really* far away. But she's happy. They've got one of the best reptile conservation programs out there, and she fell in love with the yellow-finned caimans. We still talk. As much as we can, at least."

Luciana picked a nail at her jeans, flicking off bits of hay dust. Aila squinted. It couldn't be. It was literally, physically inconceivable that Luciana, the flawless queen of the San Tamculo griffin show, could ever be...

Self-conscious.

Sad.

Maybe even a little...lonely, talking about a friend on the other side of the world.

"You've got people here to help you, too, you know," Aila said. "If you need to cancel some interviews, shuffle things around. We'll understand. I wish you'd told Tanya and me about Nimit sooner."

Luciana half laughed, half sniffed. "What could you have done?"

"I don't know. Something?" That was a lie. Aila struggled with *normal* people interactions, to say nothing of grief counseling. "We could have gotten some salted tequila shots at the Macbhairan Pub, if nothing else."

Luciana's face shriveled. "That bar near the harbor? How would that...? Wait. The fuck. Is that *your* family?"

Back to shrivel mode. "Well. Yeah. My parents, at least. I didn't follow in the family business. Obviously. I don't even know if it's really a family business. Just them." She coughed, hay dust stuck in her throat. "Have...? uh...Have you been?"

Aila cringed, awaiting the answer. Luciana cut her a dry look.

"That potato salsa makes *zero* sense," Luciana said. "But it's delicious. Probably goes great with tequila, too."

Aila staggered, the camaraderie of potato salsa too much to bear. Of course it was delicious. Spicy and savory and starchy, all the essential taste groups. She could level a whole bowl and a bag of tortilla chips on her own, with or without Tanya's judging looks.

Luciana, though.

How wrong had Aila been about her, harboring a grudge all this time?

"I appreciate you stopping by," Luciana said, a suspicious levity forced into her voice as she wiped away another tear. "Really kind of you, Aila. But I'm sure you're itching to get back to your phoenixes. I'll be OK."

Aila was, indeed, itching to get back to her phoenixes, who were still on their supervised playdate. Tanya could handle it. The birds had hardly looked at each other all morning.

"Are you sure?" Aila asked.

"Of course. Why wouldn't I be?"

"Nimit meant a lot to you." Aila pictured this barn a few

months ago, the peacock griffin's head nuzzled in Luciana's lap. "That's OK, you know. Caring about your animal. You don't have to pretend to be granite all the time."

Luciana's lower lip jutted out, defiant, betrayed by a quiver. "He was pretty wonderful."

"Super popular in the show, too. From what I heard."

"The nicest peacock griffin we ever trained."

It happened in an instant. There sat Luciana, fierce as a basilisk even in her misery, head tall and lips clamped. Then she crumpled. Drew her knees to her chest just as Aila had done, a sob sending the glossy strands of her ponytail cascading over one shoulder.

"Gentle as a mouse griffin," Luciana sobbed. "Thirty years at this zoo, and he never so much as scratched a keeper by accident. Could have put a toddler on his back, and he'd guard it like his own." She sniffed, face buried in her hands. "He was my first training assignment with the show. I was so worried about fucking up, so afraid of making a mistake on the stage. But Nimit was perfect. Like he could sense when I was nervous, and he'd just . . . press his head into my chest . . . and . . ."

The words dissolved as Luciana gave in to tears.

What was Aila supposed to do? She sat petrified, heart lurching in empathy, terrified of saying the wrong thing. She could claim she understood, but she didn't, having yet to lose one of her charges. She could crack a joke, but her jokes were shit, and this didn't seem the place. A hand on the shoulder? Aila wasn't positive she'd escape unscathed.

She opted for silence. A quiet companion to listen to Luciana's memories, to keep them safe and remembered. That was what Aila would want.

In time, Luciana's breathing calmed. She lifted her head, mascara ruined, cheeks puffy. Still gorgeous.

"He was a good griffin." She wiped her smeared make-up with the back of her hand, quick and efficient movements—as if that, too, was practiced routine. "We've been training his replacement for a while. Big talons to fill."

"I'm sure," Aila said.

"You can leave now. Really. I don't know how I can embarrass myself any further."

To the contrary. Aila had never respected her more.

She jumped to her feet and held out her hands. "Come on."

Luciana squinted up at her. "Come on, what?"

"Get up and come with me. We need to help you feel better."

"*We* don't need to do anything—"

Luciana snarled as Aila grabbed her arms and heaved. Aila was smaller. Luciana could have fought back. Despite her protests, she let Aila drag her to her feet.

"I just need some time, Aila."

"Of course you do. But what will help that time go better?"

"Liquor?"

"Fair. But do you know what *else* will help?"

Luciana looked ready to commit murder as Aila dragged her into the afternoon sunlight. She fumed while being led away from the griffin show amphitheater, and for once, the bevy of visitors was a boon—too many witnesses to risk tackling Aila into the bushes. Not until they reached the gift shop did Luciana plant her feet, face chiseled into crystallized outrage.

"What are you doing?" she hissed.

"Stay right here." Aila dove between the shelves.

The place smelled of plastic and fabric dye, salty Movas air from the open windows mixed with sunscreen and the sweet of soda cups balanced in patron hands. Every time Aila visited (not often, given the crowds), the place seemed more sprawling than the last, yet she'd never noticed so much *red* before. Racks of phoenix shirts and hats, shelves of phoenix picture frames and feather umbrellas and snow globes with little motes of ash instead of snow. Candy-coated phoenix eggs that probably tasted mediocre and definitely didn't have an accurate speckling pattern on the shell, but damn if they didn't put a grin on Aila's face.

By a stroke of luck, Luciana was trapped at the door by a little girl with a peacock-feather dress, pulling at her mother's arm.

"Are you the griffin lady?" she said in slurred child words, eyes wide. "Momma, Momma, look! It's the griffin lady!"

The girl hopped up and down as her mother led her over.

Luciana cleared her throat. The smile snapped into place like second nature. "Yes, I am." She leaned down to the child's level. "How are you today, pretty little lady? I love your dress."

Trapped by her own public relations instincts. While Luciana fielded the giggling girl, Aila swooped past the gift shop windows like a thunderhawk on a desert scarp. Regardless of season, the most popular items on display were always the animal plushes. Chubby diamondback dragons with big glass eyes and faux leather wings. Soft krakens that could be worn as hats, their tentacles dangling down to Aila's waist. More phoenixes than usual, fluffy red fabric for the bodies accented with metallic gold tail feathers. Aila might have snagged one of those, too, if she didn't already have a pair at home.

The second most abundant plush at the gift shop? Peacock griffins.

They perched on the shelves with cobalt heads dusted in glitter, rufous wings splayed to a delightful flop, a long train of green and blue tail feathers. A range of sizes as well, all the way from palm-sized companions to fabric behemoths half as big as Aila. She grabbed the largest one and hurried to the register.

A tap of her phone to pay.

A near pass on the commemorative tote bag at checkout, then

Aila saw the new phoenix design printed on the canvas and had to throw that in as well.

"I'm not sure who would win in a race," Luciana said with the patience of a goddess, the little girl hanging rapt on every word. "Plumed dragons are very fast in the air, but merlions are fast in the water. Hard to compare."

"You think?" the girl said. "But what if the merlion had a jetpack?"

"That would change things."

"But what if the plumed dragon *also* had a jetpack?"

"Hmm. In that case." Luciana winked. "My money is on the dragon."

The patrons thanked her and left the gift shop, mother leading the way, daughter bouncing more than ever. Luciana's smile tumbled off. She pressed a hand to her temple.

"All right, Aila. Can we get out of here now? Before anyone else..."

When Luciana turned, Aila stood behind her, obscured by the ginormous griffin plush held up in offering. Honestly, she couldn't see well around the thing. The sudden silence on the other side of Plush Wall gave her a moment of concern. She peeked around a fuzzy wing.

Luciana's mouth hung open. Her eyes glistened, as if teetering on the crest of more tears.

"What in all the skies and seas is *that*?"

The words came clipped as wilting rose branches, thorns at the edges, enough to make Aila second-guess the gesture. The plush sagged in her hands.

"It seemed like something you would like. But also something you wouldn't get for yourself. If you don't want it, though, I could return it—"

Before Aila could retreat, Luciana reached out. Hesitant,

manicured fingers closed around the griffin's torso, as if too tight a grip might ruin it. She spun the toy in a slow circle, inspecting every stitch like a stern school matron. Aila held her breath.

Luciana hugged the plush to her chest, hiding a quivering lip behind fabric.

"Thank you, Aila," she whispered.

What a weird fucking day.

"Don't mention it," Aila said. "Consider it a thank you, after all you've done for the phoenix program." She gestured to the phoenix-heavy gift shop. "It's, um . . . really nice to see." Something she should have seen sooner.

Luciana laughed. "We're not done yet. But I'm glad you like it." The soft tap of her nose to the griffin's head was the single cutest, most normal human thing Aila had ever seen her do.

Both their radios crackled.

"Aila." Tanya's voice came through. "Aila, pick up."

Thank the skies and seas, enough emotional turmoil for one day, time to get back to work. Aila unclipped her radio. "Hey, Tanya. Sorry for the delay. I'm on my way back."

"We've got an emergency. Get back here. *Now!*"

Aila shared a wide-eyed look with Luciana, who'd lowered her griffin plush to a more professional cradle in her arms.

"An emergency?" Aila radioed back. "What kind of emergency? Is everything all right?"

"Just get up here!"

Aila clicked her radio back to her belt in mid-stride, already sprinting out the door.

Chapter Twenty-One

An emergency at the phoenix complex.

Aila raced out of the gift shop, cursing the throngs of patrons clogging the walkways, spurred by frantic thoughts of what could have gone awry. A patron disturbance? Tanya would have called zoo security, zoo medical, a half-dozen people before Aila. An escaped animal? They had protocol for that, code phrases and chains of command. Tanya hadn't said what was wrong, either because they had no protocol for it, or she didn't want it overheard on the radio.

Or both. Aila's two phoenixes were on exhibit together. She'd left Tanya monitoring them, making sure they played nice.

Rubra. Sweet, angsty Rubra. Please, please, please, she couldn't have done this.

Then Aila heard the screeching: two warring phoenix chants. Patrons gathered at the observation window, words obscured in the din, but all ringing of alarm. Aila bypassed them and stormed into the keeper building.

Beyond the observation window, fire flashed.

"Grab a glove!" Tanya ran past, pulling a fireproof glove up to her shoulder. "Those damn birds are fighting!"

"Fighting?" Aila's mouth went dry. "What happened?"

"No idea. First, they were chattering at each other. Then chaos. We've got to get them separated."

Fights among animals weren't unheard of in a zoo. Aila's vanishing ducks pestered the periwinkle prairie geese all the time. The mirror flamingos had a stringent social hierarchy that went through infighting every season. Aila's job was to observe. Plan. Minimize. Keep all her charges healthy and safe.

Especially if those charges had fiery tails that could melt low-grade iron.

Especially if they were supposed to be *bonding* with each other.

Aila grabbed a glove and yanked the stiff material up to her shoulder. Tanya entered the exhibit, Aila close behind. Singed olive leaves coated the ground, the air sharp with smoke.

Fire flashed again as the two phoenixes tumbled to the ground, legs kicking and beaks pecking feathers, tails swirling around them like a molten hurricane. The sight robbed Aila of breath—her two precious birds shrieking in distress. As they came apart, Carmesi retreated to a corner. Rubra cackled from a tree branch, too high for Aila to grab.

"You get Rubra!" she called out.

Tanya approached with caution. At the new threat, Rubra puffed her feathers and hissed, but Tanya distracted her with one hand raised. The gloved hand snuck below the branch and grabbed Rubra's jesses, a pair of light metal cords fastened around each ankle. Rubra squawked and tried to fly off, wings thundering crimson, but Tanya held on to the jesses, gloved arm extended to keep fiery tail feathers at a distance. After a moment of futile flapping, Rubra succumbed and perched on Tanya's glove, panting and puffed, but quiet.

Time for Carmesi.

Aila found him in a corner, a nervous cluck in his throat.

Nowhere to go. That made for a dangerous situation with any animal.

Maybe Aila wasn't thinking clearly. Maybe she'd grown accustomed to Carmesi's docile demeanor, but under such duress, she should have been more cautious. Aila came straight for him, a looming human in a monstrous glove. She grabbed one metal jess on the ground.

Carmesi lunged before she could grab the second.

With one leg controlled, the other lashed out, a talon scraping Aila's cheek. He beat his wings in a bid to escape, a blur of red and gold walloping her arm, flicks of fiery tail feathers whipping past unprotected skin. The heat left her stinging.

Aila froze in panic, unsure whether to let go of the bird or hold on. Phoenixes were dangerous, but docile. She'd never dealt with one thrashing on her glove, an angry chant ringing in her ears. When Carmesi swished his tail at her, she shielded her face behind a raised arm, hissing as fire licked her skin.

A firm grip hit her shoulder.

Another glove grabbed Carmesi's jesses and wrenched them out of Aila's hand. She stumbled backward, arm stinging, eyes wide.

Luciana moved with the force of a tempest, tall and unshaken, gloved hand extended as Carmesi fluttered on her fist. Though the phoenix cried and thrashed, she stood as still as a monolith. Not a quiver. Not a crack in focus as she held that fire-lashing tail out of range.

Aila had no words for her, a woman wreathed in flame, blazing with her own surety.

"Are you OK?" Luciana asked.

Aila nodded, shaky.

"Come inside."

With unfathomable calm, Luciana walked into the keeper room, Carmesi a torrent of red and gold on her glove.

Tanya waited inside, holding Rubra. With another phoenix in sight, the once calm bird puffed her feathers and yanked at her jesses with an angry cackle.

"Put her in the aviary," Luciana ordered. "Make sure the screen is up. Is this counter fireproof?"

While Tanya took Rubra away, Luciana claimed a chair at the observation window and rested her gloved arm on the metal countertop. Carmesi squawked and yanked at his jesses. Luciana sat unmoved, not looking at him.

"What should we do?" Aila asked.

"Shh," Luciana said. "Sit down. Relax."

Aila would have an easier time leaping over the aviary. The distressed cries of her birds scraped like claws inside her head, but Luciana's order offered no room for quarter. Like another nervous animal, Aila sat at her desk. Tanya brought her an ice pack for the burn on her arm, a minor injury.

They sat in silence. Three keepers and a crying bird whose fiery tail raked the metal countertop.

Luciana never flinched. Her posture exuded calm, an unmovable force anchoring the room. Aila wasn't sure how to react to Luciana just *sitting* there. Her brain channels, once a consistent conduit of "fuck this bitch," were turning all cross-wired, short-circuiting with images of dewy lashes and plush griffins and wreaths of flame.

"Why did you become a zookeeper?" Luciana asked, soft as a breeze.

"*Me?*" Aila fought her voice down from a squeak. "Is that important right now?"

"No. Tell me anyway. Using a calm voice."

"Aila" and "calm" were not historically compatible concepts. She tried her best.

"I . . . visited the zoo when as a kid. I saw the phoenixes. I fell in love." Her whole heart, now fluttering on Luciana's glove. Nerves turned her words to a slurry, but Luciana told her to talk, so she *talked*. "They're the most beautiful animals in the world, and we nearly lost them, they were nearly gone *forever*. To be a part of that, to work toward saving something so special..." Aila clutched her hands. Picked at her nails. "That, and...animals are easier than people. It's like they understand me. They never judge me."

Aila didn't know if she'd managed the *calm* part. Or why those last words came out so earnest. Or why her heart clawed into her throat as Luciana listened, watching with dark and intent eyes.

Carmesi yanked at the glove, letting out another angry cackle.

"Why did *you* become a zookeeper?" Aila blurted.

Luciana flashed a surprised brow. Then a grin. "In high school, my guidance counselor had a mouse griffin in the office. Calming aura from the ear tufts, you know, useful for teenagers having emotional crises. It was adorable. I wanted one as a pet."

Aila's high school counselor had a mouse griffin, too. And most therapy offices she'd visited. A staple of the modern psychology field—and also cute pets.

"It was just me and my mom at home," Luciana went on. "She was working two jobs. Said if I wanted a pet, I'd have to learn how to take care of it myself. So I did. I read every handbook, researched diets, saved all my money for the adoption fee. I named him Waffle Cone, and he was the best little mouse griffin in the world. It was amazing watching him grow, thrive. That's when I knew I wanted to go into animal husbandry."

Aila listened to the tale, yet another hidden piece of Luciana, enraptured.

So did Carmesi. As Luciana spoke in her calm cadence, the phoenix stopped squawking. His fluttering turned less frantic.

At last, he perched quiet on her glove, panting. He cocked his head from side to side, finally registering that the world wasn't trying to eat him.

"There you are," Luciana said, soft as a mother's whisper. "Worked it all out of your system?" She poked Carmesi's beak. He gave an indignant cluck, followed by a finger nibble.

Aila's jaw fell toward the floor. "How the fuck did you do that?"

"Keep your voice down," Luciana chided. A semblance of normalcy. "Animals can sense your tension."

Aila knew that. Of course she knew that. This was just a stressful situation, not conducive to recalling minor important details. She forced herself still in her chair.

"Luciana. That was . . . amazing. *How?*"

Luciana brushed a knuckle down Carmesi's breast feathers, cautious movements, judging his reaction. "We handle our show birds a lot more often than you do. Have to stay calm when one gets unruly, help them feel safe again. You think this was a tantrum? Try dealing with a green-plumed dragon when they get grumpy."

Right. Horns and fangs, Aila *knew that*, too. Not something she had personal experience with, but as her brain permitted access once more, she dredged up what she'd read about similar techniques for acclimating animals. So much more . . . *artful* to watch a first-hand demonstration. Luciana eased Carmesi closer to her on the counter, rewarding him with a cheek scratch. He was a changed bird, relaxed and uttering affectionate clucks in his throat.

Now if they could get Rubra to relax the same.

"Do you think . . . ?" No, that was a stupid idea. Aila had read every approved phoenix pairing technique published in the last two decades, and none documented an approach like this.

"What do I think?" Luciana said, soft enough to not disturb Carmesi. And to send Aila's heart for a spin.

She swallowed. For once, let her have a little courage.

"Do you think I could try bringing Rubra back out here?" Aila asked. "Now that Carmesi's calmed down?"

Surprise parted Luciana's lips. Then, the soft curve of a smile. Delicate. Beautiful.

"Can *you* be calm for me, Aila?"

Aila could have been a lot of things for her in that moment, and she wasn't sure how to feel about it. She nodded.

"It's worth a try," Luciana said.

Aila didn't want to. Today had been disastrous enough, all thanks to *her* decision to put the phoenixes out together. What if they fought again? What if one of them got hurt? The weight of possible failures crashed down like an avalanche.

She couldn't let it bury her. Luciana was right. The only way she'd get this breeding program running was to get her ass in gear and keep working, even if everything went awry.

"Whatever she does," Luciana said, "stay calm. Don't feed her your nervous energy."

"Calm" was a relative term. Aila wrangled her nerves as she slipped a glove back on, walked to the aviary, and tapped the code into the lock. Rubra hopped onto her hand without hesitation, as well-mannered as ever.

The moment Rubra saw Carmesi, she puffed like a balloon. Aila tensed.

"Calm," Luciana urged, her voice honey. "Sit down with her."

Aila sat at her desk, phoenix propped as far as possible from any flammable paperwork (not going through *that* again). Rubra clucked and pranced on her glove, staring Carmesi down. Across the room, Luciana sat with perfect poise, unmoved by the phoenix's wrath.

Aila followed her lead. One breath in, another one out. She faced away from Rubra's angry dance, focusing on the pattern of linoleum tile beneath her boots. On the sun-dappled olive leaves beyond the observation window. On the glint of light across Luciana's curls.

A smile lifted Luciana's lips. Such a tiny thing, that curve of maroon pulling a dimple against one cheek, almost too subtle to notice. But Luciana wasn't looking at Carmesi. Or Rubra.

She was looking at Aila.

"Why are you staring at me like that?" Aila demanded.

Luciana's grin vanished. "Like what?"

"All . . . *weird.*"

"I was not."

"You absolutely were!"

"Aila, keep your voice down. For the birds."

Aila scrunched her nose but kept silent. Luciana was the expert.

After several heart-thudding minutes, Rubra's clucks petered out. When at last the phoenix fell silent, she tipped an indignant look around the room. Then to her keeper. Aila forced herself to stay calm, amazed as Rubra's feathers relaxed. Though the bird kept a glare on Carmesi, she settled to a normal perch on Aila's glove.

The room fell quiet. Like magic. Aila didn't dare move, lest the spell shatter.

Luciana was first, a satisfied nod as she stood with Carmesi. "A good start for today. Keep them apart for now. We can try for longer next time."

Her boots clacked linoleum as she returned Carmesi to his aviary. Tanya and Aila locked flabbergasted gazes. Luciana plucked her oversized griffin plush off the counter.

"Thanks again for the griffin," she said. "See you tomorrow. Losers."

She strode out the door.

The latch clacked shut. In the silence, Rubra ruffled her feathers and began to preen, as if she hadn't engaged in mortal conflict that afternoon.

"What was *that*?" Tanya demanded.

"Amazing," was all Aila could whisper.

Chapter Twenty-Two

"You should have seen it! She was incredible!"

Aila spread her arms, nearly knocking her plate of fish and chips off the table. A blue striped umbrella stood overhead, shade against spring mornings growing warmer. The ocean-themed food pavilion was decorated in rope nets and replica fishing traps, concrete inlaid with a colored glass mosaic of a Movasi kelp forest and merlions swimming between the fronds. Beyond the plaza, patrons gathered at a two-story-tall aquarium window, framed in timber like a shipwreck. The exhibit was one of Sam Tamculo's claims to fame, rivaled only by the gargantuan Aquarium of the Middle Sea in the Naelo Archipelago.

A tentacle shot into view. Onlookers shouted in delight as the red-ringed kraken swam past, a blur of suckers and blinking bioluminescence, sloshing cold water (pumped fresh from the San Tamculo Harbor) over the exhibit rim. Several children standing in the yellow splash zone were treated to a deluge that left them soaked and cackling.

Across the table, Connor munched his fries with brow raised, a few extra wisps of dark hair tousled across his temple by the spring breeze. Finally, a date where Aila felt at home. Work boots instead of fancy shoes. Greasy food in checkered paper. Feral pigeons bobbed at her feet, making quick work of the crumbs she dropped for them.

"Incredible, you say?" Connor sounded skeptical. Entirely warranted. Aila herself was still reeling with Luciana-as-a-tolerable-human skepticism.

"Yeah!" She crunched a mouthful of battered fish, sharp with lemon and tartar sauce. "There was fire everywhere! But Luciana waltzed in like it was nothing."

"Sounds harrowing."

"She picked up Carmesi no problem."

"Right."

"And both birds were so calm around her! I knew she was good with animals, but *wow*."

"Glad she was there." Connor's comments came timely. Polite. Not half as enthusiastic as Aila's animated hand-flailing.

Was she talking too much already? They'd barely sat down with their food.

"Oh. Sorry." She shrank. "It's just so exciting. Luciana's been helping all week, more supervised visits for Rubra and Carmesi. I wouldn't call them warm yet, but they're starting to calm down around each other."

A miracle. All thanks to Luciana.

Connor looked doubtful. "I thought the two of you were, like, mortal enemies?"

Tanya had raised the same point, resulting in several spirited conversations and secret pro/con lists on their office whiteboard. That was different. For all Tanya's teasing, she always circled back to praise for Aila "finally getting your shit together like an adult."

Connor's tone rang of disapproval, making Aila deflate like an untied balloon.

"I mean, we *were* mortal enemies. Nemeses. Something like

that." She poked a fry, mouth pinched. "Until last week, when Luciana decided to finally act like a reasonable person." And when Aila realized *she* might be holding some unfair grudges herself. "Who knew?"

"Just be careful, yeah?"

"What do you mean?"

Connor leaned forward with that melting smile, his warm hand blanketing Aila's. "People who change their tune too quickly. Sometimes, it doesn't last. Be careful." He squeezed her fingers. "You've got such a big heart, Aila. Got to take care of it."

Aila's heart pummeled her chest like the waves at the kraken exhibit.

The first in the world, Director Hawthorn loved to boast. He'd floated the idea of a new zoo experience, paid dives for patrons, but plans for protective cages had yet to earn approval from the donor board. Even if he perfected the idea, Aila would be the last to line up. She trembled at the thought of sinking below water, a kraken lurking in the depths.

She settled for a laugh. A blush as she and Connor returned to their lunch. This date was a second chance. Better not screw it up.

"How have things been with you?" she asked.

"Busy. Start of mating season for the green-plumed dragons, so they're a handful, gnawing branches off every tree in sight to build their nests."

Aila nodded. *Yes. Good.* Talking about work kept things easy.

"And Vera?" she asked. "How's she handling the change of weather?"

"Always a little grumpy when days start getting warm again." He winked. "An afternoon with the snow machine cheers her right up."

But on their last date, Connor said he didn't want to talk about work. What was this, then? Had he misspoken before? Was he humoring her now? Aila fidgeted with the edge of the plastic tablecloth, pretending to inspect her fries.

Another *whoosh* of water sounded from the kraken exhibit. Patrons cheered.

"Water must be freezing," she observed. "This early in the season."

Connor shrugged. "Doesn't ruin the novelty, I guess."

Rancid dragon spit, why was this so *hard*? All Aila had to do was speak. Hold a basic conversation with the very attractive man who was very interested in her for some unfathomable reason. A simple lunch at the zoo. That was all this was.

Phoenix fire seemed less scary.

Aila felt her last hopes slipping away as Connor laid his phone on the table—a glass screen, infinitely more interesting than a bumbling date. He frowned and tapped through some blocks of text, a few lines and colors that Aila's uneducated brain vaguely registered as stock trends. It was the only lifeline she had.

"So," she said. "Um...How did you get into stock trading?"

Connor glanced up at her. Down at the screen. Back to her. His frown stayed.

"My dad was into it."

Right. He'd told Aila that, but she'd let the tidbit drift away in the sea foam of a disastrous first date. She waited for him to call her out, to shame her for forgetting something so personal.

Instead, concern pinched Connor's face, as if he worried Aila might imminently fall out of her chair (possible).

"It's just nothing I've ever been into," she blurted. "Stock trading. Not that that's a *bad* thing. Just not *my* thing. People can be into different...things."

She ought to throw herself into the kraken exhibit. Be done with it.

Connor studied her for—even to Aila's stunted understanding—a moment too long. "No. Wasn't my thing, either." He scrolled his phone screen with one finger, not looking at it, the type of idle motion Aila knew too well. "My dad got a kick out of it, but he wasn't any good. Got into...a bit of debt. I offered to help him out." He shrugged. "Guess the hobby stuck. Finally something we can do together."

Aila sat stricken, fry grease and salt coating her fingers, mouth ajar.

She'd never asked...She'd never wondered...She'd just *assumed* stock trading was about the most mind-numbing hobby she could imagine, without ever letting Connor explain. Beneath that perfect smile, there was suddenly something softer, more vulnerable, a completely different side of him she'd never bothered looking for.

Just like with Luciana.

So why didn't Aila feel the same relief? The guilt of it left her sticky. Sour. Even more fidgety than before.

"Aila? Is everything all right?"

She froze as if caught in a crime, a tower of fries assembled on her plate.

"Well, actually." A misjudged poke sent the fry tower tumbling. She cringed. "Luciana is doing a big interview with the Movasi National News soon. I should probably be there."

Excuses. Escapes. The only things Aila was good at.

"Oh." Connor leaned back in his chair. "I didn't think you did interviews?"

"Oh, no. Not me. Skies and seas, no." Aila waved her hands, jittery at the mere thought of cameras and microphones. "But I should be around. For support, you know."

"Of course. In that case..."

He leaned to press a kiss to her cheek. The warmth of his

breath caressed her skin, laced with the pleasant scent of pine.

"Thanks for lunch." His lips teased the edge of hers.

Aila struggled to keep herself on the chair in a single, non-liquid piece. "My pleasure."

"Can we do this again soon?"

"Again? *Soon?*" Panic tightened Aila's throat. She'd spent weeks working up courage for this outing. To say nothing about her busy schedule of phoenix bonding, food ordering, pond cleaning...

"It doesn't have to be a big thing!" Connor said with a crime-worthy blush. "No fancy dinners, if you don't want to. We can keep things small. Easier, for someone like you?"

Aila felt like she'd been drenched with cold kraken water.

Aila, the simple little girl of plastic tablecloths and zoo fries, not nice restaurants. Of silly animal talk, not deep conversations. Don't move too fast, or she might spook.

"Sure," she said. "I'll...let you know?"

Connor's smile cracked her like a rotting egg.

Armed with excuses, she downed the last of her lunch, then fled toward the safety of the phoenix complex.

As she swerved through the flow of midday zoo patrons, her thoughts swarmed, more confused than ever. Clearly, Connor was into her, or he'd have dropped her like a moldy grapefruit by now. Clearly, she was into *him*, her heart fluttering like pixie wren wings in her chest, the warmth of his lips lingering on her cheek.

None of these reassurances calmed her nerves. No matter how hard she tried to enjoy their time together, she still tensed around him. Something still squirmed in her stomach (not in the good way) while she scrambled for the right thing to say. If she could just pull herself together, get out of her own head.

Someone like you. Aila had only ever been "someone like you," not someone who made sense to normal people.

The interview excuse was only a small fib. Luciana had scheduled a monster of an interview for later that afternoon, the biggest news channel to cover the phoenix story yet. That drama remained several hours off. Plenty of time for Aila to hole away in the phoenix complex, safe from the crowds and cameras.

Or so she'd planned.

When she stepped inside the keeper room, she froze.

Unfamiliar boxes lined the counter, an uncharacteristic array of chrome and fancy plastic for a zoo. Inside, Aila spied handles of several...hairbrushes? A box of tiered nail polish. Cans of hairspray and shiny tubes of liquid mascara.

Before the banquet of torture instruments, Luciana stood with a devious grin, fingers laced like a supervillain.

"Welcome, Aila," she said with cold menace.

Aila screamed and ran for the door.

Freedom. So close. Her own sanctuary, tainted. She clawed for the door handle, but a firm arm caught her around the waist and lifted her off the ground.

"Hold on, Ailes," Tanya said. "Where are you running to?"

"Betrayer!" she shouted, feet kicking.

"Now, girlie, just hear us out."

"Villain! Fiend!"

"Horns and fangs," Luciana said. "Is this normal?"

Tanya shrugged. "More or less."

Aila squirmed until Tanya deposited her into a chair, hands pinning her shoulders, the counter of bottles and rainbow pigments spread before her like pretty poisons.

"What in all the skies and seas are you freaking out about?" Luciana brandished a tube of mascara. "This little thing? It won't kill you."

So the witch's ruse of kindness proved false after all, a devious trick to lower Aila's guard. *"You're* doing the interview today. Why do I have to look nice?"

"Well..." Luciana's phoenix-red nails drummed the mascara. Confirmation of Aila's darkest fears.

"You don't have to do the interview," Tanya said in her best Aila-placating tone. "But you're Rubra's keeper, Ailes. Wouldn't it be good to at least show up? Look nice on camera? You know your ma will be beside herself."

"If we can make her look presentable." Luciana inspected a chrome-handled hairbrush that glinted like a dagger.

"You agreed to this?" Aila demanded of Tanya. "You agreed with *her*?"

A decade of friendship. How could Aila have trusted Tanya so long, only to be sold out in her hour of greatest need?

"You've worked for this how long?" Luciana said. "Don't you want to take *some* credit?"

"She makes a good point," Tanya agreed. "Glamor queen or not."

"You're calling *me* a glamor queen?" Luciana gestured to the line-up of beauty products. "Most of these are Tanya's." Then, thoughtful, "Excellent quality, too."

Tanya clicked her tongue. "You know I came late to the game, Luc. Got to make up for lost time, all those years dressing as a boy. So few options for accessories."

As they talked over her, Aila slumped in her chair with putty arms on the rests, pouting. Useless friends. Both of them.

"Every interviewer has asked for you, Aila." Luciana spoke like a prosecutor, Aila pinned to the witness stand. "You're our head phoenix keeper. I can deflect smaller requests, but Movasi National News is the biggest in the country. You need to make a public statement at least once." Her voice dropped to something goading. Something too intimate. "Do it for Rubra?"

Aila hissed at the low blow.

The witch was right. Rubra deserved the best.

"I don't *have* to talk?" Aila clarified. "That's the deal?" If all she had to focus on was not fainting on camera, she might stand a chance.

"If that's what you want." Luciana rolled her eyes. "You don't have to talk. Walk out with me, I introduce you, then all you have to do is stand up straight and not pass out while—"

"Fine. I'll do it."

Sparring with Luciana always required Aila to be on guard. No less so when Luciana's brow lifted, cherry lips wrapped in a surprised *O*.

"What?" Aila demanded.

"You never agree to *anything* that easy."

"Well...maybe...because you actually *asked* this time." Aila crossed her arms, a splintered shield against Luciana's victory smirk. "And you're right, Rubra deserves the best. Just don't make me look ridiculous. *Please?*"

Tanya, the cunning moth, gave her a side hug. "You're in good hands, Ailes."

Aila trusted one of them, at least. As for the other one...

"We'll do our best." Luciana ran slender nails through Aila's hair, making her jump. Snagging on frizz. "Why is your hair so sweaty?"

Aila's cheeks warmed. "Well, probably from—"

"Better question." Tanya pulled up a chair. "How was lunch with Connor?"

"*Connor?*" Luciana's nose wrinkled.

"Don't scrunch your nose," Tanya chided. "That boy's a snack."

"To each their own," Luciana muttered.

Aila had never considered Luciana's taste in men. Or other-wise. The woman was a stunning persimmon mantis, always a flock of boys ogling her during college, never anyone at her side. Logical to assume that was thanks to Luciana biting the head off anyone bold enough to approach. What was her taste, then?

Why did Aila care?

The thought cut off as she was dragged into the kitchen, their new industrial sink large enough for Aila's head to get shoved under the water. She yelped at the cold.

"Stop struggling!" Luciana ordered, holding her below the faucet. "This will be over faster if you sit still!"

Death by drowning, then. Aila hadn't envisioned her demise would smell so pleasant, like mango shampoo.

It smelled like Luciana.

Aila returned to her chair with a towel draping her shoulders, hair in wet auburn clumps. Luciana set to work with a blow dryer. Good luck with that. Aila owned one herself, but could never accomplish more than a frizzed mess. Tanya took the chair beside her and inspected Aila's nails, tutting over colors of polish.

"So, Connor." She brushed on a clear coat with precise strokes. "How was lunch?"

Aila groaned and slumped in her chair, earning her a pinch from Luciana. She straightened beneath the blow-dryer onslaught.

"What are you groaning for?" Tanya said. "You're supposed to come back here all giggles and butterflies."

"Do I *have* to talk about it?" Aila complained.

"Ailes. You made poor Teddy sign a contract. You'd better believe I'll look out for you the same."

"A... contract?" Luciana said.

"The BFF–Boyfriend contract." Tanya tilted Aila's nails to

inspect the coat. "There's a copy on file in the desk somewhere. We each got a notarized version."

"That's one of the most absurd things I've ever heard." Luciana's voice dipped, barely audible over the blow dryer. "Sweet, though."

If only sweet were enough.

"You know how I am," Aila said. "The simplest situation, and I go overthinking everything. I'm a hopeless mess."

"A good boy should make you a *good* mess," Tanya argued.

"It's exhausting, making sure I say the right thing."

"You shouldn't have to *worry* about saying the right thing. You should be able to act yourself."

"Myself hasn't gotten a successful date in twenty-eight years."

Tanya's scowl, Aila expected. The *hmph* from Luciana, she assumed must be frustration over her hair.

Talking about Connor left her shoulders tight, jaw set hard enough to give her a headache. She willed her muscles to relax, begged her thoughts to stop looping over what she could have said differently. None of her efforts made a dent in the anxiety.

Instead, it was the brush of Luciana's fingers through her hair that settled her.

Luciana slid a nail along Aila's scalp to part the strands. Her brush pulled the section taut, then the heat of the blow dryer sank into Aila's skin, air swimming with sweet mango. Haircuts had always seemed a chore, never pampering like this. When the first dried strands fluttered over Aila's cheeks, they seemed too soft to be real.

Before she could think better of it, her eyes drifted closed. She grounded herself with deep breaths, focusing on the solid chair beneath her, the hum of the blow dryer.

A tingle went down her neck each time Luciana's hand brushed her ear.

Tanya made a masterpiece of her nails—red and gold swirling like the flames of a phoenix tail. Luciana finished drying her hair, then pulled out a curling iron. That contraption, Aila had never attempted. Witchcraft as far as she was concerned, an easy path to burn her fingertips off.

Luciana spun it like a magic wand, wrapping Aila's hair into wisps of spider-silk. Just further confirmation of her being a witch—though maybe not entirely devious.

Tanya ordered Aila's eyes closed, then came at her with the eyeliner. Next, a brush of shadow, though when Aila tried to peek at the color, Tanya swatted her. At last, they set down their tools. Aila felt like an animal on exhibit as the pair inspected their work, nodding to each other. Her dread boiled when Tanya handed her a mirror.

Aila had never considered herself a pretty girl. She had neither the time nor skill to tame her hair, so she tied it away in frizzy buns and ponytails. Her hands jittered too much to apply the makeup she admired so much on other women, nor did she have the sharpest sense for colors. She made the mistake of wearing mascara one time in high school. Every kid in her class pointed her out. Who was the quiet girl trying to impress? Who was she trying to *be*?

She never wore make-up again.

That dull, familiar look, Aila was used to. It was safe. How absurd would she seem, wearing anything else?

Just one afternoon. Just one interview. A small price to pay to see Tanya beaming. She steeled herself, then raised the mirror.

Aila blinked in surprise.

No. Not what she'd expected at all.

"You like it?" Tanya asked, bouncing in her chair.

"It's . . ." Aila swallowed. "How is it so *perfect*?"

But of course, Tanya knew her better than anyone. In contrast to her bold colors, Tanya applied Aila's makeup in the subtlest strokes, a tasteful black to accent her lashes, the most devious hint of phoenix red above her eyes.

A red that matched Aila's hair. Gone were the frizzy strands she'd warred with in the mirror that morning, replaced by silky curls. When Aila tilted her head, the coils bounced against her cheeks in a delightful way, springy and soft. She tilted her head again, unable to stop herself.

When she noticed Luciana's smirk, Aila froze, cheeks burning.

"How . . . ? How do I look?" Aila asked.

The smirk fled. Luciana blinked, an uncharacteristic wideness in those smoky eyes.

"It doesn't matter what I think," Luciana dismissed. "Only how *you* feel."

"Well, sure." Aila's cheeks burned hotter. She twirled a finger around a perfect curl. "I know. I was just curious what you thought. Since you do the publicity thing more. You know."

Nothing weird about that. Why was Aila making it weird?

Luciana hesitated. Skies and seas, why was *she* making it weird?

"I . . ." Luciana chewed her lip. "I think you look really nice, Aila."

Aila might have fallen out of her chair, if Tanya hadn't grabbed her into a hug.

"More than nice," Tanya said. "Stunning. *Fierce.*"

"Right. Fierce," Aila mumbled, her cheek smushed against Tanya's shoulder.

Luciana stared at her. Silent. Lip caught in her teeth and lashes veiled in a way that made Aila's blood warm. Trying to gauge the mess they were stepping into?

That had to be it.

"Ready for your interview?" Luciana asked.

"Just make sure to catch me when I pass out," Aila said.
She hoped it was a joke.

Chapter Twenty-Three

Just breathe.

Stand up straight.

Don't fidget. Don't pass out.

Aila wasn't worried. Luciana would handle all the talking, which meant she just had to stand there. Just an interview. Just cameras. Just the biggest news network in the country.

Aila had lost her mind, agreeing to this.

She led the way onto the phoenix exhibit more as habit than confidence, Luciana following. Rubra and Carmesi perched on separate olive trees, not cozy, but no more fights thanks to Luciana's regimen of supervised visits. The past week had been a wake-up call, realizing how much Aila's nerves had bled into her birds. When she relaxed around the two of them, their temperaments mellowed dramatically.

Now, Aila slipped on a fireproof glove, careful not to chip her nail polish. The hair draping her shoulders caught in the high glove edge. Rubra hopped onto her fist without fuss, but once Aila had both jesses in a safe grip, her fidgeting drew a cluck from the phoenix.

Aila stilled, her stomach in knots. Luciana had proposed they bring the birds to the interview. A horrible idea. What if they misbehaved? What if they fought? What if—?

"Calm," Luciana said, soft. Carmesi perched on her glove with head cocked, but otherwise at ease. "For Rubra's sake. Show her there's nothing to be afraid of."

Cameras and people were plenty to be afraid of, but Aila forced the tension from her shoulders. She thought back to warm air on her scalp, Luciana's fingers delicate in her hair.

Rubra's feathers relaxed. She chirped in affection and nibbled the button of Aila's polo. If Rubra believed Aila could do this, she'd give it her best shot.

Just breathe. Just don't trip. Just stand there and smile.

This time, Aila let the PR Director lead the way. Luciana stepped onto the public walkway with a dazzling smile, black hair glossy against her shoulders, Carmesi a jewel of fire and gold on her glove. A crowd of patrons shifted from the observation window, phones raised for pictures of the firebirds up close.

"No flash, please," Luciana said in that dulcet public tone, at once kind and commanding. She paused on the pathway, allowing the visitors a moment to enjoy the animals.

Aila stood at her side, tiny beside such confidence. If she could hold her head half as high as Luciana . . . but with that inspiration, she did stand taller than usual. On her glove, Rubra fluffed her feathers, then preened. The crowd pressed closer for photos, enraptured.

As they should be. Despite her nerves, Aila couldn't help but smile, seeing Rubra's popularity. Her beautiful bird, a star.

Most visiting interviewers had come to the phoenix exhibit, the patio of the keeper complex, all convenient places. Not the Movasi National News. Insisting on the optimal lighting and backdrop, the film crew set up on a sunny swath of path downhill from the building. Olive trees flanked landscaped rocks, opening onto a background of grape arbors and the giant metal phoenix above the exhibit entrance.

When Aila saw the cameras, her legs wobbled.

She walked the final distance as if drifting on air and wallowing in mud at the same time. Her throat tightened, harassed by dry Movasi air and spring pollen. On her glove, Rubra cocked an inquisitive eye. *Breathe, Aila. Relax. Focus.*

"Good afternoon!" A smiling reporter stepped forward to meet them. "Angel Aguirre, they/them, Movasi National News. Thanks so much for having us here today." Their skin was light brown and they were dressed in a maroon button-down with slacks. They wore their dark hair wavy on one side, shaved on the other, displaying phoenix earrings straight out of the gift shop.

"Luciana Reyes. A pleasure to meet you in person, Mx. Aguirre." Luciana shook their hand, balancing a phoenix on the other with remarkable ease. Aila, not trusting herself, hoped a nod would suffice.

"The pleasure's all mine!" The reporter gave Aila a whitened grin. They had some of the smoothest makeup foundation she'd ever seen. "And you must be the legendary phoenix keeper? Aila Macbhairan?"

"I'm..." Aila squeaked. Cleared her throat. "*Legendary?*"

Angel laughed like it was a joke. Luciana joined, so Aila forced herself to mimic. If anything, follow the expert's lead.

The camera crew had a dizzying amount of equipment, from giant lenses on tripods to poles with fuzzy microphones, surrounded by reflective panels and blinding stand-lights (as if the sun wasn't bright enough). One crew member fiddled with the camera. Another untangled a nest of extension cords, and... Oh, great, of course Director Hawthorn was here. He met Aila with a pat on the shoulder.

"Look at these two, some of the zoo's finest! Delighted to have you showcasing our birds today. I know you'll do our institution proud."

Luciana picked up the idle chat with ease, discussing the excellent camera weather, the zoo's phoenix merchandise. Aila contributed a nod at intervals, words fading to a background drone as she watched the crowd behind the cameras. Dozens of eyes. The afternoon sun, the glaring lights, left her skin hot and clammy. She moved in a haze as a cameraman fitted her with a microphone, then led her to stand on an *X* of tape on the ground.

Relax. Breathe. Don't faint. Aila clenched her gloved fist, trying not to shake, certain Rubra would feel every movement.

Luciana stepped onto her own *X* beside her. To all outward appearances? Perfectly relaxed, perfectly loving the spotlight. She held Carmesi on her glove like it was nothing. Meanwhile, Rubra seemed to have tripled in weight, threatening to drag Aila down.

The camera crew assumed their posts. The reporter stood off camera, straightening the microphone on their collar.

"Focus on Rubra," Luciana whispered.

"What?" Aila croaked.

"If you're nervous, focus on Rubra. Think about how much you care about her. How beautiful she is. How excited you are that the world gets to see her."

A sliver of bitterness crept back, listening to how easy Luciana made everything sound. Of course Aila cared about Rubra. Of course she was thrilled to see all these cameras pointed at her bird, these people lining up for a closer look. Had eight-year-old Aila been in that crowd, she'd have pushed herself to the front, wide-eyed in awe.

Eight-year-old Aila would have also crumpled in glee at the knowledge she'd one day hold a real phoenix on her arm. For a moment, Aila lost herself in the black of Rubra's eyes, inspecting the open sky and wind-touched olive trees. She watched the rise and fall of crimson breast feathers, the flicker of flame along her tail.

The reporter stepped into place. Straightened their shirt. Tacked on a smile.

Behind the camera, a man counted down with fingers. *Three. Two. One.*

"Good afternoon! Angel Aguirre, Movasi National News, reporting today from our sunny capital of San Tamculo. Here, a heart-warming story of persistence and compassion, a mission to save the stunning Silimalo phoenix from extinction. On the front lines, our own San Tamculo National Zoo. With me today is Luciana Reyes, Public Relations Director for the phoenix breeding program. And Aila Macbhairan, head phoenix keeper."

Hearing her name sent a shock through Aila's spine. Her. On camera. A microphone scratched her collar, wire hidden beneath her shirt.

Luciana smiled on cue. "We're delighted to have you with us at the zoo today, and to introduce you to our two phoenixes."

Aila nodded. Good. Let Luciana talk. Horns and fangs, how did she pull this off on a regular basis? The woman deserved a medal.

"Beautiful birds, indeed!" Angel said. "And who have you brought with you today?"

"This is Carmesi, our male Silimalo phoenix." Luciana tilted Carmesi on her glove, showcasing his gilded neck feathers to the camera. "And Aila has brought out Rubra, our beautiful female."

Angel nodded. "Now, as I understand it, Rubra has had a home here in San Tamculo for quite a while?"

"That's right. And Aila has worked with her for several years." Luciana dropped a glance to Aila, which she assumed was a cue to smile. Aila did so, careful not to bare her teeth too wide.

"And Carmesi," Angel continued, "transferred from the Jewelport Zoo after the tragic loss of their female phoenix. Can you walk us through the past several months? How San Tamculo has stepped up to lead the phoenix breeding program here in Movas?"

"Absolutely. Our sympathies go out to the Jewelport Zoo. Their keepers have shown such dedication to preserving these phoenixes from extinction, and we're honored to continue their work here at San Tamculo. Carmesi came to our zoo about a month ago, after a thorough evaluation by IMWS inspectors..."

True to her promise, Aila kept her mouth shut. She let Luciana speak. The glamor queen knocked it out of the park. Even Aila found herself enraptured by Luciana's sympathetic tale of phoenixes on the brink, the hours of hard work sacrificed by dedicated keepers, the hope of seeing a new clutch of baby phoenixes in Movas' own capital. The handsome bird on Luciana's hand helped, as eye-catching as she was.

Just how long were these interviews supposed to last? Angel asked question after question, a pleasant chat beneath the burning sun. In all the haste of getting painted like a doll, Aila had neglected sunscreen. As she felt herself burning, her arm lagged beneath Rubra's weight. A light bird, but over time, even a few pounds was exhausting.

"And Aila?"

Aila stiffened at the shock of her name. When she blinked the world back into focus, Angel had turned to her with a pointed look, that dazzling camera smile.

No. That couldn't be. Aila wasn't supposed to talk.

Yet no one else was talking. Something flickered over Luciana's face, unease tinting her picturesque smile. The reporter stared Aila down, expectant.

Horns and fucking fangs.

"Y-yes?" Aila said.

"As head keeper for the phoenix exhibit, how have the pair

been getting along? We've heard some visitors were concerned about a little squabble a week ago?"

"Oh. That." Aila's heart hit like a hammer. Her legs bowed. "I'm sure Luciana could answer just as well."

"Nonsense!" Angel said. "You're the primary caretaker for these birds, aren't you? Please, we're eager to hear your insights!"

Aila's ears buzzed. She stared over the cameras, the lights, the horde of patrons with phones raised. She opened her mouth, but no words came out.

Not again. Please, not again.

Not in front of everyone.

"Well..." she squeaked. "That was...um..."

She couldn't do it. She'd lost her mind, letting Luciana talk her into this. Aila belonged inside, hidden away, not floundering in the spotlight. Everyone was going to see her fail. Everyone was going to—

Beside her, Luciana laughed.

In the back of Aila's mind, she recalled a cackle from the back of a classroom—a slash of sound that cut raw into her chest. This, instead, was light. Playful. A chuckle off painted lips, bright as the sunny afternoon.

"Please, you'll have to excuse us," Luciana said. "We've had several hectic weeks. It's left us all a little frazzled."

Angel joined the laugh. "I can imagine! It sounds like you've all been working non-stop. I'd be plenty frazzled, too."

They looked to Aila again, not with the derision she expected, but empathy. The humming in Aila's ears receded. Her legs wobbled, but she caught them before they gave out.

Laugh, Luciana had said. Just laugh. Make everything less scary.

Aila's chuckle came out dry, but it washed more tension off her shoulders than expected. "Yeah, that must be it."

"You should have seen her preparing for the inspection," Luciana said. "Hardly sleeping, poor thing. Up all night studying flashcards on phoenix biology."

"Is that right?" Angel asked.

Aila nodded.

"As for the phoenixes," Luciana said, seamless. "Yes, there's been some tension, as expected. Nothing out of the ordinary, considering..."

While Luciana spoke, Aila breathed.

For the moment, she'd survived, but she felt no less like a merlion out of water. Luciana spoke with such poise, such passion. Then here came Aila bumbling like a child. What news network wanted to hear that?

They wanted to hear from a phoenix keeper.

Aila buried her attention on Rubra. The phoenix sat prim on her glove, amused by the commotion, but unflustered. She'd spent her life in front of cameras and crowds. So had Aila, for the past three years. Why, then, did they still frighten her? This was her phoenix, her program. The world deserved to know how wonderful both were.

Before she knew it, Aila felt a terrible idea blooming. Insane. Doomed to failure.

"We've made great improvements, too," Aila said. "With introducing the phoenixes to each other."

She'd timed her reply to a break in the conversation, but Luciana still shot startled eyes. *Don't do that.* As if this wasn't scary enough.

Angel perked up. "What sort of improvements?"

"Well." Aila's voice shook. She breathed in. Looked at Rubra. Focused on firm concrete beneath her boots. "Territorial disputes are to be expected. This is, you know...Rubra's home."

Another deep breath. She should have put on sunscreen. Her cheeks were on fire.

"And female phoenixes tend to be more territorial than males." Aila pictured her flashcards. "But in the past week, both phoenixes have grown more at ease with each other. As you can see."

The calm birds were evidence to that point. Hopefully, viewers were more focused on the phoenixes.

Luciana wasn't. Her proud grin sent Aila's heart spiraling.

"You've good reason to be proud of your work," Angel said. "But, Aila, I'm sure our viewers are dying to know—what got you interested in phoenixes to begin with?"

Wait. That wasn't fair. Aila had to answer *more* questions?

"Interested in phoenixes? Why wouldn't I be? They're..."

And then, the words came easier. Aila pictured herself as a little girl, her first time gazing up at the metal phoenix marking the exhibit, her nose pressed to the glass of the window while her classmates chatted about lunch and chased one another around the pavilion.

"When I was a kid," Aila said, "I...I guess I fell in love with the idea of sharing this world with such beautiful creatures. To me, that was always...magic." She looked to Rubra, who stared back with wide, glossy eyes. "To think of living in a world without this beauty, without all this amazing diversity, seems tragic. Dull. There's so much we can do to keep these birds here with us, to make sure people in the future will get to enjoy them, too."

As Aila spoke, the strangest thing happened. Her voice shook less. Her legs firmed beneath her. It felt like jumping into a current and letting it carry her, instead of thrashing the whole way down.

"And what about the rest of the world?" Angel asked. "People eager to see your beautiful phoenixes, but unable to visit San

Tamculo themselves? Do you have any plans for reinstating the live camera program, like at the Jewelport Zoo?"

The mention of that damned camera struck Aila with immediate ire. Familiar arguments flooded her head. Why did they need it? Why couldn't people appreciate the phoenixes without making them a spectacle?

But as she looked over the crowd, Aila saw something different—something in the phoenix shirts and face paint she'd noticed around the zoo in recent days, something bright on the faces of the patrons who'd gathered to see her birds. Amazement. Awe. Appreciation. The same things Aila had felt while watching the Jewelport camera every morning.

Skies and seas, how had she been so stubborn? So caught up in her own misgivings?

"Well, I think that would be...an excellent idea." The moment she said it, excitement coursed through her. "Yes. For sure. We've been discussing our options for a camera, and I think now that the phoenixes are feeling more comfortable, we should move forward."

Angel smiled from ear to ear and faced the main camera. "There you heard it, a Movasi National News exclusive! I'm sure we'll all be eagerly awaiting the camera launch. Ladies, this is all the time we have for today. Thank you for sharing your stunning phoenixes with us."

A few more pleasantries wrapped up the interview. The crowd clapped. A technician unwound Aila from her microphone wires, then she was released back into her native habitat, the quiet of the phoenix complex. When she returned Rubra to the exhibit, the weight off her arm left an ache she'd be feeling for days.

One interview, survived. A horrendous experience, and Aila would rather swim with the kraken than go through that again. But she did it. Weak-legged, anxious Aila did it.

"Your ma is going to be beside herself," Tanya said, pulling her into another rib-crushing hug. "By tomorrow, she'll have a screenshot of that interview printed out and pinned on the fridge. Right next to that picture of you and Tourmaline in matching sweaters."

Aila had no doubt of that.

As afternoon chores wound to a close, Aila plopped into her chair at the observation window to watch Rubra and Carmesi, hoping a little quiet time would stop her fingers from buzzing. The birds perched on separate branches, unfazed by their public excursion, dozing in the warm afternoon. Aila always knew Rubra was a star, but Carmesi tolerated the limelight even better. More used to it, after being at Jewelport.

The door clicked open, too early for Tanya to be back from feeding her aviary.

A few weeks ago, the sight of Luciana striding across the linoleum would have put a pucker on Aila's face. Now, she grinned.

"All done with Movasi National News?"

Luciana sighed like a normal, tired human and pulled up a chair. "All done. For now. With how much Angel was gushing about this story, I'm sure they'll be back for a follow-up."

"Great. You can handle that one on your own."

"Why?"

"I think I'm done with interviews for a few months. Years. Possibly forever."

"But, Aila, you did *great*."

Aila laughed at that. Luciana didn't. "Wait. You're serious?"

"Of course I'm serious." Luciana leaned back in her chair,

arms crossed in that prissy, self-confident way. "You said you weren't even going to speak, then you gave Angel some of their best soundbites."

Aila's cheeks warmed. She studied her hands splayed on the counter. "No way. Everything you said was way more eloquent."

"But yours came from the heart."

"Yeah. I tend to ramble sometimes. Sorry. Hope it didn't come out too nerdy."

"What do you mean?" Luciana's brow arched. "People *love* that."

Aila's thoughts flitted to Connor—his bored expression when she drowned him in tangents. "Not everyone."

"That's ridiculous. It's impressive, how passionate you are about your work. I think you could inspire a lot of people, if you shared even a little bit of it."

Aila had heard a lot more nice things than usual out of Luciana's mouth the past couple of weeks. Didn't make them any easier to process. Especially when so many people's eyes glazed over the moment Aila started ranting about her passions.

"You . . . really think so?"

Aila's heart stilled when Luciana leaned closer. Exploded when their shoulders bumped.

"Stop being such a dork," Luciana said. "I'm proud of you. I've . . . been proud of you for a long time. Impressed by how much you care about your birds." She frowned, as uncomfortable with this sincerity as Aila was. "You were just too obnoxious to admit that to. But since we seem to be turning over a new leaf . . ."

Aila's heart raced faster than it had during the interview. Silence, her usual retreat, felt painful. The moment too real.

"Thank you for pushing me out of my comfort zone." Aila had to admit it at some point. Might as well get it out of the way while they were being mushy.

Luciana chuckled. "Sorry about that. I didn't think it would be such a huge leap."

"Maybe I needed it." Aila tapped her fingers on the counter, uncomfortable looking anywhere else. "And please, teach me how to curl my hair on my own. It feels amazing." The coils still bounced against her cheeks like her own personal clouds.

"Aila..." Luciana's voice came cautious.

Too friendly? Backtrack. Abort. "Sure, I mean, not right now! We're both so busy. But maybe later—"

Luciana clamped a hand on Aila's shoulder. "Aila. *Look!*"

She followed Luciana's pointing finger into the phoenix exhibit. Rubra sat on an olive branch, cheeks puffed.

Carmesi had landed on the branch above her.

He approached with caution, head tilted to watch Rubra's reaction. When she didn't burst into squawks, he took another step, until he perched above her.

Aila didn't breathe. Beside her, Luciana sat equally still.

Carmesi plucked a single olive leaf in his bill. He pondered it a moment, chewing it back and forth with his tongue. Then, in one smooth motion, he rolled off the branch and hung upside down from his feet, tail sprayed into a fiery fan, wings tight at his sides. He clucked, waving the olive leaf in Rubra's face.

Rubra watched, stone-still. Carmesi fluttered his wings, a flash of ruby and tangerine and gold, then back to folded.

"Luciana," Aila whispered, unable to tear her eyes away.

"Aila."

"That's a bonding dance."

"I know."

"It's a *bonding dance*, Luciana."

"*I know.*"

They leaned forward as Carmesi ceased swaying, his leaf held out in offering. Rubra sat unmoved, cheeks puffed to maximum fluff.

She plucked the leaf in her beak. Carmesi relinquished it with a purr.

Aila squealed behind the observation window.

She leapt from her chair, too bubbly to sit still, overflowing like popped champagne. Unable to contain her enthusiasm, she threw herself onto the closest person: Luciana. Aila wrapped her former nemesis into a giggling hug. In her delight, she hardly registered the oddity of Luciana hugging her back, laughing in equal glee.

"We did it!" Aila exclaimed. "*We did it!*"

"We're just getting started," Luciana countered with a smile.

Chapter Twenty-Four

"Well, hi there, neighbors! Don't often see you in this neck of the woods!"

Patricia, the unicorn keeper, was a ray of concentrated Movasi sunshine: charming at a distance, blinding in face-to-face contact. Her light complexion swam with more freckles than duckweed on a summer pond, framed by pixie hair dyed cotton candy pink. A rainbow of woven friendship bracelets cluttered her wrists. Thick work overalls hung over her zoo polo.

Aila and Tanya smiled for their colleague: Aila's a cry for help, Tanya's like this was the greatest day of her life.

"Hey, Patricia," Aila said. "We just wanted to pay a quick visit to—"

"To take a look at our camera set-up! Of course! Been waiting for you all week, since we heard y'all were putting a camera up for the phoenixes! Anything we can do to help out! Zoo friends! Come right this way, I'll give you the full tour!"

Skies and seas. It was as if... every sentence ended in an exclamation mark.

Patricia looped an arm through Aila's, then tugged her down the pathway. *Please, no. Why?* Aila was a defenseless little barnacle, wrenched from her rock face by a wave of unstoppable extrovert energy. Tanya, the enabling doe, followed with a smirk.

The path to the unicorn stables wound past beds of rainbow violets trapped in white picket fences. A cotton candy cart spun sugar in pastel blues and pinks. A mini gift shop showcased unicorn horn hairbands and a quartz carrot dispensary, where patrons could pay to feed the beasts. In the interest of keeping this excursion brief, Aila tried not to wrinkle her nose.

Not that she *hated* unicorns. All magical creatures were valuable.

But horns and fangs, were unicorns overdone. If Aila had a dollar for every unicorn-themed birthday party she didn't get invited to as a kid, she'd have enough to buy one herself.

Thanks to their popularity, the unicorn exhibit hosted one of the few live cameras in the San Tamculo Zoo. With Aila's endorsement of a phoenix camera now broadcast on national television, Director Hawthorn had been at their door the next day, eager to connect them with other zoo resources. A cultural exchange, he'd insisted.

"Oh!" Patricia exclaimed. "Before we look at the camera setup, would y'all like to feed the unicorns? I can walk you to the front of the line!"

Public lines were evil. The *fronts* of public lines were even worse. Aila tried to slink away, but Patricia's arm locked her like one of those strangling rainforest vines. "No, no. That's fine. We wouldn't want to eat up too much of your time."

"What she means to say is, we'd love to!" Tanya added.

How hard would it be to stab a human with a carrot? Aila considered her options as Patricia shoved one of the pale, squiggly vegetables into her hand. The bendy tip didn't offer much potential as an assault weapon.

Quartz carrots were, by the way, one of the lowest nutritional value foods in the world, and why any magical creature had evolved to eat them as a primary food source was an evolutionary mystery. Unicorns were, overall, an evolutionary mystery.

They walked to the corral. Unicorns hailed from the grassy Pennja savannah, but in keeping with the surrounding theme, their enclosure was a prim barnyard lined in more white fencing and heaps of multicolored rose bushes. Two giant, majestic-ass unicorns trotted up to meet them, all majestic white fur with majestic tassels swathing their hooves, majestic quartz horns, majestic manes and tails billowing in puffs of blue and pink that defied gravity . . . majestically.

They scarfed the quartz carrots down in two bites, an unnerving crunch between giant flat teeth. Aila scrunched her nose. Nothing but fancy horses with carrot breath and a propensity for skewering their horns on barn gates.

"Alrighty! Come right this way!"

Patricia led them into the barn behind the exhibit, stalls swathed in scents of cedar and hay bedding. But also something sweet, sugary, out of place. Unicorns couldn't even bother smelling like normal animals.

They crammed into an office that would have been snug for two people, much less three. A computer monitor sat on the desk, displaying a live feed of the unicorn corral. Another monitor was split into panels: a scrolling chat box, an audio monitor, other graphs and readouts Aila didn't recognize.

"This here's our camera feed." Patricia pointed to the screen.

"Sure," Aila squeaked from her corner, half-skewered by a Tanya elbow. "Makes sense."

"Got the camera set up over the corral."

"Right."

"Runs during visitation hours. After that, we loop highlights 24/7. Last week, we got the most adorable footage of Sarsaparilla rolling around in a dust bath! Got dirt all over her coat. Was the cutest thing."

Aila held Patricia's gaze for a long time, assaulted by the expectant grin. "Uh-huh."

"And over here's the live chat box. Monitored by zoo volunteers, of course. Wouldn't want folks saying anything naughty!"

Behind Patricia's back, Aila mouthed an exasperated *fuuuck*. Tanya clapped a hand to her mouth to suppress a giggle. Patricia was sweet. The tour was nice. But Tanya and Aila had already visited the camera at the moss martin exhibit, lens trained on the burrow where the moss-furred weasels curled up to sleep beneath their heat lamp. Another camera at the gilled antelope, underwater, catching the spindly creatures as they walked upside down, browsing algae from the surface of their pond. She'd be better off back at the phoenix complex, where Luciana's tech team was setting up their own camera today. Aila bounced, eager to check the progress.

Huh. Eager? Weird how fast that snuck up on her.

Patricia showed little sign of slowing. "Biggest hurdle's gonna be setting up the right viewing angle. You can see, plenty of area cut off on the sides, even on the wide-angle lens. Gotta make sure you get y'all's animals in frame, or else you'll miss the most important—"

"Hey, Patricia?" came a voice behind them.

Aila swiveled to find Connor in the doorway. No space to enter, so his arms braced either side of the frame, tensed to show the perfect hint of muscle. Not that she would ever stare at something like that. He cut her a grin, then back to the unicorn keeper.

"Connor!" Patricia greeted him with the spunk of a bubble machine. "Need something?"

"Yeah. That bag of apples in the fridge—are they yours?"

"Oh, shoot!" Patricia pressed a hand to her heart. "I got those as treats for the girls, was going to hand them out today. You need the space?"

"Just got a shipment of fish in, was figuring out where to put a couple of extra boxes."

Aila shot him wide eyes. Convenient timing? Or a rescue mission? Skies and seas, give her either one and get her out of this stuffy room.

"Well, gee, I'll take care of it right away!" Patricia gestured to her guests. "I've got to finish a little tour for these ladies, then I'll race over there."

Not a chance. Not with freedom this close.

"Please!" Aila interrupted. "Don't let us hold you up."

"You sure, hun?"

"Absolutely. We've learned so much about your camera already. Truly inspiring."

"You'll let me know if you need any help setting yours up?"

"Oh, for sure." Only if the zoo got attacked by zombies and Patricia was the last person standing. Even then, Aila might be squashed by the enthusiasm.

"Fantastic!" Patricia clapped her hands, a perennial smile on her face. She shuffled out of the room, then hurried off with overalls jingling.

At last, an escape.

Aila raced to freedom outside the barn. She'd spent most of the morning touring the zoo, half-listening to camera lingo, half-dreaming of her two phoenixes cuddled on a branch together, Carmesi handing Rubra token leaves of affection. Luciana's team had griffin shows to run, but would they have started work on the camera yet?

She didn't realize she was bouncing until Connor chuckled behind her. Aila stilled, an embarrassed heat on her cheeks.

She appreciated the rescue. She wasn't sure she was excited to see him—not when she'd yet to recover emotional inertia from their last lunch date.

"Busy schedule?" Connor asked. He avoided eye contact with Tanya as she fixed him with a withering, not-good-enough-for-my-girl scowl.

"Yeah," Aila said. "Thanks for bailing us out."

"No problem. Patricia's a doll, but she does know how to keep talking."

"Sure does." Aila swayed backward, contemplating her retreat.

"But hey!" Connor lit up, that dazzling smile that caught her like a fish hook every time, that curl of hair on his temple like a flashy lure. "I hear congratulations are in order! The phoenixes are getting along?"

"Oh, yeah. We've had them on exhibit together and everything."

"That's fantastic!"

Aila squeaked as Connor wrapped her into a hug and lifted, twirling her boots off the ground. Her stomach knotted tighter.

"See?" Connor released her. "I said you could do it. Always worrying too much."

Aila planted her feet. Chewed her lip. "I wasn't..."

"What?"

"I wasn't worrying too much."

Connor's grin turned bemused. "Of course you were. Remember all that pouting you were doing? But you got through it! Easy."

Easy.

Easy?

The word snapped something in Aila.

"It *wasn't*," she said, firmer.

Too firm, she realized at the flash of Tanya's wide eyes. Aila reeled back but stayed indignant. "We had hurdles, Connor.

Real hurdles worth worrying about, that could have jeopardized the whole phoenix program."

"Oh. Of course. I didn't mean—"

"It took a lot of hard work to get over those hurdles. We still have a ton of hard work ahead. We still need eggs. We still need chicks."

"Right. I wasn't—"

"None of that's going to happen by just throwing up our hands." Aila did, just for dramatic effect. "Now...if you'll excuse us, we need to check on the camera installation. Thanks again for warding off Patricia."

Connor blinked, a stunned look she'd never seen him wear. "Sure. Catch up later?"

"Sure."

Aila marched off, leaving him in the middle of the path, a clatter of cotton candy machines and carrot dispensers in the background.

She wasn't happy about it. Alarmed was a better descriptor. Terrified, even. Stern Aila emerged so rarely from her timid shell, letting go like that in front of a guy she was kind-of dating seemed like self-sabotage. Aila couldn't help it.

Sometimes, Connor could be so...frustrating, the way he insisted she made too big a deal of things. She *did* make too big a deal of things. Sometimes. But not like she could twiddle her thumbs and wait for the worst to blow over—not when her phoenixes were on the line.

Once the path curved away from the unicorn exhibit, Tanya jumped on her like a rabid marmoset. Aila yelped in alarm.

"Look at you, Ailes!" Tanya beamed. "Standing up for yourself. Always knew my girl was fiery, but damn."

Aila slumped. "I guess."

313

"You *guess*? Told that fine boy off something fierce. What a sight."

"You're *glad* I told him off? You're the one who wanted me to talk to him in the first place!"

Tanya waved a hand, flashing sky-blue nails. "I want you with someone who makes you happy, Ailes. If Connor doesn't? Throw that boy wayside."

Aila scrunched her nose. "I'm not sure I'd go *that* far. Maybe I was too mean to him. Maybe I should have . . ."

"Ailes." Amid their swerving path through distracted patrons, the curves of concrete walkways, Tanya's hand clasped Aila's like an anchor in stormy seas. "You know I support you. The *real* you. There's nothing wrong with being a little quiet, a little reserved. But *sometimes*, you get so caught up in your own head, you stop seeing the world around you properly."

Tanya was right. Aila knew she was right. But what was she supposed to see properly, through the anxiety haze? Just how Connor frustrated her more than she'd like?

Or how he made her feel like her interests were silly.

Or how he talked down to her like a child who couldn't be fully trusted in public.

That was how most people treated Aila—nothing exceptional on Connor's part.

Though . . . shouldn't she ask more from someone she might offer her heart to? The chance to share herself without a veil? Aila needed a moment to think. To breathe. Time for the world to slow down so she could deal with Connor in a better headspace. As if that would ever happen, with phoenix breeding season fast approaching.

"Though I've got to wonder the occasion, finally speaking your mind." Tanya squinted down at Aila, tapping her chin. "You have your eye on someone new?"

"*What?*" Aila blurted. "Of course not. What would give you that idea?"

Tanya held her stare.

"Tanya, if there was someone else, you'd be the first person in the *world* I'd tell."

"Sure. Of course."

That level of dripping doubt, even Aila's stunted social radar could detect. What of it? Aila didn't have her eye on anyone else. She'd know if that was the case. No reason at all for her to feel defensive.

Tanya broke away when they reached the phoenix exhibit arbors. "I should get over to the admin building. Good form to show up a little early. You still fine covering my afternoon food rounds?"

Another meeting about the volunteer keeper program. Tanya had a few of those recently, but Aila didn't mind. "Of course, no problem. I'll see you back for closing?"

"You're the best, Ailes." Tanya flicked her ponytail before pushing off into the crowd. "Have fun with the camera! Don't be too mean to Luc, you hear?"

That stipulation depended *significantly* on Luciana, but... yeah. Aila would try.

The crowd of patrons at the phoenix exhibit grew larger every day, swathed in red feather headbands and T-shirts. Aila spotted Rubra and Carmesi through the glass, hopping through an olive tree and offering each other branches to inspect. She shoved aside the knots Connor left in her stomach and hurried inside the keeper complex, eager to get to work.

Inside, a tease of mango hit her nose. The first thing her eyes landed on was glossy curls.

Aila had cultivated such an efficient fight-or-flight response to Luciana, her heart still did a little twirl to see her maybe-former

315

nemesis seated at the metal counter by the observation window. Tame. Knees crossed primly as she tapped away on a laptop. At the desk beside her, Nadia from the griffin show sat at a brand-new computer monitor, headphones resting around her neck, discarded cling wrap and foam packaging scattered around her chair.

"Hey, Aila," Nadia greeted. "Back from your world camera tour?"

"*Finally*. How can I help?"

"Help?"

"With the camera setup?"

Nadia let out a puff of air. "Oh, that? Already done."

"*What?*"

Aila rushed to the desk, dodging landmines of cardboard and discarded user manuals strewn about the floor.

"Aila, please," Nadia said around a wad of chewing gum. "I updated your entire CCTV system in a day. You think I need more time for a single live camera? Those things are a snap to set up."

Beside her, Luciana tilted a brow.

"I know that for professional reasons, *thanks*." Nadia rolled her eyes.

Aila shoved between them, grip tight on the desk, words quick. "But what do you mean done? Like *done*, done? Did you run into any problems? Is everything working OK? Skies and seas, is it live yet? Are the birds behaving? Did you make sure to get them in the frame and—"

"*Aila.*"

Who was that, who'd just spoken Aila's name so soft? It couldn't be...

Luciana's grin curved perfect crimson lips, some scrunch to her eyes Aila wasn't used to seeing. A weapon of some kind, surely. Preparing to deliver a slicing remark. Aila braced for the inevitable ridicule over her childish behavior.

"Take a look." Luciana slid her laptop over.

Wary, Aila took it.

One glance, then she practically pressed her nose to the screen. The webpage interface had been updated since the Jewelport camera: a sleek black frame with the San Tamculo peacock griffin logo at the top. Center stage, a video of familiar olive trees, Rubra and Carmesi in the frame as they chased each other through the branches.

Aila inhaled a long breath, ready to scream.

"I got some inspiration from a friend in Ziclexia," Luciana said. "Kristina? From college? We caught up last weekend. She told me all about this layout they use for the yellow-finned caiman cam at their zoo, sent me the web template." She smirked, a slow curl of crimson lips. "She says hello, by the way. And all her best wishes for the phoenixes."

Yeah. Aila remembered. A friend from college, the one Luciana had worked so hard to support, who'd gone on to a kick-ass reptile conservation program in Ziclexia. Aila couldn't believe any friend of Luciana's remembered *her*. She couldn't believe the gorgeous new webpage. While she gawked at the screen, Rubra hopped out of frame.

The camera shifted to track her.

"*It moves?*" Aila exclaimed in half words, half squeaks.

"Oh, yeah." Nadia leaned back in her chair, feet propped on the desk. "Updated a few things since that old unicorn camera got set up—higher resolution and basic motion tracking. Welcome to the modern age."

Aila fumbled to take it all in. The monitor by Nadia displayed a similar screen to what she'd seen in the unicorn barn, though sleeker: a video feed from the camera, an audio monitor bouncing with playful phoenix clucks. Luciana's laptop showed a separate web page, the public interface for viewing the camera. Live for less than half an hour. Few people had trickled into the viewer tally, but already, the chat box moved as a steady scroll.

Look at them go!

So glad to see them getting along.

Loved watching the Jewelport cam, so happy this one is finally up!

Omg, did one just grab a leaf?

The talk went on and on, viewers growing by the second. Questions about the breeding program. Gushing over the birds. Greetings from Movas, Renkaila, Silimalo, Vjar. Every line, bursting with enthusiasm and support, festooned with smiley faces and little phoenix emojis.

All for Rubra and Carmesi.

All for Aila's birds.

"Well? What do you think?" Luciana leaned her elbows on the counter, that strange eagerness scrunching her eyes as she awaited Aila's reply.

Aila broke the silence with a heinous sniff.

"It's all right, I guess," she said, wiping the tears off her cheeks.

Nadia walked Aila through the camera program and settings. Luciana regaled her with the branding, the contact info for the chat moderators, then several distressingly kind words.

"This is a huge step forward for the program," Luciana said in those honeyed tones that, for once, came out sweet. "You won't regret this, Aila."

Aila didn't. The phoenix transfer became real the day Carmesi arrived. Yet this was the moment, watching her two birds on the camera feed, Aila finally felt the ashes stirring, her childhood program rekindling. All they needed now were eggs.

Once the griffin keepers left for their afternoon show, Aila barely tore herself away from the camera long enough to speed through her own chores. Then she was back with eyes glued to the screen, mesmerized to see *her* phoenixes preening on the feed, their names scrolling through the chat box.

She barely noticed the click of the door when Tanya returned. The heavy scrape of boots on linoleum finally broke her reverie.

"Tanya! The camera's up! Come look, it's *amazing*!"

"Oh, that's nice, Ailes."

Tanya didn't race over to admire the camera feed. She moved to her desk, a rustle of papers filling the room.

"Come on, Tanya. You've got to look!"

"I'm sure it's fabulous, Aila."

"It's even got motion tracking!"

"That's wonderful news." Tanya crossed the room toward the kitchen. "I'll come look in a second. I just need to..." She stopped in the kitchen doorway. Stared. "Aila. Did you feed my afternoon rounds?"

Had she...?

Shit.

The food bowls for Tanya's aviaries sat on the kitchen counter, forgotten in Aila's haste.

"Tanya," she peeped. "I'm sorry. I'm so, so sorry! The camera set-up took longer than expected, and you know how I can get distracted, and I got a little carried away, I guess, and I didn't mean to forget, but the camera's amazing and you should come..."

Tanya slumped against the doorframe, head in her hands, slim braids tangled around the blue of her nails. The sight sobered Aila like a pail of kelpie water to the face.

"Tanya," she asked with the might of a mouse. "How did your meeting for the volunteer program go?"

"Not great, Aila."

"What happened?"

"We didn't get the grant we applied for. Can still ask for funds during the next donor meeting. I need to work on my proposal tonight, make sure everything's airtight. Would have been nice to close up on time."

Tanya's distress drilled into Aila's ribcage, leaving a squirm of mealworms where her heart ought to be. Tanya, the majestic giraffe, her eyes dull and shoulders caved forward. The sight was unfathomable. Impermissible. How could this have happened?

"Why do you need money for a volunteer program?" Aila asked, because she couldn't think of anything else.

"For training. For uniforms. Updates to the computer system. Takes a lot of work to start something new. You know that, Ailes."

Of course Aila knew that. She'd been mired in that mud for months. "It will be OK, Tanya. You have time to get this sorted out. We've been so busy with the phoenix program."

"We have. I've given you *a lot* of time."

Aila shrank at the clip in Tanya's tone, the bite of that accusation. They'd renovated this building together. Filed the paperwork together. Applied for the camera together. Her desk chair squeaked, spurred by an anxious swivel.

Tanya softened. "And I *chose* to give that time. I wanted to. But the phoenix program is your project, Ailes."

"It's *our* project."

"It's *yours*. Those are your birds, your dream. This volunteer program is something of mine. It's important to me."

Aila's nose scrunched to a painful caricature. "Then why have you hardly said anything about it?"

"I *have*, Aila. I've been in meetings for months. But you've been so focused on the phoenixes, you hardly notice anything else."

Tanya didn't raise her voice. She didn't have to. The keen edge on her words was enough, that wispy little warble on a couple syllables that only meant one thing.

Aila had disappointed her.

Aila's ears rang. Not Tanya. She couldn't fight like this with Tanya.

"I can help," she pleaded. "I could...write something. For your proposal? I'm good at reports now!"

"I don't need you to do this *for* me." Tanya's words cut between the clack of metal food bowls, a pile of pellets and defrosted fish chunks in her arms. "I just need some time of my own to get this done. And I need to get this food out before closing."

"I can—"

"It's fine, Aila. I'll take care of it."

Tanya swept out the door like a gale, leaving Aila a crumpled leaf in her wake.

Chapter Twenty-Five

Aila didn't see Tanya again before the zoo closed.

By the time she locked up her side of the World of Birds aviary and moved Maisie into her back tank for the night, Aila returned to the phoenix complex to find Tanya's bag gone. Several folders of paperwork had vanished from her desk.

Rubra and Carmesi had already settled into their back aviary, snuggled together beneath the space heater, two puffs of crimson feathers bathed in rosy light. Aila slid closed the gate to the exhibit, checked all the locks, grabbed the old food bowls and carried them to the kitchen.

There, she found Tanya's peace offering: the sink piled high with dirty dishes.

Aila set to work, paying her penance in suds and scalding water, in mirror flamingo krill mush and stubborn clumps of food pellets crusted to the bottom of the bowls. A simple apology. In the morning, Tanya would arrive to spotless dishes and a spotless kitchen. She'd thank Aila for cleaning up, forgive her for their little spat, then they'd go about their day like everything was fine.

Everything didn't feel fine. Aila had let Tanya down. Today, and for the past few months, not giving the support her friend deserved for her volunteer program.

Once the sink was empty, floor swept, counter cleared of every scrap of leftover kale, Aila and her pruned fingers returned to her desk. She pushed her chair into a slow swivel, taking in the quiet of the room, the hum of the fridge and new electronics.

She faced her phoenix poster. The crinkled edges looked extra yellow in the drift of fluorescent light from the kitchen. Not twenty feet away, Aila's phoenixes slumbered in their aviary, a dream finally being realized.

None of this would have been possible without a battalion of griffin show keepers pitching in to bring the building up to snuff. Without Connor helping to wrangle the linoleum flooring into place. Without Nadia rewiring their computers. Without Luciana calling out the marching orders and singing sweet words to the news cameras.

But Aila *especially* wouldn't be here without Tanya, her untiring work and ceaseless emotional support.

Just that afternoon, Tanya had warned Aila not to get so caught up in her anxiety, she stopped seeing the world around her properly. Yet that was exactly what she'd done with Connor, refusing to heed how small and unsettled he made her feel. With Luciana, failing to see what positive things she could bring to the phoenix program.

Now, with Tanya, blind to how much her best friend was struggling.

It seemed unfair. The moment Aila clawed a step forward, she slipped back again. She thought about going home, hiding like she always did, waiting for a new day when Tanya would return to her chipper self, then they could pretend this never happened.

Tanya deserved better than that.

She deserved better than Aila, honestly. But if Aila was all

Aila had to offer, she'd better find the best version of Aila to put forward. Made more palatable with chocolate, at least.

To the grocery store, then.

Aila locked up the building and departed the zoo. She took the eastbound train, hopped off, then swept through a supermarket like a scavenging kelpie, emerging like a coat rack loaded with overfull canvas tote bags. Then back on to the train. Into the suburbs.

Tanya lived in a quieter part of the city than Aila, shorter buildings and wider lots on twisting cul-de-sacs, crickets buzzing beneath the streetlamps. Aila—whose eyes had been perhaps too large for her spindly arms—wobbled herself and her heavy bags up the concrete walkway, past Teddy's latest attempts at water-wise landscaping (mostly gravel and some succulents), onto the porch hung with yellow string lights. She knocked on the door.

Theodore answered it.

He stood on the threshold in flannel pajama bottoms and a faded T-shirt printed with some movie Aila half-remembered marathoning with Tanya a few years back. As Teddy appraised the visitor—her heavy breathing, the canvas bags steadily dragging her toward the ground—his brow twitched upward.

"Oh, OK," he said mildly. "Unexpected. But we can work with this."

"Hi, Teddy," Aila panted. "Has Tanya told you what happened?"

"I got the highlights."

"Good. If you're caught up, we can get straight to—"

Before Aila could step inside, Teddy planted himself in the doorway, barring entry.

"What are you going to say?" he asked.

Aila blinked. Readjusted the bag handle on her wrist to avoid cutting off circulation. "Um...I was...gonna go for something from the heart? Whatever comes to my brain?"

Teddy's brow rose higher.

"Shit. You're right," Aila groaned. "That's a horrible idea. I'm a horrible idea. I had the whole train ride here, and I didn't even—"

"Practice on me."

"What?"

Teddy stood at full height, arms crossed in what could only be—comically—his Tanya impression. "Practice what you're going to say."

Why not? Aila sucked in a deep breath.

"Tanya, I was an idiot, and so dumb, and careless, and I didn't think about your feelings at all, which is ridiculous, because I care a lot about your feelings, and they're good feelings, possibly the best feelings, but then I went and ignored you, but I did do the dishes like you wanted, but that didn't seem enough, so..."

Aila paused to breathe. Teddy's brows stretched toward his hairline, forcing his glasses to slip down his nose.

"Can we pare that down a bit?" he suggested. "Add some punctuation, maybe?"

Definitely. Good advice. "Tanya. You magnificent tropical merhorse. Your volunteer program is amazing. And you're amazing. And anyone who thinks otherwise is flamingo poo."

"Closer. Can you make it less weird?"

Aila's nose scrunched. "I don't...I'm not..." She slumped. "I'm sorry, Tanya."

Teddy snapped his fingers. "That's the one. Lead with that."

He stepped aside.

The place was homier than Aila's apartment, more decorative pillows on the couch, more photo frames of Tanya and Teddy sharing ice cream at the San Tamculo Pier, hiking the mountains behind the city, dressed in sunhats for a vacation to a sandy beach in the Naelo Archipelago. Warm light glowed from a terrarium, a small palm dragon curled asleep like the world's cutest pine cone. Aila tiptoed past, down the hallway.

She found Tanya in her office, the room dark, desk lit by the computer screen and a little lamp with a base shaped like a kraken tentacle. Whatever movie posters Tanya hung at the zoo were ones she didn't mind getting flecked with food or phoenix embers. Here were her framed and signed editions, her prop replica monster masks lined up in glass cases.

"Ailes?" Tanya straightened at her desk, eyes wide, concern slipping quick into her syllables. "Is something wrong? I put my phone on silent, just to get some work done." She flashed the screen on, searching for emergency messages. "I didn't think—"

Aila dropped her bags to the floor and dove into a hug. The action sent them both spinning in Tanya's chair, Aila's elbow banging against the desk, but she held on tight.

"I'm sorry, Tanya."

A long moment stretched. Over Tanya's shoulder, Aila spied Teddy in the doorway, making a *"more"* gesture with his hand.

"I'm sorry I flaked on you today," Aila said. "But more than that. I'm sorry I haven't been supporting you enough. You were right, I've been so wrapped up in the phoenixes, I hardly paid attention when you talked about your volunteer program. I didn't ask how you were doing."

"Oh, Ailes. You came all the way here to say that?" Tanya patted her back, then urged her gently into a seat on the desk, disentangling their hug. "Thank you. There's no hard feelings, though. Those phoenixes mean the world to you. They're your dream."

"Sure. But that was eight-year-old Aila's dream. Eight-year-old Aila was also convinced cherry markers would taste good, if I tried hard enough."

Tanya pursed her lips. "Hmm..."

"*And* eight-year-old Aila didn't know how hard running a phoenix program would be. She didn't know she'd have an incredible friend to help her get here. I wouldn't trade you for the world, Tanya. I wouldn't even trade you for..." Aila's nose scrunched. "OK, I was going to say the phoenixes, but maybe that's not true. You're all tied for first. But that's a high bar!"

"Ailes..." Tanya's voice made a strange sound, her eyes pinched at the edges. "Now that's sweet of you to say, but you don't have to."

"It's *true*. I wouldn't have made it this far without you, Tanya. I want the phoenix program to succeed, sure. I really, really do want that to happen. But I want the rest of the zoo to succeed, too. I want *you* to succeed. I can't pitch the volunteer program for you. But I can proofread your proposal. I can sit here and let you practice your presentation. I'll be here all night if you need me, and to keep us going..."

Aila dug into her shopping bags, piling the items into a heap on Tanya's desk.

"I brought everything we need. Chocolate bonbons. Potato chips. Hot puffs. Kettle corn. Those little strawberry candies you like with the chewy centers. You can do this. *We* can do this." Aila faced Tanya with head tall, fists full of junk food. "Where do we start?"

For a moment, the light from the computer screen made Tanya's eyes seem to glisten.

"Let's start with those bonbons," she said. "And tell me what you think of this proposal so far."

Chapter Twenty-Six

"Just...a...little...more..."

Aila braced her boots against damp soil and heaved a wrench until the bolt refused to budge. She stepped back and swiped a hand across her brow, slicked with sweat in the humid aviary air.

"Well? What do you think?"

Archie perched on a branch above her, cobalt crest raised. He fluttered down to inspect her work: a shiny metal mobile of spinning mirrors and chimes, *bolted* to a platform alongside one of the observation decks. No errant pieces this time. For all the effort she'd dedicated to her phoenixes, she couldn't neglect the rest of her animals.

Archie landed on a rotating metal arm and pushed himself into a twirl, honking in glee. Next, he chomped a dangling metal rod and tried to abscond. The fixture didn't budge. He settled for pecking his reflection in a mirror.

The aviary came to life around them. The screaming mynas hopped down next, trading toddler-like squeals as they jingled the metal chimes. The periwinkle prairie geese watched from the path, their lavender aroma swelling the air with a relaxing aura. Even a timid cinnamon bird popped out to peck at a mirror. He wore fresh curls of bark stuffed into his tail, a successful bid at romance (Aila discovered the season's first nest in a cinnamon tree that morning).

Her favorite season. And this year, something even more special to look forward to.

Aila swung her legs over the edge of the observation deck and pulled up the phoenix live cam on her phone. The video focused on the wooden nest platform, where Rubra and Carmesi had spent the past weeks collecting sticks and squabbling over how to arrange them just right. In most cases, Rubra seemed to get her way.

Every summer, instinct drove Rubra to construct a nest on her own. She'd roost in it for a few days, but of course, no eggs.

This year, IMWS was in Aila's email every day, asking for updates (oh, how the tables turned). *Any eggs yet? How about now?* Nothing was a given until the clutch appeared, and despite how well everything seemed to be going, Aila didn't dare jinx herself.

As a distraction from existential dread, she scrolled the video chat.

Viewership skyrocketed when the nest appeared—so much so, the zoo had to add more volunteer moderators to the chat. A raging success, Director Hawthorn had raved at the last staff meeting (which Aila forced herself to attend), all thanks to the news interviews extolling the phoenix program, a snowballing campaign on Griffingram.

In other words, all thanks to Luciana. If not for her, the camera wouldn't be half as successful. It might not exist at all, nor the flood of donations it had already brought in for the phoenixes. A few months ago, Aila would have chewed her own arm off rather than admit it, but this publicity thing wasn't all bad. She'd even started taking notes on Luciana. *Professional* notes, about professional things like public speaking and not yelling at patrons and how to smile even when people asked stupid questions. Speaking of which...

Aila checked the time. With her chores finished for the morning and Archie spinning on his new toy, she decided to do something horrendous.

She headed to a griffin show of her own free will.

One night of supporting Tanya and her volunteer program wasn't enough. Getting back to staff meetings wasn't enough. Aila wanted to do better, *be* better than the cloistered little fern lizard she'd always been, even if that meant stepping outside the safety of her aviaries.

Summer came fast in Movas. In the hills beyond the city, grasses greened by fleeting winter rains faded toward desiccated gold. Zoo visitors swarmed shaded paths beneath the tall conifers of the Vjari section, the lush Fenese bamboo, the thick Renkailan banyan trees. Misters lined major intersections and eating areas, supplemented by large overhead fans and handheld contraptions clutched by patrons. Among them, Aila was delighted to see a large proportion of red and gold phoenix designs.

As she approached the griffin show amphitheater, a recorded announcement came over the loudspeakers.

"Good afternoon, ladies and gentlemen! Please find your seats. The world-famous San Tamculo Zoo griffin show is about to begin!"

At the entry gate, a keeper had to turn several groups away: no more room in the stadium. While the patrons grumbled and dispersed, the keeper—Aila recalled him flecked with fire-resistant orange phoenix paint during the renovations—waved to her.

It was strange, having colleagues greet her with smiles, rather than the wide eyes of a rare animal sighting. She kind of liked it.

"Hey, Aila! Don't see you here often. If you want to slip in, I can find you a seat?"

"Nah. This is fine." Aila joined him at the railing, standing room only, but a clear view of the stage, the wide swath of lawn, the tiers of stadium seats packed to capacity. More visitors to the zoo meant more visitors to the griffin show.

Drum music picked up from the speakers. The crowd murmured, then on cue, the flock of mirror flamingos flew out in their choreographed swoop around the amphitheater, colored spotlights glinting off reflective feathers like disco balls. Patrons swiveled to line up photos. As the last flamingo glided out of sight, a laugh sounded from the crowd as a Vjari auk waddled out a trapdoor near the stage, flapping flightless flippers as it ran across the lawn.

The two-headed falcon, Aila didn't see often, an oddity of the lowland Ziclexian rainforest. It appeared while most attention followed the auk, a dart of dark pointed wings to perch upon a pole near the first row of seats. One head trilled to one half of the crowd. The second head chirped to the opposite half.

As the falcon took off toward the backstage area, heavier wings beat the air. Stratus, the young thunderhawk, swooped over the crowd on his ten-foot wingspan, rustling a couple of hats before ascending to a minaret. From his perch, he let out a shriek that laced the air with ozone, spinning sparks along his crest feathers, summoning a bolt of lightning that turned every light on stage blue.

When the crowd applauded, Aila joined. Still the gaudiest production she'd ever seen, but she had to admit, watching all the birds perform their routines was *kind of* cool. She imagined the structured chaos backstage, Nadia and the technicians in the AV booth rolling out every light and sound change, keepers shuffling animals for their stage calls.

Lights dipped to the stage. As the music dimmed, the crowd settled as if in preparation for a storm. They weren't wrong.

331

"Welcome, everyone, to the San Tamculo Zoo!" Luciana strode onto the stage with arms raised to the crowd, black hair cascading over her shoulders as her microphoned voice soared through the amphitheater. "I'm Luciana, your host today for our incredible, our awe-inspiring, our one-of-a-kind griffin show!"

Aila had half-watched the griffin show several times, never noting much beyond the cheap tricks meant to lure the audience into a sense of adventure. Plenty of cheesy jokes and surprising animal appearances, no performance lingering too long to strain the short attention span of the average visitor.

But the closer Aila watched, the more she was surprised to see. Buried beneath the showmanship, the green-plumed dragon leapt from post to post around the amphitheater just as it would the tree trunks of its native jungle, burrowing into cubby holes with hidden plastic snakes. The thunderhawk returned for a prolonged performance, hovering along the wall of the stadium as if navigating a Movasi rock scarp. Even the vanishing ducks, with their ridiculous obstacle course, chased after fish in swimming pools. Little tidbits of biology wrapped in the shell of performance.

Through it all came Luciana's infectious enthusiasm, pairing witty attention-grabbers with trivia about each animal's life history and conservation, how zoo guests could help protect these disappearing species through donations and activism in their everyday lives. Check your pillow tags for sustainable goose down. Insist on alternatives to dragon-scale counters during your next kitchen remodel. Never support pet shops selling hatchling cockatrices.

At some point, Aila stopped paying attention to the animals. She leaned on the railing, studying Luciana's every movement and intonation like a masterclass. Enthralled by her smile.

Wings rumbled the air, the heaviest yet.

"And now," Luciana announced amid a shroud of green and pink spotlights. "The star of our show. The resplendent mascot of the San Tamculo Zoo. Our peacock griffin!"

Ranbir, the young peacock griffin, owned the audience the instant he soared into the amphitheater, his tail splayed behind him in an explosion of emerald, blue, and gold eyelets.

Awed by such a majestic creature, it would be easy to miss the curtailed angle of his swoop over the seats. His landing too far right on the stage. The pause between Luciana's command and his reaction to fan his tail for the applauding crowd. Well trained, but not a full replacement for Nimit yet.

Luciana's smile never dropped—only a flicker at the edges with each of the griffin's missteps. Not flawless. Not untouchable. Just practiced at what she did.

Once the peacock griffin exited, Luciana drew the show to a close. As the drum music swelled once more, droves of patrons funneled out of the stands, channeling through the amphitheater gate or down to the edge of the lawn where keepers gathered to accept donations. Aila shuffled against the current until she reached the head of the line.

"Well, look at you." Luciana stood at the edge of the lawn, separated from patrons by a low rope fence. She gave Aila a dry look. "Made it all the way out here, and you haven't even burst into flames yet?"

Rather than humor that with a reply (of which Aila had none), she dug for her wallet and pulled out the one crinkled bill she happened to be carrying. Aila held it between two fingers. Luciana gave a soft whistle.

A mouse griffin popped over her shoulder, ear tufts lifted. It leapt into the air on fluttering blue and green wings, snatched the paper from Aila's hand in one tiny front talon, then deposited the donation into a box held by another keeper.

"OK," Aila said. "I'll admit, that's pretty cute."

"Isn't it?" When the mouse griffin returned to Luciana's shoulder, she booped its beak.

"How does anyone refuse you donations?" Aila asked.

"They don't, really."

"So you're basically a mob boss."

"Pretty much."

They shared a laugh. Aila could have forgotten about the crowd around them.

A jab from a shoulder brought her back to reality. Some people lingered to give the mouse griffin their donations, others to ask questions of the keepers. Not wanting to take too much time from real customers, Aila moved out of line.

Luciana caught her hand.

She leaned across the rope fence, soft voice fighting the surrounding din.

"Stick around. Just for a bit." She tipped her chin to the stands.

Light fingers brushed Aila's thumb as Luciana stepped back. Mango lingered in her nose, a pleasant sweetness. Aila needed to upgrade her shampoo. Why else had the scent been on her mind lately?

She found a seat in the front row, center stadium. Aila had never *sat* through a griffin show before. No wonder the program stayed short, if people had to tolerate such uncomfortable concrete benches. The last patrons emptied from the amphitheater. Music faded, and the keepers disappeared into back exhibits. As Luciana stepped up on stage, Aila fidgeted in her seat.

"Hey?" she called across the lawn. "Is this...? You want me to sit out here?"

"That's perfect," Luciana called back. "Stay right there. And then..."

Wingbeats rumbled the air.

Aila squeaked in alarm as Ranbir exploded out of the sky, talons swooping over her head, far closer than he'd looked during the show. Then, shock molted into exhilaration. The buffeting air off his wings, the fantastic view of iridescent feathers. What patron wouldn't adore this?

Just like in the show, the griffin cut his arc short, banking toward the stage without completing the full length of the stadium. When he landed, Luciana met him with hands on her hips, a more annoyed expression than she'd dared during the show. Ranbir bumped his beak against her waist pouch, searching for his mouse reward. She pointed to the stadium.

With a huff, the griffin took flight, once again swooping over Aila's head, once again cutting his path short. When Luciana refused to relinquish his treat, he pranced around her and flared his crest of blue pom-pom feathers. Luciana stood firm.

Ranbir's wings beat heavy, a spray of rufous. His next arc cut wide over the seats, encircling the entire stadium.

When he landed, Luciana tossed him a mouse. He snapped it out of the air with glee. From the stands, Aila clapped.

"Skies and seas," she called out. "Confronting phoenixes is one thing. How do you keep your cool in front of something so...big?"

"What? This oaf?" Luciana looked up at the peacock griffin, his head cocked to inspect her hands for more treats. She scratched beneath his neck, crumpling the beast into a purring pile on the stage. "He's all fluff. Pretends to act tough."

Luciana sent him on several more loops of the stadium, each one flawless. Satisfied, she led him out onto the grass.

"We've been working on something else." Luciana ran a hand along the griffin's side. "What do you say, Ranbir? Want to show Aila your new trick?"

Aila perched on the edge of her seat as Ranbir knelt. Luciana gripped his shoulders, then swung one leg over his back, behind the joint of his wings. With flattened cheeks, the griffin stood, off balance as Luciana sat on top of him.

Incredible. Vjari scarp griffins were domesticated centuries ago, common everywhere from tourist carriages to the recreational griffin rides at the zoo, but peacock griffins had never caught on the same way. More skittish temperaments and lighter frames made them less suitable for riding, yet there Luciana sat, brilliant as a queen on a throne of emerald and cobalt.

With a hiss, Ranbir bolted. Luciana yelped and toppled to the ground, straight on her ass.

"Luciana!"

Aila jumped from her seat and ran across the lawn to make sure the batty woman was all right, but by the time she arrived, Luciana was laughing so hard she had to clutch her sides. The sound had Aila grinning before she realized what was happening. She offered a hand. Luciana took it, and Aila pulled her to her feet.

"Getting better," Luciana said. "A bit more practice, and maybe we can get airborne."

Ranbir nudged her side with his beak, as apologetic as Aila had ever seen a griffin. Luciana patted his head.

"Griffin riding?" Aila said. "That's the new show gimmick?"

Luciana jabbed her elbow. "Gimmick? Don't tell me you're still stuck in that rut."

Granted, riding atop a peacock griffin *looked* awesome. The principle irked Aila, the endless toil of capturing patrons' attention, when the animals alone should have been enough to leave anyone in awe.

"Not that long ago, you wanted to *steal* Rubra for your show."

Aila huffed. "Just because you've turned from the side of evil, don't think I've forgotten."

"I did not want to steal her."

"You have another word for forcibly taking her against my will?"

"I *never.*"

"On multiple occasions!"

Luciana hardened, that familiar bristle Aila hadn't stoked in several weeks, fists curled in preparation for battle. Stubborn. But more than that, passionate, the source of the glint Aila had seen in Luciana's eyes a hundred times but never bothered to interpret.

Aila braced herself for attack.

Instead of a snarl, Luciana dropped soft eyes to the grass. This, Aila decided, was somehow more dangerous. She couldn't help but be disarmed, concerned she'd spoken too harshly once again.

Devious witch, casting some sort of spell.

"I'm glad to see Rubra put to better use now," Luciana said.

"She was fine before."

"Not better now, with a breeding partner?"

Aila scrunched her nose. Low blow. "Technically. I *guess.*"

"Skies and ever-reaching seas." Luciana shook her head, a grin lurking underneath. "You're the most stubborn person I've ever met. You know that?"

"Coming from you, of all people?"

"Fine. We're *both* stubborn. I still say a phoenix would be a fantastic addition to the show, after breeding season."

Aila would chain herself to the aviary door if she had anything to say about it, but beyond that... "Carmesi does like you," she grumbled.

"Not me, loser. *You* could bring him."

Luciana had a knack for saying absurd, ridiculous things with disturbing nonchalance. Aila gave a caustic laugh. *"Me?* On stage? Are you insane?"

Insane and beautiful. What a combination. Luciana pinned her with a smirk, all confidence. All smug. As if she had every move planned out. Aila was never any good at chess.

"You already did an interview with the country's largest news network," Luciana said.

"Yeah. But that was on a *path*. A stage is different."

"This thing?" Luciana waved at the stage behind her. "It's not so bad. Come on up, give it a try."

"What? No. We don't need to—"

Luciana took Aila's hand.

Filthy, dirty trick.

Before, in the line, Luciana's touch had been light. Fleeting. Now, she wrapped Aila's fingers in hers, soft brown skin callused along the palm. Warmth seeped into Aila's bones.

By the time thoughts returned to Aila's head, Luciana had pulled her across the lawn and onto the stage. A painted dot marked the center. Aila stood upon it, and when Luciana's hands settled on her shoulders, her heart picked up like a bus speeding off a cliff.

"How does it feel?" Luciana asked.

Aila drowned in her expectant gaze, those lidded eyes close enough to catch every facet of warm brown and velvet black in the sunlight. Luciana wore that same intent look during their interview: approval at the sight of Aila dressed up in silky curls and eyeshadow.

Except now, Luciana was looking at...*normal* Aila. That made no sense.

Goosebumps prickled Aila's skin. Her stomach tightened into knots. Prompted by imagining a crowd in the stands, no doubt. What else could it be?

"There aren't any people watching," Aila said.

"You hardly notice them. Just the lights. The animals."

Luciana stepped beside her, chin raised to the imaginary on-lookers. A majestic beast in her element.

"It's scary when you first step out," Luciana said. "Then you slip into your routine. You understand that, don't you?" When she met Aila's gaze, the world around them faded. Nothing but dark eyes and smokey lashes, a honeyed glow to the ridges of her cheeks. "All your flashcards? It's the same thing. Prepare enough, practice enough, everything gets less scary."

"It . . . still doesn't feel right."

"You can do it. I know you can."

"Not just that."

Aila clutched protective arms over her chest and walked to the front of the stage. On the lawn, Ranbir sprawled across the grass, warming his outspread wings in the sun. Aila sat on the stage edge, legs dangling over the concrete lip. Luciana sat beside her.

"What, then?" Luciana asked in a voice so tender, Aila won-dered how this could be the same person who'd haunted her college days. Who'd butted heads with her for years.

"I'm scared to death of crowds, sure. But the show is also so . . ." Aila hesitated, not wanting to be careless with her words. "Commercialized. Everything at the zoo is, but the show even more so. I wish it didn't have to be that way."

Luciana braced her hands on the concrete edge, gaze down-cast. "I didn't realize. I always assumed the bad attitude was more . . . personal."

"Well. That, too," Aila muttered. "But these animals are incredible on their own!" She pointed to the peacock griffin, vibrant feathers splayed in sunlight, enough to rival any jewel. "Why all the showboating? Why all the lights and attention grabbing?"

"You're a rarity. Some people need a reason to care."

"But *why* do people need a reason to care?"

Aila's voice rose, no fault of Luciana's. The question had harrowed her since she was a little girl, wide eyes staring up at a phoenix on the other side of the zoo glass, unable to understand how anyone could let such a creature disappear from this world.

Why was she telling Luciana all this? Again?

Once again, Aila expected chastisement. Once again, Luciana's slow nod surprised her.

"I know what you mean."

Aila blinked. "You...know?"

"How frustrating it is." Luciana strummed coral nails against her knees. "In high school? I put together a whole bake sale to raise funds for a griffin conservation group. I don't think more than ten people showed up. I wanted to *scream*."

"You?" Aila blurted. "People didn't show up for *you*?"

Luciana laughed. "I told you, dork. I didn't just *appear* with a stage persona. It took work. Is that so hard to believe?"

Absolutely. Dumbfounding, in fact, to think that past Luciana wasn't always in control. She wasn't always in control now—a real human with flaws, even masked.

"Not everyone needs a reason to care," Luciana said. "You and I don't. These animals are priceless to us, just for existing." Her tone tightened. "On the other side, some people will never care. Too selfish. They care about what this world can do for them, and nothing else."

Like the phoenix thieves at the Jewelport Zoo. The poachers who made off with that shipment of hatchling dragons. Magical creatures for profit and nothing more. Aila's stomach twisted.

"But other people," Luciana said, the softest yet. "*Most* people are somewhere in between. Not destructive on purpose, but they don't have a reason to care yet. They don't realize why they *should* care. And no one cares about anything they can't connect to. That's our job, Aila. Connecting people to these animals, giving them a reason to care. Whether it's an exhibit or a show, it's all the same goal in the end."

"You think so?" Aila said, quiet.

"Of course. Griffin shows. Exhibits. All the breeding programs and wildlife preserves around the world. We can have all of them. We *should* have all of them. Not competing, but multiple tools in our arsenal."

Warmth drifted off her, the sweet of mango and sun-kissed skin.

"I never..." Aila gulped. "Realized how much you care about this." How had Aila missed it? No one took a mid-salary job mucking out barns on a daily basis if they didn't care. No one cried over a lost griffin if they didn't care.

"It's easy to see how much *you* care. Even when you're being stubborn." Luciana painted the words as a tease. "Use that. It's scary, I know. But your passion is the best way to get other people excited, and that excitement is what your phoenixes deserve."

This woman's kindness was more devastating than any snark. The slightest curve of her smile lulled Aila into an ease she didn't recognize, didn't understand, a sort of settling in her bones like sun-warmed concrete.

Why weren't things ever this easy with Connor?

"Stop it," Aila pleaded.

"Stop what?"

"Stop saying such nice things! It's already torture, listening to Tanya's smug lectures. *You see, Ailes? I told you Luc wasn't so bad—*" Aila stiffened, the nickname slipping off her tongue without thought. "Sorry. I didn't mean to. Tanya calls you that, but I would never..."

Luciana stared at her too long. At last, a shrug. "It's fine."

"It's...*fine*? What's fine?"

"Used to be only my mom called me Luc. Then some of my friends. Always bothered me when random people used it, trying to suck up or something."

Aila's brain short-circuited. "But you don't mind if I use it?"

"Why would I?"

"Because we're..."

Friends. They were friends.

At the edge of the stage, their hands brushed. Luciana glanced down, studying her pinkie splayed alongside Aila's. Aila stared in equal fascination and horror.

Tanya had asked if Aila had her eyes on someone other than Connor. For a breathless moment, she couldn't look anywhere else: the perfect drape of Luciana's hair, the curve of her lips, the spark of passion in her words.

Oh. No.

Aila was not prepared for this sort of ground-tilting revelation.

"I...uh...I'll think about it," she stammered. "The phoenixes and the show, that is. Maybe after breeding season, we can...um...work something out."

Luciana squeezed her hand. Aila withheld a yelp.

"Don't worry about it now," Luciana said. "You'll have your hands full this summer, once Rubra starts laying. She's more important than anything else."

She released their hands and pushed herself off the stage, a space between them that left Aila dizzy. While Luciana crossed the lawn to retrieve Ranbir, Aila stayed behind, warmth lingering on her hand.

Light-headed.

Aching.

Utterly screwed.

Aila had a hard time finishing work that day, thanks to the butterflies trying to chew her stomach from the inside out.

She'd had a crush on Luciana in college, but that was a silly little thing. Unobtainable, and therefore harmless. Aila could daydream all she wanted about sable hair and crimson lips, then go back to real, feasible things that didn't require working up the courage to confess feelings for the single most intimidating woman she'd ever met.

But as Aila shifted the kelpie into her back exhibit for the night, all she could think of was the warmth of Luciana's hand against hers. When she locked up the World of Birds aviary, she saw the spark in Luciana's eyes as her griffin circled the stadium. As she stepped into the phoenix exhibit, Luciana's words rolled through her head—talk of passion and purpose that left Aila warm inside.

All the things Connor had never made her feel.

This was—and not to be dramatic about it, or anything—possibly the most upsetting realization Aila had ever made in her life.

"All right, lovebirds," she called out. "Time for bed."

Carmesi flew into a tree beside her, but when Aila opened the entrance to their back aviary, he cocked his head and stared. Rubra remained on her nest platform, an annoyed puff to her cheeks as she stared down her keeper.

"The nest is coming together great. I agree. You can work on it some more tomorrow."

Rubra didn't budge. Aila groaned and hiked over.

Thoughts of slender hands danced through her head, the brush of Luciana's fingers through her hair. She swatted them away like gnats.

A wooden ladder led up to the nest platform, narrow and angled to avoid disrupting the "immersive visual experience" of the patrons. Aila shut her eyes and forced herself up the creaking rungs, refusing to look at the ground below. Upon reaching the top, she braced her arms on the platform and gave Rubra a chiding look.

"Rubra. Honey. It's time to go in for the night."

Rubra sat in her nest of olive branches, pressed flat like a feather pancake. With a plea to skies and seas, Aila pushed on Rubra's warm breast, trying to dislodge her. Rubra pressed back, refusing to budge. The bird could be adamant, but never like this.

Carmesi landed on the platform, greeting Aila with a nervous trill.

"Rubra?" Aila said in a hush.

She reached out again, gentler this time, slipping a hand underneath the furnace of Rubra's belly. Rubra resisted, but Aila tilted the phoenix high enough to glimpse beneath her.

A single egg lay in the nest. Large enough to wrap in Aila's palm, the shell a porcelain turquoise speckled in gold.

"*Rubra!*" Aila shouted.

Her exclamation echoed through the glass aviary, devolving into a peal of triumphant laughter that nearly toppled her off the ladder. She clutched the wooden rungs and drowned herself in mirth, basking in the perfection of Rubra in her nest and Carmesi perched proudly beside her.

Below, the door swung open as Tanya burst into the exhibit. "Aila?" she called out. "What are you yelling about? Everything good?"

"An egg!" Aila called at the top of her lungs. "An egg! An egg! An egg!"

344

One egg. Two eggs. Three eggs. Four.

One day at a time, the clutch grew, until Rubra sat upon a full nest of five turquoise eggs, palm-sized and glossy as porcelain, speckles heaviest at the wide end, then lightening as the shell came to a taper. Aila plucked each treasure from the nest to measure and weigh. She held them to a flashlight to check their contents. When she returned the eggs, Rubra settled back down, a little shimmy of breast, then tail to get her feathers laying right.

"Yes, that's right, Director Rivera," Aila said on the phone, excitement making her twirl in her chair until she neared dizziness. "Five eggs. And they all appear to be fertile."

"This is fantastic news, Aila!" Rivera replied. "You've blown us away with your success thus far. Please, if you need anything at all from IMWS, don't hesitate to call."

"Of course, Director Rivera."

When the call ended, Aila laughed and twirled until Tanya had to collect her off the floor. The remedy for such a grievous injury was ice cream, they agreed. They popped over to the Birds of a Feather Slushie Hut beside the aviaries, an open-air shop with thatched roof and mannequin parrots on the eaves. After acquiring cups of pineapple sorbet whipped into high swirls, they sat back at the observation window with a laptop open, watching the live chat explode with excitement over the successful nest.

Congratulations Rubra and Carmesi! What good birds!

"They are," Aila agreed around a mouthful of ice cream, big enough to give her brain freeze. "The best birds in the zoo. Best birds in the *world*."

And congrats to the zookeepers! They must be so thrilled.

"Damn straight," Tanya said, boots propped on the counter. "I think we deserve a party. You think Director Hawthorn will throw us another party?"

What will the chick names be??? Ruby?

Flambé?

Burnatrix?

"Holy *shit*, Tanya!" Aila nearly fell out of her chair again. "Names! We have to name the chicks!"

Tanya laughed. "Relax, Ailes. We've got a whole month before hatching. Now's the time to eat sorbet and be happy."

Aila was. So happy, she could barely tear her eyes off the observation window, smiling like an idiot every time she spied Rubra fluffed on her nest. So happy, she bounced through the train ride home, then raced to her apartment to tell her animals the good news.

So happy, she almost stopped thinking about how warm Luciana's hand felt against hers.

Almost.

Chapter Twenty-Seven

The bright wood-and-eggshell lobby of the administration building always made Aila feel restless. She perched on the edge of a polished oak bench, studying her fingernails, then the stitches of her work polo, then every single spiky leaf of the mounted succulents that spelled *San Tamculo Zoo* on the opposite wall.

Theodore sat beside her, idly scrolling on his phone. How in all the skies and seas could he look so *calm*? Aila traced the line of a floor tile with her boot, then flinched as the rubber sole squealed against the linoleum.

She looked up. So did the receptionist. They locked eyes in a blistering glare.

"Oh, wow," Teddy whispered. "What's *that* about?"

"It's nothing," Aila murmured, eyes back on the floor. "I shouted at a patron in here once. Or twice. We're mortal nemeses now."

"You've got a few of those, huh?"

Aila didn't realize she was bouncing in her chair until Teddy's hand clamped her shoulder. "Relax," he said in that calm, kind, speaking-to-a-high-strung-kitten sort of way. "You're not even the one in the meeting."

No. Aila wasn't. She'd never imagined such a scenario could feel *more* stress-inducing than sitting in the spotlight herself.

Last night, Tanya pitched her volunteer keeper program to the donor board. This morning, Director Hawthorn called her in to share the results of their vote.

Between this, and the success of the phoenix cam, and the *five whole* phoenix eggs sitting in Aila's exhibit, she ought to carry a dustpan around, a courtesy to whoever had to clean up her remains when she inevitably exploded out of excitement.

Because Tanya deserved this. She deserved it so damned much, Aila might scream, glaring receptionists notwithstanding. No matter how Aila balked at the idea of more volunteers skittering around the zoo, she knew Tanya would build the program into something phenomenal, something they could all be proud of.

"She'll be fine," Teddy said.

"How do you know?" a mildly vibrating Aila returned.

"Hm?"

"It's hard work. And nothing's guaranteed."

"Sure. But we know Tanya. We know how much she's put into this. That it's a great idea. And even if things don't come together this time?" He shrugged. "She'll keep trying until it happens."

Aila...liked that. She liked the idea of Tanya succeeding, obviously. But more, the idea that maybe some things didn't work out as intended right away. That this wouldn't be, contrary to her usual expectations, the end of the world. She sat a little easier.

Until the instant she heard the director's office door open, at which point she bolted to her feet like a snapped rubber band.

Tanya and Director Hawthorn walked down the hall and into the lobby. Shook hands. The director nodded to Aila, then returned to his office.

Tanya was smiling.

Aila made a high-pitched squeal that somehow syllable-ized into "*Well?*"

"It's been approved!" Tanya sounded out of breath. "Just a pilot program, to start with. We'll need to show good results to earn long-term approval, but we can get going in a couple of months with—"

Aila launched forward, trusting Tanya to catch her. Tanya did. They spun together in a tight, laughing embrace.

"*Tanya! Congratulations!* You're brilliant, and beautiful, and you deserve this more than anyone in the entire world, and you're going to get this program going and it's going to be *amazing*, and of course they'll approve it for forever, they *have to*!"

Tanya chuckled, a bubbly sound like fresh summer soda pop. "Thanks, Ailes. It's . . . Skies and seas, I can't believe it's really happening."

It took a moment, but Aila finally allowed herself to be dislodged from Tanya like a beloved burr. Teddy came forward. He tipped onto his toes and pressed a kiss to Tanya's lips, the slow and lingering kind that made even the eavesdropping receptionist lighten her glower.

"Proud of you, Tani. Nothing new there."

Tanya beamed like Movasi sunshine.

They headed outside—Tanya's hand woven with Teddy's, Aila bouncing ahead of them like an unleashed puppy.

"This deserves a celebration," Teddy said. "Have they still got those seasonal churros? The ones with the strawberry filling?"

"Teddy, that sounds blissful," Tanya said. "But I've got food prep to—"

"Oh, *shut up*," Aila said. "I can take care of food prep. Go get a treat!"

Normally, Tanya would argue. She *must* be beside herself, to only smile in reply. And was that a little bounce in Tanya's boots Aila detected?

"We'll celebrate proper tonight," Teddy said, tugging Tanya away toward the food court. "Meet at the pub? Get some margaritas?"

"And party hats!" Aila proposed.

"And *party hats*!" Teddy agreed, alongside a Tanya who was laughing too hard to reply.

Aila watched them go, smiling wide enough to leave her cheeks aching for a week.

That evening, she danced through her closing routine.

She whistled down the stairs of the back kelpie exhibit, gleeful notes echoing off concrete. At the bottom control panel, she hit the button to open the gate. Maisie swirled into her tank like a drift of flotsam, algae-wreathed hooves prancing through water as she flipped by the observation window.

"I've got amazing news, Maisie!" Aila hit the button again, closing the gate and sealing the kelpie in her back holding for the night. "Tanya's volunteer program got approved!"

Aila had told every one of her animals the exciting development. Most responded with the expected (if disappointing) nonchalance. Maisie was polite enough to press her snout to the glass and puff bubbles in acknowledgement.

"*Right?*" Aila agreed. "It's almost as if..." She hesitated, hand pressed to the cool window of Maisie's tank. "As if everything's finally coming together."

Maybe it was. San Tamculo had its first nest of phoenix eggs in over a decade. Tanya's hard work had paid off. Aila was still buzzing with the sight of her friend victorious, of Tanya's radiant smile and her hand woven with Teddy's as the two of them frolicked away for an impromptu churro date.

At how ceaselessly Teddy supported Tanya. At how easy they acted with each other.

And there, to Aila's dismay, a little pang in her heart soured her otherwise perfect day. There was *one* thing still not going right in her life, a weight like iron around her ankles.

Aila trotted up the stairs and made sure the upper door to Maisie's tank was locked. In the kitchen, she laid out a goat to defrost, then shut off the lights. Checklist complete, she swung through the outside door.

And barreled straight into her biggest problem in the entire zoo.

"Holy. Crap!" Aila staggered, clutching her racing heart.

"Sorry!" Connor raised his hands. "I didn't mean to startle you."

"What did you expect, hiding around corners?"

"I was just standing here."

"Well, how was I supposed to know that?" Aila threw up her hands. Her fault, not watching where she was going, but a heart attack was the last thing she needed. Who'd take care of the phoenixes? "What are you doing here?"

"Hoping to talk to you. If you have a minute?"

There came that pang in Aila's heart again, like a shard of ice trying to burrow through her ventricles.

Tell him no. Tell him you're busy. It's not a lie.

"Yeah, sure," she said. "What is it?"

Coward. Aila cringed at her indecisiveness.

"I want to show you something. We'll be back in a flash." Connor took her hand.

Aila and her spineless back followed without protest.

Even before the Tanya/Teddy showcase of love that morning, Aila had dragged herself to a painful realization: she had to break things off with Connor. It wasn't right, the way he made her stomach squirm. The way their interests passed each other at angles askew. Aila knew it, and Tanya had given her enough raised eyebrows to say *she* knew it, too. The question of how to enact this decision debilitated her. Aila couldn't stand the thought of disappointing people.

Now, hang on there, Aila, a sane person might say, *wouldn't leading him on cause even more disappointment in the end?*

Why, yes. What an accurate and paralyzing observation.

Connor led them across the zoo, patrons gone for the day, paths empty except for a handful of workers closing up food stalls or sweeping up stale fries. This couldn't be another meal date. He'd planned something else.

When they arrived at the dragon aviaries, Connor grabbed a bucket of thawed fish from the keeper kitchen.

"Ever fed a maned dragon before?" he asked.

Aila squinted at him, trying to find the joke. "No . . ."

"First time for everything, then."

The back holding area for the maned dragon was the size of Rubra's entire public exhibit, outfitted with a swimming pool and several hard plastic toys riddled with chew marks, enclosed in metal bars the width of Aila's arm. Connor slid open a latch, then slipped inside. Beyond, the door to the main exhibit stood open. Aila froze on the threshold.

"Connor! What are you doing? You can't just walk into an exhibit with a predator!"

He laughed. "She eats fish, Aila. Perfectly harmless."

His confidence threw her for a loop. Aila was, by every stretch of the imagination, a strict rule-follower, and she could guess with reasonable certainty that this was breaking zoo protocol (fish-eater or not, dragon teeth and claws were no joke). Then again, Connor was the dragon's keeper. He ought to know her temperament better than anyone.

When else would Aila get such an opportunity?

Wary, she followed Connor out the door to the exhibit. He

glanced back, all bravado. Pink blossoms swirled at their feet, falling from cherry trees along a rocky hillside. A pond lay at the center, black water dotted with flower petals and floating green duckweed.

Daiyu, the maned dragon, raised her head at the sight of visitors. Her serpentine body relaxed in a loose coil, scales like polished jade. Flower petals sprinkled her gold and onyx mane like confetti. A few pieces stuck to her antlers.

In addition to their weather-altering abilities, old tales claimed maned dragon hair brought good fortune. Scientific research had yet to prove the claim conclusively, though a recent study found people wearing dragon mane bracelets reported greater happiness on average. Then again, wouldn't Aila be happier if she got to wear a kick-ass dragon bracelet?

The dragon rose on short legs, claws digging into the rocky soil, neck towering ten feet over Connor and Aila.

"Evening, sweetheart." Connor lifted an offering of fish. "Hungry for a snack before turning in for the night?"

Hot breath puffed from the dragon's nostrils, a smell like humid air before a storm. She bared her teeth, then pinched the fish from Connor's fingers, swallowing it whole. Aila's mouth hung open wide enough to catch flies. Forget all that relationship anxiety nonsense. This was one of the coolest things she'd ever seen.

"Wouldn't want to get on her bad side." Connor patted Daiyu's mane. "But she's a peach. Want to try?"

Did Aila want to try hand-feeding a dragon? What a dumb question.

She grabbed a fish from the bucket, cold and slick, scales rough against her fingers. With Connor standing by for moral support (not sure what else he could do, if the dragon decided to snap), Aila held up her offering.

She'd never realized how big dragons were up close.

Daiyu sniffed Aila's hair, no doubt spotted with feather dust and kelpie algae. The air cooled around the dragon, like fresh rain without the hassle of getting wet. When Daiyu opened her mouth, teeth the size of Aila's palm grazed her hand, gentle. The dragon gulped the fish, then stared her human visitor down with expectant eyes, black flecked with gold like stars.

Aila bounced on her heels, electrified by the thrill. Connor chuckled and handed her another fish.

"How are the phoenixes?" he asked.

"Couldn't be better." Aila offered the next fish to Daiyu. The dragon snapped it up, then nudged empty hands with her snout. "Five eggs, all viable so far."

"That's fantastic news. When's the hatch date?"

"Average incubation time is twenty-eight days. Considering Rubra didn't start full incubation until the fifth egg was laid... I'd say the timer started yesterday. We'll be on immolation watch in a little under a month."

Saying it out loud sounded terrifying and exhilarating in equal measure. After months of preparation, almost a year since the fated break-in at the Jewelport Zoo, Aila and her run-down breeding program had come so far. When those phoenixes hatched, there wouldn't be enough ice cream in the world to celebrate.

Connor handed her the last fish.

Aila held it up to Daiyu. Once the dragon gulped it down, she tipped her snout into the empty bucket. Huffed. With a ground-shaking plop, she lay down and curled her tail around her, brushing the fanned tip through cherry blossoms.

Connor stroked her snout. He beckoned Aila closer.

Scarcely breathing, she traced her fingers over Daiyu's nose, the ridge of her eye. The dragon didn't just look like jade, her scales were smooth as polished gemstones and cool as spring water.

"I'm sure you have a busy month ahead," Connor said. "I've been meaning to drag you over here for a while. Figured now was a good time to get some things off your mind."

"This is incredible, Connor." Aila stroked the dragon's silky mane. "She's incredible."

Daiyu huffed and tilted her neck toward Aila, enjoying the scratches.

"I thought you'd like it." Connor grinned.

"I do. I really do." Aila bit her lip. "But..."

The word tainted the air like kelpie fog. Aila struggled to finish the thought, guilt heavy on her tongue.

"I've noticed," Connor said for her, and that was worse. "Things have been a little...strained between us."

Of course he'd noticed. Anyone with a sliver of social awareness would have. She stared at Daiyu's polished jade scales, smooth beneath her fingers. Why didn't Connor do this for their first date? Aila would have been hooked.

But he hadn't. Aila might like this side of him, but what about the rest? What about the side that made her feel embarrassed? Self-conscious? Aside from Tanya, Aila had come to expect that kind of treatment from other people, that she'd never quite fit in right. Expecting anything more was asking too much.

Then she'd gotten to know Luciana better these past few weeks.

Around her, Aila didn't feel embarrassed. She didn't feel self-conscious. That freeing feeling, she hadn't thought possible. And that was the core of the problem, wasn't it? Even alone here with Connor, surrounded by cherry blossoms and enamored by a dragon, Aila didn't have the butterflies in her stomach she'd had just sitting beside Luciana.

Be a big girl, Aila. You can do it.

"It's very thoughtful," she said, meek. "But I'm not sure things have been working out between us."

Connor studied her a moment. Scrunched his mouth. "I see."

"That's it?" Aila clutched her hands to her chest, awaiting something worse.

He shrugged. "If that's how you feel."

Aila hadn't known what to expect. An angry outburst, maybe not, but she'd anticipated something more than this. Connor's level tone left her reeling.

"Connor, look, I'm sorry," she blurted out too fast. "You have so many amazing qualities, and I appreciate the time we've spent together. I feel awful that it's taken me so long to say this, I really do. I just think that sometimes—"

"Aila." Connor cut her off without ire, a tight smile on his lips. "It's fine. Really. I'm glad you told me."

"It's . . . *fine*?" Aila chewed the word. Where was the argument? The pushback?

"No hard feelings." He picked up the empty bucket and nodded toward the door. "Come on. I ought to finish locking up."

Somehow, Aila dragged herself out of the dragon aviary without keeling over from awkwardness. Connor locked up the exhibit. He bid her goodnight with a smile.

They went their separate ways.

Horns and fangs, what just happened?

Aila walked back to the phoenix complex at a slug's pace, the afternoon slipping into twilight, her world a haze. She'd never broken up with someone before. She'd always been the one rejected, the one dumped to the curb, and she'd never handled it with such poise. A guy thing, maybe? Or was Connor putting on a brave face, trying not to make awkward waves when they still had to work together? No worries there. Aila planned on avoiding the dragon exhibits for a year, at least.

Tanya had left for the day, a text on Aila's phone promising to meet at the Macbhairan Pub in an hour. Aila plopped into a chair behind the camera monitors, head in her hands, zombie eyes half-focused on the screens. Should she tell Tanya about Connor—a guaranteed downer no matter how many margaritas and party hats she dressed it up in? No. Tanya deserved tonight to celebrate. Aila could muster a smile until morning.

She reached for her backpack, but ended up squinting at the video feed instead.

The camera focused not on the nest platform, but the opposite corner of the aviary. Not unheard of. With Rubra on her eggs, Aila had started leaving both phoenixes out on exhibit overnight. Sometimes, the motion-sensing camera tracked Carmesi as he hopped around the olive trees.

Except now, the camera focused on an empty frame. Aila stared at the screen for several seconds before the video shifted back to the nest platform, where Carmesi perched at Rubra's side, head cocked.

Weird. Aila stood from her chair and pushed on tiptoes over the counter, peering out the observation window into the exhibit. Nothing but quiet olive trees. She returned to the monitor.

A flicker of movement caught her eye on one of the outside security cameras.

Aila straightened in her chair. She stared at the feed from the back loading dock, unblinking, breaths shallow. Could Tanya still be here? She checked her phone, but Tanya's text had come through a half hour ago, and no bag sat at her desk.

Nothing else moved on the camera. Aila unclipped the radio from her belt.

"Aviaries to security."

After a pause, her radio clicked back.

"Zoo security," a man's voice replied. One of the night security guards.

"Hey, Antonio. Could you take a peek at the loading dock behind phoenixes?"

"Roger that. Everything all right, Aila?"

"I thought I saw something on the security camera."

"Be right there."

Aila set down her radio and tapped her fingers against the desk. After the Jewelport break-in, all of San Tamculo's security measures had been updated, from higher resolution cameras to the latest locking mechanisms on the phoenix aviaries. Even with all those precautions, Aila would be lying if she claimed the poachers had stopped haunting her mind. She tried to reason the worry away. The true danger wouldn't come until closer to immolation, the eggs useless until a female hatched them. When that time came, IMWS had arranged an extra security patrol from the San Tamculo Police Department to be on standby.

As the seconds ticked by, Aila stared at the security feeds, the exhibit camera. Nothing looked amiss.

At last, a figure stepped into the loading dock camera. Antonio circled the back of the building before looking up and waving. Aila's radio clicked.

"Everything looks clear," he announced. "You want me to stick around for a bit?"

"No, that's fine." Aila propped her tired head on one arm. "I must have been imagining things. Thanks for checking."

"No worries. I'll walk around the perimeter, just to make sure."

"Thanks, Antonio."

Aila set down her radio and rubbed her temples. Just a long day. Hopefully, some time with Tanya and Teddy would take her mind off things for the night, and she could get these jumbled thoughts sorted out in the morning.

Hopefully, she could put this whole mess with Connor behind her.

Chapter Twenty-Eight

Aila expected a pleading message from Connor the next day. Maybe a heart-wrenching phone call. Or even a visit to the phoenix complex, where he begged for a second chance with a bribe of chocolate. After several weeks of pursuit on Connor's part, a clean break seemed too much to hope for.

Yet Aila heard nothing.

No phone messages. No Connor lurking around corners at the staff office, or the aviaries, or the loading dock of the phoenix complex any of the dozen times Aila hiked out to make sure the security cameras were working. No more strangeness on the video feed after that night.

Crickets would have been preferable to the unsettling silence. Maybe she'd read Connor wrong, and he'd been eager for a way out. Maybe he was wallowing in the dragon exhibit, waiting for her guard to drop before he struck. Aila spent the rest of the week flinching every time her phone buzzed.

A suitable reaction, when an email from the IMWS director popped into her inbox.

That shouldn't be allowed. Those kinds of heart-dropping messages ought to come with warnings, whistles. Not cheerful salutations and *Hello Aila! I'm in town for a conference. Would you mind if I stop by tomorrow to check on the nest? Best, Maria.*

Aila couldn't decide whether to celebrate or faint at the first-name-basis with Director Rivera. She settled for a half-assed attempt at curling her hair (recalling as much as she could from Luciana's demonstration, plus an online instructional video), then a thermos of coffee doused with enough sugar to leave her buzzing for the morning meeting. Needless to say, she hadn't slept well. A dose of prescription-strength periwinkle prairie goose sleeping syrup took the edge off, but even magic couldn't work miracles.

The lavender smell lingered in Aila's nose. She had that going for her, at least.

Morning routine complete, she waited in the zoo entry plaza, bouncing on the balls of her boots as the first patrons wandered through the gates. Heat baked the concrete, sunbeams glaring off the bronze peacock griffin statue.

Connor ought to be working by now. That common sense didn't stop Aila's head swiveling like a mirror flamingo, uncomfortable with the open terrain, alert for an ambush.

Stop it, Aila. A nest full of phoenix eggs gave her plenty to worry about already.

She straightened when Director Rivera appeared at the side entry window, reserved for special zoo guests. She wore a maroon business skirt and blazer, dark hair starched into a ponytail without a strand out of place. Self-conscious, Aila twirled a curl of auburn hair around her finger, the ends crimped where she'd held the heat on too long. Luciana did such a better job.

"Aila!" The director crossed the plaza with a smile. "So good to see you again!"

"You too, Director Rivera. Welcome back to the zoo."

Aila offered her hand. Rivera shook it, then came in for a hug that made Aila's brain short-circuit. The email pleasantries, she could write off as casual office fluff. But a hug? For someone who hadn't even hatched a phoenix egg yet?

A swell of warmth hit Aila's chest.

"Excellent. Shall we...um..." Aila cleared her throat. "Take a look at the nest?"

"Please." Her guest beamed.

As they walked to the aviaries, Aila kept alert for any Connors hiding behind vending machines or cycad trees. When that hazard failed to appear, she cut side glances at the visiting dignitary. Most big donors and board members focused on themselves when they visited, chatty parrots in suits and pencil skirts.

Director Rivera clacked her heels with the same confidence, folded her hands behind her back in that way that suggested she had her shit fully together. Yet her eyes darted over every patron they passed. She peered into every exhibit, from the gilded swans honking on the lagoon, to the yellow-finned caimans lounging by their pools. The caiman keeper was giving a talk to a group of patrons, explaining how the creatures wore gold dust to attract mates, demonstrating how the scales were magically magnetic to gold but no other metals (yellow-finned caimans were common shop pets in jewelry stores to demonstrate quality wares, and absolutely essential to most pawn shops).

"You used to be a phoenix keeper here?" Aila asked. "Before the breeding hiatus?"

"I was!" Rivera's smile crinkled lines around her eyes. "That was...oh my, some fifteen years ago? I miss it some days, working hands-on with the animals."

Aila couldn't imagine leaving them behind. "Why'd you leave, then? Not that I'm complaining! I appreciate having the job, and all."

The director laughed. "I can assure you, scrubbing aviaries is kinder to young knees." She patted her leg, a stiffness to her gait. "Moving on to administration is a normal part of pro-fessional growth. At this rate? I'm sure you'll be on to bigger things before too long."

Aila's nose wrinkled. "I like what I do now." The polite way of saying she couldn't imagine doing anything else, much less—she shuddered—*administration*.

"Of course you enjoy what you do." Rivera turned tender, the tone Aila's mother had used when her child brought home crayon drawings of phoenixes from school. "I expect you'll do much more excellent work here in San Tamculo. But who's going to be the next Aila? One of our most important jobs is making way for the next generation. And we need keeper experience at IMWS, people who know the animals best because they've worked with them."

Aila wasn't prepared for this dilemma. She'd dreamed about breeding phoenixes since she was eight years old. What came after that? A second nest. Then a few more. Moving farther into the future, things turned fuzzy.

Their arrival at the phoenix complex rescued Aila from her existential crisis. Director Rivera walked to the observation window, giving Aila time to pile binders in her arms, then spread them along the counter.

"All right. Here we've got"—Aila pointed to each item—"egg measurement data. Nest temperatures and exhibit climate. Diet supplements. Lay date probability scenarios."

The director nodded without looking at the paperwork. She leaned toward the window, craning to see Rubra on her nest platform, Carmesi preening beside her. "How is Rubra handling the incubation?"

"Um..." Aila flipped open another binder and dragged a finger down a table. "Her weight has gone down a little, but still in a healthy range. Appetite is fine."

S. A. MACLEAN

"She and Carmesi are getting along well?"

"I don't...have any data on that. But we've kept up our behavioral monitoring shifts. And we've recorded the expected pairing behaviors."

"And the eggs. Gorgeous, aren't they?"

"The measurements fall within healthy parameters for lay weight and length—"

"Aila, relax." Rivera laid a hand on her shoulder. Smiled. "This isn't an inspection."

"Excuse me?"

Why else would an IMWS director pop in for a surprise visit, if not to check on their prized investment? To make sure Aila wasn't screwing things up? The email had kept her awake most of the night, running through lists of whether her protocol binders were up to date, how their egg measurements compared with program standards.

"You've done an exceptional job with the phoenixes already," Rivera said. "Getting them to breed within the first *year*? Skies and seas, we have established programs that would struggle to achieve such a feat after a transfer. The Renkailan program has been trying for years without success. Such unpredictable birds, you know."

Another test. It had to be.

"Sure," Aila said. "But I've still got to get the eggs to hatch. And take care of the chicks after that. I know there's a lot of work left, but I'll do my best to prove you were right to choose San Tamculo for the transfer."

That they were right to choose Aila.

She didn't expect the director's eyes to widen.

"Aila, we're already pleased with our decision to transfer Carmesi here. You've more than proven yourself up to the challenge. Why, just earlier this week at our regional conference? Director

364

Garumano was talking about the nest with such enthusiasm, I could have sworn his mustache would fall off."

"But—"

"We're here to support you, Aila. It's a difficult transition, seeing administrators as anything other than boogeymen. Skies know I went through that struggle, when I first stepped into the program. But please, think of us as colleagues. We're all working for the phoenixes."

Aila's thoughts went blank. A power outage. A swift reset back to factory standards.

Colleagues. A couple years ago, Aila could barely work up the courage to speak to Director Rivera.

To *Maria*.

Now here they stood, on even linoleum, a pair of phoenix nerds admiring their birds.

"Was it hard," Aila asked, quieter than intended, "shutting down the program?"

Director Rivera had moved on to IMWS just four years before the last successful phoenix nest at San Tamculo. She'd been part of the committee that transferred Rubra when the previous pair passed away of old age. She'd denied the male transfer request.

"The hardest decision I've ever made," Maria said, equally soft. "Impossible, it seemed. Rubra, we pushed through easy enough, couldn't let an exhibit go to waste. But when the male transfer application came in, I agonized over it for a month, ran every genetic pairing, evaluated every active breeding program. San Tamculo simply wasn't the best fit." She took in a long breath, hands folded in that mostly composed way at her waist. "Sometimes, we have to make those hard decisions, the ones that are best for the birds."

Maria turned to Aila, the somber notes vanishing as she donned her warmest smile yet. "I'm delighted to see a healthy phoenix pair back at San Tamculo. And even more delighted to see them under the care of such a compassionate keeper."

That fleck of warmth crept back into Aila's chest. It couldn't be...pride? Proud of her birds. Proud of her work.

Proud of her people.

"I couldn't have done it alone. Tanya, the Bix phoenix keeper? She's been with me every step of the way. Luciana's been a goddess on the publicity front. So many other keepers pitched in to get the breeding complex renovated."

"Of course." Maria beamed. "Teams always make us the most successful, all our different talents applied to the same goal. I'm so glad you're building a strong team here. Hopefully, that will mean many more successes to come."

Aila joined Maria at the observation window. Morning sun slanted through the aviary, casting dappled shadows through olive leaves.

"You came here *just* to see them?" Aila asked.

Maria smiled wider. Her eyes never left the phoenixes. "They're incredible, aren't they?"

United in that sentiment, Aila relaxed (apart from the buzz of caffeine). "What was the exhibit like, when you worked here?"

"Less vibrant." Maria smirked at the orange walls. "Though I'd call this an improvement. My phoenixes were Carnella and Pyrio. Beautiful birds. When I let them out in the morning, Carnella would hang upside down from her favorite branch and make this delightful trill..."

Aila fell quiet, content to listen to Maria's stories. With this much passion? Maybe hers wasn't a bad path to follow—administration and all. Aila could get a few successful breeding seasons under her belt. Publish some husbandry studies. Maybe even get involved with the IMWS effort to reintroduce phoenixes to their native range.

That was years down the line. For now, Aila enjoyed her birds and the company of a colleague who understood how special they were.

By the time Aila returned Maria to the zoo exit—and survived a goodbye hug that sent her pride rocketing—her stomach snarled for lunch. Even more so, when she returned to the phoenix complex and smelled fried food.

"That you, Ailes?" Tanya's head poked in from the patio.

"Nope. I'm a merlion in disguise." Aila waggled her arms like flippers.

"Ha! Sassy Aila's back. I've got a surprise for you."

"It better be waffle fries, because I'm—"

Aila yelped as the patio door flew open. Her mother attacked in a bolt of red hair and cinnamon-laced cardigan, wrapping Aila into a hug. She hadn't expected a family visit, her crushed ribs unprepared for the assault.

"Hi, Mom," Aila greeted through smushed cheeks. "Didn't know you'd be stopping by today. Is everything all right?"

"O' course!" her mother returned in a sing-song cadence. "Since when do I be needing an excuse to pop in on my favorite daughter?"

"I'm your only daughter. And I . . . can't . . . breathe."

From the doorway, Tanya chuckled. "I got waffle fries, too."

Parental visits to the zoo weren't uncommon, particularly when new food items arrived at the restaurants, or baby animals in the exhibits. To show up unannounced (and without scheduling into Aila's social obligations calendar at least one week in advance) rang suspicious. Betrayed by her rumbling stomach, Aila let it slide. They returned to the patio, where she plopped down at the table behind a plate of waffle fries piled high with coleslaw and spicy chicken. Her mouth watered before she had a fork in hand.

"Hope you don't mind." Aila's mother sat beside her. "Me popping in unannounced and all. Tanya called, said my little girl could use a pick-me-up."

"Oh yeah?" Aila said around a mouth stuffed with chicken. "That's really sweet, Mom. But my meeting this morning went better than expected! Director Rivera—Maria, I think I'm allowed to use her first name now, so weird—anyway, she *loved* seeing the phoenixes. And she's super cool! Can you believe they used to let kids roast marshmallows over phoenix tails during summer camp?"

"Did they? What a right treat! So glad you two are getting along."

"But *we're* here"—Tanya skewered a forkful of fries—"for the bigger thing."

Aila paused, food halfway to her mouth. "Bigger?"

A trap. She knew it.

Her mother laid a hand on her arm. "Break-ups are hard, sweetie. But we're here for you, whatever you need."

Even waffle fries couldn't stave off cruel reality. Aila wilted, her temporary high from Maria's visit replaced by that knot in her stomach when she thought of Connor, the guilt she felt for leading him on.

"I appreciate it." She poked her food. "But could we... maybe...not talk about that?"

Her mother shared a long look with Tanya. "Of course, sweetie. We don't have to talk about it if you don't want to. We just worry. You tend to keep things to yourself."

Harsh, but true. Aila's tears belonged in the safety of her apartment, a pact between her and her ice cream cartons.

"I know I do. And I agree, break-ups *suck*. But..." Aila took another bite of chicken. "I think I did the right thing. I had to stand up for myself."

Hello, confidence, where did you come from? The entire situation sucked, and Aila was nowhere close to finishing her current anxiety spiral, but the surety of her words surprised her. Tanya and her mother looked on with raised eyebrows, smiles that drew the warmth back into Aila's chest.

"It's so good to hear you say that," her mother said. "It's not easy to do what's best for ourselves. I'm proud of you."

"Thanks, Mom." Aila dropped her eyes to the table, fidgety beneath the gooey attention.

"And you look lovely as well." Her mother ran a hand through Aila's curls. "You did your hair?"

"Oh. Yeah. You like it?"

"I love it!"

Aila blushed. "Luciana taught me."

Tanya's squint threatened to turn Aila redder than her spicy chicken.

"Luciana?" Her mother frowned. "Where have I heard that name?"

"She's one of the keepers here. At the griffin show." Horns and fangs, Aila talked too fast. Tanya kept staring, as if scrutinizing her beneath a microscope. "In fact, while you're visiting, you should go see the show. It's really popular."

"Oh, Luciana!" Her mother snapped her fingers. "That crush of yours from college?"

Aila prayed for a meteor to strike her down. Perhaps an errant tree branch to sweep her off the patio. Of course she'd been dumb enough to admit to a crush back then. The doubt and inferiority, she'd kept closer to her chest.

"Yeah. Her." Aila stuffed a waffle fry into her mouth. "But, you know . . ." Another. "That was a long time ago."

"Oh?" Her mother's voice lilted. "I don't hear you mention many colleagues other than Tanya. You enjoy working with her?"

Deny. Flee. These were Aila's defense mechanisms.

But what had that ever gotten her? Maybe it was the boost of confidence from Maria's visit. Maybe it was the nervous adrenaline of cutting ties with Connor. Maybe Aila had lost her mind.

"Well, I . . . might still have a little crush on her. I think."

The world came to a standstill. What. Had. Aila. Just. Said? *Out loud,* of all things? To speak something so blunt and vulnerable into existence left a spike of panic in her chest. It felt raw. It felt terrifying.

It felt . . . freeing.

Tanya shot both fists into the air. "I fucking knew it!" she shouted, loud enough they'd probably get complaints from a couple of parents at the exhibit by the end of the day.

Aila shrank in her chair. Her cheeks burned like phoenix fire. "It's nothing! Just a dumb crush. Who knows if she even feels the same way? Probably not. No big deal."

"Oh, Aila." Her mother beamed, digging dimples into her cheeks. "If it makes you happy, nothing to be ashamed of! Life's for dreaming big and taking chances."

"To be fair," Tanya added, "gorgeous women are a damn scary chance."

"Gorgeous, is she?" Her mother smirked. "You'll have to bring her by the stall at the Pepper Festival in a couple weeks. I'm sure your pa would be beside himself to meet her."

"Yeah, Aila." Tanya's grin was wicked. "I'm sure your parents would *love* to meet her."

Curse them both. While Tanya and her mother gossiped about dating prospects, Aila crumpled in her chair and skewered more food, attempting to bury her blush behind waffle fries.

"So?" Her mother leaned in. "Are you gonna tell her how you feel?"

A dream. A nightmare. The mere prospect threatened to split Aila's stomach open with butterflies, jittering her fingers, until she could barely—

Breathe.

One deep breath, and with it, a calming memory of mango shampoo. Of dark eyes glinting in sunlight, until there was nothing else left in the world.

"I . . . guess I'll have to," Aila said.

PART FOUR

Recent thefts of captive-
bred DIAMONDBACK
DRAGONS have
hindered reintroduction
efforts
significantly,
imperiling not
only the species,
but the larger
ecosystem of the
Vjari boreal forest.
DIAMONDBACK
DRAGONS are
now understood to be a
keystone species, their
roosting caves creating
warm microclimates that
serve as habitat to over a
hundred unique species
of plants, fungi, and small
animals found nowhere else in
the world.

Leather wings

Diamond Markings

International Magical Wildlife Service. REGIONAL REPORT:
DIAMONDBACK DRAGON POPULATION STATUS AND
IMPACTS ON VJARI ECOLOGY.

Chapter Twenty-Nine

With summer came the excitement of breeding birds, but also Aila's favorite holiday: the Movas Pepper Festival.

This was not to say Aila had the best (or any) genetic tolerance for peppers, but the pain was exhilarating. After sunset, the zoo reopened for a special night of chili-themed food and crafts. The catering department went all out: churros in chili jam, stuffed jalapeños shaped like diamondback dragons with bacon wings, cayenne-chocolate phoenix cake pops, volcanic salamander sundaes, kelpie bog punch spiked with something fruity that made Aila's head spin if she indulged in more than a cup.

Beyond the zoo's offerings, local restaurants set up stalls with their own concoctions. A fixture among them: the Macbhairan Pub and Tequileria, returning every year to serve classic chile relleno, plus a fusion cheesy scalloped potato relleno that generated a confused buzz, if nothing else.

Aila's mother stayed at the restaurant to oversee dinner service. Her father lugged a grill to their zoo stall, towering behind the counter, frizzy red hair and beard wrangled within a comical number of sanitary nets, wearing the phoenix-print apron Aila bought him for his last birthday (at perhaps a size too small). He'd decorated his stall with a canopy of paper phoenix feathers. A papier mâché bird perched on the cash register, tail feathers catching in the drawer every time it opened.

"What do you think?" he asked Aila. "I made it myself!"

She leaned on the counter, struggling to take it all in. "*You* made it? Since when do you do papier mâché?"

"Worked on it all week! My little girl and her phoenixes are famous now. Had to do something to show off!"

He beamed down at Aila the way he always had, as if she were the brightest ray of sunshine on a cloudy day. Her chest warmed, not just because of the spicy potato on her plate. From the register, a lumpy phoenix stared her down with uneven eyes.

"It's great, Dad. Some of your best work."

While he preened, Tanya shoveled a mouthful of her chile relleno. Her eyes widened as she clapped a hand to her mouth.

"Skies and seas," she said around the food. "What are you stuffing this with?"

Aila's father returned a wicked grin. "Dragon tongue peppers. Got a nice kick, eh?"

"*Horrendous.*" Tanya downed another bite. "You mind setting aside a plate? Teddy would be devastated if he missed this."

Teddy had messaged their group chat that he was running late, bemoaning a rather difficult phantom cat dropped off at the Humane Society right at closing, threatening both Tanya and Aila with cold shoulders if he missed out on any good food because of it.

Aila nibbled her meal, relishing the spice on her tongue, for once enjoying the hum of the busy zoo. The festivities were centered in the zoo's main food plaza, lively guitar music playing from the speakers, the Movasi-style stucco facades strung with little red chili lights and wreaths of fragrant sage. Patrons shifted from stall to stall, children clambering for a ride on the conservation carousel. Many wore handmade masks of zoo animals, manufactured at a glitter-strewn craft table. Another group gathered around one of the griffin show keepers, who'd brought their thunderhawk out for a public demonstration. The bird perched on a sturdy cart, eyeing small children like potential meals.

A hot summer breeze tousled Aila's hair.

Scents of grilled peppers, sugary confections, enough to spend all the night eating.

When the griffin show keeper caught Aila's eye, she waved. Timid, Aila waved back.

"Who you waving to?" her father asked, craning over the counter to inspect the crowd.

Aila shoved him back with ineffective stick arms. "Just some work friends."

"*Friends?*" Her father's face lit up. "Call them over! I'll give them a discount!"

"It's not that big of a deal."

"Not a big deal? I've never seen you out of your exhibit longer than ten minutes!"

"*Dad!*"

Aila looked to Tanya for backup.

"He isn't wrong." Tanya shrugged. "I'm surprised you haven't snagged food and run off hiding behind a bush by now."

Aila huffed at the assault. Sure, she hadn't made many friends growing up (zero friends, if she discounted animals). And sure, seeing her dad smile so wide left a fuzzy feeling in her ribs. No reason to make a public spectacle of it.

That was the least of Aila's worries. Her heart stuttered at the sight of sable hair emerging from the crowd. Smokey eyes with crimson shadow. A quirk of ruby lips.

Was it *hot* tonight? Or just the chilis making Aila sweat?

"Scalloped potato relleno?" Luciana approached the stall, brow cocked at the chalkboard menu. Like Aila and the other keepers, she still wore her zoo uniform. The night turned her hair to ink, loose curls glistening beneath string lights tacked along the canopy.

Aila's favorite festival. Without question.

"That's right!" Aila's father said, a couple of decibels too loud. "A Macbhairan family creation. You've never tasted anything like it."

Both her parents had more extrovert energy in one breath than Aila could muster in a month. She shrank at the counter. "Oh, hey, Dad? I don't think you've met. This is Luciana, our PR Director for the phoenix program."

Her father's eyes widened at the name. Aila cursed herself for telling any of these betrayers her secret.

"Luciana, you say?" He shared a look with Tanya that made Aila want to shrivel into dust. "Food's on the house for any friend of Aila's!"

"That's very kind," Luciana said, "but you don't need to—"

He shoved a plate of potato relleno into her hands before she could say no. Had to be faster than that in the Macbhairan household. True to form, Luciana accepted with a gracious smile and dug a fork into the cheesy concoction.

She took a bite with perfect, aching poise, the daintiest flick of her tongue to clean the fork. When Aila stared too long, Tanya shot her two scandalous brows. Aila heeled her foot.

"That's *fierce*." Luciana's brow furrowed. "Dragon tongue peppers?"

"The lady knows her spice!" Aila's father clapped an approving hand on the counter. "You like it?"

"You have any hot sauce?"

"Good woman!"

Aila's father offered a bottle of homemade hot sauce. Luciana poured it over her food, then took another bite, relishing the heat that would have burnt Aila to a crisp.

She was burning up already. Tanya's egging looks weren't helping.

"Got your email, Tanya," Luciana said around another dainty mouthful. "Count griffin show in for your volunteer pilot. We could always use some extra hands."

"You're a peach, Luc," Tanya returned, smirking ever wider. "A real asset to the zoo. To all of us, really."

"Happy to help." Luciana wiped her fingers clean with a napkin, leaving every crimson nail flawless. She turned to Aila. "Ready for the demonstration?"

Skies and seas, Aila better be. Too many people around for her to melt in public.

After finishing their food, Aila and Luciana hiked to the phoenix complex. The paths beyond the festival plaza were quiet, scents of chilis replaced by mango on the night breeze.

Rubra stayed snug on her nest, but at Aila's whistle, Carmesi landed on her glove, greeting his humans with a cluck. Luciana led them out. Aila matched her in stride and, she hoped, borrowed confidence. Couldn't wimp out now. Especially since this was *her* idea. The proposal bowled Luciana over when Aila suggested it, paired with every "*are you sure, Aila?*" under the sun. The challenge made her all the more determined to see it through.

They returned to the plaza.

"Ladies and gentlemen!" Luciana announced. "Thank you for joining us at the zoo this beautiful evening. We have a special guest tonight who'd love to say hello."

At Luciana's signal, Aila raised her fist with Carmesi. The crowd turned. Gasped. A wave of patrons surged for a closer look, but Luciana's griffin show colleagues were ready, spread out to maintain a safe buffer.

A chill raked through Aila as dozens of eyes latched onto her. Her throat turned dry. Her legs wavered.

But she kept standing—just like during the interview. Dozens of eyes weighed her down, but brightest of all, her father leaning out of his stall. Her favorite fire bird and her favorite festival, a perfect match. A perfect chance to share her phoenixes beyond their aviary.

"Our male Silimalo phoenix, Carmesi." Luciana's voice soared above the plaza, even without a microphone. "Don't worry, his partner is taking good care of their eggs as we speak. Female phoenixes handle all the incubation until they immolate, then Carmesi will take over once the chicks hatch. In the meantime, what better way to spice up tonight's festivities than with the hottest bird in the zoo?"

Luciana held out her glove.

At the signal, Aila tilted her fist, prompting Carmesi to leap into the air. He flew the gap between them, wings like liquid sunset, tail dripping fire across the pavement. When he alighted on Luciana's arm, she held him up for the crowd.

The cheers rumbled Aila's chest, terrifying at first. So many eyes, so many voices, so many cameras trained on every move. Beneath that, a new feeling. She had to dig deep to find it, buried under years of closed exteriors and scurrying into corners. Excitement. Pride. All these people, thrilled to see *her* phoenix.

Aila wanted to show them how beautiful he was.

She extended her hand. Carmesi pushed off Luciana's glove, a languid arc back to Aila. When he landed on her fist, warm air beat off his wings, soft against her cheeks. The flame of his tail lit a golden halo on concrete. She'd carried phoenixes in and out of aviaries hundreds of times, but never flown one like this.

Free. Simply for the spectacle of being. The sight took her breath away.

She tilted her arm and sent Carmesi flying again. The crowd swayed with each passing.

"Silimalo phoenixes are one of the most critically endangered species at our zoo," Luciana said between flights. "Once, you could see these beautiful birds throughout the western Silimalo coast. Today, no wild birds remain. Breeding programs like ours are crucial to keeping this species alive, and you can help. This month, the Movasi legislature is considering a new law that would place harsher penalties for the sale and possession of protected magical creatures and their products. You can contact your local representative and tell them you support these measures to defend our phoenixes."

The crowd hung on every word.

So did Aila, a flutter in her belly thanks to more than the beautiful bird on her glove.

She'd always assumed Luciana's smile was plastered on, an act to coddle praise from the public. Maybe sometimes, it was. But now? Each time Carmesi lit on Luciana's hand, her smile was a beacon, her eyes engulfed in phoenix light.

After the flight demonstration, Aila brought Carmesi to the edge of the plaza. He sat on her glove with a pleased puff while Luciana stood nearby, curating questions and most of the public's attention—aside from Aila's father lumbering by to snap a hundred photos.

"*Dad*," she hissed.

"Just one more for your mother. Look at you, out in public with your bird!"

"Who's watching the stall?"

"Tanya, of course!"

"Tanya can't be trusted with grills, Dad."

Once Aila's father ceased his pestering, Luciana took the spotlight. She moved from patron to patron on airy steps, kind and patient with every question, smiles blooming in her wake like flowers following the sun. Aila was happy to step aside, catch her breath while Luciana worked her outreach magic.

Until a little girl pushed to the front of the crowd.

She emerged in messy pigtails, scuffed sneakers, overalls dirty with grass stains and craft table glitter. Tiny hands clasped a handmade mask, red with finger paint and decorated with a beak and feathers.

"Hello, little lady." Luciana crouched down to her level. "Do you have a question about our phoenix?"

The girl didn't answer. Her mouth hung open, eyes glittering with reflected flame off Carmesi's tail. At a nudge from her mother, she inched closer.

"Hi, Miss Keeper?" Her words stumbled with child embarrassment.

The question wasn't for Luciana. She looked up at Aila.

"Y-yes?" Aila said, slow to catch her tongue. "What's your question?"

"I was wondering...you know...How can I become a phoenix keeper like you?"

The world around Aila stood still.

A thousand eyes could have been boring into her, but she felt the weight of only two, wide and brown and uncertain. The little girl swiveled with hands twined at her waist, pigtails swinging like pendulums, clattering the phoenix hair ties at each end. She couldn't be much older than eight.

What would Aila have wanted to hear when she was eight

years old? The weight of responsibility threatened to wobble her legs out from under her. Luciana was so much better at this. What if Aila said the wrong thing? In seconds, she flew through a dozen potential replies.

Overthinking. Always overthinking.

Aila looked to Carmesi, regal on her glove. She crouched in front of the girl, lighting her astonished face in phoenix glow.

"You have to care a lot about your animals," Aila said.

The girl nodded.

"And you have to work hard. Do you like science classes in school?"

"Of course!"

"Good!" Aila matched her enthusiasm, the words coming easier. "A good zookeeper is a good scientist, so learn as much as you can. If you'd like, you can learn even more in college."

The girl's eyes widened. "College . . . for *zookeepers*?"

"Sure! Luciana and I both went to zookeeper college. What's your favorite animal?"

After a moment of staring at her feet, the little girl pointed to Carmesi.

Aila smiled so wide, it hurt. "Hey. That's my favorite, too."

Chapter Thirty

Aila posed with Carmesi for a photo. The little girl giggled at her side while her mother lined up the shot on her phone. After a huge thank you, the future zookeeper disappeared into the crowd, swinging her mother's arm, gushing about which science classes she wanted to take.

Aila felt the need to pinch herself.

Luciana did it for her, a teasing poke at Aila's arm. Festival lights glittered in her eyes like stars. The proud curve of her lips left Aila simmering.

They lingered in the plaza for another half hour.

If someone told last year's Aila she'd survive this long at a keeper talk, she'd have laughed her ass off, then gone back to hiding in a back exhibit. Now, her departure from the festivities almost seemed too soon. Almost. Aila's arm ached beneath Carmesi's weight. Luciana led their exit, parting the crowd for Aila and the phoenix.

"That's all for tonight," Luciana told the dispersing visitors. "Thank you for supporting the San Tamculo Zoo, and be sure to stop by the phoenix exhibit the next time you visit!"

Once they escaped the plaza, the smells of roasting chilis faded. Laughter and music dimmed to a background hum, replaced by crickets and the tap of Luciana's boots. Night-shrouded pathways soothed a brewing headache—too much social exertion for one night.

Totally worth it.

Now, Aila looked forward to hunkering down for the evening, snagging more food and a quiet place to enjoy it. She might stop by the craft table if the crowd thinned. Maybe say hello to the other griffin show keepers, thank them again for helping with the renovations.

"Your dad seems nice," Luciana said, soft.

"He does?" Aila peeped. "I mean, he *is*. Very outgoing. Both my parents are, I'm the weird one. And he always remembers faces, so if you ever stop by the restaurant, I'm ninety percent sure you'll get free drinks at least." She shrugged. "You know how dads are."

Luciana gave a low laugh. "I'll take your word for it."

Griffin shit.

Too late, Aila recalled what little Luciana had shared about her family: sparse comments about growing up with just her mom . . .

"I'm so sorry!" she said, panic speeding her words. "I didn't mean to—"

"It's fine." Luciana waved a hand. "The standard deadbeat nonsense—left when I was a toddler. I hardly remember him."

She sounded as poised as ever, as calm as ever. As good at hiding things as ever. Fathomless as the sea beneath a placid surface.

And just as breathtaking, the pathway lights glinting off every sable curl.

"So . . . what does your mom think of you being a zookeeper?" Aila asked, desperate to salvage some scrap metal from this car wreck.

"A little confused," Luciana admitted with a smirk. "But supportive. I'm the first in my family to make it through college."

"Hey." Aila smiled back. "Me too."

Luciana held out a fist. Aila bumped it, careful not to disturb Carmesi on her other arm.

"She usually comes to stuff like this," Luciana said. "Couldn't get off work tonight."

"I'm sure she's super proud."

"Yeah." Another grin, softer. "She is."

They reached the aviary. Moonlight danced in glass panes, slanting silver through the olive trees as Aila released Carmesi to the exhibit. He flew to Rubra's side, where the pair exchanged muted clucks. Lovebirds. The sight never got old.

Inside, the lights in the keeper building had shut off, just a computer screen glowing in one corner. Moonbeams trickled through the window. Aila tossed her glove to the counter, then sat atop the cool metal surface, enjoying the quiet. Enjoying what the year had brought.

Luciana swatted her shoulder.

Aila swatted back. "What's that for?"

"Look at you! I've never seen you smile so wide!"

It did, in fact, hurt. Aila's cheek muscles weren't used to this exertion. "I'll admit, the whole demonstration wasn't as bad as I thought it would be."

Self-conscious, Aila shrank, drawing her legs up onto the counter. She startled when Luciana slid beside her, a bump of elbows cracking her shell.

"You were *fantastic*, Aila."

That smile again—a weapon, painted in ruby.

"It was fun," Aila admitted. "Even if some of the questions were weird."

"They always are."

"Like, that one about phoenixes using their tail fire for propulsion? How do people come up with that nonsense?"

Luciana laughed. "That's half the fun of talking to the public. You never know what you'll get."

"And that little girl."

"Adorable. I think you made a good impression."

"Maybe. I wish I'd had a zookeeper to talk to when I was that age."

Luciana nudged her arm. "That's the point, you dork. *You* can be that person."

Aila uncurled, coaxed like a snail with a strawberry dangled in front of her. Luciana leaned against the counter, a brush of heat off her arm. Mango drifting off her hair.

Usually, this was the time of night Aila sought solitude like a covetous hermit crab, the mere thought of company enough to send her head throbbing. People (even people she liked) took energy, draining her battery until she had to retreat to recharge. Even her beloved Tanya recognized when to send Aila off to a warm blanket and a quiet apartment.

This easy feeling, Aila wasn't used to. A person seated beside her without drain, without demand. Luciana's smile was energizing. One look, and Aila's grin refused to fade.

"Thanks...Luc."

The name was a firebrand on Aila's tongue. Sweet like honey. Even sweeter: the pleased curl of Luciana's lips, catching the words like a secret whispered to the dark.

They ought to head back to the festival. Neither of them made the first move to leave.

Aila wasn't sure how to act in moments like this. Quiet? Earnest? She tried to make the words come out right. "I never dreamed I could stand in front of a crowd like I did tonight."

"You're the one who did it," Luciana countered. "Not me."

"But you helped me step outside my cranky little shell. I owe you."

"You don't owe me anything." Luciana dropped her eyes and tapped crimson nails against the counter, a fidget Aila wasn't used to. "I'm grateful, too."

Aila's brows rocketed upward. The griffin show witch, proud and perfect Luciana, acting self-conscious? Maybe Aila had slipped in the kelpie exhibit months ago and hit her head. All this would make more sense as a hallucination.

"Grateful?" she asked.

"It's been a hard few months. Ever since Nimit..." Luciana paused. The scrunch to her brow didn't belong.

Aila wanted nothing more than to reach out and brush her thumb over that soft skin.

Panic jolted through her. Another night, nerves would have sent her fleeing. Now, her hammering heartbeat rooted her in place, unwilling to break this moment between them.

"But working with you and Tanya," Luciana said, "it's been nice. I...uh..." She chuckled. "Was nervous at first. I knew how you felt about me. Tanya and I used to be OK, but I assumed she'd take your side. I thought the two of you were going to hate me."

"To be fair, we did." *Smooth, Aila.*

Luciana rolled her eyes. "You came around."

"So did you." More than Aila could have imagined.

"Please. I'm not as bad as you made me out to be."

"Are you kidding? In college, people *fought* in group chats over who'd get to be your partner for animal practicals."

Luciana crossed her arms, a pout on her lips. "I heard about that."

"The school newspaper interviewed you at least once a year."

"Sure. That's not—"

"Our outreach professor kept a recording of your final project as a class example."

"I know, I know." A defensive edge crept into Luciana's voice. "To be honest? It's all pretty...isolating."

"*Isolating?*" Aila pictured Luciana basking in a teacher's praise, trailing adoring fans, raising her arms to a packed amphitheater.

"Of course. People expect you to be perfect all the time, successful all the time. You stop being a person to them. Instead, you're just something shiny on a pedestal."

Exactly how Aila had treated her. For *years*.

"But then," Luciana went on, "you feel like everyone is always watching you. Judging you. Like all it will take is one small mistake and..."

"And you'll let everyone down," Aila finished, a whisper in the dark.

"Yeah. That."

Luciana hunched into herself. Shrinking. Vulnerable. Aila knew the feeling, yet seeing the shell on another person was baffling.

"I never realized." Aila floundered for something to break the tension. She dared to poke Luciana's arm. "For the record? I like human Luciana better than pedestal Luciana."

That got a low chuckle. Success.

"The griffin show is great," Luciana said. "But nights like these are my favorite. Talking to people. Spending time with the animals."

Aila could tell. That smile was infectious. "Don't get me wrong, you're amazing on stage. But listening to you field the craziest phoenix questions? Watching you scratch Carmesi's cheeks so good, he purrs? That's...a side of you I never saw before." A side she should have seen. Aila dropped to a murmur. "I'm sorry I was so mean all these years."

"Not just you. We were both . . ." Luciana chewed her lip.

"Trapped in a cycle of bitchiness?"

"Sounds right."

They shared a laugh as light as moonbeams, a dark room and a counter cool beneath Aila's fingers. She didn't recall leaning closer to Luciana, drawn in by the warmth of her skin. The unconquerable pull of a star.

"I wish we'd gotten off to a better start," Luciana said, soft. "We had so many classes together in college. You should have said something."

"Are you fucking kidding me? I was *terrified* of you. No matter how bad my crush was, I never could have—"

Aila clamped her mouth shut so fast, her teeth creaked.

Which, of course, drew more attention to the horrendous words she'd blurted. A stream of expletives screamed through her head. Maybe it was fine. Maybe she could salvage this. She risked a glance at Luciana, hoping the slip had gone by her.

Luciana's eyes went wide as moons. "What did you say?"

"Nothing!"

"You had a crush on me in college?" Her brow furrowed. "*You?*"

"Shut *uuup.*" Aila dragged the word out, pleading. For Luciana to give her a break, or for some black hole to swallow her. She wasn't picky. "It was a dumb little thing."

"Why didn't you say anything?"

"Because I'm me?" Nothing more needed to be said, but Aila went on. "I'm awkward. Shy. A complete disaster at ninety percent of social interactions, if we're generous. Meanwhile, you're confident. Accomplished and popular and . . ." *Oh no. Here it comes.* "Beautiful."

Horns and fangs, Aila hadn't even dived into the festival's kelpie bog punch yet. *Sober Aila, what are you doing?*

Luciana held too still. She should have run away by now, should have drowned Aila with excuses to escape this awkward conversation.

Instead, Luciana leaned closer, pressing their arms together.

"I think you're confident," Luciana said, words soft on the lips Aila couldn't stop staring at. "When you want to be. About things that matter to you."

Aila didn't know what thoughts were. "You don't have to say that."

"It's true. And I think you're..." Color warmed Luciana's cheeks. "Cute."

Absurd. Unfathomable. The prospect left Aila's heart vibrating in her ribcage.

"You do not," Aila said.

"Why would I lie about something like that?"

"I don't know, because...Really?"

A few seconds drew out to eternity. Aila dragged her gaze away from Luciana's lips, only to stumble into the greater hazard of her eyes—deep as ink in the dim light, veiled in thick lashes and bold red shadow. More frequent phoenix colors, since Luciana started working with them. Another detail Aila took too long to notice.

Slowly—so slowly, like braving a wild beast—Luciana raised her hand.

Something exploded inside Aila when Luciana brushed her temple.

"These frizzy things your hair does?" Luciana curled a strand around her finger. "I think they're adorable."

Aila's panic hit full force, hot as lava through her veins, restless as a hundred thousand butterflies trying to flee her stomach.

At the same time: a stunning calm. Counter-intuitive. Like

something settling inside her, the feeling of pieces clicking into place. A beautiful night. A quiet room.

Just the two of them.

"You and Connor." Luciana toyed with Aila's hair. "Are you ... still a thing?"

"No." A simple word, fizzling with anticipation.

"Good to know," Luciana agreed.

In that moment, Aila only knew the sweet smell of mango. The enchantment of half-lidded lashes. The allure of full lips, cruelly parted. Achingly close.

Do it. Do it, you coward.

Aila might have liked some semblance of thought to drive the moment, perhaps a romantic observation or poetic reverie. Her deafening mental scream would have to do.

She tipped her head up and kissed Luciana.

Her lips were soft. Pliable. Willing in an instant, pressing back with an eagerness that made Aila's head spin. The watermelon lip balm was unexpected, but pleasant. A veritable buffet of tropical fruits, this woman. Aila tasted her for one deep breath before reeling back for air. The sweetness lingered on her lips, Luciana watching through dark eyes, mouth parted for a low exhale.

Aila giggled, nervous.

"Was that ... OK? I mean, for me, obviously it was OK. More than OK. It's just that reading signals is weird, so I want to make sure I'm not—"

Luciana cupped Aila's cheeks in light fingers. "Aila. You're the biggest dork I've ever met."

They laughed together.

Luciana kissed her again.

The warmth of those lips sank Aila to her core, like she could melt beneath the heat yet not bemoan the life of a puddle. She wound her hands into Luciana's hair, the accomplishment of a life's ambition. Flawless silk slipped between her fingers. This woman's moisturizing routine was on a level beyond Aila's comprehension.

All of this, beyond Aila's comprehension.

She'd kissed other people before. Of course she had. But by the endless, merciful skies and seas, no one had ever brushed a thumb so soft along Aila's jaw. No one had ever ghosted a tongue along her lip, light enough to make her forget how to breathe. No one had ever cupped a hand to the back of Aila's neck, dragging her closer the way Luciana did, as if she was something to be relished, as if she was finally something to be fucking *wanted*.

Luciana shifted, standing to face the counter where Aila sat, towering over her with deepening kisses. This moment, theirs to indulge, theirs to draw out as long as the room lay quiet and dim around them, the crowds and festival booths out of sight and out of mind. Aila was already teetering on the edge of disintegration. Why not be a little daring? She brought up her legs up to hook around Luciana's waist, pulling her closer.

Luciana paused. Smirked.

Then pushed Aila onto her back against the counter.

Aila gasped as the butterflies in her stomach stormed free, fluttering into every extremity. The surprise of it left her breathless. Left her heart pattering an entirely new rhythm. Aila had never been a top in her life. She was a meek, groveling little creature.

She'd not lament this woman crushing her into pieces.

They both stilled, Aila pinned on her back. Luciana leaned over her, letting her glossy black hair fall around Aila's head. Her eyes were dark and deep like night sky as she bit her lip, brushing the errant curls from Aila's temple with soft fingers.

"When do you want to head back?" she asked. "Someone will notice we're missing."

"Not yet," Aila pleaded. "Just a little longer."

Later, there'd be time for festival food. A cup or two of kelpie bog punch.

In this moment, Aila's entire world was mango-scented hair. The press of warm lips as Luciana bent to kiss her again. Cool metal against her back.

And a flutter in her heart that told her this was, at last, what she'd wanted for so long.

Chapter Thirty-One

Aila had never floated like this.

The rest of that festival evening. The days that followed.

She sailed the zoo paths as if they were made not of summer-baked concrete and old chewing gum but of ocean waves, wisps of cloud, beams of silver starlight. The sludge in the kelpie exhibit seemed less grimy. Collecting moldy fruit from the World of Birds aviary became an afternoon stroll. When she stood in her phoenix exhibit, she basked in the light through the glass.

In the nest, five perfect turquoise eggs on the brink of hatching.

In her hair, remnants of mango that teased throughout the day.

Once, she'd dreaded Luciana's visits. Now, each one stoked butterflies in her stomach, a smile that didn't fade.

On a sweltering afternoon, Aila braved the porch of the phoenix complex, in need of cleaning after a windy day filled it with twigs and olive leaves. As she swept around the table legs, Aila whistled. She wasn't even good at whistling. Off-key notes stumbled through her teeth with reckless abandon as she *swish-swash-swished* her broom across the tiles.

"How long am I gonna keep catching you like this?" Tanya said behind her.

Aila startled, her whistles twisting into a squeak as she fumbled with the broom handle. Clutching it to her chest, she spun around. Tanya leaned against the doorframe, watching Aila with brows raised.

A familiar gesture, by now. When Aila confessed to kissing Luciana, Tanya had (as was her duty) joined in the initial squeal called for by such an occasion. After that? The teasing. Constant and merciless. That "I-knew-longer-than-you" smirk of Tanya's had burned into Aila's retinas.

"Will you stop sneaking up on me?" Aila snapped.

"Only when you stop acting like a love-drunk idiot," Tanya countered with a grin.

"Am not!"

"Are too."

"Oh, real mature."

Tanya brandished a teal fingernail. "Ailes. You only whistle when you're multiple shots into tequila." A second finger shot up. "When you see a cute animal on the internet." A third. "And now, apparently, when you're thinking about kissing terrifying women."

Aila plopped into a patio chair, the broom handle too narrow to hide her blush. This brand of whimsy, she had no experience with. Most of her relationships consisted of awkward small talk or anxious glances around corners before crashing and burning in a heap.

Happy Aila didn't know what to do with herself. Part of her scrambled for her shell, waiting for all this joy to crack beneath her.

Tanya pulled up a chair. Despite Aila's best pouting, Tanya propped a chin on her shoulder and weaponized a smile. Aila crumbled, and they both tumbled into a fit of laughter.

"Sorry." Aila kicked the broom from foot to foot, scowling at new debris blown out of the trees. "I'll try to be less obnoxious."

"Ailes. You know I'm teasing."

"Still."

Tanya swatted her shoulder. "You stop that right now, girlie! Look at you! I've never seen a smile like this!"

Aila rubbed her cheeks. "It's exhausting. Do normal people smile this much?"

"Love-drunk idiots do," Tanya countered. "This is exactly what I was hoping to see from Connor. Who knew Luc would be the one to bring it out of you?"

Aila remembered a few fleeting butterflies from Connor. Her infatuation with that smile. Nothing like this warmth that settled in her belly like a furnace.

Luciana.

Her phoenixes.

All of it, perfect.

This moment Aila could live in forever.

She leaned back in her chair, smiling like an idiot as she breathed in the warm, olive-laced air, with a hint of sweet kettle corn and salty fries from the nearest snack shop.

"Do you ever wish," Aila said, "you could go back and tell your younger self to just keep going? That it will all get better in a few years?"

"Absolutely," Tanya said, equally wistful.

Aila wished she could have been her friend sooner. It was hard to imagine Tanya as anyone other than the vibrant, confident woman she'd grown into, but everyone had their own rocky road. At least they had each other now. Each other, and the phoenix program they'd built.

Tanya reclined against the table, a pensive look at the trees overhead. "Do you think she's a top or a bottom?"

"*What?*" Aila sputtered. Her moment of reverie, shattered.

"Luciana. One would assume top, but people can surprise you."

"Tanya!" Aila's cheeks burned.

"Only one way to find out, you know." Tanya waggled devious eyebrows.

Aila had no chance of a dignified comeback, but any attempt at it was thwarted by the well-timed click of the door inside. Boots tapped against linoleum, a confident tempo they both recognized. Tanya shot Aila her most scandalous smirk yet.

Aila tackled Tanya in her chair.

A futile assault, as always. Tanya had her beat in reach. And muscle. And underhanded tenacity. Tanya pinned her by the armpits, snickering as Aila flailed her spindly arms.

Luciana stepped onto the patio. Stopped. With squinted eyes, she appraised a relaxed Tanya, Aila squirming like an indignant chicken on the verge of gnawing a hand off.

"Hey, Luc," Tanya greeted. "You come to pick up our sassy gremlin child for ice cream?"

Aila gave a puny battle cry as she kicked her legs. Still no freedom.

"Yeah...no." Luciana held up a flash drive, her tone dry. "Nadia sent me to drop off the audio files we have rights to. For your phoenix video project?"

At last, Tanya released her struggling prey. Aila stumbled out of her arms and onto her feet, making "gimme" hands at Luciana. All insults forgotten. Eyes bright on the flash drive.

Luciana held it just out of reach. "First, I'm going to need the two of you to act like professionals for *at least* thirty seconds."

Off to the side, Tanya smirked and mouthed an affirmative "*top*" to Aila. They swatted each other once more.

Aila snatched the flash drive from Luciana. The project idea came to her a couple of days ago, and as with most strokes of inspiration, Aila had been consumed by it ever since. As popular as their live phoenix camera had become, who wouldn't love a highlight reel of the best preening moments? The cutest phoenix clucks? Edited to music, of course. Of which the griffin show had plenty to share. As Aila clutched the flash drive, Tanya chuckled and headed inside.

"See you later, Luc." Even facing away, Aila heard the smirk.

Luciana stared after her. A scowl puffed her lips, nose wrinkled into the most adorable lines Aila couldn't stop staring at.

"Is she . . . mad at me?" Luciana asked, confused.

"Oh, no. There would be way more knives involved."

"That's unsettling."

"Yeah." Aila sighed, wistful. "I don't deserve her."

The moment turned more earnest than expected. Aila cast her eyes down, but before she had time to feel awkward, Luciana laughed. A line of rescue, hauling Aila up from the deep. And when Luciana booped a finger to Aila's nose? She soared again.

They'd kissed at the festival. And several times since then. Afterward, Luciana hadn't said it was a mistake, or tried to avoid Aila, or anything sensible like that.

"I love this video idea," Luciana said.

"Really?" Excitement turned Aila's words to a squeak. "Did you watch any highlight videos for the Jewelport Zoo? Don't get me wrong, they were amazing, and I watched each one ten times. But could have had better production value, you know? Not that I'm an expert, but I've been watching a lot of instructional videos, and I think I can put something together."

Aila paused for breath. A blush followed: the realization she'd been talking too much, too fast. Again. *Don't blow it.* She couldn't risk scaring Luciana off when they'd barely—

"I can't wait to see what you come up with."

Before Aila's anxiety could spiral, Luciana leaned down for a kiss.

Aila fluttered. Fell. She couldn't seem to remember what she'd been worrying about when Luciana's arm wrapped her waist. Soft fingers cupped her cheek, the brush of lips like a watermelon breeze.

Perfect. All of her. All of this.

When Luciana pulled back, she wore a smile. Not one of those polite, humoring smiles Aila was so used to seeing. Genuine.

"Those songs are all you need?" Luciana asked.

"I think I'm good for now," Aila said, breathless. Floating.

"Well, if you think of anything, let me know. Ranbir's keeping me late tonight, trying to train this new routine when it's not so hot out."

Luciana brushed her nose to Aila's before pecking a parting kiss. When she left, the sweet of mango lingered on the air.

As the day wound to a close, Aila settled cross-legged in her desk chair to work on her video project.

The patrons had gone home. Her animals were all safe in their back exhibits (with the exception of Rubra and Carmesi, diligent at their nest). The new computer in the phoenix complex offered better ergonomics and processing power than a laptop on the couch in her apartment.

"I swear, I'm going to throttle that bird one day," Tanya complained from her desk, packing up her bag to head home. Fresh mud clung to her work polo, a mark of defeat in the latest squabble with her Bix phoenix and his hiding hole.

"At least your deterrent strategies are lasting longer?" Aila offered. Her eyes stayed glued to the computer screen as she clicked through folders of phoenix video clips.

"A whole month, this time!" Tanya let out a teeth-grating sigh. "How'd that little bastard dislodge a *metal plate*? Screws and all?"

"Persistence?"

"Could do with a drop less of it." Tanya hefted her bag to her shoulder, then loomed over Aila. "Been staring at that computer screen like it owes you something. You sure you don't want to take a break tonight? Come out with us?"

A kind offer. Tanya and Teddy were headed for their monthly outing to the drive-in theater, a standing invitation Aila had succumbed to on rare occasion—and rather enjoyed herself, not having to worry about fighting movie crowds.

"We can get some of those almond chocolates you like?" Tanya taunted, seeing Aila's frown of indecision. "It's a double feature, too. They're playing *Night of the Killer Unicorn* and *Krakenado 2: The Rising Tide*."

Aila scrunched her nose. "Didn't we already watch *Night of the Killer Unicorn*? Why do you need to see it a second time?"

A gasp. Tanya pressed a hand to her heart. "Aila. I'm going to pretend you didn't say that, in the interest of our friendship."

Aila snickered. Tanya nudged her shoulder, a sign of no hard feelings.

"You have fun with Teddy," Aila said. "I'll tag along next time."

"Of course, Ailes." Tanya shifted to a squint. "How late are you staying here tonight?"

"Um..."

Aila's hesitation made Tanya click her tongue. "Don't work yourself too hard. You need your sleep for when those phoenixes hatch."

"I know. Just another hour..."

Aila got lost in projects too easily. Tanya knew as much, as shown by her glare.

"Or *two*," Aila conceded. "This computer is so much better than mine at home! Blame Nadia for picking out excellent hardware. Plus, in a couple of days? The police will be here for immolation watch. How am I supposed to get work done when there are strange people around?"

"I'll call to check in," Tanya said. "Two hours. You better be home by then, Ailes."

"Sure, sure. Enjoy your movies."

The door clicked closed as Tanya left.

Then, quiet. From the kitchen, the refrigerator hummed. The overhead lights flicked off, leaving the room lit by a phantom glow off the computer screen, cool white across metal counters and the dark pane of the observation window.

Aila loved the zoo at night. So much space to focus.

She popped open a bag of potato chips left over from lunch, crunching away as she pulled together video clips for her highlight reel. Film editing didn't rank high on her skills, but learning something new brought a calming, meditative focus. Her mouse clicks marched through the room as she pulled together her favorite moments of Carmesi preening Rubra, the pair playing with leaves, squabbles over the perfect sticks for their nest platform. In the background, she layered a cheerful guitar jingle, borrowed from the griffin show's media catalogue. Aila tapped her boot to the rhythm, trying to time the video transitions.

All of this, a warm-up for the coming act. In three days, Rubra was due to immolate. Aila couldn't believe how the time had flown, yet here she was, dreaming of her next video compilation filled with peeping chicks, their first steps out of the nest, their first flight.

The night ticked by. As fatigue dragged Aila's eyes, her thoughts drifted to other things.

She ought to ask Luciana out on a date.

Well, there went the calm of a late night at the zoo. Aila's heart picked up speed, crashing her focus. She'd fessed up to her crush. She'd dared the kiss and, skies and seas, did it turn out nice. Next step was, logically, to pursue some kind of relationship. A terrifying prospect.

Within the scope of the zoo, Aila felt safe. Beyond that, the world got scary. People opened into all sorts of brilliant and rotten complexities.

A stream of "what ifs" hit Aila like a windstorm. What if Luciana thought she was boring outside of work, like Connor had? What if Aila tripped and made a fool of herself in front of Miss Perfect Poise? What if she laughed too hard at one of Luciana's jokes and choked on her water and had to be rushed to the emergency room? What if—

Aila groaned and leaned back in her chair. She could find a million things to worry about, a million ways to make a fool of herself. But Luciana already knew Aila was a dork. She already knew Aila talked too much when she got excited, or that rooms with lots of people made her nervous. Despite all that, Luciana had kissed her. Several times.

A trickle of calm settled over Aila. It seemed impossible that someone could see the real her and not run off screaming. Tanya had given her that reprieve. Could Luciana as well? The warmth in her belly returned, a welcome change from her usual anxious somersaults.

In the aviary, a phoenix shrieked.

Aila nearly fell out of her chair. She clamped the edge of the desk in clawed fingers, halting her swivel, heart thundering against her ribs.

S. A. MACLEAN

Another shriek rattled the glass—and her frail heart.

What in all the skies and seas?

Phoenixes weren't nocturnal. The moment the sun went down, they roosted for the night, not a peep under normal circumstances. Yet there came a cackle echoing through the aviary, notes of a familiar staccato. Carmesi.

Aila had *never* heard that call before.

She hurried to the window.

After hours of staring at a computer screen, it took her a moment to peer through the glass, tired eyes struggling to parse shadowed silhouettes. Outside, the exhibit lurked dark and quiet, moonlight dim through glass panels and olive trees. But there, at the far side, a halo of light. Carmesi perched on the nest platform, his tail flared to golden flame. He called out at full volume, head bobbing, every gilded feather puffed.

Beside him, Rubra lay flat against her nest, the flame on her tail dimmed to red embers in the dark. She splayed her wings, gold and tangerine flight feathers tangling with twigs and insulating down. Her breast rose and fell, breaths heavier than usual.

She let out a low, sharp cluck.

Then she burst into flame.

A flare of gold engulfed the aviary, pure daylight in the middle of the night. Aila squinted and shielded an arm across her face, blinded by the light, breath caught in her chest. Normal fire didn't burn with such intensity, wreathed in tendrils of blue and crimson and gold in ever-changing swirls. Sunlight didn't shine with such heat, enough to bake Aila's cheeks even from across the exhibit, even through the heat-reinforced glass.

Just as quickly, the light snapped out. The exhibit went dark again, starker in contrast.

Spots danced across Aila's vision. She blinked them away with pained fervor, fighting to focus on dark trees. Dark aviary

404

struts. Across the exhibit, only a dull orange smolder lit the nest platform.

She stood at the window, frozen in disbelief, hands shaking against the countertop. Aila had read every book. She'd read every paper, watched every video online and in the IMWS archives, had *heard* it described two dozen different ways. Nothing that could prepare her for . . .

Fuck. Fuck. Fuck.

This was early.

Rubra had immolated *early*.

Weeks, months, years, she'd prepared for this, yet the moment threatened to topple her. Terror and excitement were warring bears, clawing for supremacy. Through the haze, Aila floundered for clarity in mental snapshots of flashcards. Her protocol binders sat organized along the wall, every word memorized.

She jumped into action.

Click, click, click, went down the line, her fingers jittery as she flipped on the incubators. Carmesi would handle most of the chick-rearing, but this first night after immolation? Crucial. The highest mortality window for young phoenixes. The chicks, exposed to that extreme heat, risked cooling down too fast, even with an attentive father roosting over them. Aila's priority was getting them inside, moderating their temperature in the incubators until they stabilized.

She pulled fireproof gloves onto both arms, then grabbed a metal basket, lining it with towels she didn't mind getting singed. As Aila stepped into the exhibit, her heart raced like pixie wren wings.

It's time, it's time, it's finally time.

The acrid smell of burnt olive leaves clawed Aila's nose. Charred twigs crumbled to ash beneath her boots, piling in gray drifts beneath the nest platform. She hefted herself up the ladder, wood hot beneath gloved hands. The fire-resistant treatment held up, though bits of platform popped and creaked in protest.

At the top of the platform, the nest had vanished. Only ash and blackened branches remained, traces of a cataclysm. Carmesi roosted at the epicenter, his crimson wings splayed gray with soot, wide eyes looking up at Aila. Full of pride? Understanding? At least one of them seemed calm in this situation.

"Good bird." Her voice rattled, constrained by tight cheeks. A smile, she realized. Aila's smile stretched wider than any she remembered. "You've done such a good job, Carmesi. Let me take care of them for the night, then you can have them back. I promise."

He clucked in protest as Aila reached beneath him, lifting the bird off the ruined nest. With a flutter of wings and a puff of ash, Carmesi hopped to the edge of the platform, pacing as he watched her.

They both stilled at the sight of moving ashes.

A muted peep struggled into the world. Aila dug through the soot until her fingers brushed something tiny, squishy. The chick emerged in a wriggle of wet gray down, eyes shut, nubby wings floundering. Aila cupped the treasure in her palms. It weighed nothing. It smelled of woodsmoke.

She had to move quickly, before tears clouded her eyes.

One by one, she dredged five chicks from the ash and set them in her metal basket. Carmesi nestled up to the side, peering down at his brood with puffed cheeks. Last, a bigger lump shifted within the nest. Aila brushed the bird clean, large enough to fit in both her hands, covered not in slick down but a bustle of ruby pin feathers.

Rubra. Gone in flame, returned as a chick, though more grown than the others. She raised her head, greeting her keeper with a tired peep. Aila hugged her phoenix to her chest.

"Sweet bird. You did so well." Tears slipped from Aila's eyes, slick down ash-stained cheeks.

Once Rubra rested in the basket with her chicks, Aila descended the ladder. Carmesi followed her across the exhibit, clucking anxiously. The sight broke her heart, but she'd get the chicks back to him soon. Tonight, she'd keep them safe at any cost.

Inside, the line of incubators filled the room with orange light, buzzing as the heaters worked. Aila placed Rubra and her precious chicks inside. Five times, she checked all the knobs and panels, making sure the temperature was right, the schedule set to gradually return to ambient. Nestled in their boxes, the chicks' egg-wet down dried into the poofy coat that would keep them warm.

Aila stood back from her work, heart hammering. Breaths quick.

All quiet.

All well.

As the fog of fight or flight receded, reality struck. On the wall above her desk, a crinkled phoenix poster glowed in orange light. In the incubators, five phoenix chicks peeped as they settled into sleep.

Aila's fingers jittered. Her boots bounced against linoleum. Five phoenix chicks. *Her* five phoenix chicks. Who cared if they were early? So long as Rubra and her brood looked healthy—

A laugh erupted from Aila's chest. Remembering to breathe became an issue. Wiping the smile off her face before her cheeks split open? Impossible. She had to call Tanya. She had to tell Maria. Director Hawthorn. Her parents. Everyone in the *world* was going to hear about this. San Tamculo's first phoenix chicks in over a decade.

And what about the live camera? Some viewers must have

been watching. Aila flipped open her laptop on the counter, giddy to see the excitement in the chat.

When she pulled up the page, the video failed to load.

Frowning, Aila reloaded. Still nothing. A black screen sat at the center of the page, flanked by the scrolling live chat. Viewer comments streamed past in confusion, questions of why the video was down and when it might return.

Technical difficulties. That was all. Aila's attempt at self-assurance didn't stop her mood from plummeting, elation replaced by a squirm in her stomach. She glanced at the incubators, her phoenixes nestled safe inside. With the initial transfer complete, she had a laundry list of hatch-day protocol to check through, chick health to inspect and IMWS to notify.

That could wait five minutes. For Aila's own sanity.

She yanked open the door and stepped outside.

Night shrouded the zoo like velvet, heavy in the trees, broken by dim light from the lampposts. No din of patrons. No squawks from the sleeping aviaries. Aila relished most quiet, but now, the lonely patter of her boots against concrete left her jumpy.

Ridiculous. She was worrying too much, like always.

A jog brought her to the loading dock behind the phoenix complex. She flipped open a metal box affixed to the wall, containment for the nest of wires that fed into the camera. Something loose. Something disconnected. That was all she'd find.

When she opened the box, the wires curled in neat bunches.

Except for one: the camera's internet connection, cut in two.

Aila's mouth turned dry as she inspected the severed cable. Infiltration by a destructive purserat? She saw no other damage within the box, no obvious point of entry into the metal case. Once more, Aila berated herself for overreacting. She *had* to be overreacting.

She needed to call the police. Rubra was *early*, too early for their scheduled patrol.

"*Fuck!*" Aila patted empty pockets and empty belt, her cell phone and radio cast upon the counter while she'd worked on her video project. Forgotten in the mad rush to rescue phoenix chicks. She sprinted around the building to retrieve them.

When she rounded the corner, she smacked into someone at full force.

"Horns and fucking fangs!" Aila sprawled onto the pavement, catching her fall with scraped palms. She hissed and flexed her fingers, angry red stinging her skin.

Looming above her, the absolute last person she wanted to see.

"Aila?" Connor's polo was rumpled, the curl of hair against his temple cast askew by their collision. He stared down at her with wide eyes, as if he'd run into a ghost.

If only. She'd made herself scarce since they broke up, calculating paths and staff office check-ins to avoid him at all cost. Slamming into him on her own doorstep, a dick move.

"Will you stop that?" Aila scrambled to her feet, wincing at every joint that had hit concrete. "Lurking around corners. You're going to give me a heart attack!"

"Aila, what are you doing here this late?"

"Working! What are *you* doing here this late? Actually, no, never mind. Crisis first!"

Taking fish inventory, cataloging dragon scales, bleaching swimming pools—Aila didn't care what obnoxious inconvenience had tossed Connor into her path. She had to make sure her phoenixes were safe.

"What crisis?" Connor called out. Jogging after her, she noted with annoyance.

"Rubra immolated!" Aila hurled herself at the breeding

complex door. "The chicks are out, but the live camera's down. Looks like someone messed with the wiring. I need to call the police."

"The police? Aila, take a second to calm down."

"*Calm down?*" Aila reeled on him, boots squeaking against the linoleum.

"Take a deep breath." Connor stepped closer, hands raised. "There's no need to overreact."

"I'm not overreacting, Connor! These are my phoenixes. My responsibility. I don't care if I have to dredge the entire police department out here to investigate a single purserat. I'm not letting anything happen to them. Not after Jewelport."

Aila finished with chest heaving, words ringing against the empty room. Skies and seas, that felt *good*. She should have stood her ground with Connor ages ago, not tiptoed around like a frightened rabbit. Empowered by the swell of confidence, she reached for her phone on the desk.

Connor grabbed her wrist.

"What are you doing?" Aila yanked back, annoyed, but his grip held. "Connor, let go—"

Her words slipped into a yelp as he pulled her across the room and shoved her into the phoenix aviary, slamming the gate behind her.

Chapter Thirty-Two

"Connor, this isn't funny."

Aila rattled the bars of the back aviary, but the metal didn't budge. Renovated and sturdy, like everything else in the phoenix complex. By the observation window, Connor tapped on his phone, ignoring her.

"Stop being such a prick!" Aila shouted. "This whole 'you worry too much' bullshit is getting old. Let me out!"

Connor flicked an annoyed glance at her before holding his phone to his ear. He stared out the window, arm braced on the counter, boot tapping against linoleum.

Aila jammed her shoulder against the bars and flailed her hand out as far as she could, but not enough to reach the keypad. Connor would have to let her out. *Asshole*. She should have slapped herself for fawning over him. If this was some kind of dumb power play for her breaking up with him—

"Hello?" Connor spoke harsh into his phone. "About time. How soon can you be here?"

Aila scrunched her face in confusion. The zoo closed hours ago. Why was Connor acting so strange?

"I know." Connor paused, scowling through the reply Aila couldn't hear. "I *know* it's early...No, the chicks are already out...No, it has to be *tonight*." He glanced at Aila, then ran a hand through his hair, messing the dark locks. "Just get here with the portable incubator. *Soon*. I'll set up the phone jammer...OK...*OK*."

He clicked off his phone and shoved it into his pocket.

Aila's hands fell slack against the bars, the metal cold on her fingers. Understanding came colder. She looked to the line of incubators humming along the wall, Rubra and her chicks inside. Then back to the window, the hunched silhouette of someone she'd thought was a friend.

"Connor?" she said, quiet. Pleading.

"Why the fuck did you have to be here tonight, Aila?" His words carried that annoyed brevity she'd heard from so many people. Never this biting. "You should have gone home hours ago. Like a *normal* person."

Aila gripped the bars tighter, grasping for stability. "Connor, please. Let me out."

"We both know that's not going to happen, Aila."

"You can't! Not my phoenixes, Connor!"

Speaking the words shattered her composure. Aila yanked at unmoving metal, knuckles white, panicked breaths hitching up her throat. What was Connor doing here so late? Why had he locked her away?

What was he going to do to her phoenixes?

On the counter—across the world—Aila's phone screen lit up. A cheerful jingle played, the tune she'd assigned to Tanya. Hope lit Aila's chest. Tanya could help. Tanya always came to Aila's rescue when she was powerless.

That hope sputtered as Connor clicked the call to voicemail, then tossed her phone back to the counter. Why hadn't Aila kept the phone with her? *Stupid, stupid.*

"Connor." Aila's voice shook with entreaty as she tried to make sense of all this, tried to fight down the heart racing into her throat. "If this is because... because of what happened between us, I'm sorry. I didn't want things to end that way. I was selfish, and afraid, and I should have said something sooner, but I did like you. I just don't think—"

"Skies and seas," Connor said, "you still think I *wanted* to date you?"

The barbs hit every mark—the husk of Aila's chest, the chaos swirling in her head. She gripped the bars. Released. Flexed her hands over and over, yet every movement came numb, her joints like a little toy girl made of wood and straw for a brain.

"What?" she squeaked.

"You think anyone enjoys listening to you ramble about animals all day? You think I wanted to spend time with you when I'm the only one who can hold a conversation?"

Aila's heart was crumbs cast to pigeons. Bits of dust clogged in the patio corner.

"But... but you kissed me. You asked me on a date. You kept after me for weeks!"

"Yeah." Connor sneered, his smile no longer gorgeous, but sickly white. Cruel. "Thanks for making things as difficult as possible, making me simp and fawn over you. All that, just to get a fucking hatch date."

It couldn't be. Connor had come to their aid with the building renovations, sacrificing his time to help them roll out linoleum. He'd helped cart their fridge inside. He'd tuned up the incubators, lugged camera cables, cleaned purserat remains from under the cabinets.

He'd helped Aila install the new keypad lock on the aviary.

He'd bolted the security cameras in place.

He'd pushed her to get the live camera set up.

Locked behind bars, her phoenixes beyond reach, Aila shriveled at all the things she'd shown Connor. The horror of how close she'd brought him. He'd laughed with her at lunch breaks. He'd celebrated with her after the phoenix transfer got approved, string lights in his eyes and that dazzling smile. Even when she'd shunned him after their date, he'd pursued her as no one ever had.

But, of course, he hadn't wanted Aila. What made her believe such a ridiculous thing?

He'd only wanted what she could give him.

"You did it to steal my phoenixes?" The truth turned Aila's tongue to mud, a lump in her mouth. A wildfire roaring in her head. "Those smiles. Those...*compliments*. They were all fake? This whole time, you were planning to steal my phoenixes?"

"Don't do this, Aila. There's no point trying to—"

Her phone rang. Tanya again. Connor scowled and sent the call to voicemail once more.

"How could you?" Aila demanded. "I don't care what you think of me!" A lie. "But how could you do this to the phoenixes? After all you did to help us. After what happened to your dragon hatchlings."

Connor braced his hands on the counter. Hung his head.

"It was so much money, Aila."

Realization hit her like a jolt of thunderhawk static. Sick. She was going to be sick. Or strangle these bars until they crinkled beneath her fingers.

"*You*," she hissed. "It was *you*? You sold your own dragons to *poachers*?"

"Do you have any idea what a diamondback dragon hatchling is worth?" Connor's voice rose. His palm slammed the counter. "My dad dropped himself into so much debt with those fucking stock trades, it would have taken me a decade to get him out of it. A single hatchling paid off the whole thing. The entire *fucking* thing, Aila!"

She recoiled. To think he could be so desperate. To think she never knew.

"But Vera!" Aila pleaded. "She's *your* dragon! Don't you care about her?"

"Of course I care about Vera." Connor stepped closer, brow pinched. Tone condescending to a stupid animal. "I cared about those hatchlings, too. I stayed up all night while they were in the incubators. Hand-fed them when they hatched. All that, just for the zoo to send them away?"

"They were *babies*," Aila said. "They were supposed to go to Vjar, released into the diamondback dragon preserve."

"What—so poachers could snatch them up from the wild instead?" Connor threw up his hands. "It's pointless, Aila. You can have playtime with your precious animals in the zoo all you want, but none of them are going to survive in the real world. At least I made sure my dragons went to private collectors, rather than cut up for parts and scale dust."

Collectors? How chivalrous of him.

"Fine," Aila gritted. It wasn't fine. It was about as far from fine as a glop of shit to the face. "You sold your dragons. You paid off your debt. Leave *my phoenixes* out of it."

She thought her clenched teeth might crack when Connor pointed at the incubators.

"Do you know what those chicks are worth?" he said.

Unimaginable. Aila's heart rioted to even humor the calculation. Five perfect peeping chicks, defenseless, not an hour old. Some of the last of their kind. What monster could put a price on them? A paltry amount, nothing beyond the cost of their feathers.

"I would never," Aila said.

"The dragons were a lifesaver. But a single Silimalo phoenix"—Connor held up a finger—"enough to retire. Enough to escape to some island in the Naelo Archipelago, stop scraping fish guts and dragon shit all day."

A meaningless life, built on bones.

"That's what this is about? Scraping fish guts? You knew what you were signing up for when you went to *zoo college!*"

"Of course I did. And we all thought the work would be worth it, when we were young and naive." His voice cracked. "What are you doing now, Aila? Delaying the inevitable. Holding on to a species that's already headed down the drain. Might as well make some money off it while we can."

"You're *disgusting.*"

"And all you care about is a bunch of stupid birds that couldn't cut it on their own."

If only shouting could open bars. Aila's vice grip made no headway against the metal. She contemplated spitting at Connor instead, that slithering orchid viper. But no, that wasn't fair to orchid vipers. At least they had a symbiotic relationship with their host trees—venom that boosted flower growth. Connor was nothing but trash.

For a third time, her phone rang.

Tanya. Beautiful, persistent Tanya. Through Aila's boiling rage at Connor and his flat champagne personality, a sliver of hope returned. When she didn't answer her phone, Tanya would worry. Not like a normal person would worry. This was *Tanya-level* worry, direct as an afternoon sunbeam to the retina. She'd drive back out here, cussing the whole way, just to drag Aila home herself. Maybe, she'd even bring help.

Connor must have realized the same thing.

He stared at Aila's phone, cheerful jingle playing from the speaker. He held it out to her, too far to grab, finger poised over the "answer" button.

"Tell her everything's fine," he ordered.

"Or what?"

His voice dropped low. A warning. "Or I'll take the chicks now, and fuck the portable incubator. We roll the dice on how many survive."

Aila's stomach twisted like kraken tentacles. Connor had one trump card: she'd do anything to keep those birds safe. When she conceded a nod, Connor clicked to accept the call.

Focus, Aila. Don't fuck this up.

"Hey, Tanya." She couldn't stop her voice from quivering. Connor's glare didn't help.

"Ailes?" Tanya snapped back. "Are you home yet?"

Her voice exploded from the speaker, fighting a background of screams and unicorn neighs set to slasher music. The reprimand oozed venom, dripped with loving concern. Aila choked back her tears.

"I, uh..." *Think, Aila, think.* Something to say. Something to let her know what's wrong.

"You're still at the zoo?" Tanya accused.

Aila never could lie to her, like her best friend had a radar for when Aila was working too hard. "Yeah. I am."

She glanced at Connor. He circled his finger in the air, signaling her to wrap up the call. Aila didn't have much time.

"The live camera's down," Tanya said, a hint of worry. "Everything all right?"

"Sure. I checked the wiring. Purserat must have gotten into the box. We can fix it."

Come on, Aila, that's not good enough!

"Tomorrow, Aila," Tanya said. "Time to go home now."

"Sure. I...just need to take care of that leaky water tap in the exhibit, then I'll head home."

A long silence played over the speaker.

Aila held her breath, hands locked around the aviary bars. In her head, she begged, pleaded. *Come on, Tanya.* She'd never let Aila down before.

"You sure everything's all right?" Tanya said at last.

"Totally." Aila used the false chipper voice reserved for patrons she couldn't wait to escape from. "Thanks for checking, Tanya. You're ... a lifesaver."

Another pause. "All right, Ailes. Take care."

"Bye, Tanya."

When Connor ended the call, Aila slumped against the bars.

Connor powered off her phone and stuffed it in his pocket. He grabbed her radio from the counter as well, yanked the internet cables from the computers, then slung a bag off his shoulder and pulled out a black box crowned in antennas. As he fidgeted with the dials, Aila cursed.

A cell phone jammer.

And the live camera cut.

Bastard copied the entire playbook from the Jewelport break-in. All their updated security, useless against someone who knew it in and out. Their planned police patrol, scheduled for the expected immolation window days away.

"Connor," she called a final time. Even then, she wasn't sure if it was anger that shook the words, or her pleading heart, frail to the last.

On his way out the door, Connor paused. Faced her. "For what it's worth, I didn't want you to be here tonight."

Not out of compassion. Out of convenience. Aila heard that finality in the slam of the door. She sank to her knees, hands clasped around the bars of her aviary. Tanya would understand. She *had* to understand.

Help still might not arrive in time.

418

Chapter Thirty-Three

Aila had to escape. She had to save her phoenixes.

For the dozenth time, she jammed her arm through the aviary bars, pivoting her shoulder against unyielding metal until her joints ached. Reaching. *Reaching.* Her hand swiped empty air several inches from the keypad lock. For all her pride at their renovated security measures, she'd never foreseen them betraying her like this.

With a cry of rage, Aila paced the aviary, searching for options. She tried the smaller gate that opened onto the phoenix exhibit, hoping she'd gotten lazy and left it unlatched. Another pipe dream. Meticulous, obsessive Aila had checked and double-checked all her locks, ensuring everything was closed up tight for the night.

Aila returned to the bars and shouted for help. She screamed obscenities at Connor and his piece of shit personality. When no one responded, Aila melted down to her knees, a puddle on the floor. Less effective than a puddle, which could have escaped beneath the gate.

Hands raw, coated in aviary dust, Aila drew her legs to her chest and scrunched into a ball. Tears ran hot down her cheeks, tightening her throat until she labored to breathe. She was supposed to keep these birds safe.

She'd failed.

While she cowered in a cage, they'd be whisked away in front of her.

What would she tell Tanya, when her friend arrived too late?

How would she explain to Maria that she'd lost their phoenixes?

Not just lost. Aila handed them to Connor like an educational slide presentation, complete with a question-and-answer session on phoenix nabbing.

She flinched when the door across the room clicked open. Connor returning with the portable incubator? Aila couldn't look, couldn't bear to watch her phoenixes taken away. She clutched her knees, wincing as boots tapped linoleum.

A confident stride.

Familiar.

"Aila?" Luciana called out.

Aila stood up so fast, her elbows slammed the metal bars. The impact shot through her bones.

"Luciana!" she shouted through the pain, through the tears. "Here, here, here, *I'm back here!*"

She'd never beheld such a beautiful sight: Luciana frozen in the center of the room, mouth agape and brows raised to the ceiling as Aila bounced inside the aviary, screaming at her via some half-intelligible combination of words, laughter and sobbing.

"Aila?" Luciana hurried toward her. "What are you doing in *there?*"

Aila didn't pause for breath.

"The eggs hatched but Connor is evil and he cut off the live camera because he's been planning to steal the phoenixes all along and when I figured it out he locked me in here and he took my phone and my radio and he'll be back any minute for the chicks and you have to get me out of here now now *now!*"

"*Excuse me?*" Luciana's manicured nails flew over the keypad, typing in the combination. "The phoenixes hatched already? And Connor is doing *what*?"

"He's trying to steal the chicks. *My* chicks, Luciana! We have to stop him!"

When the gate clicked open, Aila hurled herself onto Luciana, wrapping her into a desperate hug. Fresh tears slicked Aila's cheeks as she buried her face in Luciana's neck, warm skin and the comfort of mango. Her fingers dug into Luciana's back, tighter when Luciana's arms wrapped around her. Solid. Safe.

"I'm so glad you're here," Aila said, her throat thick. "*Why* are you here?"

"I was working late with Ranbir," Luciana said through a mouthful of Aila's hair. "Then Tanya called, insisted I check up on you."

Tanya, that clever tropical parrot. She'd never let Aila down.

Time was short. Aila sprang out of the hug so fast, Luciana yelped in surprise. Again, when Aila dug through Luciana's pockets like a mute monkey with no concept of personal space.

"Aila! What are you—"

"Aha!" Aila held up Luciana's phone. She clicked the screen on. "*Fuck!* No service?"

"It went out in the middle of my call with Tanya."

"Fucking cell phone jammer. Ugh, what a *prick*!"

Aila could have yanked her hair out. She shoved the useless phone back into Luciana's hand, then hurried to her incubators. The phoenix chicks dozed inside the heated compartments, oblivious to the threat awaiting them.

"OK, no phones." Luciana spoke slowly, a woman trying to piece together mad ramblings. "You said *Connor* locked you in there? Like, the dragon keeper, Connor?"

"Yes, *him*! Lying piece of shit bastard doesn't even care about—"

"Shhh." Luciana patted hands to Aila's cheeks. "Focus time, Aila. Where is he now?"

Aila was starting to understand Luciana's gift for calming angry animals. She forced a deep breath, focusing on the grounding bite of nails curled into her palms. "He left a few minutes ago. I think he's working with someone, heard him talking on the phone. They're supposed to bring a portable incubator to transport the chicks."

"OK. OK..." Luciana's words trailed off. As the situation sank in, her posture stiffened, worried eyes on the incubators.

"What do we do, Luciana?" Aila bounced from foot to foot.

"Why are you asking *me*?"

"You're the responsible one of the two of us!"

"Sure! That doesn't cover how to apprehend criminals!"

Luciana was supposed to be the adult in the room, the white knight coming to Aila's rescue. To see the queen crack her cool stoked Aila with fresh terror. Her phoenixes weren't safe yet. Not by a long shot.

"We need to call someone," Luciana said. "Let them know what's happening?"

"Right. *Right*." Aila scanned the room, weighing options. No phones, no internet, but...She squeaked and pointed to Luciana. "Your radio! We need to call zoo security!"

"Shit! You're right. Sorry." Luciana scrambled to pull her radio off her belt. Under less dire circumstances, it would have been cute, seeing her so flustered. She held the radio up, finger poised over the call button.

Then hesitated.

"What's wrong?" Aila asked.

Luciana's face soured. "Does Connor have his radio on him?"

"Yeah . . . and mine, too."

"Do you want him to know we're on to him?"

"What other options do we have?"

Aila stamped her boot, an insulting squeak against the lino-leum. Luciana was right. Of course she was right, but what good did that do them? Still out of options. Still clicking down on time. Aila dug fingers into her hair and snapped her eyes closed. Thinking. Thinking. Sure, the zoo had whole binders of protocol for animal escapes and fires and patrons falling into exhibits, but not for black-market poachers stealing phoenixes in the middle of the night? What a frustrating administrative oversight.

"So we go in person," Aila said. "To the staff office. If Antonio isn't out on patrol, he should be there, right?"

"Right!" Hope lilted Luciana's voice. "He should know what to do?"

"Maybe even have a working phone?" Aila matched her enthusiasm.

"Let's go, then." Luciana clipped the radio to her belt and headed for the door.

Aila stayed, unable to move.

"Aila?" Luciana's hand paused on the handle. "Come on. Connor could be back any minute, right?"

"Exactly." The dread growing in Aila's stomach threatened to crumple her to the floor. "He could be back any minute. If he comes before we find help . . ."

She faced the incubators. Watching her phoenixes whisked away in front of her was unimaginable, but to lose them while she wasn't even there to fight back? Never. She couldn't leave them behind.

"We need to move, Aila," Luciana pressed.

"I can't abandon them!" Aila's heart tore in two, pulled by her phoenix chicks in one direction, their salvation in another.

"The best we can do is *get help*. They won't survive outside the incubators, will they?"

Flashcards flicked behind Aila's eyes. Temperatures. Cooling curves.

"They can," she said. "Not all night, but . . . for a little while at least."

She looked to Luciana with wide eyes, not just pleading, but a question. Was she making the right decision? Was she being stupid?

"You're sure?" Luciana asked, a quiet to shatter what remained of Aila's heart.

"I think so," was the best Aila could offer.

Luciana didn't question her further. No hesitation. No doubt. With a nod, she hurried to fetch the fireproof gloves.

Aila might be a little bit in love with this woman.

The phoenix complex had no portable incubators. Aila had to scavenge. From her desk, she dug out the phoenix tote bag she'd brought from the gift shop, thick canvas with convenient carrying handles. Inside, she stuffed every insulating towel she could fit, creating a nest.

With a silent plea to skies and seas, she popped the first incubator open. Heat blasted outward, a hit like a raging campfire as Luciana reached in with her protective gloves. The sleeping chick, now covered in poofy gray down, peeped in protest as it was stuffed into the towels. Aila and Luciana assembled the chicks in a pocket to keep as warm as possible. Last, little Rubra, wriggling and covered in awkward pin feathers.

"She's so small," Luciana breathed, cradling Rubra a moment before slipping her into the bag with the others.

Aila wrapped the towels over the top. Not a full incubator, but the set-up would keep the chicks warm enough for the journey to the staff office. She slung the bag over her shoulder, impossibly light. Impossibly precious.

Luciana led the way outside.

Once again, the dark zoo pathways met Aila not with their usual calm, but an ominous quiet. Too empty. Too many shadows. All but the most essential path lighting had been dimmed for the night, leaving her and Luciana to navigate via memory. They crept from one junction to the next, careful not to tread too loud against the concrete.

The smoothie hut passed them by, mannequin parrots on the roof looking down like phantoms. In the trees above, leaves shifted, wild purserats and racoons disturbed by the human interlopers. The zoo exhibits sat quiet, all the animals herded into back exhibits for the night.

No sign of Connor. Aila couldn't decide if that was a comfort or a worry.

As they neared the staff office, golden light slanted out the door. Salvation. Emboldened, Aila jogged the last several paces, phoenix tote cradled to her chest. She burst inside to beautiful beige walls, the boring rows of protocol binders and bulletin board with staff notices.

At the desk, Antonio leaned back in his chair, dressed in his security uniform. Snoring.

"Antonio!" Aila stumbled against the desk in her haste. Caught herself. She grabbed the man's arm and shook it. "Antonio, wake up! It's an emergency!"

He didn't budge. Aila shook him harder.

"*Antonio!* We need your help!"

"Aila..." Luciana said behind her.

"Are you kidding me?" Aila grabbed him by the collar and poked his cheeks. "No one has any right to be this hard of a sleeper. Antonio? Antonio!"

"Aila."

Aila turned. Luciana stood across the desk, nose wrinkled over a coffee cup.

"Does this smell like lavender to you?" Luciana held the cup out.

Sure. Not like this was a situation wrought with dire peril, or anything. Plenty of time to waste on sniffing *coffee*. When Luciana insisted, Aila took an impatient huff.

"OK," she said as the most delicate lavender aroma lifted above bitter coffee. "Super weird flavor combination. Not a great time to judge, Luciana."

Luciana glared back. At least one of them could think straight. Aila stumbled way too long before the realization hit her.

"Periwinkle prairie goose lavender?" Aila spit out. "You think someone *drugged* him?"

Not normal sleeping pills, either. Concentrated periwinkle prairie goose oil was a small step down from medical grade anesthesia. Judging by Antonio's snores, how hard Aila had shaken him, they'd be lucky to see him awake by morning.

Luciana swirled the cup. "Seems these thieves have really planned out—"

"Argh!" Aila snarled as she pushed past Luciana to the land-line on the wall (a cheap plastic telephone, pastel blue and green in imitation of a peacock griffin). Aila yanked the headset off its cradle and pressed it to one ear.

She was halfway through punching in the emergency number before she registered the lack of dial tone.

"Are you fucking kidding me?" Aila slammed the useless phone back to the cradle. The next time she saw Connor, he was getting punched in his stupid, clever face.

Within her tote bag, the phoenix chicks peeped. Whether in protest of the cold or Aila's shouting, she didn't care. They needed a new plan. Luciana tapped a red nail against her chin while she thought.

"We leave the zoo," she proposed. "We've got the chicks. If we can get to the parking lot, we can drive to the police station. Or at least get out of range of that cell phone jammer."

Thank the skies and seas Luciana showed up. Aila's brain was too much rage pudding to generate a coherent strategy. Leaving the snoozing security guard behind, they delved back into the zoo, heading for the gate to the employee parking lot. Not a long jaunt from the staff office. Aila pulled her tote bag close as they power-walked, eager to lend any body heat she could.

They rounded a corner, the employee gate lit by a solitary lamp post.

Half a yelp escaped Aila before Luciana clamped a hand over her mouth and dragged them both into the shadows of some shrubbery.

Connor stood at the open gate. With friends. Two men Aila didn't recognize spoke to him in hushed tones, their attire all black, gloves and long sleeves unsettling on the warm summer night. One wore a clunky backpack, box-shaped with plastic siding. The portable incubator. Such a cramped space would barely fit the full clutch, but of course, scum like this wouldn't care.

That wasn't the biggest problem.

Both men wore handguns on their belts. Dark metal glinted in the harsh overhead light, making Aila's breath hitch.

"Luciana," she squeaked.

"It's OK, it's OK." Even Luciana's voice shook.

The three men turned, setting a brisk pace toward them.

Luciana pulled Aila along the path, back into the zoo.

They had nowhere else to go. The immersive layout of the zoo stressed meandering pathways, a feeling of faux wilderness, but the core design remained artificial. Patrons were herded from exhibit to exhibit with little opportunity to stray, a track with masked edges. Aila and Luciana hurried away from the intruders, but also away from escape. At the first branching path, they shifted onto the walkway across the entry lagoon, hoping they hadn't been spotted. Hoping Connor would lead his accomplices back to the phoenix complex.

With the men no longer in sight, Aila flinched at every shadow.

"Shit, shit, shit," she hissed, cowering behind the cover of a frozen banana billboard. "You think they saw us?"

"Hopefully not." Luciana peered around the corner, scanning the path they'd come from. "We can let them pass. Sneak behind them and still make it out of the gate?"

"But what if they spot us?" Aila worried.

"We might have to take that chance. Where else can we go? Once they see the chicks are missing, they'll be on to us."

And what would the thieves do? Cut their losses and run? Or would they comb the zoo, searching for their prize? Aila hugged her bag of phoenixes to her chest. Risking herself in the escape was one thing, but delivering her birds into Connor's hands, she couldn't stomach.

"We can try to sneak past them," Aila said. "But not with the chicks. We need to hide them somewhere, in case anything goes wrong."

Luciana made a frustrated huff. "Hide them? Where?"

Great question. As much as Aila despaired to think of parting with her precious chicks, she flew through a mental map of the zoo. Somewhere warm. Somewhere safe, where those poachers wouldn't think to look. They didn't have to stay there long, just enough for her and Luciana to escape and get help.

Aila straightened like a rod.

"Holy shit," she breathed. "I think I know the perfect place."

She pulled a startled Luciana after her.

The glass aviaries loomed ahead, both danger and salvation. Aila wouldn't last five minutes in most action movies, her heart too frail, temper too timid, but she did feel a little badass sneaking down zoo pathways, peering around every corner as if Connor the Jackass might be waiting to slam into her again. They passed the sleeping mirror flamingos, beneath the dark banyan trees of the Renkailan section, arriving at a dark, quiet aviary.

The Bix phoenix.

Aila pulled out her keys and unlocked the door. Moonlight brushed the exhibit pool, the feathery papyrus reeds along the shore.

"Are you sure about this?" Luciana whispered.

"Like, eighty percent?" Aila hissed back. Not as high as she'd like, but . . .

She clutched her tote bag and clambered up the muddy incline, too quiet with the waterfall shut off for the night. When she reached the hole in the rocks, a tattered sheet of metal lay over the opening, screws bent, the remnants of Tanya's latest defeat by her stubborn bird.

"Horns and fangs." Luciana poked the metal, warped as if by a water jet. "Is this what she's always complaining about?"

Persistence at its worst. And best. Aila braced her shoulder against the metal sheet, pushing it aside enough to look into the hole.

Khonsu, the Bix phoenix, greeted her with an irate croak. He roosted in the back of his cavern, head tucked against the gray feathers of his body. Cheeky little bastard.

"Khonsu," Aila whispered.

He croaked again, angrier.

"No, no, no, it's OK!" She held up a hand in peace. "You can stay this time."

A softer croak, irritated, as he pulled his head down tighter. "But I have a big favor to ask. Like, the biggest favor ever."

Aila reached into her bag. The interior of the towels was like an oven, hot against her fingers. She scooped up a protesting phoenix chick, then leaned into the hole, offering it to Khonsu for inspection.

His head lifted, cheeks puffed in alarm. With neck extended, he twisted an eye to peer at the crying baby bird. Khonsu had never raised a nest himself. Tonight, Aila relied on instinct.

She nudged aside Khonsu's breast feathers and slipped the phoenix chick underneath, into the warm pocket of down. Khonsu clucked in protest, but after a moment of puffed feathers and swiveling head, he settled down. Beneath him, the chick's peeping quieted.

Aila could have kissed this muddy bitch of a bird.

One by one, she moved the rest of her charges into the hole. Khonsu shifted atop the new occupants, but so long as Aila wasn't trying to drag him out of his den, he didn't protest. Luciana watched from the sidelines, silent. Only once Aila finished did she notice her companion's mouth agape.

"Incredible," Luciana said. "They'll be safe here?"

"For a bit. Bix phoenixes run cooler body temperature than Silimalos, but not by much. Nice and toasty."

Aila hoped. It was all gambles and hope at this point, but Luciana's proud hand-squeeze offered a boost of confidence. Within his cave, Khonsu croaked, then settled his beak against his back, dozing. With the chicks safe (for now), Aila slung the empty tote over her shoulder and snuck back out of the aviary.

They'd still not seen the phoenix nabbers, but by now, Connor must have made it back to the complex. He must have seen the empty incubators, Aila vanished from her prison. Time pressed her and Luciana faster than before, hurrying toward the staff entry gate.

"Short cut?" Aila suggested, pointing to the World of Birds aviary. They could cut through the exhibit, out the door on the far side. At Luciana's nod, Aila pulled out her keys, fingers shaking as she slid them into the lock.

Before she could pull the door open, footsteps sounded behind them. Luciana went rigid.

"Shit!" Aila scrambled for the door handle.

Then froze at the sound of a cocking gun.

Chapter Thirty-Four

Aila turned.

Facing her was the barrel of a handgun.

In the movies, the books, true heroines stood tall in times like this. Their moment to shine in the face of adversity, to turn the tables and save the day. Staring down a gun in real life, Aila experienced no such burst of courage. Only dread, released in a quivering breath as she and Luciana raised their hands.

The unlocked aviary door slipped from her grasp. So close to escape.

In the path stood Connor—truly, fuck him—and two conspirators Aila had never seen before, young men in black attire and black gloves. The one pointing a gun at her sported the goatee classic to all douchebags. The shorter had a bald spot he'd attempted to comb over with a coif of wispy hair.

Connor regarded Aila with, of all things, an annoyed expression, that I'm-so-much-better-than-you scrunch to his brow she'd come to recognize too late. His scowl flicked to Luciana.

"Hey, Luc," Connor greeted, flat. "You working late tonight, too?"

"Don't fucking call me that. Prick." Luciana's voice was a level keel, a manicured tempest of derision. Skies and seas, let Aila borrow a sliver of that confidence.

She fought to keep her wobbling legs from collapsing. And she'd thought crowds were bad. If, somehow, she got out of this scrap in one piece, Aila vowed to never complain about public speaking again.

"Where are the chicks, Aila?" Frustration painted Connor's words. As if that was anything new.

Aila clamped her mouth shut.

"We're not here to hurt anyone," Connor pressed. "If you'd have gone home like you were supposed to, this would be over by now."

"Sure," Luciana said. "That's why you came *armed*."

"Y-yeah!" Aila added. *Very smooth.* "You and your..." She squinted at the unfamiliar men flanking Connor. "Friends?"

"Friends?" Connor frowned. "Associates. They reached out to me with a business proposal, and we found mutual interests. That's all."

That was even *worse*. No camaraderie? No exciting heist montage? All of this, just for the money. Just to rip away Aila's heart.

Goatee Douchebag brandished his handgun, impatient. "Let's move this along, please?" The weapon pointed to Aila and Luciana, but his annoyance fell on Connor.

Beside them, Balding Coif tipped back a sleeve to scowl at his watch.

"Yeah, I *get it*." Connor eyed the tote bag slung over Aila's shoulder. "Hand them over."

Aila clutched the bag. No doubt, Connor thought her grasp a throe of defeat, one last effort to shield her phoenixes with spindly arms. She hugged the bag to her chest, the nest of towels bulky in her embrace. Beyond that, empty. Her chicks dozed in the Bix phoenix exhibit.

A moment of panic, nonetheless.

Connor didn't realize the bag was empty. He was about to.

As he approached, Aila's thoughts raced into overdrive, at risk of smoke pouring out her ears. He'd look in the bag. He'd demand where she'd hidden the chicks, a gun pointed at her head. Between those two inevitabilities? A sliver of opportunity. One chance to act.

Connor walked in slow motion. One step. Two. His boots cracked against the pavement, soles sticky with spilled soda.

Oh no. Oh no. What should she *do*?

He paused in front of her, that curl of hair on his temple so obnoxiously handsome. Eyes slitted. When Aila refused to hand the bag over, he yanked it off her shoulder. As he dug into the towels, her legs jittered with the urge to run.

Scowling, Connor dug deeper into the bag.

He yanked the towels out, spilling them to the concrete. When he tipped the empty bag over, his eyes went wide, the most delicious look on that punchable face.

Well. Ought to go with instinct.

With a shrill battle cry, Aila punched Connor's stupid nose.

A wet crunch. Two yelps. Connor doubled over, clutching his not-so-handsome-anymore face as blood seeped across his lips. Aila winced at her throbbing hand.

Punching people *hurt*? Why had no one ever told her?

As Connor staggered and cursed, his accomplices looked on with startled eyes. OK, but honestly? They were *that* surprised to see Aila put up a fight? She scowled at the insult (and her screaming knuckles).

The gun wavered, drifting sideways as Connor stumbled into its path. Aila grabbed Luciana's hand and charged them both into the World of Birds aviary.

An excellent plan, if Aila did say so. The cherry on top came from Luciana, who had both the sense of mind and dexterity to smack the door lock closed behind them. Connor slamming into

434

the door at full force was the second most satisfying sound Aila had heard that night, after his face crumpling.

Less satisfying: the jingle of metal as Connor ripped his keys from his belt. Curse this organized zoo and its universal aviary locks. At least Aila had a head start.

She never let go of Luciana's hand.

The paths inside the aviary curved and intersected like the rest of the zoo, but once again, escape options were limited. Aila led Luciana off the concrete and into the cover of vegetation, wide leaves slicked with moisture from the afternoon misting, soil spongy beneath their boots. Hundreds of times, she'd trekked through the aviary plants—rooting around for Archie's discarded toys, searching for items stolen from patrons, hiding from those same patrons—enough to know every trunk and slope as well in dark as in daylight.

Fleeing for her life, she had less experience with. Aila channeled her inner phantom cat—skies and seas, what she wouldn't give for the ability to go incorporeal right now. Adrenaline made the shadows beneath the cecropia trees pool deeper. The vines snagging Aila's wrists seemed alive with malice. Blinded by dense underbrush, Aila couldn't see their pursuers.

So she had to listen.

She and Luciana paused beside a knotted fig trunk, clothes damp, shoulders pressed together in the dark. Aila strained to hear anything above her ragged breaths, the blood beating in her ears. Near the aviary entrance, her vanishing ducks quacked in alarm. Closer, the screaming mynas hopped through the canopy, following an intruder.

Aila crouched with Luciana amid the bushes, waiting to see if the interloper would pass. The aviary had two other exits. If they could find an opening, they might slip out unnoticed.

Except the thieves knew their prey were trapped. Near one

door, the periwinkle prairie geese joined in irate honking. Toward another, the screaming mynas hollered with the shrieks of a middle-aged man. At the third, a squawk from Archie.

Surrounded.

Aila curled into a ball with her back against the mossy tree trunk. She'd only wanted to play with her phoenixes, only wanted to save an entire species from extinction. Was that so much to ask? Now, she wanted to hide away like she always did. She could cower here in her musky exhibit, wait for someone else to take the stage. Someone *better* to save the day.

But no one else was coming. Aila's phoenixes needed her. If this was a do or die moment, she had a long list of life accomplishments she'd hoped to check off.

One of them knelt beside her.

"Hey, Luciana?" Aila whispered.

Luciana shushed her, one finger tapped over crimson lips. All that red and gold makeup since joining the phoenix program. The shades looked gorgeous on her. Most things looked gorgeous on her, but fiery colors matched a fiery personality.

"So, um..." Aila's heart picked up speed, a hindrance to coherent words. "Would you...want to get dinner some time?"

Luciana gawked. Surprise, anger, joy, all beautiful on that face. Unfair, really.

"*Excuse me?*" Luciana hissed with such force, Aila imagined the decibels she was being spared, thanks to their current peril. "We're hiding in a bush from armed intruders trying to steal your phoenixes, and you're asking me on a *date?*"

"Yeah, well, you see..." Aila flinched at a rustle of leaves above them. A flutter of wings. Just one of the cinnamon birds, inspecting the kerfuffle. She steeled her nerves and pressed on. "I'm not all that great at this dating thing."

"Really," Luciana said, flat. "Skies and seas, I never would have guessed."

"Usually, I bumble my way into messing things up."

"Aila, this isn't the best time to—"

"But I like you. I think I...*really* like you. I don't know how we lucked into getting you for the phoenix program, but I'm so happy we did."

Luciana paused at that. Annoyance twitched her brow, but the expression softened as she squeezed Aila's hand, grungy with sweat and mud. None of that mattered. Aila focused on the warmth of Luciana's skin, that sweet of mango.

"So I have to ask," Aila said. "Usually, I psych myself out. I get terrified of all the things that could go wrong. This time, I want to be different. I want to have the courage to at least *ask* you on a date, and I figure I better do it now, just in case...I don't get to ask later."

In case the worst happened. Aila shuddered to think, but planning for worst contingencies ranked high among her skills. Years of rejection had her bracing for Luciana's response, the possibility of refusal. Now would be a perfect time for back-tracking. What better excuse than dire peril to snuff a budding relationship that was a mistake from the start?

"First of all," Luciana said with that mix of haughty and annoyed. "How dare you talk like that. Second of all...I'd love to go on a date."

Aila blinked. "With...me?"

Luciana swatted her. "Who else? About time you asked me. Dork."

The mynas squawked overhead, moving through the trees as Connor and his conspirators combed the aviary. Aila's knuckles throbbed, and a growing chill on her ass suggested she'd sat in something moist.

None of that stopped her heart from soaring.

"Once we get out of here," Aila said. "Once the phoenixes are safe. A proper date? Outside the zoo?"

"Wow. Splurging for me already?" Luciana's smirk turned Aila to putty. "You have a restaurant in mind? Or would you prefer something quieter?"

"Oh, thank the skies and seas—quiet, *please.*" Aila could work her way back up to proper social interaction. After tonight, she'd be lucky to pry herself out of blanket cocoons for a month. She chewed her lip, working up the greatest courage yet. "We could...um...relax at my place? I've got a carbuncle who gives excellent cuddles. And I make a passable chicken parmesan."

"The selling points. Incredible." Luciana pressed a hand over her mouth, stifling a laugh. "Sounds perfect. I'll bring dessert?"

"You're on."

In the dark of the aviary, damp with mud and surrounded by doom, Aila kissed Luciana.

Soft lips stirred embers in her belly, a moment of desperation and unshakable calm. She could imagine it, couldn't she? A night alone with Luciana, drowning in the depthless dark of her eyes. She ran her fingers through the tight roots of Luciana's ponytail and imagined the curls unbound, falling against her cheeks.

Maybe Luciana would wear a dress. Skies and seas, Aila might perish.

Then Aila's hand was on her waist, measuring the flawless curve. She could imagine more. Bare skin, hot beneath her fingers. Soft thighs. Soft everything, lulling her into oblivion.

All they had to do was make it through tonight. Aila clung to that promise, willing it to give her courage for her next plan.

"Get out of the zoo," Aila whispered against Luciana's mouth. "Get help."

Luciana frowned. "Right. That's our plan."

"*Your* plan. I'll make the distraction."

Aila leapt up and ran before Luciana could grab her.

The hiss of her name through Luciana's lips struck just as hard.

Brave? Debatable. Foolish? Most likely. As much as Aila wanted to shrivel like a worm in the mud, *one* of them needed to escape, and the aviary was a trap. If she could drag one of their pursuers away from a door, Luciana could get out. Help might arrive in time to save her phoenix chicks from being tossed in a box and smuggled across the world.

Or freezing in a hole. Hopefully, Khonsu didn't mind the company.

Three aviary doors to choose from. As the splinters of a plan came together in Aila's head, she sprinted toward the door where Archie croaked in the canopy. Maybe luck would cut her a break, and she'd run into Connor again. Getting to punch that stupid face a second time wouldn't be the worst outcome.

Luck was not so kind.

Aila skidded around a curve in the path, boots slick on damp concrete. Ahead of her, Mr. Balding Coif guarded the door. He yanked the gun from his belt and pointed at her.

"Hold it! Hands up!"

Aila froze and did as he said. Not the sharpest plan she'd ever had, but all she needed was a little time. She hoped.

Above her, leaves rustled. Archie called out an inquisitive wheeze.

Balding Coif blinked at her, baffled by the lackluster escape attempt—a little *rude*, but Aila wasn't about to call him out on it. He approached on wary steps, gun level with her chest. The shiny metal caught a sliver of moonlight, lighting up like quicksilver in the dark.

Come on, come on, come on...

A squawk was his only warning.

Archie hit his target like a gray bullet. A phantom in the night. A fearless archibird with his beady black eyes locked on one of the biggest, shiniest objects to ever enter his aviary.

Maybe Aila wasn't out of luck yet.

The gunman cried out, flinching as gray wings beat the air in front of him. Valiant Archie, eyes always too big for his claws, grasped the gun in his feet, then tried to fly off with it. This endeavor failed, owing to the oversight of said object being grasped by an adult man with more weight than an archibird. Thwarted but not defeated, Archie hollered and puffed his crest to full height. Then came the onslaught: pecked fingers, fluttering wings, ear-piercing shrieks. The gunman cursed and swatted at his attacker.

If only Archie was that easy to deter, Aila would have fielded a lot fewer guest complaints over the years.

She seized her opportunity. With the gunman pointing his barrel to the ground as he attempted to rip Archie off his arm, Aila lurched forward. Arm strength, she had none, but raw body weight was enough to shove Balding Coif off balance and tumbling through the vegetation of the adjacent slope.

Archie landed on a branch, a couple of feathers ruffled, but looking more annoyed than harmed. What a good bird. Deserving of *all* the mango slices and shiny buttons later.

For now, Aila's exit stood unguarded.

She smashed the lock open and stumbled out of the aviary, making sure to bang the door behind her. The sound echoed through the glass dome, enough to alert the other thieves that she was on the move. Escaping. Better run after her, and don't spare any mind for the hot griffin keeper who was, hopefully, hidden away until her opportunity came.

The crash of bushes and curses behind Aila told her at least one of her assailants took the bait. She glanced back to see Balding Coif lurching out of the aviary several paces behind her. Aila set her boots to the concrete and sprinted.

Escape, she wasn't sure of. Her goal was to lead him away.

Past the smoothie shack and its judgmental mannequin parrots. Over a bed of ornamental shrubs. Through the junction to the kelpie exhibit. Aila steered the other direction, circling around the World of Birds aviary, hoping to loop her pursuer along for as long as possible. She could branch sideways at the dragon aviaries, or take a detour into the Renkailan section.

Instead, a figure charged into the path ahead, gun in hand. Douchebag Goatee. He spotted Aila and set toward her at a sprint.

She yelped and backtracked down the kelpie path.

Not good. Not good. Balding Coif was still somewhere behind her, and now Douchebag Goatee was closing fast from the other side. Boxed in. If Connor caught her from a third direction, she'd have nowhere to go.

Aila already had nowhere to go, the beat of footsteps closing too fast behind her.

"Stop running!" he shouted.

Aila might have to. Her meager muscles weren't made for cardio. Huffing and exhausted, desperation drove her to a tight turn off the path and into the closest shelter.

The kelpie exhibit.

In the moment, the safety of the keeper corridors seemed irresistible. Aila had always been able to hide from the world here, her personal sanctuary. Not until the door shut did she realize her mistake.

Ahead of her, the corridor branched on one side into the

kitchen, the other leading downstairs to the kelpie tank. Only one way in or out.

Maybe she'd lost her tail. He'd keep running, thinking she'd continued down the path.

A *thud* from the other side of the door made her shriek. So much for laying low.

Aila ran down the hall. Fluorescent lights flickered overhead. The kitchen was too small, nowhere to hide. She hesitated at the top of the stairs, looking down to the observation window for the kelpie tank. A dead end there, too. As keys clicked in the door she'd entered through, one last option remained. One that made her blood run cold.

She hefted the heavy latch of the door into the kelpie chamber. Metal scraped concrete as she escaped inside.

Within the room: quiet.

Placid water lapped the pool. Aila's breaths tumbled ragged out of her chest. Each exhale twisted into mist, merging with the thick fog coating the floor. Back holdings tended to be plain, this one dominated by the massive water tank. The door entered at a shelf of concrete flush with the water's surface, scattered with algae and bones from the meal Aila left out that evening.

She tried to calm her breath, tried to keep as silent as possible. The black water didn't move, an uncanny stillness beneath waves of fog. A good place to hide, just not for long. No one in their right mind would think to follow her in here.

In the meantime, Aila just had to get her heart rate down.

She breathed deep, grounding herself with solid concrete beneath her boots, cool metal against fingers—

Aila yelped when the door behind her boomed, a heart-stopping echo through the room. Note to self: mindfulness exercises, not *superbly* effective during life-or-death situations. She'd complain to her therapist later. When the latch turned,

Aila planted her feet, trying to stop the door swinging inward, but her boots slipped on slick concrete.

The door burst open. She fell back, hitting the floor with ass and palms. Balding Coif strode into the room with eyes on fire, peck marks on his face, gun leveled at Aila.

"Get up," he ordered. "Tell us where those fucking birds are, or I'll put a fucking bullet through your head."

He clicked something on his weapon. Aila didn't know enough about guns to say what, exactly. She understood the threat just as well.

Only ... she couldn't quite bring herself to care.

A calm fell over her. Over the room. Her heart, once hammering in her throat, settled with remarkable speed. Her breaths slowed, smooth and quiet as black water.

Aila looked away from the gun, away from the looming man. All of a sudden, the pool seemed ... mesmerizing. Inky black, though little lights danced on the surface like drops of stars. Brighter. Wider.

Two eyes peered back at her from beneath the surface, ringed in a mane of hair and algae.

The kelpie raised her head without a sound. Without a ripple.

Her black eyes fixed on Aila like a starless sky, like wells into the pit of the world. Her mane hung like mussed silk, swirling at the water's surface. Aila wanted to run her fingers through that mane. To slip into the pool. Weightless. What a wonderful feeling that would be.

She shifted onto her knees. The kelpie tilted her head.

The spell snapped like a twig.

Aila's knuckles throbbed. Her breaths had worn her throat raw, and her bony legs ached against concrete. Ahead of her, Maisie floated in the pool. Aila fell back on her hands, survival instinct screaming at her to crawl away from the carnivorous horse still staring, still holding her kelp-strewn head in an inquisitive tilt.

No longer hypnotizing, though. One of the deadlier ways kelpies lured prey into their native bogs. Aila had never realized a beast could break off the trance.

Or why one would.

Beside her, Balding Coif held his gun limp, staring at Maisie with unblinking eyes.

Aila's breath caught in her throat.

She lurched forward, but not in time. The man stepped toward the pool. Maisie reached out, tipping her snout to grasp his pant leg in gentle fangs. A single tug, and he slipped into the water. Before Aila could shout, both man and kelpie were gone, the inky pool returned to a glassy surface, the room silent.

Aila sprinted out the door.

Panic and fatigue had baked her thoughts into pudding, yet a single goal drove her forward. Into the hall. Down the stairs to the base of the kelpie tank. Faster. Faster. She didn't have much *time*.

Beyond the glass of the observation window, Maisie drifted like flotsam, strands of mane and tail encircling her unusual prey. Not a goat. Not severed deer legs. This seemed to intrigue the kelpie. While she inspected him, the man hung in the water as if in suspended animation. No flailing. No struggling. A single gurgle of bubbles escaped his lips and floated to the surface.

Not today.

No one had ever died in one of Aila's exhibits, and skies and seas be damned, she was *not* losing that streak. Not even for a poacher. This, at least, she had zoo protocol for.

Aila slammed her palm to the gate release button. Inside the pool, the water shuddered as machinery moved, opening the gate to the main exhibit. Maisie paused from inspecting her human, casting a curious glance at the gate instead.

"All right, Maisie." Once the gate opened, Aila moved to the window and pressed both hands to the glass. "Come on, sweetie. It's not the usual time, but you know what to do."

Most animals in the zoo didn't have the training the griffin show did. Move to exhibit, move to back holding—that was the extent of it. Aila hoped that would be enough. Within the tank, Maisie hesitated, mane swirling in eddies as her hooves pawed the water.

"Maisie, please." Aila pressed closer to the glass, until her nose scrunched the cold surface. "Go out to your exhibit. I will give you . . . the juiciest goat leg ever tomorrow."

The kelpie peered at her through the glass, unable to perform any charms across the barrier, but those depthless eyes held Aila's heart still. The silence stretched too long. Another burst of bubbles escaped the hanging man.

With a kick of hooves, Maisie flowed through the gate, into the main exhibit.

Aila's victory shriek bounced off concrete walls. The moment the kelpie passed out of the back holding, she slammed the button to close the gate. It whined shut on hydraulic levers, falling still with another shudder of water. The pool turned placid once more.

Until the man started thrashing.

He came awake with a violent jerk, flailing arms and sputtering water. His gun already lay at the bottom of the pool, but the rest of him, Aila wasn't thrilled to deal with. Saving his life ought to be favor enough.

While he swam to the surface, Aila ran back up the stairs to the door she'd left open in her hasty retreat. Inside the room, the man hunched on the concrete slab, coughing and spitting up water. Still alive? Excellent.

Aila slammed the door shut and heaved the latch into place, sealing him inside. He shouted and banged from the other side, but with Maisie out on exhibit, he'd be safe for now.

One down, two still lurking. Aila took a moment to gather her breath before plunging back into the zoo.

Chapter Thirty-Five

Aila peeked around a corner.

The path to the aviaries lay quiet. In the height of the Movasi summer, the sun-baked walkways held their warmth well past sunset, heat radiating against her boots. An army of crickets serenaded from plant beds and underneath vending machines. This could have been a normal night: her staying late after work, a tranquil zoo that seemed hers alone.

It wasn't.

Somewhere down the dark and twisting paths, two phoenix thieves still lurked, hunting Aila and her chicks. So far, her plan to run distraction had worked out better than anticipated (barring, of course, nearly being shot and/or eaten by a kelpie). But what about Luciana? Had she escaped while Aila kept their assailants busy?

The answer came faster than Aila wanted: a shout from across the zoo.

Aila ran. She should have stayed stealthy, should have kept her eyes keen for Connor or his remaining accomplice, but all that sensible nonsense fled when she heard that shout. *Luciana's* shout, the velvet timbre unmistakable even at a distance. As Aila ran, yelling sounded ahead. A door banged.

The commotion led her into the Renkailan section. At that,

Aila's panic fizzled like over-shaken soda. Luciana was supposed to get out, get help. Sure, their brief farewell hadn't been enough time to *say* all those directions, but Aila thought the specifics had been implied. Why, then, had Luciana run in this direction, *away* from the zoo's staff gate?

She must be in trouble. Someone must have spotted her.

Aila kept running.

Ahead, the monolith of the griffin show amphitheater loomed, shadows deep in the concrete alcoves and twisting vines. Fitting. Aila had sought safety on the familiar ground of a carnivorous horse lair. It stood to reason Luciana would flee here under duress, her kingdom of barns and show corridors. Hopefully, familiarity would give her an edge against pursuers.

Aila, on the other hand . . .

She sprinted around a corner and slammed into Connor.

Rancid. Dragon. Spit.

Aila yelped as he grabbed her. The smell of pine turned sickly. Toned arms became a thing of ire. For all the times she'd caught him lurking around corners, she'd never appraised it as an actual skill, much less one that would spell her doom. While she flailed and cursed, Connor lifted her by the waist, leaving her legs kicking air.

"Give it a rest, Aila! You've caused enough trouble already."

Still annoyed. Still condescending. As if all she could ever be was a bumbling idiot.

Aila twisted in his arms and bit him.

As Connor shouted, she lurched from his grip and hit the ground running. To where? Another circuit of the zoo, hoping he'd follow? Behind the stage to find another place to hide?

Her ears perked at a distant rumble. A beat of wings.

Please let that be real, not a figment of her adrenaline-rattled brain.

Aila's boots thudded concrete. Next came grass, the squishy lawn of the griffin show. In a last push, she sprinted into the open, boxed in by the empty maw of amphitheater seats and the curve of the stage. She hadn't covered half the distance before Connor tackled her. They tumbled to the grass, wet against Aila's knees, stinging her scraped palms.

She kicked, but Connor dropped his weight on top of her, pinning Aila to the ground.

"Where are the chicks?" he demanded.

Aila spit toward his face. Not the best angle. Half of the mucous glob ended up on her cheek, the other half sprawled across grass.

"They're just birds, Aila! How are they worth all this?"

"Just . . . birds? *Just birds?*"

Of all the things he'd said—all the veiled boredom and passive insults—nothing had ever struck such rage into Aila's chest. Let Connor insult her. Let him complain about her talking too much, or her unhealthy work habits, or her inability to appreciate snobby restaurants.

Not her birds. *Never* her birds.

"They're *my* phoenixes," Aila sputtered, spitting out grass that lodged in her teeth. "You're not taking them!"

Connor's weight shifted atop her, a stupid slump to accompany that stupid sigh. "Fine. You want more incentive? I'll cut you in on the deal. Ten percent market cost per bird. You hand them over, I make you fucking rich, then we never have to speak of this again."

"Are you out of your mind?"

"Ten percent is more than generous, Aila."

That was it. That was the moment Aila truly understood how, despite faking smiles and pretending to be her friend, Connor hadn't bothered to learn a single thing about her. Shouldn't that have made her sad? Defeated? Like she ought to curl up and never risk dangling her heart on a string again?

No.

Aila wouldn't give him that satisfaction. She wouldn't give him that power over her when he'd done nothing to deserve it.

"You think this is all about money? You slimy piece of dragon shit. Those phoenixes are priceless! I will *never* tell you where they are. You'll have to turn this entire zoo upside down, and even then, good fucking luck."

Connor twisted Aila's arm, a sharp pain at the joint. She bit back a whimper.

"You're in no spot to negotiate, Aila."

Fair. An understatement, even. Aila was nothing but pasty limbs and weaponized awkwardness, though neither seemed an advantage in this situation. No matter how she wriggled, Connor's weight kept her pinned.

Fortunately, Aila only had to play the warm-up act.

Connor flinched when a defrosted mouse splatted his cheek, the fur still wet enough to stick to his skin. He grimaced and peeled it off.

"The fuck is this?"

His only warning was a wingbeat. A flash of gemstone green and blue feathers.

A gust of air buffeted Aila as a peacock griffin toppled Connor off her. Ranbir pinned his target to the grass beneath dull talons, dark eyes wide in focus, wings splayed and tail iridescent even without the glare of amphitheater lights.

Upon his back perched Luciana.

An icon. A queen upon her throne, never one to miss a cue. She sat behind the griffin's wings, hands wreathed in feathers, a mane of black curls having broken free of their tail to drape her shoulders. The glare she leveled at Connor could have knocked the venom out of a basilisk.

He screeched when the griffin's beak snapped down at him. An ass, to the end. Gentle as a kitten, Ranbir gobbled the mouse off Connor, then pecked every inch of him, searching for additional treats beneath his shirt, armpits, within the messed coif of his hair.

"Get this thing off me!" Connor shouted.

Luciana dismounted, humoring Connor with the brush of a scowl.

"Aila! Are you all right?"

She rushed to help Aila to her feet. Beyond grass cuts and a sore shoulder, Aila appeared unscathed. She gripped Luciana by the arms, holding her close, drinking her in.

"That was . . . *incredible*! You *rode* a peacock griffin?"

Luciana dropped her eyes beneath a veil of lashes, adorably bashful. "I did. The act we've been working on, you know."

"An act? That was amazing! Please tell me you get to tackle a member of the audience in the real show, because that would be *memorable*."

"Oh no, that's just Ranbir. He can get . . . excited."

Connor grunted as he ripped himself out of the griffin's talons. While Ranbir inspected him with a curious head tilt, Connor shifted onto his knees.

"You two and your stupid birds," he panted. "Who do you think . . . ?"

Luciana reached into a bag at her waist, reeled back her arm, then tossed a second mouse, smacking Connor on the forehead. Ranbir lunged, pinning him with another yelp.

"We've got to work on that," Luciana observed, already digging into her satchel for another mouse. "Unpleasant trait. Useful tonight, though."

Gorgeous, both of them. Aila cupped Luciana's cheeks and scoured her from head to toe, searching for any sign of injury.

"Are you OK? I heard yelling!"

"Fine, fine. A little frazzled." Luciana gave a nervous laugh. "They gave me a run."

She wasn't hurt. That gave Aila full rein to whip out a puppy-dog scowl. "You were supposed to escape!"

"And leave you behind? Don't be ridiculous!" Ah, that familiar chiding tone.

"I was being *resourceful*, not ridiculous, thanks. Where's the last thief?"

"Last I saw, he was—"

A *click*.

Aila hated that she recognized the sound now.

Douchebag Goatee stood at the edge of the lawn, gun drawn, appraising Connor's struggle beneath a peacock griffin. He pointed his weapon at Luciana. Unless another secret griffin waited in the wings, this appeared to be a problem.

"Call that thing off him," the thief ordered.

"Took you long enough!" Connor spat. "Just shoot the damn thing!"

"Don't you dare!" Luciana stepped in front of Ranbir, one hand digging into her satchel. The only person Aila knew who'd take on an armed intruder with nothing more than defrosted mice, but damn if that wasn't attractive. Attractive, yet in this moment, terrifying.

Unamused, the thief cocked his gun.

Several more clicked behind him.

An unexpected sound. And puzzling. The thief looked equally baffled as he glanced over his shoulder.

Boots thudded into the amphitheater. A flash of lights and radio chatter. Aila blinked, not trusting her eyes: a squad of five dressed in dark blue San Tamculo PD uniforms, badges glinting silver, guns trained on the intruder.

"Police! Put the gun on the ground! Hands above your head!"

Aila's heart skipped, unable to comprehend. Unable to believe. She and Luciana hung back with wide eyes as the officers advanced. When the cursing thief dropped his gun to the grass and raised his hands, two policemen restrained him. Another pulled out a pair of handcuffs.

Three thieves down.

None left.

Aila's relief threatened to melt her onto the lawn.

"The police!" She snagged Luciana's arm, words dripping disbelief, hands trembling with adrenaline. It was over. Help at last meant this nightmare was *over*. "Luciana, *the police are here*! Who called the police?"

She tilted up an expectant look, anticipating another miracle by this woman.

Luciana shook her head. "I tried. The signal's still out."

"Then who—"

"*Aila!*"

The voice sent a jolt through Aila's spine, tears into her eyes. With the thief subdued, Tanya burst through the line of police officers, batting aside their protests as she sprinted to Aila and lifted her into a giant, leg-swinging hug. Aila clasped her friend's shoulders, already sobbing into her neck.

"Tanya!" She sniffed, horrendous. Tanya had seen worse. "What are you doing here?"

"You sounded like you were in trouble!" Tanya said with a click of her tongue.

"So you called the *police*?"

"Girlie." Tanya took Aila's cheeks in firm hands. "Aren't I always telling you the importance of trusting your instincts?"

Aila could have crumpled. "I'm glad you did."

"Me too, Ailes."

Their teary reunion was cut short as the police circled them, guns holstered, some curious looks at the dead mouse Luciana still brandished like a weapon.

"Good evening, ladies," one of the officers greeted. "We received a report of a disturbance?"

"He's trying to steal the Silimalo phoenixes!" Aila shouted too fast, pointing to the Goatee Douchebag glaring up from the lawn.

"He's working with them." Luciana pointed behind them, where Connor languished beneath a frisky peacock griffin.

"There's a third one!" Aila said. "Trapped in the kelpie exhibit!"

"Trapped in the . . . *where*?" Luciana shot her a startled look.

"It's OK. Maisie didn't eat him. I mean, she might have, but she seemed about as confused about it as I was."

"All right, all right." The flustered officer made a calming hand gesture. "We'll take care of all that right away. You're fortunate no one was hurt. Once you've had a chance to settle down, we'll need a statement from each of you about what happened."

Aila was already racing out of the amphitheater.

"Right, right!" she called back. "Statement, sure. We'll tell you everything. Just let me take care of something real fast!"

A few shouts at her back entreated her to wait. Nothing could stop her.

She ran all the way to the Bix phoenix exhibit. With cramping legs, rasping breath, she pushed through the door and scrambled up the embankment. Papyrus reeds snagged her hair. Mud squelched beneath her nails. At the hole, she heaved her shoulder against the metal grate and pushed it as far as it would go.

Khonsu greeted her with a croak. He hadn't moved from his

roost in the back of the hole, his cheeks puffed in annoyance at having been disturbed a second time in one night.

His breast feathers ruffled. A peep sounded within the down, followed by the poke of a tiny, wobbling head. Aila dug her hands into the pocket of warmth, ignoring Khonsu's protests as she plucked the young phoenixes out from under him. As the full clutch nestled in her arms, their smoldering feathers singed her skin. She didn't care.

Aila laughed, the sound dancing through the aviary.

The door slammed open a second time. At the base of the hill stood a worried Tanya and Luciana, flanked by two bewildered police officers.

"Aila!" Luciana called up. "How are they?"

"Fine!" Aila called back, tears of joy in her eyes as she stroked the hot down of her baby phoenixes. "They're all fine."

Epilogue

"Food time, everyone!" Aila shouted. "Come and get it!"

She and Tanya stepped into the phoenix aviary, decked in full battle gear: fireproof gloves on both arms, fireproof overalls, metal trays stacked with chopped fruits and vegetables. The summons were unnecessary. On its own, the click of the door summoned calamity.

A horde of month-old phoenix chicks stampeded toward them. Adorable peeps had been replaced by loud, braying calls from gaping mouths. Most of their gray down had been shed, growing into pin feathers of russet and tangerine. Skies and seas help their poor keepers when these monsters grew large enough to fly. They hopped and scraped at Aila's legs, stubby wings fluttering. When she set down her food tray, the chicks inhaled chunks of mango and kale like feathered vacuum cleaners.

Aila loved them more than anything in the world.

After a harrowing hatching night, the zoo hadn't fielded any further break-ins (thanks, in large part, to a bolstered night patrol by the San Tamculo Police Department). Aila's trials had just begun. That first week, she averaged enough hours of sleep per night to count on one hand, bundled in a makeshift bed on the breeding complex floor, jerking awake at the softest peep to help Carmesi feed the chicks and check temperatures. Once

Tanya found out, Aila received a firm lecture. They camped out together after that, trading off chick-watching duty and stints of rest.

The hatchlings grew fast. Their down filled out, allowing them to scamper around the exhibit, chewing olive leaves and tripping over branches. They learned to eat on their own, though anytime Carmesi or Aila entered proximity, five begging mouths surrounded them.

Every day, Aila and Tanya tracked their weight, their beak length, their feather growth. Five growth charts on their office whiteboard, twice-weekly reports to IMWS. And the onslaught of interview requests—Luciana had her pick of national news networks vying for footage while the fluffy chicks were at peak cuteness.

A month in, their awkward teenage stage involved less cute toes and more gangly legs, headdresses of red pin feathers and mouths too large for their faces. Aila adored them all.

While the chicks devoured their meal, Tanya set a smaller platter into the branches of an olive tree. Rubra fluttered down, an awkward landing as she wobbled with her new wing feathers. Age-wise, she sat about a month ahead of her chicks, though she joined the younger brood in harassing her keepers for food. Well-deserved pampering, after bursting into flame for the sake of her nest. Aila scratched Rubra's crimson breast feathers as the bird chomped a mouthful of mango.

Carmesi landed last, a haggard hunch to his shoulders, gilded breast feathers dimmer than usual. When Aila held out a gloved hand, he hopped to her fist, a haven from his chaotic brood where she could hand him a juicy grape. Seeing the injustice, the chicks scrambled at her feet, hopping and gaping in a vie for attention.

"You quit that!" Tanya chided, sending the chicks scampering as she set down a final tray of food. "Poor Carmesi. Amazing *he* hasn't burst into flames, harassed by these demons."

Aila chuckled. "No kidding. How about a little break, Carmesi? Would you like that?"

At the lilt in her voice, Carmesi bobbed his head and trilled. She took that as a yes.

As they worked in the exhibit, a crowd pressed at the observation window, eyes and phones jostling for the perfect view. Several younger patrons waved to Aila and Tanya.

Aila waved back.

At some point, the gesture had stopped feeling forced. She held Carmesi out to the observers, beaming as patrons snapped their photos.

Rubra and the chicks would keep the exhibit lively. Aila walked Carmesi inside the keeper complex and held him to a metal carrying crate. Once he'd hopped inside, she closed the door and slipped off her bulky gloves. Then, a deep breath.

"Horns and fangs," Tanya said with a dramatic exhale. "Never been so busy around here. Can't wait for the first keeper volunteers to show up next week."

Aila grinned—actually *grinned*—at that. Just ten volunteers for Tanya's pilot program, but they'd passed the interview process and initial training session. One more week, and there'd be a batch of fresh faces at the zoo.

Tanya crossed her arms, lips curved to a smirk. "You ready?"

Aila's grin plummeted. Ready for volunteers? Sure, she'd give it a whirl. Ready for what had Tanya grinning? "Well, *no*, obviously not. But it's going to happen anyway, isn't it?"

Tanya punched her shoulder. "That's the spirit, Ailes."

Tanya lifted the carrying case, then they set off across the zoo.

On a weekend in late summer, the paths couldn't be busier.

Patrons swarmed in waves scented of sunscreen and fizzing soda, fried churros and lemon sorbets in animal-shaped cups. The latest fads in the gift shop were phoenix-colored parasols, a perfect match for sunglasses with fiery feather rims. For a short time after the chicks hatched, Aila and Tanya made a game of how many pieces of phoenix merchandise they could spot in one day. They had to quit after running out of room for tallies on their whiteboard.

As they passed the dragon aviaries, the crowd funneled into a plaza. Aila paused in the path, a stone amid the current.

In front of the diamondback dragon exhibit stood the zoo's newest keeper, encircled by the attentive crowd. He was a young man with Movasi-brown skin, scrawny as Aila, all beanpole arms and fidgeting fingers as he sped through his list of dragon trivia.

"What's the hold-up, Ailes?" Tanya called from a couple of paces ahead. "We've got places to be!"

"Sure, sure." Aila vacillated in the path. "Just . . . hold on one minute, OK?"

The keeper talk ended. As the crowd dispersed, Aila squirmed past strollers and elbows. The dragon keeper waited for the patrons to leave, bouncing on his boots in an impatient fashion Aila knew all too well. Martin, she recalled his name was. He wore a black polo still stiff out of the plastic wrapping, already globbed with pine resin and fish scales.

Aila popped out of the crowd like a gopher. The dragon keeper startled.

"Hello!" Aila gave a little wave, tight at the wrist. "Yes, hey, hello there! I'm Aila. We . . . um . . . met at the staff meeting?"

"Oh! Of course!" He vacillated between handshake and fist bump before offering a strange amalgamation of both. "I'm Martin."

"Ha! I remembered!" That came out too loud.

Martin shrank. "You're the Silimalo phoenix keeper?"

"That's me! And here's Tanya, Bix phoenix keeper." Aila waved to the bemused friend standing beside her.

Martin greeted them with a polite grin, though a different light hit his eyes when he spotted the carrier.

"No way! Is that...?" He knelt to peer inside. When Carmesi poked his head to the screen, Martin gasped. "Can I...?" He held up a finger.

"Of course," Tanya said. "This one doesn't bite."

Giddy, Martin poked a finger to the front of the carrier. When Carmesi nibbled back, he chuckled. If the mess on his shirt wasn't reason enough to expect good things, Carmesi's vote of confidence spoke volumes.

"Anyway," Aila said, "we wanted to stop by, welcome you to the zoo and all that. We're not, you know, dragon experts, but seeing as how your predecessor is in prison on charges of international animal smuggling"—Aila wasn't normally big on true crime TV, but she'd watched *that* live court hearing with a bucket of popcorn—"let us know if we can help out?"

Martin stood, eyes wide. "Really?"

"Sure! I mean..." Aila clasped her hands behind her back and swiveled. "We're exhibit neighbors. We ought to look out for each other?"

She glanced to Tanya, just to make sure this was the right move.

"Absolutely!" Tanya beamed. "In fact, why don't you pop over for lunch? We can run you through all the best places to eat in the zoo."

Aila perked up. "Oh, and how to run the snow machine for Vera!"

"And some pointers on wrangling refrigerator space from Patricia."

"Anything you need."

"That sounds fantastic." Martin darted a smile between them, then at the dragon lounging in the exhibit. "I'm sure Vera will appreciate it, too. We're still getting to know each other."

Good deed accomplished.

But Aila was on a time crunch. She and Tanya bid farewell to their new colleague before diving back into the crowded pathways. Tanya spared the friendly teasing about Aila's growing social competency, but a proud elbow nudge sent Aila's heart soaring.

She'd always loved this zoo like a home. Now, it felt full like never before.

They arrived at the griffin show amphitheater as a fresh crowd funneled into their seats, adventurous music beating from the speakers. Aila and Tanya slipped through the side entrance and into the bustling corridors behind the stage.

"Aila's here!" Nadia shouted from the tech room, somehow spotting the newcomers without looking up from her screen.

A shame. Aila had been contemplating whether this was all some colossal mistake and she ought to hide in a dark corner before anyone noticed her.

A hurricane swirled around her: keepers setting animals into their boxes and perches, strapping on microphones, filling waist pouches with mice and fruit. At the center of the storm stood Luciana, immovable as ever, head tall and hair a cascade across her shoulders. She turned to Aila with those piercing brown eyes, that weighted stare that could crumble a person to dust.

Then, a smile.

"You made it. Just in time."

Even now, Aila couldn't comprehend how Luciana sounded

so calm—*excited*, even. Aila harnessed all her focus just to keep breathing, to keep the walls from spinning around her.

"How's my hair?" Aila worried, running her hand through the wavy auburn locks. "I tried to curl it this morning, but we both know I'm not half as good as you are. I think I smelled a little burning. That's not bad, is it?"

Luciana twirled a strand around her finger. "It looks lovely, Aila." Then, a whisper in her ear. "Though I prefer how messy it was at your place last weekend."

Aila squeaked in reply. She, too, enjoyed how her hair had felt last weekend, particularly the contribution of Luciana's fingers running through the strands. If she dwelled on that, she'd keel over.

Instead, she bounced on her heels. Twisted her fingers. She squeaked again when Luciana settled two warm, grounding hands on her shoulders.

"Aila," she said, close and quiet, as if they stood separate from the surrounding chaos. "You don't have to do this if you don't want to. I won't think any less of you."

Aila believed her. Instead of hiding, taking the out, she bobbed her head in determination.

"I can do it," Aila said.

Luciana grinned. "I know you can."

From out of the storm, another keeper materialized. "You've got Carmesi?" she said to Tanya. "Go ahead and set the carrier right over here. That's perfect."

Tanya put Carmesi's carrier on the table. Aila sat beside it, quivering.

Too soon, Luciana was called away. The music soared. The chaos of pre-show preparation shifted to a well-oiled machine as keepers glided in and out of the room, setting each piece of the production in motion. At her cue, Luciana stepped on stage.

"Welcome, everyone, to the San Tamculo Zoo! I'm Luciana, your host today for our incredible, our awe-inspiring, our one-of-a-kind griffin show!"

Oh no. This was happening. Aila had actually agreed to this for some reason.

Tanya gripped her shuddering arms. "This is your time, Ailes!"

Aila nodded, staring at the floor, her boots.

"You are fierce!" Tanya said. "As fierce as a manticore!"

"I'm not sure about—"

"As fierce as a kraken in the depths!"

Aila gripped the table with white knuckles and willed herself to believe it.

"Aila?" one of the keepers called. "You're on deck!"

Now or never.

Aila breathed deep, put on a glove, then pulled Carmesi from his carrier.

"Up next," Luciana's voice sang over the speakers, "we have a special surprise for you today. A griffin show first!"

The world moved in slow motion, muted and blurred around the edges. Aila told herself not to look at the crowd. As she stepped onto the stage, she focused on her boots against the concrete, the glare of flame-colored spotlights. Carmesi perched on her glove, feathers flattened, head cocked to the stadium.

If he could look, so could she. Aila had survived the inspectors. Survived the interviews. Survived gun-wielding intruders. She could handle this.

She looked up.

The sight of packed stands threatened to stop her heart. Blood thudded in her ears, as loud as the gasps and applause, as loud as the Silimalo string music blaring over the speakers. Stuck in the spotlight, Aila's legs wobbled.

Wobbled, but didn't collapse. Though her heart thundered, it didn't burst. Before her sat a sea of onlookers, every one of them smiling ear to ear. The two largest smiles sat in the front row—Aila's parents, rising out of their seats as they snapped photos.

She smiled back.

"Ladies and gentlemen!" Luciana stood across the lawn, hand raised to quell the rambunctious crowd. "If you haven't already visited our Silimalo phoenix exhibit, make sure you do so after the show. San Tamculo is one of the only zoos in Movas to breed this critically endangered species, and it's all thanks to your generous support."

She held her gloved hand high. Aila tipped her wrist, Carmesi's signal to take flight. He glided across the lawn, sparking gasps from the stadium as spotlights turned his tail into a river of fire.

Once he alighted on Luciana's fist, she held the bird aloft for the audience.

Then, with a twist of her hand, Carmesi dove off her glove and flapped back to the stage, landing on Aila's arm in a flare of red and gold.

Aila faced the crowd, their applause a thunder in her heart, a phoenix brilliant on her glove.

Her phoenix, to share with the world.

Acknowledgements

I'd like to think that, if Aila was asked to write the acknowl-edgements section of a debut novel, it would cause her no small amount of panic. She'd probably pull all the recent books off her shelves, study the way other authors wrote their acknowledge-ments, and correlate the patterns to make sure she did it "right."

Thank goodness Aila and I aren't anything alike...

I never could have imagined, while I was drafting *The Phoe-nix Keeper*, how many amazing people would be involved in bringing this book to print.

To my incredible, enthusiastic, arm-flailing agent, John Baker, thank you for taking a chance on me. You talked about my char-acters like they were lifelong friends and believed in my "hug of a book" with infectious gusto. I forgive you for living in the UK and making me wake up at 6 a.m. for Zoom meetings.

To the loquaciously eloquent GIF-queen, my superstar editor Bethan Morgan, thank you for bringing me along on your quest for world fantasy domination (and for filling my inbox with a frankly ludicrous number of bird and sword photos). Thank you to the entire stellar team at Gollancz for bringing this book to life in a capacity that exceeded my wildest dreams. Thank you to Priyanka Krishnan for starting this incredible journey with me on my side of the world, to Tiana Coven for taking over the reins and keeping Team Phoenix burning bright, and to the entire team at Orbit U.S. for spreading our flames ever wider.

To my mother, the first person I ever shared my stories with, who's been reading my silly words for ten whole years, thank you for encouraging me along every step of this long and difficult path. And to my father, who couldn't be here to see this journey—I started writing to cope with the grief of losing you, and I know you'd be so proud of the person I've grown into.

To my partner, Michael, thank you for your endless patience, for smiling and doing a *very good* impression of pretending you understood when I gushed all the details of good book news—and for handing me tissue boxes and boba tea as I despaired over bad book news.

To Lore Austin, my good friend, my peerless critique partner and theme-plotter extraordinaire, thank you for helping me polish this book to a diamond glow in our hours-long brainstorming sessions, for all your suggestions on how to make Connor *even more* awful, and for believing in me through every emotional breakdown along the way.

To Virginia Fox, friend and boundlessly enthusiastic writing buddy, thank you for your endless cheerleading, for rooting for me through edits and copy edits and bonus content even on the days I wanted to throw my computer against a wall.

Thank you to the beta readers who volunteered their time and feedback to chisel this book into shape: to Vanessa Le, Griffin Freitas, and D. P. Douglas for your incredible developmental feedback; to Del, Kaylie, and Taylor for some of the best line comments I've ever read ("he needs to be fucked by an angry cactus" will forever live in my hall of fame).

To David Bonter, my college research mentor, thank you for inspiring and guiding my path to biology. I'm sure you didn't envision *this* outcome while you were teaching me to band birds and clean gull poop off my jacket, but your patience and love of nature lives in every page of this book.

To Alexa, the first therapist who was able to speak my language, thank you for giving me the support and tools to grow from an anxious wreck into...well, still a little bit of an anxious wreck, but a far more functional version, which I take as a victory.

Thank you to Pauline, the hybrid falcon who taught me exactly how prissy princess a bird could be. To Banshee, the peregrine falcon, who taught me exactly how *terrifying* a bird could be. To Peanut Butter Cookie, the seagull, and your awe-inspiring ability to steal food from unsuspecting lunch eaters at the Shoals Marine Lab. To every single mischievous animal I've had the joy and angst to work with over the years, who inspired the cast of creatures in this book.

And last but not least, thank you to you, the reader, for coming on this journey with me. I wish all of you the perfect day at the zoo, a churro in hand, a beautiful bird on the other side of the glass that just might inspire you to help make our world a better place.

extras

orbit

meet the author

Tiffany Doan

S. A. MacLean is a romantasy author from sunny California. Infatuated with magical worlds since her days of brewing mud potions in her childhood garden, she fell in love with the romantasy genre after realizing all her favorite fantasy novels had kisses in them. Her stories invariably feature quirky humor, sassy animal companions, and queer casts who represent her voice as a chaotic bisexual woman.

Find out more about S. A. MacLean and other Orbit authors by registering for the free monthly newsletter at orbitbooks.net.

473

if you enjoyed
THE PHOENIX KEEPER

look out for

SORCERY AND SMALL MAGICS

by

Maiga Doocy

From debut author Maiga Doocy comes the charming tale of an impulsive sorcerer and his curmudgeonly rival as they must venture deep into a magical forest in desperate search of the counterspell that can break the curse binding them to each other—only to discover that magic might not be the only thing pulling them together.

Leovander Loveage is a master of small magics. He can summon butterflies with a song or turn someone's hair pink by snapping his fingers. Though such minor charms don't earn him much respect, anything more elaborate always

*blows up in his face, and so Leo vowed long ago never to
use powerful magic again.*

*That is, until a mishap with a forbidden spell binds Leo to obey
the commands of his longtime rival, Sebastian Grimm. Grimm
is Leo's complete opposite—respected, talented, and absolutely
insufferable. The only thing they can agree on is that they need a
counterspell, and fast.*

*Chasing rumors of a powerful sorcerer with a knack for undoing
curses, Leo and Grimm enter the Unquiet Wood, a forest infested
with murderous monsters and dangerous outlaws alike. To break
the curse, they'll have to uncover the true depths of Leo's magic, set
aside their long-standing rivalry, and—much to their horror—
work together.*

CHAPTER ONE

It was not my intention to cause mischief immediately upon
arriving back at the Fount, despite what anyone else may tell
you. And yet, by the time the night was over, I was drunk,
my nose was bleeding, and Sebastian Grimm was furious
with me.

It should be noted that only one of these things was unusual.

In order to understand these happenings, you must first
understand the circumstances of my return to the Fount.
Chiefly, that I was lucky to be there at all. My previous year of
study had come to a close with an unfortunate incident involv-
ing a spell that caused one of my instructors to think she was
a duck for a full hour, and no matter how much I argued that
this was how the spell was *supposed to work*, no one seemed to

agree that explanation made things better. I'd been allowed to come back, but it had involved quite a lot of hand-wringing and promises of good behavior (on my part), as well as some stern lectures and threats of immediate expulsion if I did not meet certain standards (on the part of the Fount's academic board).

In short: I was on thin ice before even stepping foot on the Fount grounds.

The sun was setting as I passed through the city gates, and I delayed further by grabbing my violin case and hopping out of the carriage, directing the driver to deliver the rest of my belongings without me. ("Care of Agnes Quest, if you please. She'll know where to put them.")

The Fount was situated in the city of Luxe's southern quarter, with towers of pale stone that rose high above the surrounding buildings and paper-choked depths that sank far below the city streets. Inside those walls existed a separate world that revolved entirely around magic and discipline. Not being in the mood to subject myself to either of those things a moment sooner than necessary, I veered off course and made my way to the boisterous streets of the northern quarter, where I proceeded to distract myself with music and cards and good company.

The night air was mild when I stumbled out onto the street hours later, summer still clinging to it. I decided to take the long way back in order to enjoy both the breeze and my last few moments of freedom. Despite that, I'm certain I would have reached the Fount gates before the midnight bell struck were it not for two factors:

One: I was slightly tipsy. Only slightly, but that was enough for me to be distracted by the moon, peeking out from between the building spires above me, and I took a wrong turn.

Two: I was followed by two of my companions from that night's card table.

Perhaps they were upset by the amount of their coin I'd managed to walk away with, or perhaps the celebratory winner's song I'd played whilst perched on top of the bar had rubbed them the wrong way. Who's to say? Usually, I was better at spotting sore losers, but I'd entered the game already inebriated, which improved my opinion of most people.

I had just enough presence of mind to make a few quick turns and then scramble up a drainpipe before my followers could match my pace. Perhaps if I was a caster a more direct approach would have been possible, but there are two kinds of sorcerers: those who cast spells and those who write them. I was the latter—and not even an impressive scriver at that.

I held my breath as my two erstwhile gaming companions rounded the corner and looked around wildly.

"Lost him," the man with the deep voice said.

"Well, we know where he's going," the woman replied. She wore tall red boots that I had complimented her on, back when we'd been friends an hour ago. "The Fount is back in session tomorrow, and only a sorcerer would be seen about town in one of those hideous coats."

I bristled at this. My coat was midlength and black, with many pockets both on the outside and running along the inner lining. A sorcerer's coat is a wonderful thing to have, with spells on the pockets so you could carry far more than the space should have allowed for and more magic woven into the fabric to keep the wearer cool in summer and warm in winter. I also thought it happened to be an unquestionably stylish piece of clothing and that I looked quite dashing in it.

My would-be robbers, unaware of my outrage, continued on in the direction of the Fount. Once their footsteps had faded,

I pulled myself from the gutter and onto the roof proper. It wasn't the first time I had avoided attention by scrambling over Luxe's rooftops, and it was a faster (if more dangerous) route.

The journey went mostly without incident, though I did lose several minutes untangling my boot from a wash-line full of someone's clothing. Nevertheless, when I finally caught sight of the Fount's grand front gate, my followers were still nowhere in sight.

I shimmied down another drainpipe with more haste than grace, clutching my violin case awkwardly, then darted across the road. It wasn't until I slid to a stop in front of the gate that I realized something that should have been clear to me from first glance—it was shut.

This was a fairly new development. Until recently, the Fount's doors had been open all hours of the day, but the previous year a troop of Coterie members had gone rogue and broken into one of the library's locked vaults, stealing an undisclosed number of extremely rare spells. Needless to say, security measures had been heightened in the wake of the robbery. These measures included closing the gates at midnight, as I now belatedly recalled.

I swore softly and looked over my shoulder.

"You missed the midnight bell by twenty minutes at least."

The voice was flat, remarkable only for its deep tenor and the unmistakable disapproval lacing each word. I flinched in surprise and looked back toward the door just as a figure stepped forward from the collected gloom of the gate's arch.

"Oh. Hello, Grimm," I said with little enthusiasm.

Sebastian Grimm lived up to his name in every way imaginable, like a thundercloud in human form. His hair was a shockingly pale gray and had been that way even when we first met at seventeen. A permanent line of displeasure was etched between

479

his dark brows, and his mouth had a habit of settling into a thin line, turning his expression sour. Or at least, that was the expression he wore whenever he caught sight of me.

Grimm's usually immaculate sorcerer's coat was covered in a thin layer of dust, and the indigo caster's sash wrapped around his waist was creased. A bag hung from his shoulder, packed so tightly the seams were straining. It looked heavy. Grimm looked tired.

Grimm was always easiest to annoy when he was tired, and I have always been unable to resist low-hanging fruit.

I shook my head and made a tutting sound with my tongue. "Sebastian Grimm, out cavorting the night before our final tier commences. What is the world coming to?"

Grimm's lips tugged down at the corners. "My return was delayed when a stream decided to forge itself a new path directly across one of the main roads. It took the Coterie nearly two hours to spell it back in place." He gave me a once-over, making note of my rumpled clothes and flushed face. "What's your excuse?"

"Lost track of time," I said, and winked for good measure. "What are you waiting here for?"

Grimm looked down his nose at me like I was a particularly stupid bug he was thinking about stepping on. "No one answered when I knocked."

I laughed. "Do you mean to say, in nearly five years of attending the Fount, you've never bothered to find another way in besides the front gate?"

Grimm, tellingly, said nothing. It was not so surprising, considering what I knew of his habits. No reveling with friends in the streets of Luxe for Sebastian Grimm. I could not imagine he had ever found himself in a situation that demanded sneaking back into the Fount after hours.

It was tempting, very tempting, to turn around and leave him there without another word. It's undoubtedly what Grimm would have done to me, had our positions been reversed. But I couldn't help but think what would happen if my pursuers arrived and found Grimm outside the gate instead of me. I wasn't concerned for his safety, understand, but the last thing I needed was for Grimm to discover I'd been gambling. I was sure he'd be only too eager to share my transgressions with the Fount's board of sorcerers, and I'd already received a very clearly worded letter from them detailing exactly what would happen if I so much as thought about breaking a rule this year.

I sighed heavily. "Come along, then. Or do you intend to sleep in the dust of the street tonight, simply to avoid following me?"

Then I turned on my heel and started walking, not bothering to wait for an answer.

After a moment I was rewarded by the sound of Grimm's footsteps, leaving the gate to trail reluctantly after me down the road.

Around the eastern side of the Fount, there is a particularly pretty stretch of wall where trees border the walkway and their branches stretch up and outward, leaning over to kiss leaves with the trees overflowing from the Fount's garden within. By day, this area is a popular place to stroll because of the shade and the view. By night, it's the perfect place to sneak over the wall, making use of the natural handholds provided by greenery.

There were, of course, spells in place to prevent outsiders from doing this, but Grimm and I were not outsiders; we were simply residents resorting to inconvenient measures. I'd climbed these trees many times on my own since the midnight bell's implementation, when I'd been unwilling to let the Fount's rules deprive me of a full night of fun.

"There's no need to climb with me here," Grimm said impatiently, once I'd explained this. "A lightfoot charm will see us over the wall easily." He looked at me expectantly.

"Oh," I said, surprised. "You want me to write it?"

"It's only a charm, Loveage," Grimm said. "You should be capable of that much, yes?"

Yes, I could write charms. Cantrips too. I could even transcribe other scrivers' Grandmagic spells without issue. It was when I wrote my own that things went wrong—that was what Grimm was hinting at. Grandmagic had a habit of turning out so poorly for me that I avoided writing it altogether. My last brush with it had been an accident in second tier, when I'd unintentionally written a wind spell with a bit too much power built into it. The demonstration of said spell had destroyed an entire classroom, knocked one person out a first-story window (Grimm), and resulted in the cracking of three ribs (my own). This had earned me a bit of a reputation, as well as a fair amount of laughter and whispers behind my back. A Fount-trained scriver who couldn't write Grandmagic? What was the point?

I had said something very similar to my father when he insisted I enroll. In fact, I believe my exact words were "Why would I want to spend five years as a laughingstock?" I'd been considered a scriving prodigy when I was young, but that talent had withered on the vine. I'd held more promise as a child than I ever would again, but my father had yet to accept this.

"You've had a place at the Fount since you were born," he'd said.

"Well, I don't want it," I told him, which had led to a week of heated arguments and ended with him making it clear that, if I didn't attend the Fount and become a fifth-tier sorcerer like my older brother had, I could kiss my portion of the inheritance goodbye. The money, the title, the land holdings, all of it.

I didn't much like to think about that confrontation, but sometimes my father's parting words still echoed in my ears.

You will learn to control your magic and your attitude and become a fully trained sorcerer, or you will become nothing at all.

After four years at the Fount, I rather thought my father had overlooked the possibility that I could become a fully trained sorcerer and *still* amount to nothing at all. But Grimm was right; I could write charms, at least.

I reached into my pocket to retrieve paper and quill. The words of the lightfoot charm Grimm mentioned were lost to me—I was shit at memorization—but it was the work of a moment to come up with my own version of the spell, combining what words in the old language I remembered with a few more I found fitting. When it was done, I blew the ink dry and handed the spell to Grimm.

"Your penmanship is awful" was the first thing he said. There was plenty of light from the street for him to read by, so I thought the show he made of squinting and frowning down at the paper was a bit much. "This is incorrect."

"It's not," I said. "I just couldn't remember the words to the light-foot spell so I wrote my own. It should work the same. Mostly."

Grimm stared at me. "Surely you've memorized something as basic as that by now?"

I shrugged. "Didn't stick."

Grimm looked horrified by this admission. He took ages reading over the spell again, probably searching it for traps. This was insulting but perhaps not entirely unwarranted. Grimm and I had been collecting grievances against each other since first tier, like honey catches flies. I'd once tricked him into casting a charm that turned his pale hair a delightful shade of pink. I'd thought it rather fetching, but he vehemently disagreed. That incident had been the launching point for the enmity that had stuck like a thorn between us ever since.

Once he'd assured himself the spell was as I said, Grimm motioned me closer and gingerly grabbed my left arm with one hand. With the other, he held the spell paper between thumb and forefinger and began to cast. His brow furrowed in concentration. Smoke gathered in his hand and rose up into the air as magic ate the words I'd written, burning away the paper as it went. He didn't even have to speak the words of the spell aloud.

I will passionately deny admitting this if asked, but Grimm is a brilliant caster. Most sorcerers can't cast silently, but he did it as a matter of course. If he'd been even a little bit better-natured, this kind of careless display of power might have been attractive. As it was, I found Grimm about as appealing as the austere marble statues that graced the Fount's hallways—just as haughty and twice as cold. Most of our tiermates disagreed with me on that front. Grimm had plenty of admirers who were willing to overlook his personality in favor of his talent. Little good it did them. Grimm had just given more attention to studying my spell than I'd seen him devote to any of his followers over the years.

The paper wasn't even completely finished burning when Grimm tugged me forward and our feet left the ground. This spell was undoubtedly more exciting than a lightfoot charm, which floated you upward with all the urgency of dandelion fluff drifting on a light breeze. *My* version hit with the same adrenaline as a gutless drop, only in reverse. A sort of falling upward, if you like. We had nearly cleared the wall when Grimm's free hand shot out and grabbed the nearest tree limb, halting our progress before we could descend on the other side. I was hardly tipsy anymore, but our landing was awkward enough that only Grimm's unsteady grip on my arm kept me from tumbling down. I wobbled on top of the wall like a toddler, laughing and giddy, buzzing from the rush.

"That was brilliant. Why did you stop us?"

"We were going too fast," Grimm said, scowling. "Your spell likely would have catapulted us headfirst into the ground had I let it continue."

A little of my rush faded, replaced by annoyance. It was one thing to have everyone turn their noses up at me for something I was admittedly bad at, but my charms worked just fine. I wouldn't have dared let anyone use them otherwise.

"Climb down on your own then, if you don't trust my scriving." I pulled my arm away with a quick tug, intending to move toward the nearest tree and away from Grimm. But *hardly tipsy* is not quite the same thing as absolutely sober, especially when one is standing on a narrow bit of stone ten feet above the ground.

I leaned.

First one way, then the other. My balance was further thrown off by my violin case, heavier than usual thanks to the winnings I'd stashed there. My free arm flailed for something, anything, to hold on to, and the only thing within reach was Grimm.

My fingers caught on the sash at his waist, causing Grimm to cling even tighter to the branch he held, rather than offering me any assistance.

"Let go," he snarled, but I clutched that sash like a lifeline, silk twisting in my grasp. Briefly, I thought it would hold, but the fabric was too delicate. It gave way under my fingers with a hushed *riiip*, and I tumbled over the wall.

It was fortunate that there was grass beneath me, rather than stone, but the impact still rattled my bones and sent the case in my grasp bouncing forward to connect with my face, hard enough to leave me seeing stars. I lay there, dazed, as something wet trickled down from my nose and the metallic tang of blood bloomed at the back of my throat.

By the time I managed to sit up, Grimm was just finishing making his way down one of the trees, landing with an elegant hop. He slowly leaned over to pick up the pieces of his sash. It had been torn neatly in two.

Sorcerers decorate their sashes, you know, or at least most of us do. I'd never bothered, but Grimm's sash was covered in careful stitches that depicted droplets of water and waves. Now the threads trailed through the air, ripped down the middle of the design.

Grimm folded the pieces carefully and put them in his pocket. Then he looked down at me, coldly furious, and said, "I don't know how you manage to keep your place here. You're useless, Loveage."

There were many things I had argued with Grimm about over the years, but this was not one of them. I didn't say anything now, either, as he walked away. My own uselessness was something I'd spent years perfecting. Not all sorcerers could be like Grimm. Some of us had powers best left untouched.

Follow us:

f /orbitbooksUS

X /orbitbooks

▶ /orbitbooks

Join our mailing list
to receive alerts on our
latest releases and deals.

orbitbooks.net

Enter our monthly
giveaway for the chance
to win some epic prizes.

orbitloot.com